They tried to improve the human genome, but nature took things into its own hands!

Echoes: For every ten embryos they genetically enhance, nature would return nine to their unaltered state. They remained echoes of humanity's limitations.

Deltas: Only one in ten would be born with and keep all of its altered traits. They were an improvement to humanity, but only within limits that were considered a reasonable step beyond normal evolutionary growth.

Charlies and Betas: But for 1% of those Deltas, nature wasn't done; it threw a genetic curveball brought on by puberty. They were faster, stronger, and smarter than was thought to be humanly possible.

If that had been the end of it, science would have been satisfied: its goal had been achieved. But they just couldn't leave it alone. And what they did next would start the final war—the war to end all wars.

THE REGNANT WAR

BOOK ONE

THE
REGNANT
WAR

R. J. Hunter

Curriculum
That Matters

The Regnant War

Copyright © 2023 by Rayanna Hunter

Cover art by Kaitlynn Hunter
Cover art © 2023 by Kaitlynn Hunter

Interior Illustrations by Rayanna Hunter
Interior Illustrations © 2023 by Rayanna Hunter

ISBN: 978-1-7353113-2-6

First Edition: July 2023

For my girls: Kaylee, Kaitlynn, and Jessika
and for my wonderful husband.

Thank you for your support and encouragement.
You are the reason this made it to print!

"The moth to the flame: An appropriate description of man's draw to power. Once a man permits himself to be drawn in by power's allure, he will fail to acknowledge the inherent danger of its touch until the very last moment when he becomes consumed by it.

This, then, was the cause of the Pernicious Bellum War. North Korea refused to admit the possibility that the inherent outcome of their desperate pursuit of power was their own destruction and the devastation of the world around them. And the rest of the world's superpowers were so drunk in their own strength that they did not clearly see who else had joined them in their dangerous dance around power's flame.

The result of their blindness? A war that would surpass all others: a Regnant War if you will. A war that would dominate, reign, and rule over historical records for all time. For no other crusade, campaign, skirmish, or battle in all of the world's vast history ever had, or could ever hope to have such far-reaching consequences."

Ganton, D. (PB 124) The Regnant War: The Philosophy Behind the Pernicious Bellum War. Journal of Philosophies, 243.

THE REGNANT WAR

The
United Federation

Directorate Zones

Zone 1: NW. North America
Zone 2: NE. North America
Zone 3: SW. North America
Zone 4: SE. North America
Zone 5: Central America/
  N. South America
Zone 6: S. South America
Zone 7: W. Europe

# of Countries
Directorate Zone Map

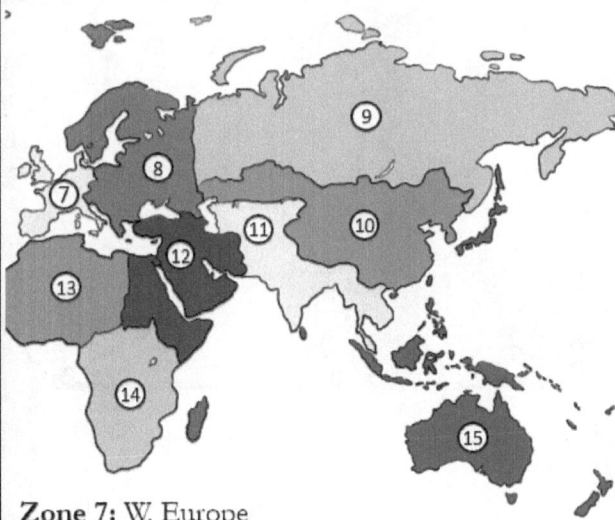

Zone 7: W. Europe
Zone 8: E. Europe
Zone 9: N. Asia
Zone 10: Central Asia
Zone 11: S. Asia
Zone 12: NW. Africa/W. Asia
Zone 13: N. Africa
Zone 14: S. Africa
Zone 15: Australia/Oceana

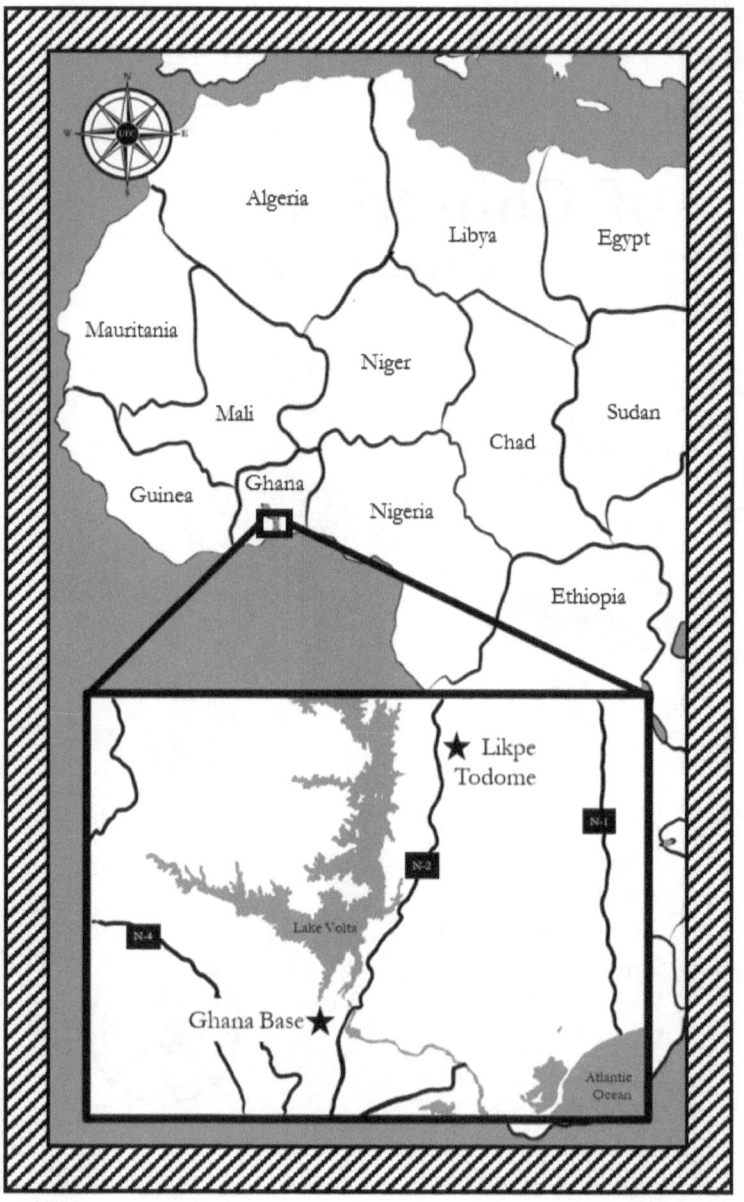

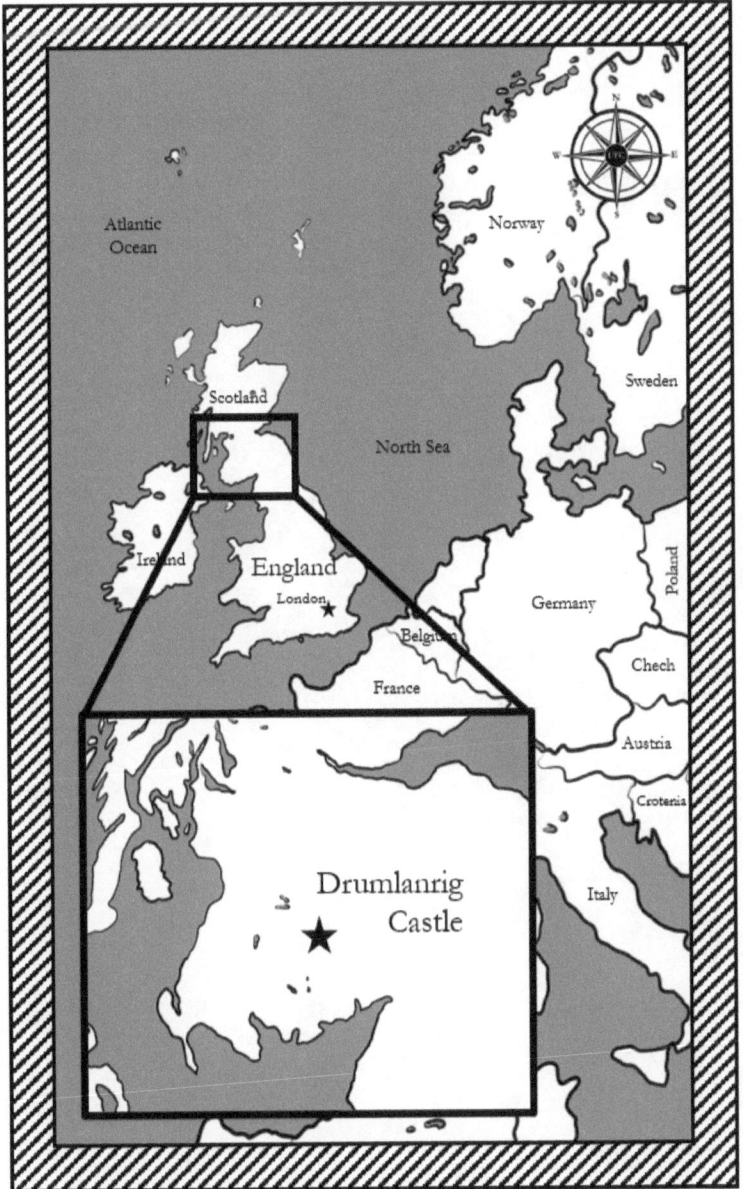

Prologue: Alexandria Jaquette

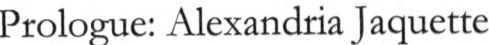

I READ A history book recently. It talked about the wars this world has fought through the ages. It said that the earliest men fought over food and shelter; the Romans spent more than a thousand years fighting for honor, land, and wealth; the Americans fought for freedom during their Revolutionary War of the eighteenth century; and, during the two World Wars of the twentieth century, the major countries of the world came together to end Germany's quest for world domination.

I suppose those wars were each noble wars in their own way, but by the Pernicious Bellum War, the war that reset the world's calendars, man had digressed to fighting wars for revenge. Not a very noble reason to fight, yet that hadn't stopped them from destroying the world they claimed they were trying to defend. The book went into great detail about the Pernicious Bellum War, but I already knew that part by heart; every school child did. The world had underestimated North Korea's leader until it was too late.

North Korea had played them. They thought the country was still throwing its little tantrums, using a fledgling nuclear program as leverage to get concessions out of the United Nations. What they didn't realize was that one of Pakistan's

3

terrorist groups had been silently egging them on in the background. For nearly three years, they had secretly shipped weapons-grade uranium, plutonium, and tritium gas along with components for an intercontinental missile into North Korea. Along the way, they had stoked the unstable country's ego into the mistaken belief that they could use the weapon without fear of retaliation.

In Post-Bellum 1, they had done just that. They launched their missile over the Pacific Ocean and straight into downtown Los Angeles. The thermal radiation alone had obliterated everything within a five-mile radius. The radioactive fallout had then destroyed most life within another one hundred and twenty-five-mile radius beyond that.

It had taken nearly twenty minutes for North Korea's missile to cross the almost ten thousand miles of sparkling blue ocean. It only took two minutes for America to exact its revenge. Thirty minutes after pushing the launch button, North Korea burned in its own firestorm from the sixty-some-odd Tomahawk Cruise missiles that the Ohio-class submarine, the USS Michigan, had launched from its hidden position in the East China Sea.

Unfortunately, one of those sixty missiles overshot its intended target of a nuclear facility in Pyongyang, North Korea to instead hit the nearby Chinese resort on Moon Island in Dandong, China. It turned out that China's president had been there vacationing with his family when the missile struck. America tried to claim it was an accident, and who knows, maybe it was. But whatever the cause, an hour later, China launched its revenge, and the Great War began.

Just as they had during World War I, the world split apart as allies came to each other's aid. Unlike World War I, which extended into World War II for nearly twenty-seven years of war, this war was over in a matter of twenty-seven hours.

It was once estimated that nine countries possessed a total of fifteen thousand nuclear weapons. In just over twenty-four hours, the world's nuclear arsenal had been spent. In just over twenty-four hours, the world's population was reduced by several hundred million people. While that was only five-hundredths of the world's population, the full extent of the devastation would not be realized for another twenty years as the radiation poisoning's effects began to be noticed.

Twenty-five percent of children born over the next twenty years were born with unnatural mutations that deformed their bodies and warped their minds. They were a bloodthirsty, self-destructive generation that despised the seventy-five percent who did not suffer as they did.

The war of revenge played out once more as the M-Gens, short for the Mutated Generation, viciously hunted every non-M-Gen they could find. The good news was that most of the M-Gens were sterile and weren't able to pass their twisted mutations on to future generations. The bad news was that some of them were not.

For the next fifty years, it looked as though man wouldn't make it out of its self-induced extinction cycle. Then a miracle happened; a generation of mutated children was born who didn't inherit their parents' crazed blood lust and warped minds.

That generation began to grow up and seek a better life for themselves than the one their parents had ordained. They studied the textbooks that hadn't been destroyed, and their minds opened up in ways that had never before been seen. They were brilliant by the standards of the twentieth century.

Technology, medicine, and science became child's play to them as they mastered their understanding of the human genome, created energy sources that were self-sustaining and clean, and discovered an enzyme that ate radioactive materials and left clean, nutrient-rich growing soil in its place. Within ten years, they had learned how to manipulate a growing embryo's DNA so that it was free of all inherited diseases, especially the mind-warped craze that had afflicted their parents' generation.

Within twenty years they began experimenting with selectively adding a few of the more desirable characteristics they had mapped out. Children were born taller, stronger, faster, and at least as smart as their parents. But unlike their previous successes, and in spite of all their collective wisdom, they found they couldn't guarantee the results.

For every ten embryos they surgically altered, one would be born with, and keep, all of the intended traits. The rest would appear to be born with the alterations, but then around the age of eight, the child would suddenly, and inexplicably begin to lose the intended traits. It was as though the human race, in spite of man's best efforts, insisted on following its own course of evolution and would take matters into its own hands to ensure that these children grew along the "natural" course nature intended for them. They came to refer to these children as Echoes of the Past, or Echoes for short because, despite the scientists' best efforts, these children were no different from the other unaltered children around them.

Then there were the ten percent; those who retained their altered advantages after the age of ten. Most of them continued to age and grow for the remainder of their lives with only the advances that had been engineered into them. They were faster, stronger, and smarter than previous generations, but only within limits that were considered a reasonable step beyond normal evolutionary growth. They referred to this group as the Deltas because they considered them to be an improvement on the Echoes, but they were otherwise like the Echoes in most ways.

If that had been the extent of the advances, they would have considered their work a success; but nature wasn't finished interfering. It wasn't long before they began to notice nature's next surprise. For every hundred Deltas, one of them would hit puberty and discover that one of their unique genes was taking matters into its own hands. For some, it was their speed. Where they had been fast before, they would suddenly discover that they were capable of even greater bursts of speed than had previously been thought possible. For others, it was their endurance. Where their bodies had previously tired after an hour or so of sprinting, they found that they were capable of sustaining high speeds for hours on end. For yet others, it was their strength, or their mind's capacity to remember things, or their speed with calculations, or their ability to see things at long distances, or their vastly superior hearing, or...well you get the idea.

That one percent of the population entered puberty with all its normal problems only to discover that they had been thrown a genetic curveball that had not been originally planned for and was completely unpredictable. It could show up anywhere between the age of ten and fourteen in girls, and twelve to nineteen in boys, and there was no way to know ahead of time who it would hit or in what way it would manifest itself. They called this group the Charlies and Betas depending on the scale of their increased abilities: Charlies if they only had one advanced ability; Betas if they had more than one. The only common thread they were able to grasp in predicting who would fall into this category was that each of the Charlies and Betas had a direct ancestry traceable back to an M-Gen.

In Post-Bellum 138, a scientist named Elwick Müller made a breakthrough. He discovered that if the fetal offspring of two Betas was genetically altered during a critical growth phase between six and seven weeks when the five parts of the fetus' brain began to develop and separate, it was possible to enhance the child's brain growth so that a sixth part of the brain would develop.

This part of the brain, it was soon discovered, permitted the child to see things in a way the rest of humanity could not. Light waves, sound waves, gravity, things that were there, but were completely invisible to the naked eye, were clearly visible to these children. And what was more, they could be trained to manipulate those unseen forces that were nearest to them.

Unfortunately, it came at a cost: infertility. Alphas, as they dubbed this group, were completely, one hundred percent, incapable of having children. Unlike the Betas and Charlies who could pass their traits on to future generations, Alphas could only exist if they were created in a laboratory. Add to that the complications inherent in an invasive procedure that was occasionally known to result in a braindead child, and the extreme cost of the procedure, it is understandable why so few Alphas exist today.

I guess that makes me one of the lucky ones. I'm one in a million. I'm an Alpha, or at least I was. Turns out that an injury to the brain can take it all away far more easily than it was given; and that for all of our medical advances, we still don't have a perfect understanding of how the brain works, or how to fix it when it's damaged. In an oddly twisted sort of way, that narrative could also be used to describe the chain of events that resulted in my injury.

The M-Gen's children had worked hard to end their parents' war with the result being a reasonable peace that lasted for nearly a hundred years. During that hundred years, the world did a pretty good job of recovering from the effects of the Pernicious War.

Nature and medicine had worked together to eliminate most of the bad mutations. A few not-so-bad mutations were permitted to stick around. Hair so black that it shone blue, blue eyes so deep that they looked more violet than blue, and skin that was so pale it was almost translucent was now a regular occurrence. But the twisted bodies and warped minds of the M-Gens seemed to be a thing of the past.

Unfortunately, anyone who had studied genetics should have known that an occasional recessive allele can sneak its way out into the open. They thought they had eliminated all the bad genes. They were wrong.

By 158 PB, the first generation of Alphas had reached adulthood. There were five of them in that first generation, with another twenty-three in various stages of childhood behind them. For the most part, they were scientifically minded individuals whose gifts allowed them to expand their scientific knowledge of waves and light well beyond what had previously been understood. They, like the children of the M-Gens, focused their efforts on improving the world. But there were one or two of the younger ones who questioned why their abilities should only be used to advance science. Why not use them for advancing their own interests?

I guess we should have seen it coming. After all, history is full of crazy men and women who craved power and would go to any cost to get it. Caligula, Cleopatra, Napoleon, Hitler, Stalin, and Kim Jong Un were some of the early ones. Icarus is ours.

From an early age, there were indications that Icarus was not interested in the greater good: selfish tendencies, cruelty in his treatment of other children, and an unwillingness to do his part. Yet the hints were either missed or they were ignored in a desperate hope that he would outgrow them; he didn't.

In addition to his Alpha abilities related to radio waves, he had also inherited some Beta traits from his parents. His gifts weren't so much physical, although they do say that he is unusually handsome. (Personally, I don't see that he is any different from most other men I've seen, but that could just be my personal hatred for him getting in the way of my opinion. It does that sometimes.) Anyway, his other gifts are listed as being more along the line of mental prowess above and beyond the normal. He is said to be incredibly smart and a brilliant strategist. He also has a way with words that causes people to want to listen and believe whatever nonsense he is spouting off.

By the time he was in his twenties, he had developed quite a circle of followers who would hang on to his every word and were ready to jump at the slightest indication that there was something he wanted them to do. He was the top student in his classes, and he loved the attention he was getting. Then the unthinkable happened.

He had set his sights on a girl named Letha. She was beautiful, well-liked, had an incredible singing voice that was literally dual-toned, and she wasn't the least bit interested in the cocky young man that she perceived as a stuck-on-himself jerk. He pursued her, she ignored him, he proposed, she told him, "Not on your life," he didn't take her rejection very well, she turned up dead with her vocal cords torn out of her throat. It was a gruesome murder that shocked everyone.

Icarus was never officially charged, but then he didn't stick around long enough for the charges to be made. He and most of his followers seemed to disappear overnight and, for a time, things were relatively normal. That probably should have raised someone's suspicions. Once again, it didn't. Bad guys don't just disappear; they go into hiding as they plan their next move.

It came four months later. He and his followers appeared out of nowhere to attack a school in northern France. It was a school for Charlies and Betas. The school was unprepared, unguarded, and unsuspecting. By the time help arrived, hundreds were dead, and fourteen kids between the ages of twelve and seventeen were missing. A few months later, another school in Russia was attacked. This time twenty-three kids were found to be missing.

After those two attacks, most schools got smart and began hiring guards, but that didn't stop the third school in America from getting hit two months later. Seventeen kids went missing this time.

It was about then that someone finally put two and two together and noticed that all of the missing kids were Betas; no Charlies had been taken. And what was more, the vast majority of the missing kids were girls. Why would someone be kidnapping teenage Beta girls? I guess humanity wasn't as smart as they had come to think they were, or maybe they had just become so far removed from the "evils" of their parents' world that the answer was unthinkable to them.

Whatever the reason, no one came up with the right answer until one of the kidnapped girls managed to escape and make her way back to safety. She was fourteen years old and seven months pregnant with an Alpha.

She told a horrific story of tiny cages, brutal treatment, and nightmare surgeries that would leave a grown man trembling. She had only escaped because a careless guard had been in a hurry and failed to notice that the locking mechanism on her cage had not properly latched. That, and her Beta gifts were to walk silently, run fast, and jump high. Still, her escape had not been easy or without injury.

She had been doggedly pursued through the frozen wastelands of northern Russia, fear spurring her on to even greater speeds than she had ever known before. She was barefoot, underdressed, and without supplies for the arduous trek. She barely made it to civilization, frostbitten, severely dehydrated, on the verge of collapse, and terrified of anyone coming near her. She was a tiny wraith with a bulging belly who didn't speak a word of Russian and was babbling incoherently in French.

It took a whole day to find someone who could translate and another eight hours to get any coherent information out of her. By the time authorities found Icarus' facility, he was gone. He left behind him a scene of gruesome carnage that reinforced the French girl's morbid claims.

They found most of the missing Beta children: forty-seven corpses confirmed dead at the site, brutally murdered in their cages during the course of Icarus' retreat; three more corpses strapped to surgery tables, left to bleed to death after rushed cesareans; during later autopsies, it was found that every one of the murdered females was either in the first six months of pregnancy at the time they were killed or had given birth within the last two months; in a shallow grave, just outside the compound, investigators found the decaying remains of some twenty-two new-born infants, all showing signs of the surgery that was intended to produce Alphas, but all having clearly not survived the process.

The obvious conclusion was that Icarus had kidnapped the Betas for the purpose of producing Alphas. Not so obvious was his reason for wanting the Alphas, or what he was planning to do with them. It would be many more years before that became clear.

In the meantime, the wraith of a French girl survived her ordeal long enough to give birth two weeks later to a reasonably healthy Alpha girl, then she slipped peacefully into death a few short hours after that.

The tiny infant spent the first two weeks of her life in a heated incubator with oxygen and IVs before she was strong enough to survive on her own, then another three months in the neonatal unit while the authorities argued over what to do with her.

During that time, the Russian nurse who cared for her dubbed her Alexandria. It means defender of mankind. It's an appropriate name, since that is what I do, defend people that is. Except that I never go by my full name; everyone just calls me Alex.

Chapter 1: Alexandria Jaquette

WHEN I WAS three months old, I was named a ward of the United Federation of Countries and was shipped off to a special school for Alphas in England where I grew up under the constant tutelage of a group of teachers and scientists who alternatingly mentored me and monitored me. Periodically a military official would show up to check my progress, but for the most part, the military showed little interest in me; especially since they were being kept busy by the escalating activities of Icarus and his group.

The summer before I turned thirteen was an especially memorable one. Up to that point, Icarus had kept the military on its toes as he randomly attacked schools for Betas all over the world and seemed to make it his personal goal to generally wreak havoc on any and all forms of government. But that summer, he introduced a new weapon that no one saw coming.

It was a child. The boy was the same age as me, only his education had clearly not been the same as mine. While I was sitting in a classroom learning how to read and write, solve physics calculations, memorize the history of the world, and how to use a few of my unique talents as an Alpha for the advancement of science and the betterment of society, he was learning how to use his Alpha talents to destroy things. With this new weapon at the forefront of his army, Icarus began to step up his attacks.

By the time I was fifteen, war with Icarus' army was in full swing. They started in Russia where they literally brought the building down on the Russian Federation's State Duma and Federation Council during a joint event in which both houses were present. Russia's military put up a gallant fight in the following months, but they were no match for an army guarded by an Alpha who had learned to control sound waves far beyond what any Alpha before him had done.

The boy, I don't know his real name, but everyone referred to him as DEAN (short for Devastating Emanations of Amplified Noise), could send focused sound waves with destructive capacity toward enemy soldiers, buildings, and equipment.

By the time I was seventeen, Icarus had either marched through, or been joined by, Kazakhstan, Afghanistan, Iran, Iraq, and Syria. He tried for a time to conquer China, but they had a few tricks up their own sleeves and developed a sound-dampening field that dramatically reduced the boy's ability to use sound waves against them.

Around that time, two other Alphas began to make appearances in his attacks. One was a girl a little younger than me who had figured out how to focus infrared light waves into a heat beam that could start fires and make a man's blood boil. The other was a boy only a few months older than me who could see air currents and coax them into massive storms that he sent roaring against his enemies.

It was around then that I got curious. If they could do things like that, why couldn't I? I started simply enough. I could see low-level gravity fields, and even manipulate them to move objects nearest me. So, I began stretching my reach, trying to manipulate the fields around objects across the room from me.

My first few tries were pretty much a joke. But I kept at it and within a month could lift a book off of the table at the other end of the room and bring it flying through the air to my hands. Next, I tried something a little bigger, the table itself. Within three months, I was getting pretty good at rearranging furniture while sitting on a rug in the center of the room. And that was about the time I got caught.

It turns out that one of the things the scientist had been monitoring me for was just such an event, and the military was ready for me. I was given a choice: join the United Federation of Countries' military or, well…there really wasn't another option offered.

Three months before my eighteenth birthday, I was shipped off to a special UFC facility in Ghana where a group of three other Alphas and about thirty Betas and Charlies were working with the military to "weaponize" their gifts.

The Betas and Charlies were a mixed group of individuals. There was a smart-mouthed thirteen-year-old girl from Mexico who could hear a pin drop in a haystack from a hundred yards away and a fifty-four-year-old Korean man who could follow a faint scent for miles on end. There was a sun-tanned Australian surfer who could hold his breath underwater for almost thirty minutes and a tiny pale-faced Chinese acrobat who could scale the side of a wall with such deceptive ease that you might mistake her for a spider. The rest of the group boasted a wide variety of skills including speed, strength, accuracy, heightened senses, and increased mental faculties.

Then there were the Alphas. Although I had been in a school for Alphas, the truth is that there were very few of us, and all of the Alphas I had previously seen had devoted their lives to the sciences and forwarding world cooperation, using their skills for research and the sharing of information. They were very different from the three Alphas that worked with the UFC.

Callia Ubuqua was an ebony-skinned beauty from Liberia that made every woman jealous. All she had to do was bat her long, thick eyelashes and purse her perfectly pouty lips to have every man in the room swooning over her. It turned out that her Alpha talent had more than a little to do with that.

Her gift was to see and manipulate light waves. She could change her appearance by bending the light waves around her. Whether it was to give her body that little extra glow that she liked to tease men with, or to completely alter the appearance of her face and body structure so that she looked like someone else; when accompanied by a voice modulator, she was the perfect infiltrator.

She was also an exceptionally skilled combat soldier who could single-handedly take down ten trained men without breaking a nail. Lieutenant Colonel Ubuqua liked men about as far as she could throw them, and took great pleasure in teasingly taunting them, then dumping them like yesterday's garbage when she was done using them. There were very few men she held in any level of regard, but Troy had somehow earned her respect, and she usually deferred to him when he was on-site, though that was rarely the case.

Brigadier General Troy Durnham was the undisputed leader of the three Alphas. Most of the base referred to him as The Brig when he wasn't present. Although he didn't make a big deal out of his rank, he was the highest-ranking military commander on the base. More than that, he was one of the original Alphas. He had been born back in 158 PB before scientists had come to fully understand the ramifications of the Alphas' sixth lobe.

It must have been frightening to grow up, able to see things that no one else could see, with no one around who understood or could explain to him why he was different. If the scuttlebutt around the base was to be believed, he had been a terror child, throwing tantrums and wreaking havoc against a world that didn't understand him. The rumors say that his parents had been unable to control him and had sent him off to a military school when he was only ten. That would be highly unlikely since most military schools won't accept kids until they are at least twelve, but whatever his age, he had quickly learned that tantrums and self-pity would only result in more push-ups and more latrine duty.

At the same time, he discovered that he liked the structured, demanding life of the military. He also finally solved the mystery of what made him so different: everyone else had to wear infrared goggles to see what he saw with his natural eyes. By the time he was eighteen, and officially able to join the military, he had already developed a name for himself: Trojan Horse, because of his uncanny ability to sneak into enemy camps and single-handedly dispatch the guards so that his platoon could then move in undetected and take over the base.

After boot camp, he served several years in the UFC's decorated SEALs unit before beginning his rapid rise through the officer ranks. Despite his rise in command, it was not uncommon to hear after the fact that he had been in the field with his troops, using his Alpha skills to ensure their success, and that they all came safely home.

The final Alpha was a little different from the other two. While they were fine-tuned soldiers, he was gangly and wiry, always tripping over his own feet and bumping into things. He was a brilliant computer specialist in his own right, but that wasn't what made him such a valuable part of the group. Cepheus Jonsson could see and control gamma waves, or rather, he could see the naturally occurring gamma radiation that all decaying atoms emit, and he could encourage that rate of decay to rapidly increase.

He had only mastered doing it on a small scale, to things that were within a hundred yards and within his direct line of sight, but when the weapon in the soldier's hands suddenly began to heat up and vaporize along with their hands, or a tank suddenly became a huge firebomb, it quickly became obvious that he was potentially the greatest weapon the group had.

For that, Callia showed him a measure of respect. But more often than not, she treated him like an annoying little brother; one she allowed to tag along, one she punched in the shoulder and rolled her eyes at, but when she thought no one was looking, she allowed a gentle smile of pride for his progress to briefly grace her lips.

Durnham likewise treated him like a little brother, only in his case, it was more like the little brother he was never satisfied with, at least on the surface. Durnham pushed Cepheus hard. He was always verbally harsh in his assessments, critiquing every little mistake he made, and only occasionally nodding his head silently when Cepheus achieved his expectations. One might have expected Cepheus to resent Troy for his treatment; I know I would have. Surprisingly, he didn't. It turned out that Cepheus idolized

Durnham. In his eyes, the General could do no wrong. All he wanted was to live up to Durnham's expectations.

The three of them formed a tight-knit core at the center of the rest of the team. In many ways, my entry into the picture was somewhat of an intrusion. At eighteen, I was just coming out of my gangly adolescence and starting to fill into the woman's body I have today. I wasn't the most beautiful girl in the room, but I was far from being the ugly duckling. My thick, auburn hair was a gift from my mom. My stormy violet eyes I can only assume came from my dad. I also had the smooth, pale skin and long, lithe lines that were characteristic among the French. I didn't purposely try to attract the attention of guys, but my outgoing and relaxed attitude made me easy to get along with so that I made friends quickly.

Callia soon decided that I was her rival. No matter how hard I tried, I was never quite able to convince her that I wasn't purposely, or otherwise, trying to take her place as the dominant female in the group. In the end, I settled for avoiding her and doing my best to stay under her radar anytime she was on base. For the most part, that was relatively easy. Coming to the base was not a vacation. They had brought me here to work and train, and the military had a plan that kept me busy.

My days now consisted of waking up at five a.m. with two hours of intense physical training, followed by four hours in a classroom learning everything from physics to battle strategies. Four grueling hours with a group of scientists who prodded and probed while pushing my talents to their limits, twenty-minute breaks for meals, then it was back to the physical training for another four hours and a final hour or two of book study and homework in preparation for the next day.

At the end of the day, they were gracious enough to give me thirty minutes to myself. Or rather, if I rushed and finished getting ready for bed in ten minutes, then I had twenty minutes to relax before the lights turned off.

I wasn't a fan of the enforced schedule, though it did have its merits. Within six months, I had successfully extended my range the length of a football field; I could easily flip a fully-grown man over my shoulder on the combat mats or take the knife out of the hand of a close-range combatant; I knew the difference between a phase pistol and a phase rifle and how to use them both. I could rappel down a forty-foot sheer wall, climb a rock wall with or without a climbing harness, and complete the indoor obstacle course in a smooth three minutes. These were the expected outcomes. Then something happened that we never saw coming.

I was taking part in a night training that included rappelling out of a helio-transport. We were supposed to make the night drop behind "enemy" lines, sneak into their base, and capture the other team's captain. It was a reasonably routine training led by a group of trainers who had done it with hundreds of groups before us, but on this night the rappel master released my rope too soon. It was an eighty-foot drop, and I was only two-thirds of the way down when I felt my rope go slack. I was free-falling, with nothing but the ground to stop my fall.

I probably should have been terrified, and in truth, a part of me was. But mostly I was angry. *How was this fair? What right did life have for putting me in this position?* I hadn't asked to join the military. Nighttime raids and extreme rappelling had never been on my to-do list. And, *How could the rappel master have made that mistake? The tautness of my line should have told him I was still on it.* All these thoughts and more raced through my mind in the space of a breath, only to be replaced in the next instant by the realization that if I didn't do something, none of my questions would matter; I was going to be dead on the ground.

Yet, what was there to do? The rope had been my only protection against the pull of gravity. *Gravity!* I could see the field of gravity that had me in its grasp. Without fully comprehending what I was doing, I reached into the gravitational field that was pulling me downward and hurried to force it into a new pattern, a wave that wrapped around my body, pushing and pulling with equal balance.

It suddenly felt like I was floating in water, my hair gently swirling in the eddies of gravity that flowed around me. My free fall came to a gentle stop three feet off the ground; I was floating on gravity. The training officer, who had watched my fall with horror, slowly came toward me. His eyes were wide with shock as he spoke in an awed whisper, "Well, that's a new one."

I didn't stay suspended for long after that. As soon as I allowed my mind to think about what I was doing, I lost my control of the gravity field and it took back its mastery, pulling me down to the Earth.

The rest of the night was a wash. My preoccupation with trying to figure out what had just happened got me "shot" before I had even entered the other team's base. The training officers, who had no sympathy for my preoccupation, sent me and four others stupid enough to get shot hiking the five miles back to base while the rest of the team finished the mission and got a ride.

We got back to our barracks just as the sun was coming up. All I wanted was to fall into my bunk. Unfortunately, the scientists back at the base were equally fascinated by my newly discovered ability, and they had gotten a full night's rest. I didn't get any sleep that night.

The next few weeks of training took on a newly intense focus as I learned to do it again, this time on purpose, and without the imminent threat of death to guide my actions. You would think it would be an easy matter to repeat something I knew positively that I could do; unfortunately, it wasn't.

Instinct is a funny thing; it isn't always quite so instinctive as the word makes it sound. The first several days I felt like I was banging my head against a wall: all I was getting from my efforts was a massive headache.

The scientists must have been equally exasperated because Dr. Eris finally called an early halt to our session eight days later after yet another unproductive day. "Enough!" she had growled. "We are just wasting our time until you get your act together and figure this out."

They were clearly disappointed by my failures. Of course, Troy was there that day, watching from the observation room; the frown on his face spoke volumes. Callia was also there; the smirk on her face said even more.

For my part, I was worn out and tired, but I was also angry, frustrated, disappointed, and embarrassed all at the same time. I admitted to myself that sleep wasn't going to happen the way I was feeling. I needed to burn off some of those excess emotions, so I headed for the gym.

Running laps on the indoor track was one of my preferred ways to burn off steam. I imagine it was another gift from my mom. The base's track wasn't nearly as popular as the weight room was, which meant I usually got it to myself.

Unfortunately, it seemed my bad luck was a step ahead of me; someone else was already on the track. He was a new guy, or at least I hadn't seen him before. That wasn't really a surprise considering the number of troops that were constantly transferring onto and off of the base, but he was running faster than most of the others did which meant I would also have to run fast if I wanted to be able to keep an illusion of solitude by staying on the opposite side of the track from him. That was fine. I was fast enough in my own right to keep a steady distance between us, and running fast actually sounded like a good idea at the moment.

The first two laps went exactly as I thought they would: my pace matched his at a smooth five-minute mile pace. But on the third lap, as I rounded a corner, I caught a glimpse of him out of the corner of my eye, not where I had expected him to be. He was gaining on me. I growled quietly to myself and sped up, assuming that would solve the problem; it didn't.

Half a lap later he was passing me. A few laps later he was passing me again. According to the speed board on the wall, I was running a 4:50 mile. He was running a 4:15. No…make that a 4:02…3:45…3:15…2:43…*Wow, this guy was fast!* He continued to lap me multiple times for the next three miles. His top speed that I saw register was a 2:36 mile.

I had heard that there were Betas and Charlies capable of such speeds, but I had never seen one running before. Even though I had come to the track focused on solitude and burning off steam, I found my eyes following the other runner each time he passed me, and I began to mentally categorize my track mate.

From the back, which was the primary view I was getting of him, I could tell that he was well built, muscular in all the right places without being too bulky, and with a light golden tan that complemented his hair color perfectly. His short hair was that vibrant black-blue that was a holdout from the M-Gens. It was a little longer than the average soldier's though, with the tips haphazardly tousled into an organized chaos that probably drove the girls wild but got him into trouble with his commanding officers.

Each time he passed me I got a brief glance at his chiseled face with its heavy brow and lightly pursed lips. His features placed him in his late teens, early twenties. There was also just a hint of a smile on his features to suggest that he was enjoying the fact that he was so easily outpacing me. My suspicion was confirmed the next time he caught up to me.

As he passed, he smoothly pivoted so that he was running backward; his pace only slowing slightly. *Ok, now he's just showing off!* I might have been annoyed if it wasn't for the mischievous twinkle in his brilliant blue eyes. *Wow! He has gorgeous eyes.*

I barely had time to register that thought before he was around the corner and out of sight once more. Less than a minute later he was passing me again, still running backward, only this time there was something different about him.

It took me a full three seconds to register what it was, and then I couldn't hold back the laughter as I realized what my peripheral vision had immediately noticed: he had crossed his eyes and the tip of his tongue was sticking out of the corner of his lips.

Chuckling to myself, I slowed my pace to a walk. Partly due to the run, but mostly due to the laughter, I was feeling much better. A few seconds later he came around the corner once more and slowed to a walk beside me.

He was breathing hard and grinning even harder. "So, th' lady does know how tae smile." His voice was a rich baritone with a gentle Scottish lilt.

I laughed lightly in return. "I guess I just needed something worth smiling about."

"Well then, glad I could be of service." He held out his hand to me. "Th' name is Aiden. And what name goes with yae?" I didn't answer him immediately. It wasn't that I was trying to be coy, but most people on base knew the Alphas by sight. No one had ever asked my name before because they already knew it.

I looked at him a little quizzically, instead coming back with a question of my own. "You must be new on base. When did you come in?"

He shrugged off the change in direction and answered my question. "Me unit is just passing through. We got in this morning, and we'll be shippin' out for Egypt before th' sun goes down. But me CO said headquarters wanted me tae take advantage of th' facilities here tae get an updated baseline for me speed." He glanced up at the speed board with a smirk. "It must be a scientist thing. They need numbers and data tae work with. They weren't satisfied with me answer when I wrote on me skills form that I was a "fast mover.""

I couldn't help but laugh. "You really wrote that?"

"Well, it did say list all of yer skills."

"Oh? What else did you list? You have me curious now."

"I also wrote down that I was dashingly handsome, a smooth talker, and a hopeless comedian, but they crossed those off sayin' they didn't qualify as skills. I guess that makes speed me one and only claim tae fame."

I shook my head, slightly impressed with his shameless bravado. "Well, your speed at least is quite impressive. My mother was a Beta who could also run fast. They tell me she clocked a 3:35 mile when she was twelve, but that wasn't a trait she happened to pass on to me."

"Oh, I don't know about that…" He turned playfully thoughtful. "Yae were recording some pretty impressive times of yer own. There aren't many women who can maintain a sub-five-minute mile for as many miles as yae did. But, yer right. That does seem pretty slow when yae compare it against that other guy's times up there on th' board. So, speed is not yer skill. That means yae must have some other skill that caused them tae assign you tae this base."

I raised my eyebrow. "What makes you think I'm assigned to this base? Maybe I'm just passing through like you."

"Naw," his smile returned, "yer stance tells me yae have been trained for combat, yer age suggests yae are tae young tae have enlisted th' normal route, and yer hair is tae long to be a typical soldier's. Th' only non-typical soldiers on this base are assigned tae th' Alphabet Unit."

Alphabet Unit? I wasn't impressed with that joke. I stopped walking this time, forcing him to turn back around to face me. "Is that in reference to the Alpha, Beta, and Charlie makeup of this base's primary unit?"

He tried to keep a straight face to match my suddenly angry tone, but he was only just barely succeeding. "Of course not. It was in reference tae the Absolutely Beautiful, Crazily Delicious, Entirely Female Group yae must be part of." His response caught me off guard. *Did he just compliment me?* I was still trying to formulate an appropriate response when a new voice startled us both.

"Cute, Private. An excellent line for picking up little girls, but a lousy one for addressing your superior." Neither one of us had noticed the third person standing silently in the doorway to the gym, his arms folded sternly across his chest. I didn't recognize the man, but Aiden clearly did. He snapped to attention; all traces of laughter gone from his face.

"Sorry, Major. I was jus—"

The Major cut him off. "I know what you were failing miserably at doing, Haskell. I don't need an excuse. You have eight miles left to go, now get back to running."

"Aye, sir!" Aiden turned smartly without another word and resumed his running at a brisk pace. The Major then turned to me and met my eyes briefly with a stern look before he grunted a gruff, "Ma'am" and turned to leave the track. Clearly, I had also been excused. It would seem they didn't want Private Haskell distracted from his run. I rolled my eyes as I moved off the track and headed for the hall.

I was halfway down it when an idea occurred to me. I stepped quietly into the observation booth, found an open computer, and typed a quick message for the speed board to display. A few seconds later, I knew he had read it because I could hear his laughter echoing down the hall.

ATTENTION PRIVATE FAST MOVER: THE ALPAHBET UNIT ALSO INCLUDES ADORABLY BONKERS, CLEARLY DESPERATE, ENCHANTINGLY FUNNY GUYS.

-ALPHABET GIRL

Chapter 2: Alexandria Jaquette

WHEN I DIDN'T see him in the mess hall later that night, I assumed he had already shipped out. I'll admit I was a little disappointed, but not very surprised. I had gotten used to people coming and going around here. The one constant I could always count on was the routine. Dinner was bland, lights out came too fast, and the next morning started way too early with a five o'clock training run followed by four hours in the classroom. The focus of that morning's lesson was battle strategies as they related to guarding facilities.

Captain Newman was directing the lesson. "Some of the possible locations you may be assigned to are educational facilities that have been designed not only to educate our world's future but also to protect them. These facilities offer a special challenge because of their dual nature. They must be safe, secure environments for the children who live and learn there while still being accessible to the families, teachers, and scientists who work with and visit those children. These are not closed facilities and so, by nature, they are more susceptible to attack.

"If you are assigned to one of these facilities, it will be because it has been determined that your unique set of skills will enhance the security of that facility above and beyond what an ordinary platoon can do on their own.

"We currently have five educational facilities under our unit's direct security: Dartmouth College in America, the University of Cambridge in England, the University of São Paulo in Brazil, the University of Cape Town in South Africa, and Peking University in China. Each of these schools is currently staffed with an OSP.

"For those of you who haven't been here long enough to become familiar with that term, an Operational Securities Platoon consists of three combat squads, assisted by one information technology squad and two Special Ops Teams. The Special Ops Team is where you come in.

"Your assignments will be directly related to your skills, and you will answer directly to the Sergeant First Class responsible for that platoon. However, you are better versed with your skills and abilities than the Sergeant is likely to be when you first arrive.

"For that reason, we are going to spend the remainder of this week discussing the layouts of each of those schools, the fortifications already in place at each of these schools, the methods Icarus' armies have used to attack similar schools in the past, and the strategies each of you can specifically employ to defend those schools should you ever be assigned to one of them."

Someone in the back must have raised their hand because Captain Newman turned to address them. "You have a question, Specialist Miller?"

"Yes, sir. Icarus has not attacked a school in several years. Is there still a need to protect them with so much security?"

"Reasonable question, Miller, and there are others who have suggested it as well; some of them pretty high up in the government. But one thing remains certain. Children are our greatest resource. They were always the future's leaders, but now they have also become the present's weapons. Some of them, like you, are literal weapons. But the vast majority of them are figurative weapons whose destructive capacity comes into existence the moment the enemy realizes they can be used as pawns, emotional leverage with the capacity to topple governments. Icarus has clearly shown that he has no problem killing children. Imagine the potential situation should Icarus get his hands on, say, one of the UFC leader's kids? The job of those assigned to these schools is to prevent that from happening."

"Forgive me, sir," another voice asked, "why not just lock down the schools? Wouldn't that make them easier to defend?"

Newman paused, his eyebrow raised and his mouth set in a firm line just long enough to remind the speaker that he had crossed a line by not raising his hand and waiting to be called on, but surprisingly, he chose to answer the question in spite of it. "While the countries within the UFC have agreed to send their gifted children to special schools for training, many of those same countries remain unwilling to give their children over totally to the care of the military. And can you blame them? Look how The Brig turned out: ugly and stubborn." That brought a good laugh from the group; even I had to smile.

"Now, seeing as we can't fully lock down the facility, we have to instead focus on enhancing the existing natural barriers with unobtrusive structures that maintain the feeling of openness while in fact more fully securing the site."

He directed our attention to the large display screen at the front of the room. "From this satellite image, you can see that the terrain around Dartmouth College consists primarily of hills, woods, and a small river. Although you can't see it, there is an IBS surrounding the whole campus.

"An IBS is an Invisible Barrier System. It uses a wireless system of volumetric passive and active infrared barrier detectors, ultrasonic and thermal detectors, and state-of-the-art imaging cameras to give twenty-four-hour surveillance capabilities to the information technology squad.

"The three combat squads rotate a 24-hour sentry in unobtrusive, but militaristically contrived locations throughout the campus. Additionally, there are multiple secure locations to which the students can be evacuated in a matter of minutes."

Captain Newman went on to describe the functionality of the IBS, bunkers, and other fortifications, but I had grown up at Cambridge College in England; I was already somewhat familiar with all of the security he was expounding on. I knew about the IBS and how it worked. I even knew about the soldiers.

As students, we had known they were there, and even knew a few of them by sight or by name. But for the most part, they had unobtrusively protected us without interfering in our lives. The one exception had been during the bi-annual drills when they had us practice rapid evacuations into the bunkers beneath the campus.

The rumor was that there were fourteen of those bunkers scattered beneath the campus, but I had only ever seen the inside of five of them. Which one you went into depended on your grade level and associated location on campus.

During those drills, the soldiers came out in full gear, no effort was made to blend in at those times. I think they did it so that we could get used to them. If there was ever a real evacuation, they didn't want us to be so frightened of them that we wouldn't obey. If that was their goal, it was an effective one.

By the time I was four, I was so comfortable with them that I had even climbed into one soldier's arms, pushing his equipment to the side so that I could lay my head down on his shoulder. I can't imagine what the soldier must have thought, but he had taken it in stride, carrying me down the stairs with one arm, while guiding the group of students with his other.

Another time, when I was fifteen, I and three of my friends had worked out a way through the Invisible Barrier System that would allow us to sneak off campus and back on without anyone the wiser, or so we thought. We made it off campus just fine and had hours of fun dancing the night away at a party that was taking place at a friend of a friend's cousin's boyfriend's house a mile off campus. But when we were sneaking back onto campus, our eyes heavy-lidded from staying up all night, we were startled to find ourselves greeted at the head of the pathway by four of the usually hidden guards.

Our attempt to "sneak" off campus had been anything but successful. They knew exactly who had gone, when we had gone, where we had gone, and what we had been doing for the past few hours. In fact, we soon discovered that we had never even been truly on our own.

We'd had a plain-clothed soldier shadowing us the whole time. After ensuring we were safe, they'd let us have our fun, but then they made sure that the cost of it was sufficiently high that not one of us was ever interested in trying it again.

I don't recall how many bathroom stalls I had to scrub, but the one thing I never forgot was the look on the face of the plainclothes soldier when I turned around and noticed him for the first time. It was the same soldier who had carried me when I was four. This time, however, there was no tenderness or patient understanding in his expression. Instead, his stone-faced disapproval was etched into every tightly clenched muscle of his face, telling me I had disappointed him. Worse, his gentle gray eyes which had always spared a smile for me on the occasions when our paths had crossed in the past, were now hard and cold with glinting anger that was barely contained beneath the surface.

I wasn't able to hold his gaze for more than a few seconds before I had to look away, a feeling of deep shame filling me; I had disappointed him. That night, for the first time, I came to realize that I valued his opinion of me at least as much as I valued my own. I determined to never disappoint him again.

I didn't have many opportunities to talk to him over the next eighteen months. Still, I think I must have won back some small measure of his good opinion because he was there the day they came to take me to the UFC base in Ghana. Or rather, I saw him standing just inside the doorway of the commander's office, talking to someone I couldn't see.

His voice was low, gruff with emotion, yet just loud enough for me to catch a small part of what he was saying as we walked past. "...she's a good kid. She doesn't deserve this...they should have let her stay a kid..."

Then, a few minutes later, as the helio-transport rose into the air, I caught another glimpse of him, standing just outside the doorway of the command center. He stayed there, watching us go until he was too small to see anymore.

I know it's unlikely that I will ever see him again, but his influence has remained a part of who I am. In a way, he became the father figure I never had. I'm determined that if

I do ever see him again, he won't have cause to be disappointed with me. That thought has driven me to do better, to become better.

Speaking of which, I doubt he would be too happy if he ever caught me daydreaming during a lecture. I pushed the memory of that soldier aside and forced my attention back to the Captain as he switched the image away from the technical details of the security arrangements and back to the aerial view of one of the school's campuses.

He was still droning on, "Earlier I mentioned the terrain. Terrain is always a double-edged sword. While geological features can be natural barriers, they also have their weaknesses. Of all the campuses, Dartmouth is the most exposed in this area. There are two primary concerns with the terrain: The first is the river on the school's west edge. IBS systems are ineffective in moving water, so the school has a sonar system in place here. There is also only one bridge within a ten-mile radius that crosses the water, and that bridge is secured by a two-man guard at all times. The problem comes with the difficulty of guarding against underwater infiltration. The second concern is the hills, or more particularly the ravines and caves that are a natural part of hills. These naturally occurring landforms create a thousand hiding places that an approaching enemy can utilize. As advanced as the IBS system is, it would be virtually impossible to install one that is full-proof under these circumstances. This is where you come in."

He paused as he gazed around the room, allowing his eyes to rest on each of us just long enough to emphasize that this was important. "For the next few hours, I am going to break you into four-person teams to discuss this scenario. Your objective is to identify what defenses could be used to address this school's weak points as well as the weak points of the other three schools, and how each of your skills could be applied to close the gaps within those schools' security plans."

To tell the truth, I enjoyed the breakout session. I had been paired up with three other specialists who took the assignment seriously but could still chuckle when someone suggested that a few mutated sharks in the river could solve a lot of problems. By the time the class ended, we had developed what we felt was a reasonable plan that pitted each of our skills against the natural barriers the Captain had identified as well as a few more that we noticed as we studied the detailed plans.

Rockman, it was a nickname we had all given the 26-year-old German because of his extraordinary skills as a rock climber and his uncanny ability to recognize the fault lines in rock structures, would be best suited for the Peking University where he could either scale the mountainous terrain around the city or one of the nearby skyscrapers. His climbing skills would give him an eagle-eye view of the school and the terrain around it while his mind would more accurately identify potential dangers than the IBS could.

Estradé, a fifty-year-old Mexican woman who could hear a pin drop a mile away but had only recently been recruited to the group, would do well at any of the schools listening for sounds that didn't belong. But would likely be especially effective at the University of São Paulo because her skin tone and facial features would allow her to easily blend in with the local population and allow her to covertly do her job without standing out. In addition to her native Spanish, she also spoke Basic, Portuguese, English, Farsi, and Russian.

Smith, not to shame Estradé's language skills, was the base's resident language expert, and was also reasonably suited to any of the campuses, but his language skills would be especially useful in a region that boasted a diversity of spoken languages. His record stated that he was fluent in thirty-two languages and had a rough grasp of eight more. Of the four schools, the University of Cape Town had the most diverse cultural makeup, and Smith currently spoke nine of the twelve languages most common in that region.

That left me. What could I do with gravity that would help guard a school? It was Rockman who came up with the idea, so blame him, but the rest of the group agreed it was brilliant: I could throw snowballs. Granted it would only work during the winter, but that was six months out of the year in New Hampshire. I would use my control of gravity to move snow around so that it didn't interfere with the IBS systems, or to create walls made of snow and ice that would then become additional barriers, and of course, I could throw ice balls with deadly accuracy and speed. I did grow up in snowy England, after all, where snow fights were a winter tradition. Though to be truthful, I had never actually tried throwing snow with gravity, so I couldn't say for certain that it would work, but the theory was sound. Captain Newman had actually cracked a smile when Estradé outlined our plan for the rest of the class.

I was in a good mood by the time class ended and I headed for the next part of my daily routine: the "torture" lab. I would be spending the next four hours trying to, and likely once again failing to, figure out how to get my feet off of the ground.

At least the scientists also appeared to be in a much better mood when I walked into the training center. I caught snatches of conversations that suggested their excitement had to do with a new Charlie joining the group and something about a new record having been set. But the smile on Dr. Eris' face faded quickly when she saw me.

"Well, are we going to see any improvements from you today?"

I almost rolled my eyes but caught myself at the last second. I really hated that lady. It wasn't like I hadn't been trying. It was just proving harder to nudge the gravity under me than the gravity in front of me.

"I'll tell you what," I said instead. "When I make progress, I promise you will be the first person I let know about it."

Her deepening frown told me she wasn't at all impressed with my sarcasm. I ignored it and swept past her without meeting her eyes.

"So, what are we working on today? Shall I rearrange the furniture for you, or would you prefer I sit in the middle of the mats Zen style until I get another headache from failing to lift myself into the air?"

But it wasn't Dr. Eris' that answered my question. "Oh no, dear." The smug purr of Callia's voice sent chills down my spine. I spun around to see her leaning against the wall. I was certain she hadn't been there when I came into the room, so she must have been bending the light to keep me from seeing her.

"Today you will be working with me. Troy thought you could use a little help focusing. He asked me to give you a hand."

She didn't give me a chance to respond before turning to Dr. Eris with a look of conspiracy. "If you don't mind, Doctor, Alexandria and I would like the room to ourselves for a bit."

Eris smiled back just as sweetly. "Of course, dear. I'm sure I can find something productive to do elsewhere for a while."

The training room door shut behind her with an ominous thud that was only slightly louder than the sudden pounding of my heart. It's amazing how quickly a good mood evaporates when faced with an undesirable situation; I was not looking forward to what was coming next.

Chapter 3: Alexandria Jaquette

CALLIA PRACTICALLY PURRED as she sauntered away from the wall and walked around me, looking me up and down, stalking me like a cat stalks a bird. I turned my body slowly to follow her movements head-on, not stupid enough to turn my back on her.

At the same time, I was aware that her movements were skillfully leading me away from the door and closer to the center of the training mat with herself standing between me and the exit. I almost laughed at that one. If she thought I might try to run, she needn't have worried. I wasn't one to run from trouble, even if it meant that I would take a beating because of it.

"So, what comes next?" I asked as casually as I could, trying not to betray the uneasiness that had settled in the pit of my stomach. In the last few months, I had become reasonably good at hand-to-hand, but I knew I wouldn't stand a chance if Callia went on the attack. Seeing through my charade, she smiled wickedly in response.

"Now we push you to the edge."

Despite my effort to be ready for the attack that was obviously coming, I was far from prepared for it. She moved impossibly fast so that her hands were little more than a blur as her clenched fist lashed out to catch me just below the ribs.

I stumbled backward several steps, gasping for air as I struggled to not fall but Callia was immediately beside me, not giving me time to catch my breath. She snarled ferally and swept her foot behind me to kick my legs out from under me. I fell to my back with a thud, my head banging hard on the ground. If there hadn't been a workout mat beneath me to soften my landing, there's a good chance I would have been knocked out.

As it was, my head gained a new spinning sensation that left me feeling slightly off balance as I rolled to my side and stumbled back to my feet. It also seemed to be messing with my sense of distance. I could have sworn that Callia had stepped back, presumably to give me a moment to catch my breath, but in the same instant her image blurred, and she was striking out at my hip from right next to me. Despite the maelstrom in my head, a sudden realization clearly echoed: Callia was bending the light so that I couldn't accurately see her attacks coming.

I snarled in frustration. I hadn't stood a chance under normal circumstances, now she was taking it too far. "How am I supposed to defend myself if I can't see you coming?"

Her throaty laugh only served to irritate me further. "What? You thought Icarus was going to play fair? Wake up child," she sneered, "this is a war we're fighting. If you have a gift that gives you an advantage, use it." She snarled that last part as she suddenly lunged at me, wrapping her arms around my waist and tackling me.

In that moment, it was like time slowed down inside my mind. I was still falling backward, but in the space of a single breath, something suddenly clicked: I have a gift. I can see

41

the ebbs and flows of gravity, and, not only can I see them, I can control them.

It was suddenly so easy to see; so perfectly obvious that it didn't make sense why I hadn't realized it before. People were no different from furniture or training balls as far as gravity was concerned. The same force that allowed me to lift those inanimate objects flowed around living things as well. The only difference was that living things caused swirls in the flow of gravity as they moved. If I accounted for those swirls, then there was no reason I couldn't continue to control the gravity around Callia or the gravity under me.

The exquisite look of surprise on Callia's face as she was torn backward from me and dropped to the ground several feet away was undeniably satisfying, though short-lived as Callia rebounded back to her feet with a cat-like grace that matched the predatory grin on her face.

"Good," she purred. "Now do it again."

She stalked forward and then I saw her body begin to blur as she bent the light around her once more. This time I was ready. Instead of watching her, I watched the flow of gravity throughout the room. Bending light had no effect on those.

In the last second, before she was within reach of me, I pushed off with the gravity at my feet, launching myself backward several feet. It wasn't exactly floating the way I had done the night I fell from the helio-transport, but I had definitely been in control of the gravity beneath me this time as I used it to move my body away from Callia's.

For the next hour, we played a game of cat and mouse. I became increasingly confident in my skills as I bounced from place to place, gaining height and control in equal proportions. She still got in quite a few blows, but I was now avoiding at least as many as were catching me.

I can't say that I was happy about her methods, but I could not deny their effectiveness. I would have several ugly bruises tomorrow to attest to the cost of my newly developed skill, and it was worth every one of them.

I was grinning from ear to ear, using the gravity to lift myself well out of the range of the staff she was swinging at me when the door at the front of the room unexpectedly opened and in walked Private Haskell followed by General Durnham and two of the base's scientists. They stopped mid-stride, a low whistle escaping Aiden's lips as he looked up at me in amazement. I was hovering seven feet off the ground, with nothing beneath me but the air.

Durnham, with his usual air of unsurprised expectation, only nodded his head once in gruff satisfaction before turning to say something to the scientists behind him that sent that woman scurrying from the room.

Suddenly embarrassed, I came down a little harder than I meant to. An hour of training had taught me how to get myself into the air but coming down was still pretty rough.

Aiden's eyes were still wide with surprise when the General turned back to him. "Haskell, allow me to introduce you to Lieutenant Colonel Callia Ubuqua and Specialist Alexandria Jaquette."

Haskell shook his head as if to clear the shock of what he had seen as he looked away from me and stepped forward to shake hands with Callia. "It's a pleasure tae meet yae, ma'am."

Callia took his outstretched hand in both of hers as she stepped ever so slightly closer to him. "The pleasure is all mine." The purr in her voice and the seductive way she was looking at him made my stomach churn, but Aiden hardly seemed to notice it as he briefly shook her hand and then stepped around her to approach me.

"Hello again." His eyes were twinkling as he offered me his hand. "Specialist Fast Mover at yer service."

His lilting words were as charming as they had been the day before. Despite my embarrassment over my fumbled landing and my disgust at the game Callia was playing, I found that I couldn't help but chuckle in response. "I guess you took me up on my suggestion. What did you tell them that convinced them to let you stay? That you have a talent for being on hand when damsels are in distress?"

He was grinning even bigger as I accepted his outstretched hand. "Well, I did happen tae mention that I had managed tae tweak a smile out of a particularly frustrated young lady, but I suspect it had more tae do with the time I clocked a few minutes after yae left."

"Oh?" I asked. "Did you break the speed board?"

"Somethin' like that," he chuckled. "I set off some alarms and managed tae interrupt the sleepin' habits of half th' scientists round here by breakin' th' two-minute mile barrier."

Now that truly was impressive. The two-minute mile had been an impenetrable barrier that runners had been striving to break through for the last fifty years. Some scientists had even concluded that it was physically impossible for humans to move that fast.

"Wow," I said in awe, "remind me not to enter into any races with you." I was about to ask him if the scientists had allowed him to get any sleep after that, but General Durnham interrupted our banter before it could go any further. His commanding voice carried easily across the room. "Haskell has agreed to add his speed to our team. He will begin training with us starting in the morning. However, for the rest of the afternoon, I am assigning Jaquette to show him around the facilities and introduce him to the rest of the specialists."

I was a little surprised by this. There were personnel responsible for the job of orienting new recruits and it was very unusual for the assignment to be given to someone who didn't hold the position. Yet I knew better than to question his orders.

"Yes, sir," I replied, a little confused, but not at all upset. It meant that the General was satisfied with what I had achieved today. Not that I cared what the General thought about my successes or failures, but I believed that if he was pleased with my success, then so would have been the soldier from my youth. If I had been a little wiser, I would have stopped to wonder why I was the one he asked. I might have even considered that Callia would not have been pleased with the order.

Unfortunately, at that moment I was so excited by my success and the opportunity to escape the lab, not to mention having some time to get to know this humorous Private who really did have a knack for making me smile, that the questions didn't even so much as flit through my mind.

Instead, I nodded my head toward the door to indicate to Haskell that we should move in that direction. He seemed only too happy to oblige as he jumped forward to pull the door open for me. As we passed, Callia did something I should have seen coming.

She leaned toward us, speaking just loud enough so that Haskell and I were the only ones who could hear her. "Do be careful in the barracks, Jaquette. We don't need you to injure another man. After all, Private Lance never fully recovered from your last one-on-one tour."

I stopped in my tracks, my cheeks suddenly flaming red, my fists balled up in anger. How dare she bring that up! She had no right to even insinuate that anything had happened there! I didn't pause to consider the consequences, just the amount of force it would take to slam her against the wall and break every bone in her miserable, spiteful body.

Fortunately, Haskell saved me from my anger by reaching out to put his arm through mine and force me away from Callia before I could act on the thoughts. He chuckled lightly as he did so, while at the same time muttering under his breath just loudly enough for Callia to hear him. "Thank yae for th' warnin'. Now I know where th' real danger is on this base."

The door closed solidly behind us and for several moments I allowed him to lead me, my anger blinding me to where we were going. It wasn't until there were several hallways between us that the realization of what he had just done sank in.

I stopped suddenly, pulling my arm from his. "Why would you…" I started to ask him why he had done it, only to find that I didn't know how to put into words what I really wanted to ask him. We had barely met yesterday. He didn't know me any better than he knew Callia. So why had he taken my side over hers? By now he must also know that I was an Alpha, and he'd seen enough to know that I was a strong one at that. Why wasn't he scared by that? Or was he? Had he meant me when he said he now knew where the real danger was? Yet that didn't seem right either. His arm through mine had not been tensed, as though holding something dangerous. It had been quite the opposite: relaxed, yet firm and purposeful. He had intentionally guided me away from Callia, putting himself in harm's way to keep me out of it. Why would he do that?

Did he not recognize that Callia was in a position of authority and had it in her power to make his life miserable? I wasn't worth that type of trouble. So why? Or, was it possible, just maybe, that for some unimaginable reason, he thought I was? I didn't see how he could. Nor could I think of any other reasonable explanation. So instead of finishing my question, I just stood there, waiting for him to turn and face me, to give me some type of explanation for the questions I didn't know how to ask.

I'm sure the maelstrom of questions must have been visible on my face because his hands were up as if to ward them off as he slowly turned to face me. "Look," he began, his eyes serious for the first time since I had met him. "I know it's not me place, but yae looked like yae were about tae get yerself into some real trouble and it seemed like a good idea tae get yae out of there."

He paused as though gauging my reaction. I didn't say anything, so he went on. "We've a sayin' where I grew up: 'Never draw yer dirk when a blow will do it.' Yae looked like yae were ready to draw a phase rifle and blast her through th' wall."

He paused once more, his eyes carefully searching mine. "I'm not new tae th' games women play. Me older sister is a master at them. She would'a put Corporal Ubuqua's efforts tae shame in there." His serious expression slowly evaporated as he explained, a sly smile creeping in to replace it. "She taught me everythin' I know about handlin' th' ladies. Seein' as I've no interest in bein' th' lady's next conquest, an offhanded rejection was th' only thing needed to set th' Corporal straight."

Despite so desperately wanting to know his reasoning, I was caught off guard by his open admission, so I said the first thing that came to mind: "Are you crazy?"

His grin really lit up at my question. "Well, if yae were tae ask me older sister she would say most definitely. And now that I think of it, that sayin' from back home probably came from a time before they had nuclear bombs because as soon as I said it, the Corporal turned so red that I could'a sworn she was about tae blow her top."

Once more, I found his smile to be infectious as my own smile slowly came back to match his. His lack of concern about Callia and her vengeance was refreshing. I had spent a long time trying to avoid the Corporal and her games when in truth, I had never really cared about them, just the trouble she could cause me as a result. But I was tired of always having to avoid her and her games. Haskell had it right. And if that was a little crazy, so be it. "She's right. You are crazy, but maybe a little crazy is just what we need around here."

"Good." He laughed. "Now that we have that established, I have just one more question: What happened in th' barracks that th' Lt. Colonel was able tae turn into an attack?"

Now it was my turn to laugh. "Quite the opposite of what she suggested. It wasn't even a tour. Shortly after I was transferred here, we were putting up temporary barracks for a visiting platoon. Specialist Lance was assigned to use his strength to hold up the main beam while I was assigned to help him balance it. They had almost gotten the beam secured in place when I made a mistake that caused the beam to tip. Lance acted quickly to return the balance, but he strained his shoulder muscles doing so. They healed quickly enough, but now and then he liked to tease me by acting like his muscles were still stiff and sore and that he needed me to do one of his duties as a result.

"At the same time, about a month after the incident, Callia tried to play the same game with Lance that she just tried to play with you. Lance already had a girl at home and wasn't the least bit interested. He rebuffed her, much like you did.

"Callia got her revenge by starting some rumors about Lance and me, suggesting that our playful banter was a result of a more serious relationship, even going so far as to call his girlfriend and share the rumors with her personally.

"A few days later I found Lance off by himself, crying over a breakup letter his girlfriend had sent him. I was furious but had no way to fix it. Whatever Callia told his girlfriend, it was very convincing. When I tried to call his girl and straighten everything out, she refused to believe anything I said. She cussed me out and hung up on me instead of listening."

"Well, that won't be a problem for me. I don't have a girlfriend, and me sister would only get a good laugh out of it if th' Lt. Colonel were tae call her."

"And if she comes up with some other type of rumor or finds some other way to cause trouble?"

Haskell shrugged his shoulders. "Most likely she'll find I'm a hard person tae get revenge on. I told yae, I had a good teacher at this game. But, hey, if she comes up with a good one, I'll have a story tae share next time I go home."

I shook my head in disbelief. But the truth was that all of the tension had finally gone. "All right then. Durnham said I was to give you a tour of the base. Where should we begin?"

"Barracks?" He said it with an even bigger grin, wiggling his eyebrows in suggestion. I started laughing. What better

49

way to throw Callia's comment back in her face than to do exactly what she had suggested would be most dangerous?

"Very well. Let's do this."

Chapter 4: Alexandria Jaquette

PRIVATE HASKELL, OR rather I should say Specialist Haskell now that he was assigned to our division, seemed to have judged his situation correctly. Over the course of the next twelve weeks, I kept waiting for Callia's revenge to come, but nothing untoward occurred. It seemed that she had either failed to find a sufficiently satisfying angle for her revenge or else her plans for revenge had sputtered out so badly that she had quietly covered them up.

Either way, Haskell quickly became a fluid part of the team. He was already well-trained by military standards. He had started his military service when he was fifteen. It was an unusually young age by most countries' standards, but he said it was the normal age to begin service in his country. In fact, he told me that the Scottish Infantry Regiments had long formed the core of the United Kingdoms' infantry and that his family in particular had a tradition of service in the regiments that went back to the 1600s BC. Over the past six years, he had seen service on the front line in several arenas, including Egypt, Iran, and Afghanistan. All that remained of his training here was to learn his place in the "ABC" unit.

His quick wit and easy-going humor made him popular among the other Betas and Charlies, while his speed and training made him valuable to the commanding officers. For my part, I was really starting to enjoy having him around, though I didn't get to see him nearly as often as I would have liked.

I never saw him during the morning runs and training sessions; I assumed the scientists had given him a different workout program from the rest of us, considering that the running portion of our daily workout would obviously have not been a sufficiently harsh form of torture upon him to satisfy their twisted sense of humor.

I also didn't see much of him during the classroom schedule as we were assigned to different training squads. And of course, I rarely saw him during the four-hour torture sessions with the science teams except occasionally when we passed each other in the hall. But combat training was another story.

Combat training was an intense, four-hour period that rotated daily between hand-to-hand combat scenarios, weapons field application, and short-run tactical exercises. During this time, all three of the base's specialist squads were brought together. Sometimes we competed against each other, and other times we were required to work together; it all depended on the training goals for that particular day. It was during those times that I saw Aiden the most.

His experience in combat skills had led the commanding officers to utilize him in training the newer recruits, most of whom had had little to no military experience before accepting the invitation to become a specialist.

It turned out that he was a particularly good teacher as well, quickly guiding other specialists to master the skills he was showing them. This turned out to be especially true when he was teaching hand-to-hand fighting techniques. It quickly became recognized that he was one of the top experts on base in that arena. There were only a handful of people who managed to get the better of him on the mats. I was not even close to being one of them.

Despite that, I enjoyed every opportunity I had to train with him. Whether he was teaching me how to properly place my feet so that I could go around a blind corner balanced and ready to shoot or showing me a better way to throw my opponent on the mat. I looked forward to each afternoon knowing he would usually be there.

This afternoon's exercise was an orienteering challenge. We had been tasked with locating a series of markers, each of which would provide us with an essential piece we would need to complete the final task of securing a small bunker located somewhere in the jungle of the base's eastern edge.

The Ghanaian jungle, a lush collection of Teak, Kapok, Terminalia, and Khaya trees, is as harsh as it is beautiful. The nearly constant rainfall in the region has allowed the closely packed trees to grow into a stunningly magnificent canopy of greenery with an occasional jungle giant that towers far above the other trees as though it were reaching for the sun above. But the vast majority of the jungle's plants and animals are left to compete for survival in the shadows beneath the jungle's green crown.

Some three million different species of plants, mammals, reptiles, amphibians, birds, and insects live in and amongst those shadows. Any number of those have evolved at least one way to injure or kill men. Despite that, man had been living in this jungle for more than a thousand years. Part of the training we were given at the base focused on how to protect ourselves from those dangers. The rest of it focused on how to become just as deadly as they were.

For this particular training, we had been divided into teams of five randomly assigned specialists and then taken out in a transport vehicle whose windows had been covered, and along a circuitous route that was designed to mix us up and confuse us as to the exact location off post where we had been dropped off. It was expected at this point in our training that we had the skills we needed to survive out here, even if it took us several days.

We were handed a bag of supplies that included, among other things, a map, a compass, a first aid kit, and an emergency satellite phone as well as an envelope with the details about the first marker's location; and then the vehicle left us there.

We looked around us to get our bearings as the vehicle drove around the bend and out of view. There wasn't much to see; just a dense wall of trees, vines, and bushes interrupted by a dirt road that curved quickly out of view in both directions.

"All right then." Hadley took the lead as he opened the envelope that had been handed to him. He was a Beta whose reaction times and reflexes were beyond incredible. Combined with his years of martial arts training, he was the undisputed combat expert on the base.

He read from the paper he drew out of the envelope. "This says the first marker is located at an elevation of 98 meters above sea level."

"That's it?" Bowen asked incredulously.

Bowen was a young, short, stocky, Australian Charlie who wasn't very bright on his own, but more than made up for it with his strength. He could clean lift four thousand fifty pounds and could deadlift another ten thousand on top of that.

Estradé rolled her eyes. "Es Suficiente Mijo," she muttered under her breath, just loud enough for us to hear. Then, in her thickly accented English, she said louder, "The average elevation of this base is fifty meters above sea level."

Bowen whipped around, clearly annoyed by her depreciating comment. "And how do you know that?"

Estradé shrugged off his attitude like she always did with the hotheads on base and replied, "I paid attention during class. Besides that, the only thing around here taller than your ego is a tree. So obviously we are looking for one of the jungle giants."

I almost laughed at Bowen's silent "Oh," as he recognized the truth in Estradé's argument. He might be a hothead, but he was also quick to acknowledge his own faults and wasn't ashamed to admit when his knee-jerk, hot-head responses put him in the wrong. I liked that about him. It placed him quite a bit higher in my esteem than he might have otherwise earned.

"All right then." Hadley took the lead once more, pointing to the sky above us. "Alex, get yourself up there and find us the tallest tree."

I had been expecting that command. So, with a quick nod of my head, I gathered the gravity field under me and lifted myself from branch to branch, up to the top of the closest tree. It only took ten seconds of scanning the horizon to locate a tree, perhaps a mile to the east, that was twice as tall as all the others around it. I lowered myself back to the ground, pointing in the direction we needed to travel. Not surprisingly, it was right through the thickest part of the jungle.

"Any chance the road curves and heads that direction?" Hadley asked hopefully.

Aiden was studying the map while Estradé oriented the compass in the direction I had pointed. "Sorry." Aiden shook his head. "I don't see any roads goin' that direction."

"All right then." I was beginning to notice that that was Hadley's favorite phrase. "Estradé, you control the compass, keep us moving in the right direction. Bowen, you have point. Aiden and Alex, you're the rear guard. Let's move out."

It took us about an hour, cutting our own path through the dense underbrush to reach the tree. I didn't wait to be told this time, immediately lifting myself from branch to branch, half levitating, and half climbing my way to the top of the tree to look for the next clue. It wasn't too hard to spot, a small box dangling from a yellow parachute, caught just within the highest grouping of branches. I easily untangled the cords and carried it down to the rest of the group.

Once more, Hadley took control and opened the small box, but he had a quizzical look as he pulled the small object from within it. The small, bronze statue of a warrior on a horse fit easily in the palm of his hand. He turned it over, examining it carefully for clues, but soon dropped his shoulders in defeat. "I'm at a loss. Any of you know what this is supposed to mean?"

Hadley looked at me. I shrugged. "Sorry. I don't have any guesses."

Bowen shrugged as well and turned to Estradé to see what she thought.

Estradé was equally mystified but was at least willing to hazard a guess. "It looks old. Maybe it represents one of the local tribes, but I'd be darned if I could guess which one."

Aiden's brows were drawn tight in thought as he looked at the small figurine. "What if," he spoke slowly as his mind whirred in thought, "that isn't th' clue?"

"Not the clue?" Hadley asked a little confused. "What else would it be?"

"Well, didn't they say that each marker would give us an element we needed tae complete the task?" Aiden sounded more certain with each word. "What if this isn't th' clue, but is th' element we'll need later? That would mean th' clue is somethin' else, like th' box. Is there anythin' on th' box?"

Hadley seemed to take a moment to digest what Aiden had said, then he reached out and handed the box to Aiden. "Your idea; you get to look."

Everyone craned over Aiden's shoulder as he turned the box in different directions to study it. There was no writing on the outside or the inside. I had just stepped back, thinking to look at the parachute or even the tree itself for further clues, when Aiden gave a grunt of satisfaction. He had cut the tape that held the box together and unfolded its flaps. Sure enough, written on the inside of one of the flaps that had been hidden when folded was a series of numbers: coordinates to the next clue.

Hadley grinned broadly as he slapped Aiden on the shoulder. "Glad to have you on my team." Then he turned to the rest of us. "All right then. Estradé, get our course set and point the way. Let's move out."

Estradé directed us north by northeast and Bowen took the point once more, using his machete to hack a trail through the bushes and vines that were in the way of the direction he wanted to go. This time we didn't know exactly what we were looking for in the way of our next marker, but we knew the direction we were supposed to travel, and we knew how far away it was.

We had been walking in relative silence for the last several minutes when Aiden's voice made me jump. "So, how dae yae dae it?" he asked. "How dae yae defy gravity?"

I shrugged my shoulders. "I don't know; I just do it." The truth was that the scientists had been trying for some time to figure out exactly how I did it. That was what most of the torture sessions had been focusing on. They figured that if they could quantify how I did it, then I should be able to somehow exert more control over my abilities. But despite their hours upon hours of studying me, the best they had come up with so far was a weak theory that my body produced an electromagnetic pulse that somehow distorted the gravitational fields around other objects. Personally, I didn't care how I did it. It was enough for me to know that I could.

I lifted a small rock from the ground and set it to floating in the air above my open palm while we walked.

"I can see the swirls of gravity that flow around and through every object. The scientists can explain that part of my skills, but they don't seem to be able to explain how I control them."

He watched the rock thoughtfully for a moment, then said, "So, in essence, yae just will an object tae lift up and it does it for yae?"

I shook my head. "It's not quite that simple. In a way, I am still physically lifting the object, or rather, I am supporting the gravitational field that pulls the object toward the earth. The bigger and heavier an object is, the more force gravity exerts on it. The greater the force is, the harder it becomes for me to control. I can currently lift up to about four hundred pounds of weight, double what I can physically pick up. But much more than that, and it becomes a mental and physical strain that wipes me out."

He seemed puzzled by what I said. "But if yae are physically liftin' the gravity, then how dae yae use it tae lift yourself?"

I laughed softly. "Do you really want a physics lesson out here in the middle of the jungle, or do you want the simple answer?"

He shrugged with a grin of his own as he stepped over a log laying across his path. "Whichever helps me tae understand yae better."

That caught me off guard. I stopped walking and turned to look at him, my head tilted slightly as I considered his response.

Of course, Hadley chose that moment to look back. "Quit standing there staring into each other's eyes like a pair of lovesick nanny goats. Get moving!" I felt a deep flush race to my cheeks, and I quickly turned away from Aiden to catch up with the rest of the team. Just behind me, I heard Aiden chuckle to himself, but he didn't say anything more on the subject as we continued toward the next marker.

Unexpectedly, Hadley held up his hand in a fist, signaling a warning. Almost as one, we froze in place. Barely moving, I allowed my eyes to search the jungle of green around us. I didn't see anything out of the ordinary, but Estradé had her head slightly cocked, clearly listening to something. Her face suddenly drained of color. Without speaking she raised her finger to her lips to signal silence, then motioned us down.

Up to this point, we had been treating the exercise more like an afternoon treasure hunt than the real mission the exercise was intended to imitate. Her next action made it clear that she wasn't playing around any longer. She held her left hand in a C-shape, just above her phase rifle. Enemy. Then she raised her hand to her throat followed by five fingers. Hostages. Five of them. She pointed in the direction we had been traveling.

Hadley nodded then pointed his finger first at Aiden and then at a point some distance ahead of us, indicating that he wanted him to go up and get a better look. Aiden signaled that he understood, then quietly unslung his phase rifle from his shoulder and carefully handed it to me. All hints of his earlier joviality were gone from his face as he reached behind his back and pulled out a phase pistol I hadn't even realized he was carrying.

Moving with stealth and speed, he silently crept forward. As I watched him rapidly disappear into the jungle ahead of us, I was slightly in awe of the fluid way his body moved. He was poetry in motion as he slid gracefully from shadow to shadow, his body a perfect balance of muscle and movement under his uniform. Suddenly embarrassed by where my thoughts were going, I forced myself to turn away and check the path behind us. It was clear. When I turned back, Aiden was gone from view.

Several tense minutes later, Aiden returned. If his face had been serious before, it was dark with anger now. We all drew in close to hear his whispered report.

"That didn't look like part of th' exercise. There's another team of specialists down there, but they aren't in good shape. Four of them are bound and gagged. The fifth is lyin' face down on th' ground, not movin'. There are also eight men in black fatigues down there. They're all armed."

"Any idea who the men are?" Hadley whispered.

Aiden shook his head. "I didn't see any marking on their uniforms, and they were all wearing masks and goggles. I'm also not sure what language they were speakin', but it's not basic."

"I think it's Farsi," Estradé offered, "though it's not quite the dialect I learned. From the sound of it, they're Iranian."

"Then let's go rescue the other team." Bowen's voice was almost too loud in his determination to start acting. Like always, he was ready to jump in without thinking through the situation and his excitement likewise overruled his common sense. Estradé gave him a stern look and placed her finger to her lips to remind him to keep it down.

He scowled at her but asked his next question in a much quieter whisper. "Fine. Then what do you suggest we do about it?"

Estradé shook her head at him, making me smile despite the tense situation. "You're like my grandson, Mijo. Always in a hurry to act, but not thinking before you do." She poked him in the forehead as she whispered her reproach. "If you thought before you spoke, you might remember that we aren't exactly prepared to take on eight armed men." She looked meaningfully at the gun in his hands.

As understanding dawned on him, Bowen's expression changed to a scowl of disgust. Estradé didn't have to explain what she meant; we already knew. The phase rifles we had been given for the training mission were meant for training purposes only. They felt and worked like regular phase rifles, but they had been designed with a clouded crystal series that could only produce low-grade beams out of their barrels. They allowed us to train without seriously injuring our opponents. Their beams could do little more than buzz the black-clad men with the force of an electric fence wire. In other words, our weapons were basically worthless against armed men whose weapons were not likely to be so equally limited.

Hadley swore under his breath. I expected to see a similar look of frustration on Aiden's face but was instead surprised to see him studying the pistol in his hands as though considering its usefulness. "This one," he finally said, "isn't a toy."

We all looked up at him in surprise. The military had not issued us phase pistols. And even if they had, I was sure they would have only been practice guns like the useless phase rifles we were all carrying. Where had he gotten an active pistol from? Before I could ask him about it, Aiden started speaking again.

"Look," he whispered, "we aren't helpless here. Estradé, yae can hear and understand them from quite a big distance. If yae take the lead, we have a chance of avoidin' surprise attacks. Bowen, yae are probably stronger than any one of those men down there, and I have seen yae practicin' throwin' projectiles on the target range. Yae don't need a weapon. Yer arms are yer weapons. Pick up some rocks and use them tae knock out those soldiers from a distance." Bowen grinned with malicious joy at the suggestion.

"Alex," he turned to look at me, "yae can send rocks flying at them as well, but if I'm not mistaken, I think yae can also pick up those men and throw them. Better yet, yae can yank the guns out of their hands first and then throw them." I nodded at him, confirming his thoughts. He was right, I was more than capable of fighting without the phase rifle.

"And Hadley, yae are more than a little good at hand-tae-hand combat. With yer faster than normal movements, yae have proved tae be one of the few people here that I have yet tae get the best of on the trainin' mats." Aiden's expression was forming into a wicked grin as he said all this. "I don't think those men are goin' tae know what hit them."

Chapter 5: Alexandria Jaquette

TWENTY MINUTES LATER, I was crouched within the concealing branches of a tree. From my position, I had a reasonably clear view of the scene Aiden had described to us. The area where the specialists had been taken prisoners was a roughly cleared area of about thirty feet in diameter. At the center of the clearing was an eight-foot-tall totem pole whose carved images suggested it was a tribal marker of some sort.

Not that it mattered anymore, but there was a bag attached to the pole made out of the same yellow material the parachute had been made of. The totem pole had been the challenge's next marker. That would explain why the other team of specialists was here. They must have made it to the marker before us, only to be ambushed by the Iranian soldiers.

I looked closer at the four bound and gagged individuals. I knew two of them, Thatcher and Rockman. Thatcher was a Beta whose uncanny accuracy with any weapon placed in his hands had earned him an invitation to the base. Not long ago I had watched him on the firing range using his phase rifle to create a star pattern on his target board. The pattern had fit within a two-inch square.

Rockman was the German rock climber who was in my classes. He was the one who had suggested I throw snowballs at the enemy. Now his head was hanging down with a trickle of blood seeping from a cut on his cheek.

The other two didn't look any better. I didn't know them, but I had seen them around. The first one was a girl a few years older than me. I think her name was Fowler or something like that. She had a short, blonde ponytail and a rich golden tan that set off her blue eyes perfectly. If I remembered right, she liked to surf every chance she got.

The other was a short, wiry, Chinese man. I didn't have any idea what his name was, but I had seen him climb a sheer cliff wall like it was a child's playground. China would have to do as his name for now. At the moment, it was obvious he was in no condition to do much of anything. He had an ugly-looking bump forming on his forehead and a slightly glassy look in his eyes. He was swaying on his knees, leaving me to wonder how much longer he could stay upright. He really didn't look good. Ponytail didn't say anything, but she shifted just enough so that she could lean against him and keep him from toppling over.

Then there was the unmoving specialist. It was a girl. Though I didn't know her name, I did know that she had come in about five months before me and was scheduled to ship out soon with her new assignment. I also knew that she was a Beta with multiple gifts in data processing and fine motor skill dexterity. I had overheard one of the teachers suggesting that she would be especially useful as a drone expert. Now as I looked at her, I didn't think she would be shipping out after all. I could see that she wasn't breathing and there was a small pool of blood under her chest.

I clenched my fists in anger and then unclenched them again, all the more grateful that Estradé's hearing was as good as it was and that she had kept us from stumbling into the same trap the first team had.

Most of the soldiers were scattered around the clearing at evenly spaced intervals. They were facing outward toward the jungle, their weapons at the ready, probably waiting for the next group of specialists to stumble into their trap. The one that wasn't watching the trees was watching the prisoners.

At first glance, there wasn't much to distinguish the soldiers from one another. They were all wearing the same basic black combat fatigues, though what Aiden had described as a black uniform was actually a Multicam black. Its shades of black, dark gray, and dark green camouflage were designed to blend into the shadows of the jungle. It was an interesting choice for a daytime jungle excursion. There were shadows here to be sure, but there were far more shades of green and brown than of gray and black. Unless that was, they planned for something that would extend into the night. I filed that thought away for later use.

Over their fatigues, they were each wearing what looked to be a standard PR-12 vest. The PR-12 is capable of absorbing up to a twelve-pulse phase shot from as close as two feet away. Unfortunately, Aiden's phase gun was probably only a ten-phase. It wouldn't be strong enough to go through the vests unless it was right up against one. That could be a problem, but then I suspected that Aiden had already considered that.

In addition to the vests, each man was also wearing a face mask, an Ops-core helmet, and carrying a phase rifle. That was where I also began to notice some differences. The man guarding the prisoners had a camera attached to his helmet.

It only took a moment more of watching to realize that the man was rotating his view in a pretty regular pattern around the clearing. Camera Man was recording footage for someone or something. Was it a live feed or just a recording? A live feed would make the most sense. This meant that there had to be someone within a forty-mile radius receiving the feed since that was about as far as those cameras were designed to broadcast.

The soldier closest to my position also had a unique fixture attached to his helmet: a tactical headset. Now that was interesting. The headset meant that he couldn't hear the sounds of anyone approaching. What could he be listening to that was more important than hearing an approaching enemy?

To the right of the soldier I nicknamed Headset, I noticed that the next soldier was carrying a slightly different rifle than the rest of his squad. It was shorter and stockier and had a bigger barrel designed to discharge something larger than the narrow pulse phase that the other weapons were designed for. I wasn't familiar with that weapon. I wondered if Aiden would know more about it.

A few feet away from Headset was a soldier who appeared to be favoring his left leg. He was putting nearly all of his weight on the right leg. My suspicion was confirmed a moment later when he took a few limping steps back toward the totem pole at the center of the clearing. He swung his rifle to his side and pulled a small flask from the leg pocket of his pants. As he did so, he paused to rub his ankle. It wouldn't surprise me to find out that he had rolled an ankle traversing the jungle to get to the clearing. Well, good, I thought. He deserved it and much more.

On the opposite side of the clearing from me, next to Limpy, was a soldier who had a pack on his back. My first thought was that he was probably carrying some basic supplies for the whole team since nobody else seemed to be carrying a pack. But then I had to reconsider. The team seemed to have stationed themselves at the clearing. Why then was the man still carrying the pack? If it was basic supplies, wouldn't he have set the pack down to give him a greater range of motion in case of an attack? No. It seemed more likely to me that there was something in the pack of more value than the team's basic supplies. I decided I wanted to get a look inside that bag when an opportunity came.

The next soldier didn't have any special gear, but he was wearing a ring on his left hand. I couldn't see much detail, except that it looked a little big to be a wedding band. If I had to guess, I would say it looked more like a class ring of some sort.

Next was a particularly tall soldier. I would guess he was close to seven feet tall. I could almost have felt sorry for him when I noticed that his helmet had a few scrapes and dents that none of the others did. It was easy to imagine that his height had caused him to bang his head on a few things along the way. I say I could almost feel bad, but then my next thought was the decision to add a few new dents to his helmet if I got the chance. I guess I didn't feel all that bad for him after all.

The last soldier was an especially bulky man, clearly a weightlifter. His muscles bulged through his uniform making it look two sizes too small for him. In another setting, it might have been comical. Here it just made me think that I did not want to get caught in a bear hug by that guy.

Studying the enemy was an interesting way to pass the time, but it wasn't the reason I was sitting thirty feet up in a tree. I was waiting for something to happen: the plan that we had agreed upon. I didn't have to wait much longer.

Bowen walked out from among the trees, his head turned back toward the jungle he had just come out of, as though talking to his teammates behind him. "Found it," he shouted. "Hurry up slow pokes or we'll…" His voice trailed off as he looked forward again to find eight-phase rifles pointing at his chest. He slowly let go of his rifle and raised his hands in a show of surrender. "Uh…is this part of the exercise?" he asked with a look of befuddled confusion. I smirked to myself at how well he was playing the part. Aiden had told him just to be himself. Well, he was certainly getting the part right.

One of the black-clad soldiers, Weightlifter, stepped forward to take Bowen's weapon and bind his hands, then directed him at gunpoint to the line of prisoners.

"So, you want me to get in line with the rest of these guys?" Bowen asked needlessly.

The soldier answered him with a kick to the back of his knee, making him fall roughly to the ground.

"Hey!" Bowen protested. "No need for that."

He was rewarded with a backhand across the cheek.

"Fine," he grumbled under his breath. "I'll just sit here."

As the soldier hit him again, I thought to myself, *Shut up, Bowen. Don't give them any more excuses to rough you up.* The soldier solved the problem for Bowen by pulling a bandana out of his pocket and roughly yanking it into his mouth then tying it tightly behind his head.

Throughout this, the other soldiers were watching the path Bowen had come from, expecting the rest of his team to be coming through right after him; no one followed him through. The soldiers began to look at each other, speaking in a language I didn't understand, but clearly confused by the lack of new prey as Bowen's team failed to appear.

Backpack turned and said something to Weightlifter who nodded his head in response then pulled back his gun and used the butt of it to take a final swing at the back of Bowen's head before turning away to join the rest of his team.

Bowen fell forward to the ground, stunned by the blow. That wasn't good. We needed Bowen up and capable for our plan to work. But thankfully the blow only seemed to shake him for a few seconds. Rolling to his side, Bowen maneuvered himself back to his knees. He shook his head as he did so, probably trying to shake off the ringing that was likely bothering him as a result of that last blow. But then I realized that he was also using the movement to allow himself to unobtrusively glance around the clearing, making sure that no further attention was on him. Certain that he was now being basically ignored, he began rolling his shoulders as though working out a kink. The truth was, he was breaking the bonds that held his hands.

At the same time, the sound of phase-gunfire rang from somewhere outside the circle. The shots were immediately followed by two separate yells of pain and the sound of something crashing to the ground. Next to Bowen, the other prisoners' heads shot up, fear in their eyes as they looked around. The black-clad soldiers all raised their guns a little higher, understandably going into high alert.

Then a woman's voice called out in Farsi, the language the soldiers had been speaking. Although I couldn't understand the language, I knew the essence of what Estradé had said: "One of you men come give me a hand."

70

I snickered silently to myself as I watched the soldiers shift on their feet, looking around at each other as though trying to figure out which of their numbers had gone into the jungle and was now calling back to them. If the soldiers had looked uncertain before, they were downright confused now.

Backpack shook his head in a negative motion, then pointed to the soldier with the class ring and the tall guy. He barked instructions at them and seconds later the two of them entered the jungle, heading in the direction of the woman's voice. I watched them go with a sense of satisfaction. They were in for a nasty surprise. I knew what Aiden and Hadley had planned for the soldiers who came into the jungle after them. They would not be walking away unscathed.

That left six enemies in the clearing. I had hoped a few more would have been drawn into the trees, but it would have to be enough. It was time for me to make the next move.

I began focusing on the gravity around the soldiers. I would have to do it one at a time; I didn't have enough control yet, or enough strength, to get them all at once. But if I moved quickly enough, they wouldn't have time to recover before they became my next victim.

Forcing gravity in the opposite direction of its natural course, I tore Weightlifter's phase rifle from his grip and sent it flying into the air above him. At the same time, I flung him backward into the totem pole. I could almost see the wind being knocked out of him as he slammed into the solid post of wood. I grinned ferally, taking pleasure in the fact that the man's bulk would do nothing to help him against the wave of gravity I had just slammed into him.

Not waiting to see him hit the ground, I turned my attention to the next soldier, the one wearing the headset, and yanked his gun out of his hands in a similar manner, then slammed it into the head of Camera Man, purposely aiming for the camera lens in hopes of shattering it and disrupting the feed of whoever was watching on the other end.

At the same time, I forced Camera Man's rifle forward causing the strap around his neck to jerk him off balance, then rapidly reversed its direction and sent him reeling backward, wildly grasping at the strap that was now choking him as it began to lift him into the air as well. I was holding him ten feet off the ground when he managed to slip free of the strap. He fell hard and was slow to move again. With the gun now free of the extra weight, I easily sent it floating down into Bowen's waiting hands. Without pause, I rapidly increased the gravity around Headset and forced him to his hands and knees, and then into a crumpled heap. I could see his body making an impression in the dirt beneath him as I increased the gravity's pull. So far so good. I was a little winded from the effort of controlling so much gravity in rapid succession, but the adrenaline spike I was experiencing was more than making up for it.

Three seconds had passed, enough time for the final three guards to register that something was happening and to have turned toward the commotion, but not enough time for them to react before I reversed the gravity once more and sent Headset flying up and across the clearing, straight into Backpack. They both toppled to the ground.

Next, I jerked the unusual rifle out of Gun Guy's hands and sent it to the ground near the other prisoners while at the same time sending Gun Guy slamming into a nearby tree. Limpy, seeing what was happening, was spinning in a circle looking for the source of the attack. Funny thing, he never thought to look up. If he had, he might have been able to dodge Weightlifter's rifle as I finally brought it slamming back down toward his head with far more force than it would have normally had. Limpy crumpled to the ground and didn't move again.

A small part of my mind was exhilarated at the thought of what I was accomplishing. I had never controlled so much, so fast. But I was breathing hard and could feel small beads of sweat forming on my brow and dripping down my back. My muscles were beginning to shake from the strain of supporting so much gravity. I wouldn't be able to sustain this level of control much longer.

Out of the corner of my eye, I saw movement. Backpack was back on his feet and bringing his gun around to aim at Bowen. I reacted on instinct, ripping the gun from his hands and sending it flying into the jungle before he could pull the trigger. I was about to throw him against a nearby tree when Bowen solved the problem for me and punched him in the face, sending him reeling backward. I knew that had to hurt.

By this time, Weightlifter had also recovered and was coming to his feet. But it was quickly obvious that I didn't need to do anything more: Rockman had one of the fallen rifles and was now using it to sharply jab into the man's chest.

"You can stay right there," he growled at him.

Weightlifter seemed to consider his options for only a moment before realizing he didn't have any. Moving slowly, he raised his hands into the air.

Behind Bowen, Thatcher was also holding a phase rifle he had recovered from where I had thrown them and was now rounding up the other battered soldiers. Ponytail was checking the fallen specialist for a pulse; she didn't find one.

To be honest, I was a little glad to not have to continue. I could feel the slight hint of the headache that always came when I tried to push too far, too fast with controlling gravity. My strength had increased a lot in the last few weeks, but it still took a lot out of me, and those soldiers had not been light.

Across the way, Estradé and Hadley stepped out of the jungle driving the tall soldier and the one with the class ring in front of them. Class Ring was limping gingerly on his right leg and Tall Guy was holding his left arm tightly against his chest. Hadley nudged them in the back with the rifle he was carrying, directing them to stand with the rest of their group.

Where was Aiden? Even as I thought the question, I became aware of someone on the ground below me. I looked down to find Aiden grinning up at me.

"I don't think I can jump high enough tae reach that first branch. Care tae give me a lift?" he asked.

I had purposely chosen a tree whose lowest branches were some twelve feet off the ground; I didn't want a surprise visitor while my attention was on the other soldiers. I grinned back at him and focused on the gravity beneath him, causing him to rise gently into the air and up to the first branches. He climbed the rest of the way up on his own and found a place to settle close enough to talk to me quietly.

"Well, that was a nice little trainin' exercise," he said with his usual grin. He noted the light sheen of sweat on my forehead. "We even managed tae finally get yae tae break a sweat."

I shook my head at his sense of humor. "So, what comes next?"

"Next, we decide what tae do with them. Notice anythin' about them that I should be aware of before I head back down?"

"Well," I said thoughtfully, "one of them has a tactical headset, one has a video camera, and a third is carrying a bag he doesn't seem interested in setting down. I also suspect Backpack is the man in charge of this group."

"Backpack?" Aiden raised his eyebrow at that name and went on to tease me. "Yer telling me a backpack is in charge?"

"Funny," I said dryly.

"Okay." His smile grew even bigger. "So, th' backpack," he emphasized the word, "is in charge and won't let anyone set it down. In other words, we probably ought tae find out what is in it, and someone off sight is likely givin' instructions tae this group and probably still receivin' a feed from th' equipment." He thought about it for a moment as he surveyed the prisoners.

With Aiden beside me, the soldiers didn't look nearly so threatening. Of course, most of them were nursing injured body parts with varying degrees of slumped shoulders. So that might have had something to do with it as well. They had been beaten, and they knew it. Backpack, however, was a different story. Although he was rubbing his chin where Bowen had punched him, his stance showed no hint of submission. Under his mask, his lips were drawn into a tight line as he studied the specialists who had managed to turn the tables on his team.

Aiden must have noticed as well because his voice took on a tone of seriousness it had not had only moments before. "I think it would be best if yae stay out of sight. I don't like th' way that one's studyin' everyone. Stay alert and listen for me cues. I may still need yer skills again before this is done."

I nodded my head in understanding then watched him climb back down the tree. He was as smooth and graceful climbing down the tree as he had been stalking into the jungle earlier. Without waiting to be asked, I gave him a light assist on his final drop down to the ground. He grinned back up at me and gave me a quick salute before jogging off to join everyone else.

I turned my attention back to the clearing and the people within it. Someone had found something to cover the dead girl with. There was a sobering reality in knowing that even though we had succeeded in rescuing the other team, we had come too late to do anything to help her.

My time at this base had always seemed a little like a game. All the practicing, training, learning, and drilling had been just that: practicing, training, learning, and drilling. Before today, it had never sunk in that there was a reason for all of it. Seeing the covered, still body of someone I had known was like having ice poured straight into my stomach. I wasn't sure this was just a game anymore.

A few feet away, Ponytail had gotten her team's satellite phone out of their bag and was talking on it. I assumed she had called base to request support. She was nodding her head in response to something someone on the other end of the line had said.

Hadley, Rockman, and Bowen still had their guns trained on the enemy soldiers, while Estradé had gone to speak with Thatcher who was checking the bruise on China's forehead. When I looked back toward the huddled group of prisoners, I noticed that Backpack had moved from the center of the group where he had previously been and was now standing at Camera Man's side, closest to where Rockman had taken up position. I was disappointed to see that the camera on Camera Man's helmet was still in one piece; I had not managed to break it.

Backpack looked around furtively for a second, then, when he thought no one was looking his way, I saw his lips move, and Camera Man's shoulders raise ever so slightly in response. Across the clearing, Estradé's head came up sharply, clearly having heard whatever it was he said. Her expression became dark with anger. *Uh oh!* I thought to myself. Whatever he had just said to his companion, it couldn't have been good.

"Oi!" Bowen pointed his gun straight at Backpack. He must have noticed them talking as well. "What do you think you're doing?"

Backpack turned to face him, lifting his chin slightly in rebellion before seeming to change his mind and instead answering Bowen's question with one of his own.

"Where is the Alpha?" His voice was thickly accented, but his English was perfect.

Bowen's eyes narrowed. "What makes you think there's an Alpha here?"

The man shrugged his shoulders dismissively. "Someone just took out my team like they were a bunch of rag dolls. Only an Alpha could have done it that way and I'd say it's safe to assume that Alpha is somewhere nearby. So, where are they?"

Aiden stepped out of the jungle and answered before Bowen could. "Why dae yae want tae know?"

Backpack sized him up as he had done the others only moments before. I was relieved that Aiden was the one responding to the soldier's question. It somehow made me feel safer to think that he was standing between me and the man's question about me.

"It's just that there is someone interested in meeting them."

"I've no interest in meetin' any of yer friends."

Backpack cocked his head slightly as though thinking through Aiden's response, then asked, "So you are the Alpha?"

Aiden's shoulders tightened slightly, and his hand clenched at his side, but he didn't answer Backpack's question. Instead, he asked, "Why are yae here?"

Backpack's lips rose ever so slightly in satisfaction. Aiden's lack of an answer was all the answer he needed. Then he shrugged nonchalantly. "We were hired by the Iranian government to do surveillance on this base."

"He's lying," Estradé stated matter-of-factly from across the clearing. She had started walking toward Aiden even before she spoke so that she was now standing next to him.

"They came here specifically looking for you," she paused ever so slightly, looking Aiden straight in the eyes before emphasizing the next word, "Alexander."

Alexander? What was she saying? I thought for a moment I must have heard wrong, but Bowen seemed to have heard the same thing.

"Alexander? Why would you..."

He didn't get to finish. Several things happened all at once. Yet my startled mind seemed to see it all in slow motion as though time had slowed to ensure that I caught every detail of what came next.

A shattering staccato of phaser fire ripped through the clearing. A phaser blast hit Bowen in the back, propelling him forward. His arms were spread wide as though he was trying to stop his forward motion, but they found only air as he toppled forward and then didn't move anymore.

At the same time, another blast caught Hadley in the shoulder, spinning him in a circle before he too fell to a crumpled heap. Rockman spun around, firing his rifle into the jungle from the direction of the shots that had taken down Bowen and Hadley, but he was almost immediately tackled from behind by Weightlifter.

Even before those two had hit the ground, Backpack was charging Aiden. Aiden tried to sidestep the charge, but Backpack changed his step mid-stride and swung down low instead to swipe Aiden's legs out from under him.

I watched in horror as a small gun appeared in Backpack's hands and the two of them began to grapple for control of it. Someone screamed, "No!" I think it was Estradé, but the truth is that it might have been me. The horror of everything going wrong all at once froze my mind. All I seemed to be able to do was watch.

Estradé lunged forward, trying to grab the rifle from Bowen's unmoving hands, but Class Ring beat her there and Estradé had to jump back to avoid the blow he aimed at her head. Across the clearing I heard Ponytail begin yelling into the satellite phone, "Mayday, mayday, mayday, we are under attack. I repeat, we are un—" Her voice cut off mid-word as she looked down dumbly at a knife hilt protruding from her chest then slowly toppled forward, the phone falling from her suddenly numb hands.

And then my mind seemed to snap into clarity, and I reacted with the speed and strength of instinct that all my practice and planning could not have matched.

Backpack flew backward as I wrenched him off of Aiden and threw him across the clearing to slam into a tree on the opposite side. In the same instant, Weightlifter collapsed to the ground as I brought the full force of gravity down on him. His mouth opened in a scream of pain as his hands and knees sunk into the dirt, but I couldn't hear him, or anything else for that matter; my blood was pounding in my ears.

The gravity under Headset and Class Ring reversed suddenly so that they were propelled twenty feet up into the air. I could see them flailing, desperately reaching around them for something to hold onto. Then I reversed the field and brought them slamming back down, as hard as I could, to the ground.

Aiden had gotten back to his feet, his face a hard mask as he looked around the clearing, silently taking in all that I was doing. Estradé stood beside him, a look on her face that could have been either awe or shock.

By this time, my head was splitting with a searing headache, and I had to push the pain aside so that I could continue the assault, yet there was no thought of letting up on the attack. Through a narrowing field of vision that was growing in direct proportion to the headache, I watched as Limpy, Gun Man, and Tall Guy tried with varying degrees of success to dodge the basketball-sized rocks and dead wood that I sent flying through the air at them.

The cold horror that had frozen my mind only moments before was now a cold fury that drove my retribution. I methodically attended to each of the soldiers, returning as needed to any of them who managed to stand up after my first attack. My whole body was shaking with the effort, though I didn't really notice it. I was too focused on the multiple fields of gravity I was manipulating simultaneously.

Only Camera Man was left untouched. Although I did not consciously decide to do it, I think some part of my mind wanted whoever was on the other end of the video feed to see what was happening. I wanted them to know what I could do and would do, to stop them from hurting my friends.

For several seconds he stood in the center of the raging attack, his jaw dropped in disbelief as his mind tried to register everything that was happening. Then his gaze came to rest on Aiden and his face hardened.

I saw the movement as he reached for one of the pockets in his cargo pants and withdrew a small gun. I saw him aim and pull the trigger in one fluid motion. I even saw the small, narrow projectile that flew from its barrel through a hazy puff of white smoke. In and of itself, it wasn't a danger. I knew I could alter the field of gravity around the projectile so that it crashed harmlessly into the ground. But in that breathless nanosecond of time that required me to react in order to save Aiden, I ran out of strength.

The dark edges of my vision suddenly telescoped inward and I felt myself begin to tip backward. Where I had been in control of the gravity only seconds before, gravity suddenly took charge once more; I was falling.

It's interesting the sense of clarity and hyper-awareness that only comes in the final few seconds of consciousness. I seemed to be able to feel the air itself as it gently caressed my downward plunging body, and every branch that touched my skin as I passed through the tree was its own whipping sting of reprimand.

I had pushed my body beyond the limit that it could handle. It was shutting down to protect itself. Unfortunately, it didn't seem to understand that I was thirty feet off the ground. Now, with only seconds left, my mind recognized what my body had not accounted for. If I didn't find one final reserve of strength to pull from, there was a good chance I would die.

With everything I had left, I reached for the few waves of gravity I could still see through my narrowing tunnel of vision and pulled them to me. Even as I did so, I knew it wasn't going to be enough to stop gravity's pull. And then I hit the ground with a painful, sickening crash.

The last thing I heard before the darkness became complete was the renewed sound of fighting and phaser blasts intermixed with a voice I recognized. It was Estradé, and her voice was desperate.

"Medivac to me now. She's over here."

Chapter 6: Alexandria Jaquette

I WASN'T REALLY conscious yet. I was drifting through layers of drug-induced sleepiness and half-awareness as my body tried to adjust to the discomfort and weariness it was feeling while balancing the need to return to awareness so that it could deal with the sense of panic that had not fully subsided. As I lay there drifting, I began to recognize several voices talking in hushed tones not far from me.

"She dislocated her left shoulder when she fell, but amazingly there are not any broken bones. We've already repositioned the shoulder back into its socket. She'll wear a sling for a few days, and it will be a few weeks before she will be ready to fully use that arm again. As for her brain, the EEG shows a promotion of theta waves and a suppression of alpha waves which suggests that she is still experiencing stress trauma to her brain. It's a little concerning, though not really all that surprising considering what she just went through. I'll need to keep an eye on it; however, I suspect it will go back to normal with a few days of rest."

That voice belonged to Dr. Eris. Not my favorite doctor, but probably the best person on base to have made that particular diagnosis.

"I'm not surprised she's showing elevated levels." That was General Durnham. "The report from Estradé suggested that she was using her abilities at levels far above and beyond anything she has yet accomplished in the lab."

"It would seem our little kitten has been holding back." That grating voice belonged to Callia. I felt my jaw tighten in an automatic response.

"Indeed," Dr. Eris agreed. "I will be interested in seeing if she can replicate that level of control once she returns to active training."

"What about the other specialists?" The Brig asked.

Callia's voice came again, "We got there too late to save Bowen, Sisco, and Falkner. I've already arranged to have their bodies returned to their families." I felt a wave of sadness wash over me. I had seen Bowen and Ponytail fall and knew then that there was little chance of them surviving. In spite of that knowledge, I had still hoped that I was somehow mistaken.

"The other seven specialists were safely recovered, though Hadley did take a shot to the shoulder…"

Dr. Eris interrupted, "We were able to repair the damage there. He will also wear a sling and need a few weeks to heal, but he will make a full recovery."

Surprisingly, Callia didn't sound offended by the interruption, and instead simply continued her report as soon as Eris finished her interjection. "Thatcher, Estradé, Waverly, and Rockman all have varying levels of injuries, but none of them are life-threatening and they will all be cleared to return to duty by the end of the day."

"And Haskell?"

I felt a chill of fear enter my heart. The last thing I had seen was the projectile flying at him with deadly accuracy and had known the frustrating certainty that I did not have the strength to stop it.

"Still unconscious. The tranquilizer dart they shot him with was laced with some pretty heavy drugs. But he's young and strong. He should be fine as soon as they wear off and flush out of his system."

A tranquilizer dart?! I felt a wave of relief flood through me. It hadn't been the deadly projectile that I had feared. As the three of them continued talking, the sense of relief I felt at hearing Aiden was going to be ok seemed to wash through me like a euphoric sedative and I drifted back off.

I can't say how long I was out, but when I opened my eyes next, Dr. Eris was standing next to me checking the readings on the EEG machine.

"So, you're awake." She didn't even look at me as she continued to study the monitor's readout. "I'm told that was quite the impressive show you gave out there. Multiple fields of gravity at the same time, all going in different directions. Tell me, were you thinking through what you were doing, or were you just reacting?"

Seriously?! No how are you feeling or does anything hurt? She just jumps right into the interrogation?! I really didn't like this woman, but I bit my tongue and answered her question anyway. The few months I had spent working with her had taught me that the fastest way to get her to go away was to answer her questions. She didn't like me any better than I liked her, and she tended to leave the room as soon as she had the answers she wanted from me.

"I just acted."

"I thought as much." She pressed a few more buttons on the machine before finally turning to look at me. She was a middle-aged woman of average height and build. Her doe-brown eyes were set in a heart-shaped face that could have been beautiful if she had ever taken the effort, but she never did. She always wore her black hair in a severe bun that only served to make her high cheekbones even more pronounced, and her steel-rimmed glasses were chosen for their utilitarian lines instead of any aesthetic improvement they could have otherwise given her. If she ever wore any makeup, I had never seen it. Her thin lips were drawn in their usual tight line as she studied me for the briefest of seconds before she turned abruptly to leave the room.

"Well, that's all I need for now. I'll come back to check your readings again later today."

Ugh! The truth was, I still had a slight headache, and my shoulder was throbbing. She probably could have given me something to help with those things, but I was honest enough to admit that my stubborn streak was just strong enough that I would rather suffer through them than ask her for help.

Luckily, I didn't have to suffer for too long. A nurse came in not long after to inject some medicine into the IV tubing that was taped to my right hand. Seconds later I felt the pain in my head and shoulder begin to fade away. Unfortunately, my alertness began to fade as well, and I drifted back off to sleep.

When I woke sometime later, I noticed that the headache was gone, though there was still a slight throbbing in my shoulder. I tried to move my arm, to roll the shoulder, only to realize that my injured arm had been placed in a sling and strapped across my torso. It was an effective way to stabilize the shoulder, but it made sitting up rather difficult. I had to use the railing to pull myself into a sitting position.

In hindsight, it would have been smarter to use the bed's controls and lift the top half of the bed into a sitting position.

However, I had never been in a hospital bed before this, and it didn't cross my mind that it could do that.

The room I was in wasn't much bigger than my dorm had been back at the school; perhaps ten feet by ten feet. The hospital bed I was sitting on took up most of the space. To my left, under a small window, there was an area just big enough for a small recliner seat and an empty nightstand. In front of me was a hand washing station and cabinets that likely held basic medical supplies. To the right of that, in the corner, was a narrow door with a small plastic sign that read: Bathroom.

Further to the right was a wall of windows interrupted only by an open doorway that led out into the hallway where I could see the nurses' station. Off to the side, there was a blue curtain that could be pulled in front of the windows for privacy, though at the moment the windows were wide open.

Over my shoulder was the small bank of monitoring equipment that Dr. Eris had been studying when I had last been awake. One screen showed my heart rate, and another the display of brain waves. A third screen showed my oxygen levels and blood pressure. Next to the equipment was a single, movable IV stand. Its tubes led to my right hand where they had been taped in place. I rubbed the insertion site absentmindedly; it was just a little tender.

The bag of IV fluids was nearly empty. I recalled that it had been full when the nurse had given me the medicine that sent me off to dreamland. How long does it take for one of those bags to empty? I didn't know. What I did know was that it had been seventeen hundred hours on October 5th when we had been dropped off at the first orienteering spot. Now the monitors next to me read October 6th, fifteen forty-eight. Almost twenty-four hours had passed.

I looked at the bathroom door again and realized that however long I had been out, it had been just a little too long for the comfort of my bladder. I was going to need to get out of the bed and make use of that small room. I looked down at my left arm, slung tight against my chest, and then over at the IV tubing leading from my right hand to the IV stand. *Great!* I thought. *This should be interesting.*

Using my one free hand, I pulled the IV stand around to the side of the bed and used it to help me get off the bed and onto my feet. I probably should have called a nurse to help me, but once more my stubborn streak led me to choose the harder path. Unfortunately, I was already on my feet before I discovered that although the headache was gone, it had been replaced by dizzying vertigo that left me wobbly and off balance.

In the back of my mind, I recognized that the dizziness must be a result of the medicine they had given me. Yet that knowledge didn't stop me from trying to walk on my own anyway. The third step I took was the one that got me. I was falling sideways before I fully registered what was happening.

Suddenly there was a pair of strong arms around me, keeping me from hitting the ground.

"Whoa there. I've got yae."

I looked up to see Aiden's roguish grin. My adrenaline had spiked as soon as I had realized I was falling. It left my heart racing so that I couldn't tell if the flush that came suddenly to my cheeks was from that or from unexpectedly finding myself in his arms. Either way, the flush most definitely got deeper as I found myself captivated by the mischievous twinkle of his pale blue eyes.

He didn't seem in any hurry to let me go as he in turn studied my face, his lips parting in a soft smile. When he spoke several heartbeats later, his voice had a slight huskiness to it, though his words most definitely did not match the mood of the moment. "It would seem it was a good thing I took that course on how tae rescue damsels in distress."

I laughed at the unexpected comment. The moment, if it had truly been one, was gone and reality had returned. "I'm no damsel," I said haughtily, "though I will be in a bit of distress if I don't make it to the bathroom soon."

"Well then," his smile grew even bigger as he lifted me back to my feet, "allow me tae help yae tae th' wee girl's room."

I shook my head, not for the last time, at his sense of humor but gratefully accepted the arm he held out to steady me as I walked the last few steps to the door and entered the small room. Then he graciously closed the door and waited for me to finish. When I was done, he helped me back to the bed. He even adjusted the bed for me so that it was sitting upright and teased me that I should've done that in the first place.

"Well, if I had known it could do that then I would have done it," I told him somewhat petulantly.

His face showed his shock at my statement. "Yer sayin' that yae have never been in a hospital bed before?"

"Nope," I said. "I've never needed one before today."

"Huh." He seemed to consider that. "Well then. Let me show yae a few tricks this bed can do."

He began to point out the buttons that were located on the handrail and even gave me a mild roller coaster ride as he adjusted the back and the feet into alternatingly up and down positions. We were both laughing when there was a soft knock on the doorframe.

We turned to see Estradé standing in the opening, a knowing smile on her face.

"All right, pequeños," she chided us through her smile. "That equipment is not a toy."

I have to admit the whole situation was a bit embarrassing, but that only made us laugh even harder. Estradé just shook her head at us as she came into the room and set a duffle bag at the foot of my bed.

"I thought you might need a change of clothes. Hospital gowns aren't that comfortable, and they don't provide nearly enough coverage."

I suddenly realized that I wasn't exactly dressed appropriately for anyone to see me, especially not Aiden. They had removed the clothes I had been wearing when they brought me in to set my shoulder and replaced them with a pale blue hospital gown that was tied at the back. I was suddenly grateful that whoever had put it on me had been thoughtful enough to securely tie it closed instead of leaving it open.

Estradé must have been thinking along that same line because she shooed Haskell out of the room. "You can wait in the hall while I help her get changed."

Estradé didn't wait for an answer and pulled the curtain closed behind him. She had a motherly tone of voice that brooked no arguments and we both acquiesced to her commands.

She helped me untie the gown and maneuver it around the IV and the sling. It was a little tricky, but the design of the gown was such that it was relatively easy to get off. The clean shirt was a different story. In the end, Estradé decided to pull the fluids bag through the sleeve first before I put my arm through it so that the tubing wasn't a tangled mess. Then she had to undo the sling on my left arm long enough to fit that arm through the sleeve.

The pants were much easier, though I had to stand patiently while Estradé tied the waist string to cinch it to a comfortable hold on my waist. She had been right; they were far more comfortable than the discarded gown had been. The pant and shirt set were made from a soft, fuzzy material that would have made an equally good lap blanket.

"You know, Mija," she said quietly as she worked, "you gave us quite a scare out there."

"I think they gave me a bigger one."

"True." She laughed gently. "But you controlled your fear well. Not everyone can claim that of their first battle."

"I didn't control my fear," I argued as I looked down at her in earnest. "I was terrified. What I did to those men…" My voice trailed off and I shuddered at the memory of what I had done to them. I couldn't say why, but it was suddenly very important to me that this tiny little woman understood what I was feeling. Perhaps it was because she had become somewhat of a motherly figure among the recruits. True, she had come in about the same time I had, but her thoughtful advice and gentle smiles had given us all the sense that she cared about us individually.

"I didn't ask for this, Estradé. I never asked to join the military and I certainly never wanted to be in a position where I had to fight or hurt someone."

She smiled at me sadly. "I know, Mija. But sometimes our choices are made for us, and we can only make the best of the situations we find ourselves in."

She patted me softly on the shoulder. "Now get back into that bed." Then she rolled up the hospital gown and set it on the counter. As she did so, she called over her shoulder, "You can come back in, Haskell."

Aiden's smile was gone when he came back in. He pushed the curtain back into its open position and then turned slowly to look at me.

"What is it?" I asked him, concerned by the unexpected change in his mood.

"Did yae mean what yae said about not choosin' th' military?"

I was a little stunned by the question. I thought he must have already known that I had not chosen the military. But then it dawned on me: Why would he? I had never told him much about myself. He didn't know the circumstances under which I had come to the base. As far as he knew, I was a recruit like he was. I floundered for a moment trying to decide the best way to explain it to him.

Estradé saw my uncertainty and solved the problem for me. "Unlike you and I, Mejo, she wasn't given the choice."

Aiden turned to question her, his confusion deepening. "How could she not have been given th' choice?"

"Oh, my dear. You are young and naïve." She said it sadly, without any cruelty. "It's part of your charm. You think that the UFC is the perfect government your parents told you it is. But the truth is much more complicated. They have insured that Alexandria has not had a choice in what she does since the day she was born."

"But why? Is it because she's an Alpha?"

"Not just any Alpha, Haskell, she is one of Icarus' Alphas."

There was a depth of sadness in Estradé's voice that spoke of pain and loss. I wondered what had happened to cause her such pain. At the same time, the way she had said it struck me like a slap across my face. With those six little words, she had redefined who I was. I was no longer Alexandria, young and free to choose my own path; I belonged to Icarus and as such was an enemy that needed to be dealt with.

Aiden looked equally stunned, then his face suddenly hardened in anger. He didn't even look at me as he turned sharply on his heel and left the room. I could hear the harsh click of his rapid footsteps as they receded down the hall.

I started to call after him, only to have Estradé place her hand on my shoulder. "Let him go, Mija. He needs to work through this in his own way."

I could feel tears welling up behind my eyes; I refused to let them fall. I swallowed hard instead and looked at her.

"Is that what everyone here thinks of me?"

Estradé didn't answer immediately. She seemed to be choosing her words carefully.

"No, Mija. Most of them believe as Haskell did that you are just an ordinary Alpha. But you are not ordinary."

She sighed heavily. "It wasn't by chance that I came to this base at the same time you did. I came here looking for you. Or, to be more precise, I came here looking for Icarus' Alpha."

"Why did you do that?" My question was almost a whisper. I suddenly realized that I was afraid to know the answer. Something in her eyes had changed as she said the last part. They had taken on a steely glint that I had never seen there before.

"To kill that Alpha." She said it bluntly, with no effort to soften the blow of her words.

Had it been a physical blow it would have done no more damage. I could barely breathe. The rational side of my mind was screaming a warning at me. It was telling me that this was not the woman I had thought I knew. In her eyes there was a predatory flame I had never seen there before; it was a fire that was aimed directly at me. But the other side of my mind, the side that would normally have allowed me to act, was frozen with shock. All I could do was whisper, "Then why haven't you done it?"

Estradé studied my face for a moment then said, "I nearly did. The night your repelling rope released early was no accident; I had rigged it to fail."

Just over my shoulder, I was aware that the tone of the machine monitoring my heartbeat was beeping faster and faster, matching time to the harsh thumping of my heart inside my chest. I rapidly accessed my situation. My failure to get to the bathroom on my own was evidence that I did not have the strength to fight off Estradé. I could yell for help, but Aiden had been gone long enough to be out of earshot, nor was I certain that he would have come back to help anyway. The look on his face when he left haunted me; it had been filled with loathing and hatred aimed at me. A quick glance into the hall revealed that the nurses' station was still empty as well. There was no one out there to answer a cry for help.

Estradé saw the direction of my gaze and seemed to know my frantic thoughts. "There is no one out there. I convinced the nurses that you would be safe with me for a few minutes."

"Are you here to finish the job then?"

She laughed bitterly at that. "No, Mija. I am not here to finish the job. I'm here to apologize."

I wasn't sure I'd heard that right. "You're what?"

"Mija, I was wrong." She seemed to deflate with those words. The flame went out of her eyes and her usually tough exterior crumpled. It was as though she suddenly aged twenty years. She stepped back and practically fell into the armchair behind her. Her voice was suddenly very frail and small.

"I spent twenty-five years in the UFC's Intelligence division. During those twenty-five years, I became an expert at judging people. With a few hours of watching, I could accurately identify their strengths and their flaws. I could tell you who was going to betray their friends and who would die for them. I became highly regarded in my field. I was so good, in fact, that I was asked by the head of the intelligence division himself to postpone my retirement long enough to go undercover for a time in Icarus' camp.

"My job was to gain intelligence on his Alphas. The UFC wanted to know what kind of threat they really were. Not just their abilities, but their personalities. Could they be salvaged if the UFC managed to separate them from Icarus?

"What I found were not innocent, misguided children, but the very worst that human nature had to offer. Icarus bred them for one purpose and one purpose only: to destroy anyone who stands in the way of what he wants. They are, as a group, a cruel, pitiless breed of creatures that are wholly devoted to Icarus and nothing else. They worship the ground he walks on and will do anything he asks of them, even murder innocent children.

"I completed my assignment and returned to give my report to my commanding officers, and then I went home. Unfortunately, Icarus found out who I was and what I had done. He decided to send a message to the UFC by sending one of his Alphas to my hometown. I came home to find everyone dead. My children. My grandchildren. He had tortured them and mutilated their bodies."

Her face appeared haunted by the memory as she said the last part. But then she took a deep, shuddering breath and continued her story. "I, uh…" She cleared her throat. "I swore that day that I would find a way to destroy every single one of Icarus' Alphas, starting with the one that I had just learned the UFC was hiding."

I didn't know what to say or how to respond. I was terrified of this woman and what she had admitted. At the same time, I felt deep sorrow for her pain and loss. I could almost understand why she had done what she had done; almost, but not enough to calm the terror that held me frozen. So, I said nothing. Estradé took my silence as permission to continue her explanation.

"Icarus hates nothing more than to have something he wants denied to him. The fact that he has been unsuccessful at recovering his stolen 'Alpha' has infuriated him for the past eighteen years. I thought that killing that Alpha and forever denying it to him was an appropriate way to send a message of my own back to him.

"But, following my first failed attempt, there was an investigation into what had caused your rope to fail. I decided that if I was going to have another successful shot at you, I was going to need to sit back and bide my time until the scrutiny calmed down. So, I used that time to watch and study you, to get a feel for the best way to get at you. But then, as I watched you, I learned something I had not expected to find: You were indeed one of Icarus' Alphas, but you were not like the others.

"You did not take pleasure in causing pain and destruction. You were not boastful and prideful. You did not place yourself above others. Instead, you stood up for and protected those who could not protect themselves. You went out of your way to help those who needed help. All of the deprivations that existed in the other Alphas did not exist in you.

"I found my opinion of you gradually changing. I realized one day in class, the day we decided you should throw snowballs at an attacking enemy," she smiled fondly at the memory, "that instead of wanting to kill you to get back at Icarus, I wanted to ensure that he would never be able to touch or taint the innocence I had discovered in you.

"If there had been any doubts about you lingering in my mind, you wiped them away yesterday when you placed a higher value on our lives than you did on your own. You were hidden and safe up there in that tree. But instead of remaining that way, you nearly killed yourself to protect the rest of us."

"I didn't have a choice," I whispered. "I couldn't sit back and do nothing while you were all fighting for your lives."

Estradé's weary face changed into a gentle smile as she stood and placed her hand on my shoulder. I flinched slightly but forced myself to not pull away. "And that, Mija, reinforces what I had already come to learn for myself: You may have been born one of Icarus' Alphas, but you do not belong to him."

Estradé said the next part gently, but the gentleness was backed by a steel edge. "Alex, I am not going to harm you; that danger has passed. But there are others for whom I cannot say the same. There are things you need to know if you are going to be safe."

Even as she was saying it, I was shaking my head in disbelief. How could I trust anything she was saying? What if she was only trying to lull me into a false sense of security so she could accomplish her true goal?

"Why should I trust you?"

"I'm not asking you to trust me; I lost that privilege. But I am asking you to listen to me." The weakness was gone from her voice. It had been replaced by a sense of urgency. "Icarus is after you, Niña, and he doesn't care who he has to go through to get to you. Those soldiers came here on his orders, looking specifically for you. Icarus must not know who you are or where you are. If he gets hold of you, he will destroy every vestige of innocence that makes you who you are. I am determined to make sure that does not happen.

"But Niña, you also cannot trust the UFC's intentions for you. To them, you are nothing more than a pawn in this war against Icarus, and they will only let you live so long as they believe they can control you."

From out in the hall, footsteps echoed into the room and I could hear faint voices talking. Someone was heading our way. I thought I should have felt safer now that someone was coming, but Estradé's last words had left me with a new sense of dread.

Her fists clenched in frustration. "There isn't enough time for me to explain everything right now."

Out of the corner of my eye, I saw her pull something from her pocket. The lights reflected off a silvery needle. I struggled to pull away, sudden terror fueling my efforts. Her strong hand gripped my arm and yanked me back. With practiced speed and deftness, she inserted the syringe into the IV's catheter and shoved the plunger down.

An instant feeling of dizziness swept over me as the drug raced through my bloodstream and up to my brain. "Please…" was the only word I was able to get out before the drug she had injected me with stole control of my body completely.

With darkness rushing in to claim me, I caught a final glimpse of Estradé's sad expression. As though it came from a great distance, I heard her say, "You're a good person, Alexandria. I wish I knew another way."

Chapter 7: Aiden Haskell

I LEFT ALEX'S side without so much as a backward glance. My mind was caught in a loop of cold fury as I heard Estradé's words echoing over and over in my head, "…she's one of Icarus' Alphas." There was a wretched sense of betrayal in those words that struck me over and over, like a fist to the gut. All I could think to do was to get as far away from her as possible.

I had left the hospital far behind me before I finally realized I was heading somewhere specific. The gym track loomed in front of me. It was here that I had first seen her. Like a specter, I could almost see her running around the track like she had been doing that first day. Her long brown hair pulled back into a loose ponytail. Her brow scrunched in frustration. She had seemed so vulnerable, so in need of comfort, and I had fallen right into her trap.

I had told her that my sister was a master at the games women played, but now I suspected that Alex was even better at it. She had lulled me into such a false sense of security that I had begun to let down my guard and let her in.

I realized that I was clenching my fists so tightly that I could feel the bite of my fingernails into my palms. I took a deep breath and forced myself to relax my hands. Suddenly,

I couldn't stand to be anywhere near the track. I turned and walked rapidly out of the building.

The most painful part of it all, I thought to myself as I crossed the courtyard, was that I had betrayed my brother by failing to see what she was. I had sworn to ensure that his death was avenged and instead I had done the opposite and willingly became friends with one of his killers. I walked on without paying any attention to where I was going; I was too blinded by my self-loathing.

Once more I was already there before I realized I had been going anywhere specific. I was standing in the doorway of the barracks, suddenly caught up in another memory. This was where she had taken me to start the tour. She had been standing right here, slightly hesitant to cross the threshold of the men's building, charming me all the more with the obvious innocence of her thoughts. *Innocence? No! No child of Icarus was innocent!* I thought bitterly.

I could practically see her, pointing out the features of the barracks. Her long, slender fingers that were surprisingly strong for being so small had pointed out the bathroom, the storage lockers, and the bulletin board where the week's schedule was posted.

I shook my head in disgust and walked back out the way I had come in. Why did I keep seeing her? I wanted nothing to do with a child of Icarus. It had been a child of Icarus that had killed my brother.

Callen had been a Charlie, like me. But unlike me, his gift had been in music, not athletics. At the age of three, he had begun to show his talent with musical instruments. At the age of eight, his gift had exploded into exceptionalism, and he had been accepted into the premier music school in England. By twelve, he was already an accomplished pianist who had won competitions throughout the world. By the age of sixteen, he was dead. It had been a bitter blow to our family.

Callen had been the baby of the family. I had been four when he was born and couldn't have been more excited that the baby was a boy and not a little sister. We had grown up great friends despite our differences. When I went off to join the military, and he was away at school, he would send me letters about the cute girls he met. He had even gone so far as to set up a double date for us during one of my holiday leaves. But that was the last time I had seen him.

He had been at school when the attack came. It had been a coordinated attack, timed in sync with four other attacks on different educational institutions scattered across the globe. At each location, one of Icarus' Alphas had been present. At each location, they had left behind a scene of wanton death and destruction. They hadn't just killed those they left behind; they had mutilated them. My father had refused to let the rest of us even see his body because of how it looked.

But I had called in some favors and gotten hold of the video footage from the attack. Two years later I could still see that Alpha clearly in my mind. She was close to Alex's age, in her late teens, with long black hair that framed her small, pale face. I could still see the malicious smile on her face as she pointed her hand at Callen. My hatred for that Alpha burned as strong today as it had burned when I watched the video two years ago.

Callen had been standing between her and a group of younger children, bravely trying to protect them. She had laughed at his efforts. And then his skin had begun to bubble and turn black as though he were on fire from within. He had screamed in agony, falling to his knees in pain. And still, the

Alpha had continued to point at him, rapturous in the vision of his body blistering and his skin peeling from his bones.

When he had finally stopped screaming, the Alpha had appeared almost disappointed. The obvious enjoyment that monster had taken from the pain she was causing had left me sick with disgust and determined to avenge my brother's murder.

The sound of a fist impacting repeatedly against the side of a punching bag pulled me away from the painful memories. I looked around to realize that, once more, my aimless wanderings had not been aimless at all. I was in the training hall.

I stared at the practice mats without really seeing them. Instead, I saw the memory of Alex, paired up against another girl, trying to master a move I had just shown them. There was a light sheen of sweat on her forehead and a distinct flush to her cheeks; it had only served to make her all the more attractive.

She was making a common positioning error with her arm, and I had joined them to correct it. I had asked her partner to step to the side while I showed Alex the danger of her error. In a swift, fluid move, I had dropped her to her back and was kneeling above her with my knife at her throat. Even now I could see the brilliance of those soft violet eyes and feel the stirring emotions that had deceived me so thoroughly. If I had only known then what she was!

I turned and punched the wall in frustration. I didn't want to see her face. I didn't want to feel any emotion for her but hatred. *So why does everything seem to remind me of her?*

I was pulled from my thoughts by a voice calling my name over the loudspeaker. "Specialists Haskell, Thatcher, Gallagher, Finley, and Sobrien report to the command center.

I repeat Specialists Haskell, Thatcher, Gallagher, Finley, and Sobrien, report to the command center."

I rubbed my knuckles as I turned to leave the practice hall. Punching the wall had not been the smartest thing to do.

I entered the command center to find it alive with activity. The stations were all manned. That in itself was unusual. The only time I had seen the command center fully staffed was during the base's monthly drills when everyone rushed to man their emergency positions. Coming from each station there seemed to be a drone of busy chatter that carried with it a sense of urgency.

"Copy that Bravo team."

"The satellite will be in alignment in T-minus 15 minutes."

"...tracks heading at a bearing of five degrees north by northwest..."

"Do not engage, I repeat do not engage..."

"Haskell. Over here."

I turned to see who had called my name over the cacophony of other voices. It was Hadley. I was a little surprised to see him up and about. He had taken a phaser blast to the shoulder during the attack in the jungle, but the blast had gone clean through the fleshy part of his shoulder, completely missing the bones and major muscles. He had been lucky. He was wearing a sling by doctor's orders, though I suspected he would have been happier to ditch it and simply deal with any discomfort that followed.

"What's going on?" I asked him when I got close enough to be heard without having to yell.

He handed the clipboard he had been holding to one of the sat-com techs and gave him some final instructions before indicating that I should follow him to the other side of the room.

"Someone breached security and stole some highly classified weapon. Couldn't tell you what it was exactly, but we're working on tracking it right now. General Durnham is putting together a recovery team and wants us on it."

Hadley led the way to a door that was guarded by two armed marines. They barely glanced at the two of us before one of them opened the door and allowed us to enter. Inside I found that we were the last to arrive. Thatcher, Gallagher, Finley, and Sobrien were already seated around the conference table. Seated between them were most of the base's high-ranking staff including the General's second in command, Lieutenant Colonel Ubuqua, Captain Dollard who was responsible for the base's security, Captain Leonard who managed the equipment yard, and Dr. Eris who was the top scientist on the base. These were just the men and women I recognized; there were several others I did not know.

"Good. Everyone's here now. We can get started," General Durnham said in a grim voice.

Hadley and I found empty seats and quickly sat down while he continued talking.

"For those of you whose security clearance is below level 3, you are hereby being granted temporary clearance to information that is classified well above your pay grade. What you will see and hear in the next few minutes is considered a state secret, and disclosure of the information contained herein to anyone outside this room will get you court-martialed and thrown in prison for the remainder of your natural lives."

Someone I didn't recognize was passing out digi-pads to everyone at the table. They were encrypted to our fingerprints and retinal scans as well as required voice authorization to activate. There was a murmur of voices as we all logged in to our pads. I was startled to see the screen open to an image of Alex.

"Ladies and gentlemen, what you are seeing on the screen is one of the UFC's most top-secret weapons. No, this is not a joke," he said when several of us looked up in confusion.

"I believe you are all aware that Specialist Alexandria Jaquette is one of the base's four Alphas. But what you are not aware of is that Jaquette is not your ordinary Alpha; she is a weapon that was bred in Icarus' lab. Like Icarus' other Alphas, this weapon had been genetically modified to have powers far stronger than the normal Alpha."

I felt my grip tightening on the pad. If there had been any lingering doubts that she might not have been the monster Estradé's words had suggested, those doubts had just been stripped away.

"The UFC came into possession of this weapon in April of 162. Testing at that time showed that the asset had distinct genetic differences from normal Alphas and a few chemical modifications that scientists still do not have a complete understanding of. For that reason, the asset has been under constant surveillance from the time it was obtained.

"Early observation and testing revealed that the asset has the ability to see and manipulate gravity fields. Six months ago, the asset began to show indications that it could manipulate gravity fields with an unusually high level of control. It was determined at that time to transfer the asset to this base where a sequence of focused training would be instituted to see if the asset could be controlled and successfully converted into a retaliatory weapon against Icarus' other Alphas."

"She, sir," Thatcher corrected the commander quietly in his slow Texan drawl. I looked at him in surprise; so did most everyone else.

"I beg your pardon?" Durnham said. It wasn't really a question, but Thatcher answered as though it had been.

"You are talking about Alex, sir, not an object. 'She' is the word you should be using to refer to her."

Several voices murmured around the table. I wasn't sure if they were murmuring in agreement or in descent. The General frowned at those who had been whispering to each other and the voices immediately stopped. "Thank you for that input, Specialist Thatcher, but according to the UFC, *she*," he stressed the word, "is nothing more than a potential asset to the military."

"With all due respect, sir," Thatcher had a lot of guts to counter the General, "the UFC lost the right to designate her as nothing more than an asset the day they put her in a position to save my team. I owe Alex my life, and I will not relegate her value to that of an object. Alex is an individual. She is the only reason a few of us are sitting here today."

A small seed of doubt settled in my mind, disrupting the feelings of anger that were quietly seething. Alex had saved my life out there as well, and it had very nearly cost her own life in the process.

Durnham's normally tight-lined lips lifted ever so slightly. "I see your point, Specialist Thatcher. Very well. I will consent to refer to her in your requested more personal form of address."

Durnham continued the briefing. "While Jaquette has only recently begun to develop a weaponized control over her raw power, analytical testing performed over the last several years has suggested that she may have only barely tapped the surface of what she is capable of."

The image on the pad was replaced by a graph that showed her confirmed control over gravity fields in a green line with a second red line showing the secondary influences on gravity fields she had inadvertently caused. The red line had multiple intermediate spikes in field activity that rose far above and beyond the green line.

The General continued as we studied the graph. "In the hands of the UFC, it is believed that Jaquette can become a powerful weapon against Icarus' forces. But if she were to fall into the wrong hands, her power used against us could be equally devastating. This belief was confirmed yesterday when she single-handedly took down a team of Iran's highly trained special ops forces. She is not a weapon we wish to lose."

"Excuse me, sir, but why are we being told all of this? If Alex is already in UFC hands, then what is the point of this meeting?" Specialist Finley had a way of breaking through the surrounding noise to get straight to the heart of an issue.

"Because," the General said slowly, "today at sixteen thirty-two, Specialist Jaquette was forcibly removed from her hospital room and taken off the base."

My head shot up. Alex has been kidnapped? How?! All of a sudden, the anger that had been burning like a raging inferno for the last hour was joined by an equally strong wave of panic. Was she ok? Where was she? What was happening to her? The two emotions began to war inside of my mind like a deadly storm.

"How do we know it was a forcible removal, sir?" Captain Leonard asked the question that seemed to be on the minds of several others. Around the table, heads were nodding in agreement. "Isn't it possible that she just decided to go back to Icarus on her own?"

In answer to that question, our screens changed to a video feed of Alex's hospital room. I glanced back down at the pad and my breath caught in my throat. It must have been made shortly after I left her room because Alex was already dressed in the clothes Estradé had brought her. There was a look of terror in Alex's eyes that tore at my conscience. I watched in stunned silence as Estradé pulled a syringe from her pocket while Alex fought unsuccessfully against her. I heard her faint, "Please…" and Estradé's, "You're a good person, Alexandria. I wish I knew another way," as Alex slipped from consciousness.

The storm inside of me suddenly froze. It wasn't that I had forgotten that she was a child of Icarus because I most definitely had not. But the cold fury I had been feeling ever since gaining that knowledge was overpowered by a sudden wave of anxiety for Alex. The terror in her eyes and her weak plea for help were burning into my mind like a waking nightmare that wouldn't go away. Deep inside, it sparked a tiny flame of guilt that steadily resisted the anger of the last hour.

Captain Dollard, the head of base security took up the briefing, but I only partially heard what he was saying. I couldn't pull my eyes away from the repeating video.

"Maria Estradé is the other woman in the image. Estradé has more than 20 years of experience working in UFC intelligence. She specializes in psychological evaluations and is considered one of the field's top experts. Six months ago, Estradé returned from an undercover mission where she supplied the UFC with invaluable psychological profiles on several of Icarus' key Alphas. Not long after returning from the field, she requested permission to come here and observe the asset.

"I will note that there was an incident shortly before her request that brought into question her motives, but it was determined by those with a higher pay grade than mine that she posed no threat to the asset and her request was granted. Her time here has been exemplary, and her review of the asset's psychological status has been quite valuable.

"That being said, shortly after the asset awoke this afternoon, Estradé presented the nurse on duty with papers suggesting that she had been ordered to perform a post-traumatic-stress evaluation on the asset. The nurse saw nothing out of order with the papers and let Estradé enter. Not long after, the nurse began her rounds with the other patients in the ward. It should also be noted that Specialist Haskell was present in the room, visiting with the asset at the time Estradé entered."

Most of the table turned to look at me; shame raced through me. I had been there. I had been in a position to prevent this, but instead, I had allowed myself to be blinded by my anger and had abandoned her at a time when she needed me. I found I couldn't meet their eyes, so I stared unseeing at the wall across the room.

Dollard continued as though he had not said anything of concern. "After careful review of the video, it has been determined that Haskell was not a party to Estradé's betrayal but was in fact manipulated by her so that he left her alone with the asset."

I remembered the words Estradé had said that had made me so angry. Had she purposely manipulated me with them so that I would abandon Alex? A small voice in my mind whispered that it was true and that I had failed Alex by falling for it. My guilty conscience grew.

"What was in the syringe?" Thatcher asked, drawing the attention away from me. I nodded at him slightly in appreciation; he nodded back.

Dollard pointed to Dr. Eris and she answered the question. "Estradé dropped the syringe on her way out of the room. We were able to evaluate it and found that she had administered Corsetron to the asset. Corsetron is a fast-acting general anesthesia that will leave the average patient unconscious for approximately four hours. Normally, Corsetron has no side effects when administered properly. However, it does have an interesting additional effect on Alphas. The chemicals in Corsetron seem to inhibit those produced by the Alpha's 6th lobe, resulting in a temporary loss of the Alpha's abilities. She will still be able to see the waves, but she will not have the control over gravity that she ordinarily does. The more doses she is given, the stronger the side effects will become and the longer they will last. You will need to keep this in mind. It is unlikely that she will be able to aid you in any way related to gravity and it is more than likely that she will be disoriented and not thinking clearly."

"Thank you, doctor," Dollard said. "Now we know that Estradé used a wheelchair to transport the asset to a Jungle Cruiser she had waiting just outside the hospital. We also know that the vehicle left the base traveling northeast toward the N-2 onramp approximately thirty minutes ago. What we don't know is where the vehicle went after it left the guards' field of vision. Further, it appears the jeep's transmitters were disabled prior to leaving the base so that we are unable to track it through that method."

The Jungle Cruiser was a rugged cross between a modern light strike vehicle and an antique Jeep Gladiator pickup. It was designed to travel at high speeds through rough jungle terrain, allowing for rapid transport of key personnel and their heavy equipment. Over rough terrain, it could quickly and easily reach speeds of up to 40 miles per hour. But on the smooth surface of the N-2 Highway, it could easily reach speeds of 120 miles per hour. If Estradé took Alex onto the N-2, the search radius was growing exponentially by the hour.

"We have Bravo team out searching for the vehicle as we speak. Initially, Estradé seemed to have chosen a jungle route, but approximately twenty minutes ago, they believe she took the vehicle through a stream, in an effort to deter tracking, before returning to a trail and finally leaving the jungle."

A map appeared on our screens showing Estradé's route.

"The most recent report we have suggests that the vehicle has moved onto a paved road. This has made tracking the vehicle considerably more difficult. However, we do have one mode of tracking the asset that is not usually available to us. The asset has an embedded tracker that was designed to remain inactive until such an emergency as this one."

There was another sudden murmur of voices. Embedded trackers were not unheard of, but they were normally reserved only for criminals, not teenage girls.

"Hold on!" My head snapped up once more and I was speaking before I had even fully realized the words were coming out of my mouth. "Yer sayin' that someone surgically placed a tracker in Alex?"

Ubuqua smirked at me from across the room. "Yes, Haskell, I believe that's what he just said. She is after all the property of the UFC. It's only natural that they should tag her like they tag all of their dogs." Durnham gave Callia a steely look. She stopped speaking in response to it, but her smirk remained.

My chair scraped loudly against the ground as I pushed back from the table and stood up. My fists were balled in anger; a new fury rose in my chest. Property of the UFC? Alex was not the property of anyone. She was a living, breathing human being, not an animal.

In a small corner of my mind, I recognized the hypocrisy of my thoughts. On one side, I was blaming her for being born as one of Icarus' Alphas as though he had ownership of her and therefore control over the way she behaved. On the other side, I was furious that the UFC thought they owned her or could control her. The contradiction only served to reignite the emotional storm inside of me and fuel the anger that raged as I glared at Ubuqua.

"Sit down, Haskell!" General Durnham ordered quietly, the cold hard steel in his voice cutting through the haze of my anger. His eyes locked with mine; not a hint of anger in them, but every hint that if I didn't immediately do what he said, I would regret my choice. I was seething, but too well-trained to disobey the direct order from my commanding officer; it was not a challenge I was ready to make.

I reached for the chair behind me and sat down angrily. The muscles in my jaw were twitching as I clenched my mouth shut to avoid saying something I might regret. Thatcher handed me back my digi-pad. As he did so, I noticed the hard, twitching line in his own jaw. I wasn't the only one who had taken offense at Ubuqua's words.

Dollard looked to Durnham for permission to continue; Durnham nodded.

"Normally the tracker would have been activated immediately upon the recognition that the asset's condition had been compromised. However, the activation of the tracking device requires a ping from one of the twenty-four sat-com B series satellites. Under normal conditions, the B series satellites provide continuous coverage allowing for activation at any moment. However, one of the satellites took some meteor damage earlier this week and is currently awaiting repairs. That means that there is a one-hour gap in the satellite system's coverage. Estradé appears to have done her homework. She timed her attack to fall precisely at the beginning of that blackout window. We are presently," he glanced at his watch, "T-minus two minutes until the tracker can be brought online and an additional two minutes before it can begin giving us a real-time feed of the asset's location."

"Thank you." General Durnham took back control of the meeting as Dollard returned to his seat. "You now know what happened. The next step is what we are going to do about it. It is imperative that we recover Jaquette as quickly as possible. So, I will be leading the recovery team in the field. Besides myself, the field team will consist of Ubuqua, Leon, Thatcher, Gallagher, Haskell, Finley, and Sobrien. Hadley, I am assigning you to assist Captain Dollard and Cepheus here in the command room.

"Each of you have previous combat and field experience; you know the routine. This operation is going to be light and tight. We will be taking off the instant we nail down Jaquette's position. Your equipment is already waiting for you in the command center's locker room, with one exception: Thatcher, go to the armory and retrieve your K-51."

Thatcher nodded his understanding. The K-51 was a Russian-made sniper's rifle that was said to have an accuracy range of three miles. Each gun was individually made and specifically altered to its owner's specifications. Somehow, I wasn't surprised to hear that Thatcher had one. I had never seen his equal on the target range, nor out in the field for that matter.

"We will regroup on the airfield in ten minutes, so get a move on it. Dismissed."

Chapter 8: Alexandria Jaquette

I WOKE GRADUALLY, rising through the fog of sedation as though I was coming up from the depths of a deep abyss. The first thing I became fully aware of was the deep thrumming hum of a vehicle engine under me and the howling whistle of the wind above. I had been hearing them for some time, but it had taken a while for me to be alert enough to recognize the sounds for what they were.

The next thing I became aware of was the cool, hard metal beneath me. It wasn't exactly smooth. There were ridges and bumps in it like the ripples of a wind-blown sand dune, but they were not so big as to be uncomfortable. I also recognized that a blanket had been wrapped around me and that the part of it that was under me helped to provide some cushioning.

A piece of my hair blew across my forehead, tickling me. I reached up to move it, only to find that my hand was caught fast by a metal bracelet looped around my wrist. Fear began to creep into my growing awareness. Something wasn't right.

I struggled to think through the fog. What was going on? I tried to remember how I had gotten here, but the last thing I remembered was Aiden laughing with me as he showed me how to work the bed's controls, and I remembered Estradé coming in to talk to me, and then Aiden leaving, and...

It all came back like a rushing tidal wave, threatening to drown me. My breathing quickened and my heart began to race. My eyes shot open only to be blinded by the glaring rays of the afternoon sun. I quickly snapped them shut again. Taking more care the second time, I turned my head to the side and opened my eyes slowly. I was able to make out the shadowed wall of the vehicle beside me while giving my eyes time to adjust to the brightness around me.

I immediately recognized the distinctively mottled green and brown roll bars of a Jungle Cruiser. I was in the bed of the vehicle, and what I had thought was a bracelet on my wrist was actually a pair of military cuffs with one end attached to my wrist and the other end around the roll bar. I pulled against the cuffs tentatively; they were securely attached. I would need the six-digit code to undo them and my left arm free from the sling to enter it. Neither one of those was an immediate option so I turned my attention to trying to identify where I was.

I couldn't see much from where I was laying; the bed of the truck blocked my view of most of the outside world. I could see the blue sky above us and scattered white clouds floating lazily across it, though that didn't tell me much about where I was. It did occur to me that the cruiser was driving on a smooth surface, and it was moving fairly fast. That suggested a road, though I hadn't heard any sounds of other vehicles, so it wasn't a major one.

I turned my head to look toward the front of the vehicle. I had thought it might be possible to see out the windshield from here; I couldn't. What I could make out was the backs of the two forward seats. The passenger side appeared to be empty, but Estradé was sitting in the driver's seat. I was immediately angry. What did she think she was doing?

Just at that moment, Estradé glanced in the rearview mirror and noticed that I was awake and watching her. The cruiser began to slow in response, and she pulled off of the road.

"You shouldn't be awake yet." She said it calmly, almost curiously, as the engine turned off.

"I shouldn't be here," I countered angrily.

"No." Her voice had a sadness to it that surprised me. It wasn't what I was expecting from a kidnapper. "You should have never been put in a situation where this was necessary, but you were."

She opened her door and came around to the bed of the vehicle so that she was standing near me. I sat up to face her.

"Where are you taking me?" I tried my best to sound tough but sitting up had been a bad idea. Whatever she had given me in the hospital, it was making the world around me shift and spin.

"Oh, lay back down." She said it with her usual motherly tone. I almost obeyed without thinking. She sighed when I resisted. "I promise you that I am not going to harm you. What I am doing is only intended to help you. I am truly sorry, Mija, but we don't have time at this moment for me to explain and I don't have time to fight you on this."

Without warning she grabbed my hand, the one that was cuffed to the roll bar, and inserted another syringe into the IV catheter I had not even realized was still in my hand.

My vision began to narrow almost immediately. I swore at her in frustration. She didn't retaliate but instead helped me to lay back down before I passed out once more. As I drifted back into the darkness, I felt her fingers stroke the hair from my forehead. "Oh, Mija, if all goes well tonight, the right people will be in place and ready to shield you from what is coming. This will all be over in a few more hours."

ALEX'S TRACKING DEVICE had been activated on schedule and showed that Estradé had indeed taken her north. It was believed that she must have at least started on the N-2 Highway because the tracker showed them to already be more than eighty miles away. But, by the time the tracker had been activated, they were no longer on the main road, or on any road for that matter. The blip on the screen showed them to be in the middle of the jungle, several miles east of a small city labeled Likpe Todome.

What was more, they were moving at a walking pace. It would seem they had left the vehicle and were now on foot. General Durnham nodded his head in satisfaction. We were in the air five minutes later.

The Daedalus Transporter we were in was surprisingly quiet. Its four turbine engines had first been introduced to the world sometime before the Pernicious Bellum War, but they had not reached the silent running capacity that this one had until recently. Of course, silent was a relative term. While the engines might be considered silent to those outside the craft, there was just enough airflow noise coming in from outside the craft's metal walls to make talking at normal levels difficult; we had to raise our voices to be heard. As a result, there wasn't much talking going on. We all sat in silence, mentally preparing for what would happen when we landed, though none of us were quite certain what that would be.

The General expected this to be a quick, easy recovery mission; I wasn't so sure about that. Estradé had never struck me as a fool. If she had abandoned the vehicle, she had a strategy behind it.

Although I had only known Estradé for a few weeks, she had a motherly way about her that instilled a sense of trust. It was not a virtue that one could easily fake; it developed from true care and concern for others. During the attack in the jungle, Estradé had been the only one quick enough to pick up on the fact that I was trying to protect Alex's identity and she had actively stepped in to help me. The look in her eyes at that time had not been one of deceit, they had been one of concern.

When she had seen us playing with the hospital bed, her smile had been so gentle. She had chided us, but it had been with a laugh of amusement. Standing just outside the doorway, I had easily heard the concern in her voice as she told Alex how worried she had been. And then her voice had taken on such sadness when she had explained that the UFC had taken away Alexandria's choices. None of those times felt like the behavior of someone who was out to hurt Alex. So why kidnap her? The more I thought about it, the less it made sense. It felt like I was missing pieces to a puzzle.

The bio sheet I had read before we left the base had briefly detailed Estradé's career. She had a Ph.D. in psychology that she had earned in her early twenties. She had gone straight into service with the UFC's Intelligence division after graduation, working primarily as a psychological analyst for the department. At some point in her service, they had begun sending her out into the field to do psychological profiles on several world leaders. Some of those assignments had been undercover and had required her to undergo specialized weapons, equipment, and survival training. In other words, she had the training to be both mentally and physically dangerous.

But then her bio sheet had gone on to detail her home life as well. She had been married for thirty-five years to the same man. She was the mother of three children and the grandmother of seven. She spent all of her vacation time at home with them, often taking time off to simply attend their athletic events and musical performances. She was described by her daughter as being "…loving and concerned for others, often setting aside her own needs while making sure the needs of others were met."

The report had been summarized by her commanding officer with words like, "…one of the best…," "loyal to the UFC…," and "…not a member of this department that has not personally benefited from her kind concern or wise counsel." There was nothing in the report to suggest that she would be one to betray the UFC, let alone kidnap one of their Alphas. Then why did she do it?

Then again, there had been a brief note at the end of the report. Two short lines stating that her entire family had been killed six months ago in an unexplained accident. Maybe something had happened there to change her way of thinking. Maybe she was looking for revenge or planning to use Alex as leverage for something. Even as those ideas were forming, my mind dismissed them as unlikely. I couldn't say exactly why, but they just didn't feel like the right answers.

"Come again?" General Durnham's voice was just loud enough to pull me from my thoughts. I glanced up to see his agitated profile as he listened to whoever was speaking to him through his headset. His countenance darkened with each passing moment, mimicking the increasingly darkening sky outside the cockpit window. He was quietly swearing under his breath by the time he took the headset off and stood to move to the transport hanger where the rest of us were seated.

"Listen up." He spoke loud enough for us all to hear. "This mission just took a turn for the worse; Bravo team has gone silent. Their last transmission was to report that an unidentified vehicle was approaching them at the site where Estradé abandoned her vehicle. In the middle of that transmission, there was the sound of an explosion, and then radio silence."

No one said anything; we all knew what that meant.

"In case you didn't notice, the sun has already set. It will be fully dark in the next few minutes. The pilot already set the craft to run dark and she is going to land us as closely as she safely can. That should allow us to reach the ground, but it's still going to leave us a mile out."

"Gallagher," he turned to look at him, "you're running point. I want you to stay a quarter mile ahead of us and scout out the region. Make sure we don't run into any surprises along our way."

He nodded his understanding. Gallagher was comparable to a hunting hound. He could identify tracks in the dirt that most highly programmed computer identification systems would miss. I had also heard it rumored that he could track by scent, though I had not had the opportunity to confirm that for myself. If anyone was naturally made for the point position, it was Gallagher.

"Thatcher, you are taking the sniper position. Set up on this point here and provide cover for the rest of the team." He pointed to a circled area on the map he was holding. He handed the map to the sharpshooter. Next to the circled location, a set of GPS coordinates had been penned in. Thatcher entered the coordinates into the data pad on his tactical band then handed the map back.

"Finley, you will be backing up Thatcher in the secondary sniper position. I want you to set up right here." He handed her the map. "Get into position fast and let us know what is down there. I want to know who took out Bravo team and with what."

Finley nodded curtly. She had a similar background to my own, having spent several years in the UFC military prior to transferring to the specialist division at this base. She had the ability to see at great distances, intentionally altering the focus of her eyes to see details that would have otherwise been impossible to see even with specialized equipment.

"Ubuqua and Haskell, you're my intercept team. Keep your eyes open and your guns sharp." In other words, we would be the ones responsible for finding Alex once we entered the caves.

"Sobrien, you're with me." Sobrien was an interesting character. He was one of the newest recruits to the unit, having come in about two weeks ago, but he already acted as though he owned the place. I had seen him pushing his weight around the barracks and the mess hall. I guess he was one of those tough guys who thought might made right, and he had plenty of strength to enforce his opinion with. Next to Bowen, he was the strongest person on base.

Bowen. I guess Alex hadn't managed to save all of us. *Sobrien is now the strongest man on base,* I thought bitterly.

"Yes, sir," Sobrien's gruff voice replied.

"Leon, you have the rearguard. Make sure no one comes up behind us." Leon nodded.

"We have another problem." He said it almost hesitantly, glancing back at Thatcher and me briefly before continuing. "Alex's tracker just stopped transmitting. Based on the path of its last few signals, it's more likely that Estradé took Alex into the caves than it is for anyone else to have overtaken them. That's the good news. The bad news is that those cave systems run miles deep under the earth and we no longer have a guaranteed way to track them. What's more, whoever attacked Bravo team knew exactly where to find them. It looks like we may have a leak at the command center."

There were a few murmurs at that announcement.

"For that reason, we will be running dark from here on out. Tune your frequencies to this channel." He held up eight fingers followed by one down and the ninth finger up: channel eighty-one. We all keyed the number into the computer on our tactical bands. As we did so, I felt the Daedalus begin its descent.

The General's next words came straight through the earpieces we each wore. "Get your fishing gear out, boys. It's time to catch us some fish."

Chapter 10: Alexandria Jaquette

I WAS AWARE of periods when a sound or a sense of movement would drift into my consciousness. Once or twice my eyes even fluttered open to darkness barely held at bay by the pale glow of an orange light stick, then they would close again, and I would drift once more. Awareness was a fickle friend that came and went, leaving behind it only snatches of sounds and impressions of images.

The fog of confusion that seemed to drift through my brain prevented any of those sounds and images from joining together to create a coherent thought. With the passage of time, awareness came and went more frequently, but the thoughts remained disjointed.

The first thing I noticed when the fog in my mind finally began to lift was the silence. It was absolute and dead, although I quickly realized that that was not quite accurate. The silence was not complete; it was being interrupted by the steady, slow drip of water on water.

The second thing I noticed was the cold. Despite the blanket I could feel wrapped around me, the surface I was laying on seemed to be seeping all of the warmth out of my body; I was shivering.

I reached up to rub my arms, thinking to use friction to warm my body, only to find that one arm was bound against my torso while the other arm was bound with a metal bracelet. Confused, I opened my eyes to see what was on my wrist. A pale orange light glinted off of metal cuffs that were barely visible in the thick darkness; one end was attached to my wrist, the other to a thick eye bolt that had been secured into the ground next to me. My confusion grew, unable to understand what I was seeing. Why was I cuffed? And the darkness? Was it night? Where was I? I searched my mind for answers, trying to remember something to explain what was going on.

The memories came slowly. We had been on the orienteering challenge. Estradé had heard something that alerted us to danger. We had discovered the enemy soldiers and developed a plan. I had hidden in the tree and used my control over gravity to disarm the men. And then? And then what?

I gasped as it all came rushing back in with the force of a hurricane. Then I had woken up in the hospital and been kidnapped by Estradé. And now I was here. Here! Where was here?

"Estradé, where am I?" my voice croaked.

There was no answer. I struggled into a sitting position. Just as it had last time, the world around me shifted and spun. The effort I had made was very small, but it felt like I was struggling through molasses to do it. I sat with my eyes closed for a minute, waiting for the world to stop spinning.

When I finally opened my eyes again, the first thing I saw was a military-grade light stick sitting on the ground nearby; it was the source of the orange light. Within the range of the light stick's glow, I could see little but shadowed rock.

Beyond that pale light was only darkness and the slow, steady sound of dripping water.

"Estradé?" My voice warbled slightly from the sudden nervousness that settled in the pit of my stomach. Again, there was no answer. Had she brought me here only to abandon me to this darkness? I pulled against the cuff that held me secure. Neither it nor the eyebolt gave any hint of weakness. My fear grew.

"Estradé?!" I yelled it. There was a definite note of panic in my voice this time. Only the echo of my voice came back to me from the darkness. The echo suggested that I was in a cave.

It occurred to me that I could move the light stick around to get an idea of the space around me. I reached out for the gravity field beneath it and lifted; the stick didn't move. That caught me off guard. I looked at the light stick again and studied the gravity field under it. The field ebbed and flowed as it always had. I focused again, raised my cuffed hand as best I could, and lifted for the second time. Nothing. The light stick didn't so much as wobble.

My heart suddenly felt like it had been replaced by a block of ice; its tingling chill spread rapidly outwards, coursing through my veins as though intent on freezing my soul. Why couldn't I control the gravity fields? I could see its pull on the light stick and on the few small pebbles that were within the light's pale glow, but no matter how hard I struggled to lift, the light stick and pebbles ignored my efforts.

It was a terrifying feeling; like a piece of me had been cut away. A feeling of panic was growing by the moment. My breathing became more rapid.

"Estradé!" I yelled it as loud as I could. This time Estradé's faint voice responded from somewhere off in the darkness.

"Mija, it's ok. I will be there in a minute."

A surge of relief battled back the growing panic. I strained to listen in the direction her voice had come from. I wasn't sure, but I thought I could hear the faint scraping sound of footsteps. I also thought that just maybe I could see the faint glow of an orange light coming from off to my left. Then I was certain I wasn't imagining it; the light was growing brighter. It became a sphere of glowing light that barely lit the darkness around it. I was able to make out a tunnel, just big enough for Estradé to walk through, perhaps thirty feet away from me.

I heard Estradé's accented voice speaking much softer this time. "This medicine is wearing off much too quickly. She shouldn't be awake yet." For a moment I thought she was talking to herself, but then a man's voice responded from the darkness behind her. "Icarus engineered her to be different. Normal rules do not apply to her." I didn't recognize the male's voice, nor could I see the speaker.

"Can we safely give her another dose?" Estradé seemed hesitant.

"Don't you dare." I growled with an empty threat. There was little chance I could stop her, but I was really getting tired of being drugged. They either didn't hear me, or they simply ignored me.

"We're going to have to," the man said in a thick African accent. "She can't be awake while I perform the procedure."

Procedure? The sense of relief that had come with knowing I was not alone suddenly vanished; anger took its place. They were not performing anything on me. I made a vain effort to pull my wrist from the cuff. I only succeeded at cutting the skin underneath it.

Estradé came out of the tunnel and saw what I was doing.

"Stop that, Mija," she chided me loudly. "You'll only hurt yourself."

I scowled at her. She ignored the scowl and walked closer to me so that she was fully within the radius of the light stick at my side. Her own light stick was still in her hand, adding to the feeble light of my own so that I could now see her clearly. A tall, thin man in a black shirt and pants moved to stand beside her. He had thinning, curly grey hair atop a nearly bald head, and wrinkles across his face and hands that suggested he was well beyond his prime. His dark skin combined with the dark clothes explained why he had not been as easy to see as Estradé had been.

"Alexandria, allow me to introduce Dr. Ekon Gbeho. He is an expert in neurosurgery. He came to help you."

"Help me with what?" I asked guardedly as I eyed the man distrustfully.

The man's lips twitched into the hint of a smile. "I'm going to remove the tracking device and the nano-explosive that is at the base of your skull."

I had been ready to give a smart retort to anything he said, but the words died on my lips; I hadn't been prepared for that.

Estradé sat down on the ground beside me and touched my shoulder gently. "We still don't have a lot of time to explain everything, but remember that I told you that you could not trust the UFC? When you were three years old you were already beginning to show signs that you were not going to be an ordinary Alpha. The testing they were doing with you at that time suggested your abilities would be far beyond anything they had seen before. Even then they intended to find ways to use you and they wanted to ensure that they would have a way to control you. So, they had a tracking device and nano-explosive surgically implanted. Both would remain inactive until they were needed; until they decided that they needed to use the threat of them to force you to do whatever they wanted you to do as you got older and stronger, or to destroy you if they found they couldn't control you."

This was way beyond belief. Surely the UFC wouldn't put a nano-explosive in me. Besides, when would they have had the chance? I couldn't think of a single situation where they might have done so. What if she was making this all up to get me to go along with whatever it was that she was planning? I wasn't sure what to believe. "How do you know all this?" I asked skeptically.

The man at her side laughed bitterly. "Because I am the one who put them there."

I looked up sharply. There was a distinct hint of sadness in his eyes that surprised me. He knelt so that he was looking at me straight on. "Not to excuse what I did, because I should have known better, but I believed the UFC was looking out for the greater good. I did whatever they asked without thinking through the ramifications. When they told me to do the surgery on a three-year-old little girl, I didn't ask why or whether it was the right thing to do; I trusted them completely. It wasn't until later that I learned some hard truths about the UFC. By then, it was too late to correct my mistakes; or so I thought."

He nodded toward Estradé. "Your friend here, found out about it somehow and hunted me down two months ago. She told me there was a chance to redeem myself and set everything up to make it possible. I came here to undo what I should have never done."

"Alex," Estradé said, "I understand that you don't trust me, but we are running out of time and need to do the procedure now. I had intended for you to wake up with it already done. Unfortunately, or maybe it isn't so unfortunate in and of itself," she smiled ruefully, "you don't seem to react to this drug in quite the same way other Alphas do. Who knows? It may turn out to be a good thing for you in the future.

"But right now, even as we speak, General Durnham is using that tracking device to follow you to this area. Yes, they activated it when they found I had taken you off of the base. But I was sure they would, so I took you into these underground caves because they block the device's transmission. At this moment, they know you are in the caves, but they don't know exactly where in the caves."

I felt a momentary hope that they might find me quickly. Estradé crushed the hope with her next words.

"This cave system is very extensive. It was used by undamaged during the M-Gen wars to hide from those that were hunting them down. They created several hidden pathways that aren't easily seen. Durnham and his men aren't going to find us until we are ready for them too. Unfortunately, they are not the only ones that were able to follow the transmission from your tracking device. It would appear that someone gave Icarus the code to follow your transmission; some of his men are also in the cave system looking for you."

Dr. Gbeho nodded his head to confirm what she had just said. "If we are going to have time to do it, the procedure needs to be done now." He paused, his smile fading away. "I'm sorry for not standing up for you when you were too young to stand up for yourself. I hope that you will forgive…"

He didn't get to finish what he was about to say. While my attention was on him, Estradé had reached for my cuffed hand suddenly, unexpectedly. The drug was in my system before I even realized that it had happened. She hadn't even given me the chance to trust her! I looked at her accusingly. She didn't smile this time as she gently lowered me back to the ground. "It's going to be ok, Mija. When you wake next, it will all be over. Now close your eyes and sleep." As the darkness closed in once more, I was left with the bitter sense of betrayal and the thought that there was no one I could truly trust anymore. I was alone.

Chapter 11: Aiden Haskell

I STOOD BACK from the edge of the line of trees, carefully studying the scene in front of me. The smoking remains of a Jungle Cruiser littered the far side of the clearing. Its side had been melted by the blast that had sent it flying through the air to land upside down where it now lay. Halfway out of its forward windshield were the fire-charred remains of a dead soldier; probably the driver, I thought impassively.

Twenty feet away from me, a second Jungle Cruiser was riddled with phaser holes. The rest of Bravo team was scattered around it; their bloodied bodies were stark evidence of the battle they had fought and lost. My jaw clenched in anger. Those had been good men and women.

Just beyond the remains of the second cruiser was the entrance to a cave. Actually, it wasn't much more than a jagged crack in the side of the hill. It was perhaps seven feet tall and three feet wide. Two soldiers stood just inside its opening, utilizing the shadows for cover. Speaking of which, we wouldn't have much cover once we left the shadows of the jungle. We would need to take out those two soldiers before we moved into the clearing.

As if reading my mind, Thatcher's quiet words came through my earpiece. "Two hostiles guarding the cave entrance. I'll neutralize the one on the left. Finley, you take the right."

"Copy that," her answer came back.

Two near-silent bursts of gunfire followed each other through our earpieces in rapid succession. I watched the phaser fire as their white light streaked across the air, momentarily illuminating across my lenses as the phaser bursts warmed the air they passed through.

Sobrien and Durnham were already moving to quickly pull the bodies away from the cave entrance. They deposited them unceremoniously behind the second cruiser. Then Durnham disappeared from view for several seconds as he went through the cave entrance.

"All clear," his voice spoke softly.

I moved to join him at the cave's entrance. We didn't bother with flashlights. Our equipment was designed to automatically disperse infrared beams in the dark. They were invisible to the naked eye but allowed the night vision lenses we were wearing to translate the returning signals as though it were daylight.

Twenty feet into the cave's tunnel, it opened into a natural cavern about the size of a small house. The uneven ground had been worn smooth by hundreds of years of feet passing over it. Even the walls showed indications that the touch of man had honed its edges into softer lines than it had likely started with. But the ceiling that hung some fifteen feet above us appeared to have been untouched. All this I noticed in the back of my mind as I rapidly searched the room for hints of danger. I saw none. On the far side of the cavern were multiple tunnels leading in different directions.

Durnham indicated that he and Sobrien would take the left branch; Ubuqua and Leon each indicated that they would take tunnels near the middle. That left the right tunnel for me.

As I moved into the tunnel, I kept my ears open for any sound of movement. There was little to be heard beyond the quiet footfalls that we carefully placed with each step forward. I followed the tunnel forward for twenty yards as it became increasingly narrow and the ceiling began to lower. Along the wall, hundreds of names had been carved into, or penned onto, the cold stone. Most were worn smooth or faded by age and the touch of human hands, but a few were newer. Some were simple initials, likely from those who had visited these caves. Others were full names brazenly declaring their existence. Here and there a short message had been written; gems of knowledge the writer thought to leave to the future. In one place, two lovers had carved their names surrounded by a heart as though carving it would somehow secure their love for as long as the stone walls stood. I shook my head in disgust. None of this was helping me find Alex.

It was beginning to look like a dead end, but just as I reached the point where I was thinking I should turn around, I noticed an unnatural line on the wall. It was freshly cut, a jagged gash that had been recently carved into the rock face. Beneath it were two words: Alphabet Girl. My breath hissed as my hand instinctively reached out to touch the words. It was the nickname Alex had given herself the day we first met, before I had even known her real name. It brought with it the flood of emotions I had thought I had buried deep at the start of the mission. I knew that I couldn't afford their distraction, but the raw emotions I had tried to bottle up were proving to be more powerful than my control. My teeth clenched as I closed my eyes and fought them back down.

It was when I opened them once more that I noticed something I had nearly missed. Beneath the words was a small crack in the wall, nearly hidden by the large boulder that was next to it. The crack got larger as it went around the stone, finally widening out to a small tunnel just big enough for an individual to crawl through on hands and knees. Instinctively I knew that I needed to go through that tunnel to get to Alex.

I typed a quick message to the team on my data pad, telling them what I had found, then I lowered myself onto my belly and began to squeeze into the opening. It was a tight fit, but far from impossible. I crawled as silently as I could, keeping my gun in front of me in case someone else had come this way before me. Some twenty feet or so in, the tunnel began to widen out and the roof got higher so that I was able to walk once more.

As I continued forward, I began to notice other small crevices branching off from the tunnel I was following. Some of them were big enough for a person to squeeze into. I checked a few of them to find that most were nothing more than cracks in the wall. But one or two of them opened up into larger tunnels. I was debating whether I needed to follow them when the sound of a boot crunching on a pebble alerted me that I was not alone.

I spun around to see a broad-shouldered soldier stalking toward me with his knife drawn. He slashed at my arm with the sharply honed blade. I pulled back hurriedly, trying to dodge it, but wasn't quite fast enough. I grunted as the blade cut through the fabric of my uniform and bit into my skin. I could feel the warm trickle of blood as it began to flow freely from the gash it left. My instincts screamed at me to clamp onto the gash and staunch the flow of blood, but I knew that if I took the time to do that, I would lose the ability to defend myself against his next attack. It came even before I had finished that thought, only this time I was ready.

As the man swung at me, I lunged forward into him, grabbing his weapon arm just above and below the elbow and locking it into the straight position. At the same time, I yanked him forward and drove my knee into his chest. He grunted with pain but used his free hand to club me in the side of the head. White flashes of light blinded my eyes as I reeled back, momentarily stunned.

Through the earpiece, I heard Durnham's concerned voice. "Sound off!" Our mikes were on a constant feed. While the computer chips automatically filtered out the simple sounds of breathing and footsteps, my grunt of pain must have registered through to the others, though they couldn't have been certain whom it had come from. In the background, I could hear the rest of the team checking in. I didn't get the chance to answer.

The other man dove forward, his shoulder ramming into my chest and pushing me up against the solid rock wall. I grunted again as my breath was knocked from my chest. I barely reacted in time to grab his wrist and keep him from plunging his knife into my stomach. We struggled for several seconds this way before I was able to free one of my hands long enough to reach the small gun I kept tucked into my belt at the back of my pants. I fired it point-blank into his chest. The man slumped to the ground, a stunned expression on his face as I stepped away from him.

I was breathing hard as I tucked the gun back into my belt, then pulled my bandana from the cargo pocket of my uniform and tightly wrapped it around my bleeding forearm.

"Haskell! Report!" Durnham's gruff voice ordered through my earpiece. He wasn't yelling, yet he somehow managed to convey his frustration through his near whisper. The whole team would have heard the sound of my gun firing.

"Clear," I answered back softly, even as I used my teeth to tighten the knot in the material. "One hostile down. I took a cut tae the arm, but it's not serious. I'm good tae continue." I had already begun to advance through the tunnel even as I said the last part, only this time I made sure to check every crack and crevice twice. It slowed down my progress while ensuring that no one else was able to sneak up behind me.

"Copy that," Durnham responded. "Any new markings?" he asked in a near whisper.

"Negative, sir." The tunnel in front of me branched into several possible paths. I was about to take the path to the right when I noticed a second jagged line similar to the first. It was low to the ground, disappearing behind a small pile of rocks next to the middle opening. I knelt and brushed the rocks aside to find Alex's nickname carved into the wall once more. "I take that back, sir," I corrected. "There's a second markin' here. It looks like someone is leavin' breadcrumbs for us tae follow."

"Careful, Haskell." Finley's voice came over the line. "I don't think any of us would have recognized that nickname. Those breadcrumbs might have been laid specifically for you. If so, they could be leading you into a trap."

"Copy that," I responded. The same thought had crossed my mind. I suppose the nickname wasn't a complete secret. After all, Alex had typed it into one of the base's computers. Anyone with the access and the know-how could have found it. But not many people would understand what it meant or have recognized its significance. No. I was sure Estradé was leaving a trail for me to follow. I just didn't know why.

I was already more than fifty feet into the marked tunnel when Durnham's voice came back on the line. "We're coming to you, Haskell. Stay put."

"Aye, sir." I responded automatically, while at the same time turning to focus on a new carving I had just noticed through the corner of my eye. It was a thinner line than the previous ones had been, but it was the same style. Like the previous two, it was also followed by a name, only this time a picture had been taped next to it. I froze, mid-step, as I looked at it. It wasn't Alex's nickname this time; it was my brother's name. I stared at Callen's face in the picture, my hand reaching up to touch it as though it somehow allowed me to touch him. My reaction was automatic, unthinking, and robotic, even as the trained part of my mind screamed, *It's a trap. Run!*

I couldn't bring myself to move. I was like a deer caught in the headlights of a speeding vehicle. I knew I was in danger, but still, I stood there staring at Callen's picture.

I guess I wasn't really surprised when I suddenly felt the cold, hard metal of a gun as it was pressed against my head just behind the ear. Instinctively I knew who it was. She had set her trap perfectly, knowing the bait that would trap me. Even as I recognized this, I felt shame and frustration at having allowed myself to be manipulated once more. I stiffened in anger.

"Hello, Haskell," Estradé's accented voice spoke softly into my ear. "Glad you found the way." It was the last thing I heard before I felt the thin probe of a taser unit pressed harshly against my neck followed immediately by the sharp sting of electricity pulsing through me, shutting down my body's systems. As the darkness overtook me, I saw Alex's face ghosting through my memory and knew that my failure to control my emotions had once more left her at Estradé's mercy.

Chapter 12: Aiden Haskell

I WOKE WITH a start to a sharp, acrid scent in the air. My head jerked up and I was immediately alert. Estradé, who had been standing in front of me, calmly put the lid back on to the bottle she was holding. She saw me watching her and nodded, then turned away to set the bottle on the small nearby table.

It only took a second for me to assess my situation. I had been bound to a chair across my chest, at my wrists, and at the ankles with thick, leather straps. I tugged experimentally against the restraints; they were secure. At the same time, I recognized that the chair I was strapped to had been bolted to the floor; I wasn't going to be able to knock it over and break free that way.

I looked around to get my bearings. We were in a room that was not much bigger than a small office. On the table next to Estradé were my tactical band, earpiece, night vision lenses, and all of my weapons. The only exit from the room was a single, thick door that had been set into the stone wall, while in front of me was an opaque window. This room had been designed to hold prisoners as a captive audience to whatever was beyond that window, and I was the captive audience.

The rational part of my brain had to admit that I was scared, but I wasn't about to show it. That wasn't hard since I was also frustrated and angry. Once more, Estradé had manipulated my emotions, and I had fallen right into her trap. I knew I wasn't infallible, but I had thought I was at least smart enough to not allow myself to be manipulated that way.

Estradé silently watched me as I pulled against the restraints once more; a strange smile playing on her lips. Finally, my attention shifted back to her. At this moment I wasn't sure whether she was an enemy or a friend. All of my training was screaming at me that she was an enemy. She had kidnapped Alex, she had manipulated and stunned me, and now I was her prisoner. And yet, despite that knowledge, I couldn't help but think that the real Estradé was the motherly figure that she had occasionally appeared to be back on the base. If so, why was she doing all of this?

"Why am I here?" I asked her as calmly as I could, thinking that if I could just get her talking, I stood a chance of finding out what was really going on.

"You know, it's not often I get the opportunity to study someone who is quite like you." She said it as though I were a curiosity that one had to study to understand.

"Is that why I'm here," I asked tensely, "so yae can observe me?"

"No. Actually, it's you who are here to do the observing," she answered cryptically.

"Then why th' chair? What is goin' on, Estradé?"

She smiled mysteriously, then changed the subject. Picking up my phase pistol she said, "You have an interesting weapon here. It's not a standard military issue. Where did you get it?"

"I found it in th' jungle on me way in," I lied.

She laughed in amusement. "I sincerely doubt that. You had it during the orienteering challenge. You know," she spoke thoughtfully, tapping her fingers absently against the gun as she talked, "it seems to me that this is a rather good quality weapon for the average soldier to be carrying. It makes me wonder if you aren't the average, ordinary soldier."

My heart skipped a beat; I was suddenly concerned with where this line of discussion was leading.

"I'm not sure what yae mean by that." I tried to sound confused by the comment, as though I truly was just like all the rest of the UFC's soldiers and had nothing to hide.

"Is that so?" She didn't believe me.

I thought it was best that the subject changed fast. "Where's Alex?" I asked.

"Oh, she's around. I'm sure you'll get to see her soon."

My eyes narrowed. Something about the way she said that didn't feel right. I was suddenly very concerned for Alex.

"Estradé, what is goin' on? Why did yae kidnap Alex?"

"Why do you care what I do with your enemy?" she countered.

"She's not me enemy." I had responded without thinking, but even as I said it, the truth behind the words caught me with unanticipated force. I had been blaming Alex for someone else's actions while ignoring her own. She may have been created by Icarus, but she had shown me over and over that she was not like him or his other children.

Despite all that had been done to her, she had retained a sense of innocence and gentleness that was evident in everything she did and spoke. She had been manipulated her whole life; first by Icarus and now by the UFC, never being given a choice in what she had to do. Yet, even as she had learned the military drills and perfected the combat moves they had forced her to learn, she had done so never intending to use those skills to harm others. Her words to Estradé had reaffirmed that when she expressed revulsion for what she had done to the enemy soldiers.

For the first time since the hospital room, I understood that the only thing Alex was guilty of was not being strong enough to break free of the manipulations of those who sought to use her. If I had not been strong enough myself, how could I expect her to be stronger? And yet, shouldn't we both have been stronger?

My internal battle must have shown on my face because Estradé's eyebrow raised slightly as though she found my response and the resulting battle amusing.

"That is not what you seemed to think when you abandoned her in the hospital room."

I had no answer for her accusation. It was true, I had abandoned her.

Estradé seemed to read my mind and said almost kindly, "I suppose we all make mistakes we regret. Speaking of which, tell me Aiden, why did you join the military? You're not the type who seeks out danger, and you're certainly not the type who likes hurting others. I'd say it was in response to your brother's murder, but you had already joined the military before that point. Could it be that you support the UFC and what they stand for? Are you here to help them?"

I almost laughed at the thought. It was so far from the truth it was absurd. "Yae don't know anythin' about me."

"I know you're an interesting person to observe." Estradé said it philosophically. "So much pent-up emotion hiding behind that bravado. But I know the real you…" She moved to stand behind me so that she was able to whisper the next part into my ear. "…Sir Alistair Naughton Buccleuch."

146

She said the name slowly, giving full weight to its formal title. And with it, I felt the wind suddenly knocked from my lungs as though she had punched me in the gut instead of whispering the words. *How? How had she known?* She knew my full name, which meant she knew exactly who I was. If I had thought I was scared before, I was suddenly terrified.

When I joined the military, it had been under a pseudonym to protect my true identity; my real name was supposed to be highly classified by the UFC. It wasn't even supposed to be available through my military records. How did she know my real name?

"Tell me, Alistair," she continued to whisper in my ear, "what is the royal son of Scotland doing in the UFC military?"

Her question sent chills down my spine, but I gritted my teeth and answered her. "If yae know me name, then yae know why I'm here."

She laughed lightly, then moved away to sit on the arm of the seat beside me. "True, I know the political reasons, but I want to hear your reason."

I was not interested in playing this game any longer. Clearly, she knew more about me than she should have. And equally clear, there was something she wanted from me. I looked at her with all the pent-up frustration of the past several hours and said angrily, "Just get on with it, Estradé. What is it yae really want from me?"

She shook her head, almost sadly. "This isn't a game Aiden; I want the question answered."

There was no safe way for me to answer her question. Anything I said would only be viewed by the UFC as a betrayal. I clenched my mouth shut and looked away, refusing to say anything.

147

"I see," she said softly. Then she stood up and moved to the side of the window.

"Let me put it this way…" She reached up to the window's frame to press a button I had not previously noticed there. The opacity of the window melted away to reveal a brightly lit operating room built into the small cave beyond. Most of the equipment was old but appeared to have been recently cleaned and restored. On the metal table at the center of it all was a familiar, deathly still form: *Alex!*

I surged against my bindings, struggling to break free of them. Estradé only smiled her mysterious smile as she watched me.

"You see, you will answer my questions, or…" She left the words hanging; they were threatening enough. My eyes still on Alex, I stopped struggling against the bindings.

"What have yae done tae her?" I was no longer struggling outwardly, but inwardly I had once more become a raging storm. Fury, fear, hatred, and repulsion all coursed through my veins.

"Look at you. The sight of her is enough to very nearly tear you apart." Estradé said it casually, as though she were talking about the weather outside. I looked up at her sharply. "Oh yes, I know how she stirs the emotions you had thought to bury when you became a soldier. You who cover your sorrow with witty jokes and sly smiles. You who decided that you would never let a woman into your heart because you refuse to bring a child into this world that would be forced to suffer your own fate. But you faltered, didn't you? You saw her and you forgot yourself. By the time you learned that she was your sworn enemy, it was too late. She had already wheedled her way in. Your father would be disgusted if he knew."

Her words struck me hard, adding fuel to the raging storm that had reignited. I was all the angrier because Estradé was right. She had perfectly described my feelings and my fears.

"Why do yae care what I feel?" I growled at her.

Her mysterious smile was back. "Because I need to know where your loyalties lie. So, I'll ask you again. What is the royal son of Scotland doing in the UFC military?"

The truth was, I was only in the UFC military because I had been forced to be. Like Alex, I had not been given the choice, not truly. Long before I had been born, the Scottish nation had risen in rebellion against the UFC and lost. In retaliation for their betrayal, the UFC had yoked them with a terrible price, one that we were still paying today: Their firstborn sons were to be given to the UFC at the age of fifteen, to serve in the military at the government's pleasure for the remainder of their serviceable years.

In other words, I was required to serve until I could no longer physically serve. Only then would I be released and sent home, damaged goods that the UFC would at last graciously return to my family. If any of us, especially me, should fail in our duty to the UFC, our families would be brutally murdered while we were forced to watch the execution.

I had seen it happen once when I was ten. From that day, I had known that I would not fail in my duty. I don't mean my duty to the UFC; I mean my duty to my family. I would do what the UFC required, but only because if I didn't, my family would pay for my insubordination with their lives. I had not wanted a military life. I had not wanted to become their puppet, and yet here I was; no freer than Alex.

I looked at Alex again, lying on the metal table; unconscious, helpless, dependent on me to answer a simple question in order to protect her from the threat that Estradé had left hanging in the air.

I was suddenly tired. Tired of being manipulated. Tired of being forced to do something I didn't want to do. All the time knowing that if I failed, someone else would pay the price for my failure. I wouldn't let that happen; I couldn't.

My voice sounded defeated, even to my ears. "I'm doin' me duty. I'm keepin' me family and Scotland alive."

"And there it is." Estradé seemed to relax, as though she had finally gotten the answer she wanted.

She placed her hand on my shoulder. I instinctively tried to pull away but couldn't.

Her voice was gentle once more. "The pride of the Scottish nation knows where his loyalties lie, and it isn't with the UFC. I wonder if Scotland can survive what's coming."

She stood up and walked to the door, her voice all business once more. "Now it is time for you to observe. You need to see the full extent of what the UFC is willing to do to keep control. It isn't just you and your countrymen that have suffered under them."

Her hand was on the handle when she turned back, almost as an afterthought. "Alistair; the Scottish form of Alexander. Isn't it interesting that you and Alexandria have similar names? Names that share the same meaning? You are both defenders of mankind; each in your own way." And with that thought hanging in the air, she left the room, abandoning me to the swirling storm of anger, frustration, and defeat that her words had set in motion.

I FELT EMPTY, defeated. Estradé had drawn the truth from me and then left me alone to the pain of that revelation. She had called me the royal son of Scotland, but there was little honor remaining in that title. In another time and place, as the firstborn son of the Duke of Buccleuch, I might have one day risen to a seat of power. But the truth was that after the rebellion, the UFC had insured that it was nothing more than an empty title.

My grandfather had been executed as Scotland's leader responsible for the rebellion. His oldest son, who had been fifteen at the time, had been forced to enlist in the UFC and had been sent to the war front immediately after basic training; he had died there. My grandfather's second son, my father, had been five at the time. He had been shipped off to a UFC boarding school and raised to believe that his father had been a traitor to the government; he still believed it. He did whatever the UFC told him to do.

He had tried to instill in me the same sense of loyalty that he felt to the UFC. And to a great extent, he had succeeded. From an early age, I had willingly prepared to serve my country, with pride, in the UFC's military. But he had also shown me the cost of failure to serve. I had watched with horror as UFC soldiers torched the home of a sobbing fifteen-year-old boy because that boy had attempted to dodge the UFC's enforced draft; his family had been trapped in their home as it burned. I learned that day that I could not afford to fail in my duty.

Only, I had failed. Once more, I had allowed Estradé to manipulate me, this time into the truth that my loyalty was more to my family and my country than it was to the UFC. In trying to protect Alex, I had made a far worse error; as soon as Estradé reported back to the UFC that my loyalties were not to them, the family I had joined the UFC in order to protect, would be executed.

A tear slid down my cheek. In the end, Estradé had insured that I would lose no matter what I did. Her manipulation had been complete.

I had been lost in my pain for several minutes before a soft beeping sound was finally able to break through to my awareness. I had been hearing it for some time in the background of my mind, but it only now registered as something of importance.

I lifted my head to look out the window. Estradé was moving around Alex, deftly attaching electrode sensors to her skin. I noticed that Estradé had already placed a pressure cuff on her right arm and that a saline drip had been attached to the IV catheter that was still in that same hand.

Several of the monitors had been positioned in such a way that I could easily see their readings as they were becoming active. A speaker in the wall of the room I was in had also been activated so that I could hear the sounds coming from the other side of the window.

The soft beeping I had been hearing was the strong, steady rhythm of Alex's heartbeat as the monitor tracked it. Even through my pain, there came a sense of relief: Alex's heartbeat was strong in spite of her deathly stillness. It was a small measure of solace: my words may have condemned my family, but Alex was alive.

That relief was replaced with absolute dread as I suddenly comprehended the full ramifications of what I was seeing. Estradé was prepping Alex for a procedure. Estradé's voice confirmed my worst fears. "Dr. Gbeho, she's ready for you."

I had not noticed the small man studying a computer screen in the corner of the room. He stood now and approached Alex's prone form. Estradé had lied to me. I had given her what she wanted but they were still moving forward with the threat against Alex that she had left hanging in the air.

Cursing, I surged forward, struggling against my bonds once more, desperate to break free of them. But no matter how I twisted or pulled, the straps didn't budge; it was a vain effort. I only succeeded at tearing the skin on my wrists and ankles until they were bleeding and raw.

All the while, in the room beyond me, Estradé and the doctor ignored my struggles and began their work. The doctor threaded a thin tube through her nasal passageways. As that tool went in, one of the screens came to life. Even as I continued to struggle, I realized that the tool had a camera and light attached to its end and that it was providing the image being relayed to the monitor. He was using that video feed to guide his progress. Then, using a combination of a keypad and a remote stick, he directed two additional tools along the same path.

I felt suddenly sick as one of the tools deftly sliced through a layer of soft fleshy skin to create an opening. The doctor moved all of the devices through that newly made cavity and into the space beyond.

My struggles slowed to a stop and my blood ran chill as an unexpected image appeared on the screen. The equipment had reached the base of her skull where her spine connected to it. Amongst the wet, pinkish tissue and the white bone of Alex's spine, the doctor deftly maneuvered the camera until two objects came into view that clearly did not belong there.

Estradé's voice suddenly came through the speakers. "What you are seeing, Aiden, is the UFC's crime against a three-year-old child." She was looking straight at me to ensure that I was listening. Pointing to the lower of the two shapes as it was displayed on the screen, Estradé said, "This one is the tracking device. It was activated the moment General Durnham became aware that Alex had been removed from the base. It is innocent enough as its only purpose is to allow them to know her exact location, and it won't do Alex any harm beyond preventing her from ever being able to escape from the UFC by means of hiding from them."

The doctor easily detached the tracking device from her spine and used the tool to latch onto it and then guide it out along the same pathway he had used to reach it. When it approached an accessible point, the doctor used a pair of tweezers to remove the tiny object from Alex's head. He placed it on a waiting tray that had been set nearby for that purpose.

Estradé only glanced at it briefly before turning her attention back to me. "Unfortunately, the tracking device was not the worst of their crimes." Her words, and the hard anger on her face, left me confused. What more could the UFC have done?

The doctor had already reinserted the endoscopic tool and was studying the second foreign object. At the touch of a button, the tip of the tube began to separate into several dozen micro-thin wires, each with a pale blue light pulsing along its length.

As one of the tool's wires came near to the object, I was startled to see a hair-thin tendril of the object's own separate from Alex's spine as though it were alive and feel its way toward the glow of the approaching wire. When it touched, the tendril seemed to hesitate for a brief moment before it continued forward to smoothly wrap itself around the wire.

"The first tendril has been successfully detached." The doctor seemed to gasp as he said it, as though he had been holding his breath waiting to see how the tendril would respond. I noticed with surprise that the doctor's forehead was damp with perspiration; he was nervous.

On the screen, more hair-thin tendrils were beginning to detach from Alex's spine. I wasn't sure if I was seeing it correctly, but it almost appeared as though those tiny tendrils were moving in a soft breeze, searching for something to grab hold of.

"What you are seeing, Aiden," Estradé said angrily, "is the failsafe mechanism of a nano-explosive. The tool Dr. Gbeho is using has been set to issue the same electrical impulses as Alex's nervous system. They are providing a competing electrical stimulus that is coaxing the explosive's tendrils to detach from Alex's spine and attach to them instead. But, if any one of those tendrils does not detach from her spine of its own accord, the explosive will be set off and Alex will die."

My heart faltered as understanding dawned on me. It hadn't been enough to implant a tracking device, as though she were a criminal; the UFC had implanted an explosive into

Alex's head as well! I was stunned. How was this possible? Did Alex know it was there?

And then I was angry; angrier than I had felt since Callen's death. This was not okay. I had seen a lot occur in the UFC that I didn't agree with, but always I had understood the reasons behind it. There was no excuse for this. This time they had crossed the line.

I watched as several more of the explosive's tendrils were coaxed away from her spine. This time I shared the doctor's nervousness as I silently begged each tendril to release from Alex and latch onto the wires; there were so many of them.

Without warning, Alex's heart rate spiked. Her breathing began to race in time with the rapidly beeping monitor and her forehead developed a thin sheen of sweat as an alarm sounded from first one machine and then another. My own heart jumped at the sound.

The doctor responded immediately, releasing the remote so that he could enter commands into a nearby machine. There was a soft whooshing sound, followed by a slight movement in one of the nearby machines as a panel slid open just far enough to allow a small, thin robotic arm to extend through it. Moving steadily, and without hesitation, the robot plunged the syringe it was holding straight into Alex's chest. As the plunger was depressed, I watched the yellowish fluid flow into her body.

My fists clenched in frustration as I helplessly watched, knowing I could do nothing for her. The range of emotions I had swung through in the last few hours was dizzying. I had gone from laughing with Alex and wanting to spend more time with her, to feeling betrayed by her and hating her for everything she represented. I had known both gratefulness to the UFC military who had made it to the clearing in the jungle in time to bring her safely back, and fury with the UFC for the fact that they had placed a nano-explosive into her head. I had felt hopefulness, helplessness, confusion, desire, and pain, all because of her.

I wanted my own pain to end, but more than that, I wanted hers to end. There was so much I wasn't sure about right now, but in the midst of my confusion, I knew one thing for certain: I didn't want this for her. Alex didn't deserve to suffer like this. Thatcher had the right of it. She was an individual; not an object to be owned or blamed. She had been a victim of Icarus' treachery and a victim of the UFC's oppression. If we got out of this, I would not make her a victim of my own misguided anger as well. I had no right to do that to her; just as the UFC had had no right to have placed this micro explosive into her.

She didn't deserve to have her life constantly threatened by the UFC or by Icarus. I couldn't say if there was a future between the two of us, or if I even wanted there to be. But I knew that I wanted her to at least have one, to be free to choose what that future would be.

As I watched her body struggling for life, fighting its own battle to survive, I knew with certainty that I wanted her to live. The feeling was so all-consuming that I realized that there was no longer anything more important to me than that one thought: *Alex needed to live. Please, let her live.*

And then the alarms stopped as suddenly as they had begun. Her heart rate had slowed once more, and her breathing returned to normal. I released a breath I hadn't realized I had been holding. Estradé also released a visible sigh of relief.

"What happened?"

The doctor didn't look up as he answered, his attention already back to coaxing the tendrils away. "One of the tendrils was tapped into her parasympathetic nervous system. When it released its hold on the nerve, it triggered a flood of epinephrine straight to her heart. I countered it with a dose of the hormone acetylcholine to slow it back down."

He continued to move the wires around the explosive, luring the tendrils away from Alex. One by one, he claimed them. It had been nearly an hour since the first tentative tendril had released its hold, but there were still so many more to be coaxed away.

And then it was done. I was watching the screen as the explosive device suddenly came free; its last tendril grabbing hold of the tool's wires. The doctor sat back, obvious relief showing on his face as he took a deep breath before leaning forward once more to finish the job. Moving more carefully than he had with the tracker, he guided the explosive away from her spine and out of her body.

Continuing his careful handling, the doctor carried it at arm's length and gingerly placed it into a large rectangular container that had been positioned in front of the window where I could easily see it. It was startling how small the device actually was compared to how much danger it had posed.

As he stepped back, Estradé closed the lid to the box and tightly secured it. Then she punched several buttons on the box's control panel. There was a loud popping sound as the box was rocked by an explosion within.

The small man nodded his head, a look of supreme satisfaction on his face. "And now my debt is repaid."

Estradé smiled at his words, then she placed her hand on Alex's forehead and said just loud enough that I could hear her words. "You are free now, Mija."

Estradé looked up at me, suddenly holding me riveted with her steely gaze as though she were imprinting a command into my very soul. "Make sure she stays that way, Alistair."

I had nodded my head before I even considered the ramifications of what I was promising. But as I sat there, unable to do anything more than think about the promise I had just made, I realized that I meant it. The UFC had no claim on her now. Nor did Icarus. And I would do everything in my power to ensure that it stayed that way.

Suddenly a blue light began to flash from just above the door, startling all of us. Estradé and the doctor glanced at each other in surprise. Then Estradé moved into action, reaching for a rifle that was leaning against the far wall. "Get her ready to move," she yelled at the doctor over her shoulder as she raced toward the door. She had only gone a few steps when there was a tremendous explosion, and that door flew inwards.

The room was filled with billowing dust that swirled and coalesced, momentarily blocking my view of the room beyond. I could hear the doctor coughing. "Estradé?" his voice croaked out. She didn't respond, but another voice did; one that I recognized.

"Yes. Just where is Estradé? Icarus would like to have a word with her." My blood ran cold at those words. They should not have been spoken by the owner of that voice.

Sobrien stepped out of the swirling dust, a sadistic grin on his face. The new recruit who should have been with the rest of our team was standing alone in the room's entrance. He looked around the room as the air began to clear, quickly taking everything in. Then he glanced down at the mangled remains of the door. "Oh dear," he said with an obvious lack of remorse.

I looked in the direction of his gaze and saw Estradé's unmoving hand, the only part of her that was visible from under the twisted remains of the door.

Sobrien bent down to look under the door, his grin growing even crueler. With slow, steady intent, he aimed his gun and fired. "Guess Icarus didn't want to talk to her that much after all," he said with a shrug of his shoulder as he stood back up. Then he turned to face the doctor.

"Now, just who are you?" He said this as he pointed his gun at the small man.

The doctor, who had frozen mid-step between Sobrien and the table where Alex lay, stiffened at his words, but his heavily accented voice was calm. "I'm the one who just removed an explosive from inside the girl's head."

Sobrien appeared only slightly impressed. "You don't say. Then you're a doctor?" The last part was more of a statement than a question, but the doctor answered anyway.

"I am."

"Well, I guess that makes it my lucky day. Not only do I get to bring his missing child back to him, but I'll get to bring him a new doctor. Icarus is always in need of new doctors." Sobrien's grin was cruel. "He seems to go through them pretty quickly, especially if they're not particularly good at taking orders. Tell you what. Why don't we start practicing now and see how well you do?"

He pointed his chin toward Alex who was still lying unconscious on the table in front of him. "Get her unhooked from all that equipment."

The doctor looked at Alex for a moment. His expression showed that he was conflicted by the order, but Sobrien made his decision easier as he stepped forward and put the gun to the man's head. "Now would be a good time to get started."

The doctor swallowed hard then turned and began to disconnect the monitoring devices. As he did so, Sobrien looked toward the window and noticed me for the first time. He took in the chair and the straps with a single look then started to laugh.

"Well look at that. I was wondering what happened to you." He stepped forward so that he was standing right in front of the window studying me. "The Brig was pretty upset when your com went silent. He pulled most of the team in to converge on your last location." His grin became predatory. "It made my job much easier."

I didn't have to ask what job that was. He was standing here alone, without the rest of our team. "What are yae goin' tae dae now?" I asked, my anger barely contained beneath the surface.

The traitor seemed to think about it for a moment, then his face lit up with an idea. He opened the door and came into the room so that he was standing behind me. It took all of my self-control to not look back at him.

"You know, Estradé went through so much trouble to get you exactly where you are. I'd hate to undo all her hard work, so I think I'll leave you just the way I found you. Unfortunately, this section of the caves is pretty well hidden. But who knows; maybe you'll get lucky and they'll find you in the next day or so." He paused to let that sink in. "But you've also proven yourself pretty resourceful in the past. And I just can't take any chances that you'll escape and follow me. So…"

I knew what he was about to do in the split second before he did it. I tried to lunge forward to avoid the blow; the restraints prevented me from moving far enough. Crack! My head exploded with pain and then everything went dark. The last thought that passed through my mind before I lost consciousness was the frustrating realization that I had failed again. Once more, I was leaving her without any protection.

Chapter 14: Alexandria Jaquette

IT FELT AS though I was floating on clouds. My body was drifting along through the air, occasionally buffeted by a turbulent breeze, but otherwise cushioned as it moved along at the whims of the playful bed of fluff.

There were sounds that went along with the movements; voices of chattering birds that didn't quite come together into words, and the harsh click of thunder as it echoed all around. *Wait.* My mind struggled with that last thought. *Thunder didn't click.*

Another disjointed thought flitted through my mind: *Since when were there clouds in caves? Caves? Why was I thinking about caves? And since when did birds speak with words?*

At one point I heard a little bird that sounded like Aiden. He was saying something about his family. It brought a smile to my face. Then I heard Estradé telling me I was free, though I wasn't certain what there was to be free from. I even heard a bird mention that a debt had been paid, as though it had proudly presented a pile of bird seed in exchange for some past debt.

My mind struggled to make sense of all the thoughts that were flittering through it, but each time a piece of clarity came within grasp, a random breeze would come along and blow it back out of reach.

I have no idea how long I drifted on those clouds. It could have been minutes, or it could have been days. Time had no meaning there. However, there came a moment when my mind finally found a shelter of clarity and knew that something wasn't right; I needed to wake up. It was then that the cloud seemed to evaporate from under me and I landed on something cold and hard.

My eyes fluttered as I landed, and then they opened. As they came into focus, I realized I was looking at a window that had been built into a cave wall. What an odd thing to find in a cave. On the other side of that window, I could make out Aiden, sitting in a chair. I smiled again at the sight of him, only to have my smile fade as I realized that he was a part of what my subconsciousness had realized wasn't right.

His expression was not his normal jovial, kind look that I was used to seeing on him. Instead, it was one of rage and frustration. His posture matched his expression. He was stiff and taut, as though set for a fight.

It was then that I noticed that there was someone standing behind him. I couldn't make out who it was, but I could hear the man's voice as though it were coming over a speaker. He was saying something about Estradé and leaving Aiden where she had put him. Estradé had put him there? What did that mean?

I looked closer and realized that Aiden was bound to the chair by thick straps. That didn't make sense to me, but then again, very little of what was going through my mind up to that moment made any sense. How had we gotten here? Where was here? Why was Aiden bound?

I was still struggling with those thoughts when I watched the man's arm lift sharply up, then swiftly down. I saw Aiden's body jerk as he was struck in the back of the head, and then slump forward, unconscious.

No! My mind screamed.

Adrenaline rushed through me as I surged into a sitting position, swung my legs off the table, and stood. My sudden movement caught the dark-skinned man who had been standing at my side unprepared. I had not noticed him until this moment, but as I stood, he stumbled backward, a shocked expression on his face.

My anger at the man behind Aiden supported me as a wave of vertigo struck. I was dizzy and unstable on my feet, but I was not about to leave Aiden at that man's mercy. Ignoring the dizziness, I set my feet and raised my hands to pull on the gravity field that swirled under the man. Nothing happened.

I shook my head to clear it, thinking the clouds that still drifted there were somehow hindering me. I focused again, this time pulling harder. Still nothing. Confused and exhausted by the effort, I collapsed back against the table. The man I had knocked over seemed to recover from his shock. He moved quickly to support me and to keep me from falling over.

The man in the shadows behind Aiden, whose expression had become one of fear when I raised my hands toward him, suddenly started laughing. I heard his voice over the speaker. "They said that drug would limit your ability to control gravity. Guess this really is my lucky day."

My mind was racing for answers that were far too slow in coming. There was something familiar about his voice, though I couldn't quite place it. And what did he mean about a drug? What drug? For that matter, where were we and what was going on here? I looked down at my hands. There was an IV taped to my right hand.

A corner of my mind took in the medical equipment around me and the fact that I had been laying on the surgical bed at the center of all that equipment. It also noted that the man supporting me had flecks of blood on his gloved hands. I put those facts together to conclude that something had been done to me while I was unconscious; something that was now preventing me from controlling the gravity fields. It was a frightening realization.

The man who had struck Aiden came sauntering out of the room to stop in front of me. He was a bulky man, with muscles that bulged and protruded in odd places. He reminded me of a weightlifter who had taken his workouts too far in the wrong direction. And then I remembered who he was: Sobrien. He had transferred to the base two weeks ago. He wasn't in my training group, but I had seen him during the combined training activities. I recalled that I hadn't liked him very much, even then.

As he stood in front of me, his posture a combination of disdain and amusement, I decided that I liked him even less now. "Not so powerful now, are you?" he sneered.

I glared back at him defiantly. "Guess we all have our bad days. What's your excuse?"

With a growl, he surged forward and grabbed my arm harshly in his powerful grip. He pushed the dark-skinned man aside as he did so. I gasped; the pain from the grip of his hand was nearly unbearable. Then he twisted my arm behind me, turning me so that I was facing the window. With his other hand he jabbed his gun forcefully under my chin so that I was forced to look up at Aiden's unconscious form.

"We're going for a walk," he said coldly into my ear, "and you are going to behave. If you don't, I'll come back here and shoot him myself. Got it?"

I nodded my head as best I could, not trusting myself to speak.

"Good. Glad to see we understand each other."

He waved his gun toward the dark-skinned man, holding out a pair of military cuffs with the other. "You, doctor. Put these on her. We're leaving."

Chapter 15: Aiden Haskell

I WOKE WITH a start to a sharp, acrid scent in the air, the same scent that Estradé had used to wake me last time. My head shot up only to be rewarded with a searing pain that continued to throb even after the initial sharp stab began to fade. Estradé was standing next to me holding the bottle, but unlike last time, she didn't look like she was in very good condition. She was leaning weakly against the counter, one arm held tightly against her side, and a line of blood running down the side of her face. She didn't bother to recap the bottle as she set it down.

"Good," she said simply, seeing that I was awake.

Without saying anything else, and still only using the one free hand, she pulled on the leather strap that held my wrist securely to the chair. She struggled to undo the clasp but finally managed to pull it far enough that I was able to slip my hand free. Then she stumbled back against the table, quietly watching me as I undid the remaining straps.

When I stood to reclaim my equipment, she made no attempt to stop me, instead shifting over slightly so that she was out of my way.

"He took her, didn't he?" I asked as I tucked my phase gun back into my belt.

She nodded her head wearily.

"How long ago?"

"Maybe five minutes." Her voice sounded tired. It had a thinness to it that sounded wrong coming from her.

I paused in the middle of picking up the tactical band and looked up at her just in time to see her knees buckle. She slid to the ground, groaning softly as she fell. I dropped the band back onto the counter and reached for her.

"Estradé!"

As I knelt beside her, I was suddenly able to see what her arm had been covering. The whole right side of her uniform was seeping with blood. Her hand had been covering the phaser wound, a gaping hole in her side.

She looked at me, a sad smile on her face. "I'm afraid I'm not going to be much more help."

I wanted to reassure her that she was going to be okay, but we both knew the truth: she didn't have much longer to live. Seeing the wound and the amount of blood she had already lost, I wasn't even sure how she'd found enough strength to get out from under the door and across the room to me.

In spite of that knowledge, I desperately searched my mind for a way to help. I knew from my field training that her wound had to be cleaned and closed. I looked around for something to use to bandage her up with. But as I started to reach for a cloth that was on the table, she grabbed my arm to stop me.

"You promised me you would help keep her free," she said calmly. "That promise begins now."

Certain that she had my attention, she let go of my arm in order to remove something from her shirt pocket. She handed me a small digi-pad that had been hidden there. It had a spiderweb of cracking in one corner but was otherwise intact. As I looked at the pad, unsure what its purpose was, the pad began an auto scan of my face.

"Aiden Haskell," the screen flashed in recognition. Then it displayed the words, "Authorized User."

I was startled that Estradé had already pre-set the pad to respond to my face. But then I realized that she would have known before I did what my reaction would be to Alex. Her training had allowed her to correctly judge which way I would go when I finally had all of the facts.

The screen flashed again as it changed to a detailed drawing of an extensive labyrinth of tunnels. I quickly realized that it was a map of the cave system. But not just any map, there were also several moving dots scattered along the corridors.

"Are these people?" I asked in shock as I watched the moving dots.

Estradé nodded. "Its system...is tracking heat signatures."

"How is that possible?" I was stunned. Technology like this was common in the military. But it required corresponding equipment to make it possible. When had all of this been set up? How did Estradé get access to it?

"Don't ask how...just go...get...Alex." I realized she was struggling to breathe. Her hand was shaking as she reached up to grab my arm again. Her eyes searched mine with a searing intensity.

"Aiden…keep her…safe." Her words were followed by a slight gurgling sound in her throat. Her hand tightened on my arm as her body stiffened, then her eyes rolled up into her head and she went limp.

I sighed with a surprising sense of loss as I closed her eyes. I had seen death before and experienced the loss of friends to battle wounds in the field. But somehow, Estradé's death felt different. I had only known her for a few short weeks, yet her influence on me during that time had gone far deeper than I would have imagined possible.

With five minutes of intense pushing, she had fundamentally changed the focus of my life. Before today, it had always been about protecting my family. Now, I realized with certainty that Alex was more important to me than even my family. I would risk anyone and everyone to make sure that she was safe.

I laid Estradé gently onto the floor, wishing there was more I could do for her, but knowing that she would have been angry with me if I wasted any more time caring for her dead body. I did, however, pause to move her arm so that it covered the gaping hole. It was just something I needed to do, as though it somehow gave her more dignity in death.

I stood back up, my determination hardening. Sobrien had a lot to answer for, and he was not leaving here with Alex. I knew I was going to be outmatched for strength, but I had speed on my side, and I had learned from our time on the mats that I was the better fighter. More than that, I had a promise to keep, and I was not about to break it.

As I finished putting my knives into their sheaths and my tactical equipment back on, I glanced down at Estradé once more. The UFC would say she had died a traitor, but what had she really betrayed? The UFC's very constitution stated that it existed to ensure the freedom and security of every one of its individual citizens. They had betrayed their core values when they had placed a bomb inside a three-year-old's head. Estradé had corrected that error. She had given her life to ensure that Alex would be free of their oppression. Now it was up to me to make sure that Alex would stay free.

Chapter 16: Alexandria Jaquette

IF YOU HAVE ever woken up in the dead of night and stumbled out of your bed half asleep, you might have some idea of what I was feeling as I stumbled along through the tunnels. We were walking through near-complete darkness. I couldn't see much more than a three-foot radius around the light stick the doctor was holding as he walked in front of me. Its pale light cast just enough of a faint orange glow on the ground of the tunnel that I was able to avoid the majority of the tripping hazards that littered the floor.

I was exhausted. My body ached in more places than I wanted to think about. The worst was my left shoulder. It throbbed with a constant dull pain that sapped me of my strength. It took most of my energy just to make sure I didn't trip over my own feet. Yet even as tired as I was, I couldn't stop thinking about all that had happened in the last few minutes.

I was confused and scared; there was no way around that. I was also totally lost. I couldn't figure out how I had gotten here in the first place. The last thing I remembered was prepping for the challenge. We had just been issued practice rifles and split into teams. Haskell, Estradé, Bowen, Hadley, and I were assigned to the same team. They had loaded us onto a transport and dropped us off in the jungle. I recalled finding the first two markers, but after that everything was hazy. I shut my eyes, trying to remember just what had taken place.

Closing my eyes was a mistake. I stumbled on a raised section of rock and fell to one knee. With my hands bound behind me, it was a struggle to get back to my feet. Impatiently, Sobrien grabbed me by my left arm and yanked me back up. I cried out as white-hot bolts of pain shot outward from my shoulder to radiate through the whole left side of my body.

Sobrien, still holding me by the arm, looked at me sharply.

"What's your problem?" he asked roughly.

I couldn't catch my breath to answer him. The pain was so intense that I was gasping from the exertion of trying to control it.

The doctor, who had been walking in front of me, doubled back when he heard my cry. It only took him a moment to realize what had happened.

"It's her shoulder. Estradé said it was dislocated yesterday. You must have pulled it back out of the socket when you lifted her up. You'll need to take the restraints off so I can set it back in place."

Sobrien shook his head with mirth, as though he found my situation amusing. "Not happening. The restraints stay on. She'll have to live with the pain for now."

The doctor frowned at him, about to say something more, but Sobrien deliberately turned away from him and shoved me in the back with his rifle. "Keep moving."

Shaking his head, the doctor took hold of my other arm in an effort to support me. I was grateful for his help as my mind turned all of its attention to controlling the pain. It was agony, but this time at least I didn't pass out.

This time! The words rang in my head as though I had just stumbled across something important. This wasn't the first time I had felt the agony of a dislocated shoulder. With a suddenness that made me stumble again, the memories and all of their attendant emotions came rushing back at me. The fight in the clearing, falling from the tree, the intense pain as I hit the ground, waking up in the hospital, Aiden leaving the room in anger, Estradé kidnapping me, and the doctor telling me about a nano-explosive in my head.

I fell to my knees, my eyes clenched tightly, reeling from the commotion of it all as my brain struggled to sort through the whirlwind of memories and emotions. Sobrien, who had no way of understanding what was happening, assumed I was faking another injury; he wasn't impressed.

He picked me up and slammed me against the wall. His face was inches from mine as he snarled, "I warned you what would happen if you played any games."

Aiden! Fear brought an acute sharpness to my mind; all the pain and emotions faded to the background as my mind focused on his name and the danger he was in. He would be helpless if Sobrien followed through with his threat. I used the only offensive option I could think of: I brought my knee up sharply.

Sobrien's face went momentarily slack with shock, then twisted into agony as he groaned in pain. Yet, in spite of his obvious discomfort, his hands never relaxed their harsh grip on my arms. I struggled desperately against his hold, kicking and squirming with all I had. It made no difference; I just didn't have the strength to break free.

His retaliation came swift and hard. A starburst of white flashed in front of my eyes as my head recoiled from his blow and cracked loudly against the wall behind me.

The world around me faded in and out of focus and my legs buckled under me. Still, he kept me pinned against the wall. Through my faded field of vision, I could see him pulling back his arm for a second blow. And then I was abruptly falling to the ground as a tremendous force slammed into Sobrien and tore him away from me. I crumpled to a heap, the metallic taste of blood in my mouth.

I think I must have blacked out. When my eyes fluttered open, the doctor was hurriedly pulling me out of the way of two combatants as they scuffled in the narrow tunnel.

Through the haze of my vision, I saw them moving in and out of the inky shadows, specters of death in a macabre dance, battling for dominance. The light stick the doctor had dropped cast a sickly orange glow on the scene, backlighting their blurred forms and glinting menacingly off the sharp blades in their hands.

The larger figure, Sobrien, was clearly the stronger of the two, but the smaller figure was lighter on his feet, more agile, and better able to avoid most of Sobrien's heavy-handed blows. The deep grunts of pain and the fierce howls of frustration told me that the fight was not going in Sobrien's favor.

The doctor tried to get me to my feet. I only made it a few stumbling steps before I fell again. The world around me was spinning so wildly that I couldn't seem to see straight. I struggled to my knees, only to have to turn my head to the side as my stomach suddenly heaved. There was nothing in my stomach to throw up, but that didn't stop it from contracting violently.

The old man stood at my side, shielding me as best he could from the danger only feet away. I had barely regained mastery of my stomach when rough hands shoved him out of the way and yanked me upwards. I was pulled forcefully back against Sobrien's rock-hard chest as his enormous arm snaked around my neck.

"Come any closer and I'll snap her neck." His harsh voice had a near desperate quality.

"Yae won't do that," a familiar Scottish lilt growled back confidently from the darkness. "I would kill yae th' moment her body fell."

Aiden stepped out of the shadows.

My world was still spinning, but his sudden appearance became an anchor in the maelstrom. I focused on him, willing everything else to hold still.

I took in the bandage on his arm, the bloodied tears in his uniform where Sobrien's knife had caught its mark, and the slight limp in his step. Each one mute evidence that Sobrien had done his best to kill him and had failed.

Now, with the single-mindedness of a predator stalking his prey, Aiden was moving forward, menace radiating from him with every step.

Sobrien took a step back almost involuntarily. I could sense his wavering indecision, but then he seemed to realize that he had another option. His grip on me tightened once more.

"You're right." His voice had a new confidence. "Killing her won't stop you. But what about this?" I cried out in pain as he slowly drew the razor-sharp edge of his blade across my collarbone.

Aiden froze mid-step, a guttural growl in the base of his throat. His face hardened and I could see the muscles in his jaw twitching angrily.

Sobrien laughed mockingly, knowing that he had gained the upper hand at last. "What's it going to be, Haskell?" he said haughtily as he set the tip of his knife against my cheek, reinforcing his threat. I felt its sharp point pressing into my skin and swallowed hard.

Aiden met my eyes for the first time. His eyes were filled with frustration, anger, and…my breath caught: fear. Aiden was afraid. I knew in that moment that Sobrien was going to win. Aiden would not allow him to torture me any more than he would allow him to kill me.

Sobrien increased the pressure on the knife. I struggled to not cry out but couldn't stop the whimper as the tip of the blade bit slowly into my skin and drew a bead of blood.

Aiden's hand opened slowly.

His knife clattered to the ground.

Sobrien released the pressure on his blade and lowered it so that it was against my collarbone once more. Laughing mockingly, he used the force of its touch to guide me as he began backing us away from Aiden.

Aiden didn't take his eyes off of me, his fists clenching in frustration. Then his head suddenly cocked ever so slightly as though he were listening to something. His face broke into a slow, wicked smile.

"Thatcher," he said coldly, "take th' shot."

I didn't have time to process his words before a soft, meaty thud sounded just above my head. I heard Sobrien's startled "Umph" and felt his body spasm in response. The spasm drove his knife into my shoulder. I gasped in pain, too stunned to cry out.

Like a movie that has been slowed for effect, his heavy body began to topple forward, his spasming arms still pinning me tightly against him as it drove the knife deeper. My world began to shift and spin once more as the ground came racing up to meet us.

And then Aiden was there, shoving Sobrien's dead body off and turning me over. "Alex!" There was desperation in his voice as he looked at the knife hilt protruding from my collarbone. He said something else, but I couldn't make out what it was. His voice seemed to be suddenly coming from a great distance; his face shifted in and out of focus. In my mind, my thoughts were clear. I knew what was happening, but the rest of my body wasn't working right. I was surprised to find that I didn't feel any pain, just cold; I began to shiver.

The doctor, who had been unable to do anything more than watch as Sobrien held me hostage, was suddenly there as well. He pushed Aiden aside and pulled open my shirt so that he could see the full extent of the wound. His expression was composed as he examined the injury, but I could see the concern in his eyes. Aiden handed him the medical pack that was part of our standard field gear and the doctor set to work using its contents to care for my wound.

And then the weariness came. I felt my eyes begin to grow heavy and a sluggishness enter my thoughts. It was as though a switch had been flipped and my body was beginning to shut down in response.

I felt a tapping on my cheek and opened my eyes to see Aiden talking to me, trying to keep my attention on him. While I couldn't quite make out his words, the sound of his voice was a lifeline I clung to. I sensed that he wanted me to keep my eyes open, to keep looking at him. I truly tried, but with each passing moment, it was getting harder and harder to do.

I was jolted back to alertness for a brief moment when I felt Aiden lift me forward. I realized that the doctor was wrapping the gauze dressing around my shoulder and behind my back and that the cyclonic spinning sensation I was suddenly experiencing was a result of that movement.

But then I felt the warmth of Aiden's body as he picked me up, encasing me in his strong arms. Unlike Sobrien, whose chest had been rock-hard with far too many bulges, Aiden's chest was firm, but not uncomfortable. My head came to rest on his shoulder. For the first time in several hours, I felt safe. Outside of his arms, the world continued to spin and fade, but against his chest, I found a calm spot in the storm. Knowing he was there to protect me, my eyes fluttered and then closed.

Chapter 17: Aiden Haskell

WE HAD TO get her out of these caves fast. The doctor had done what he could, but he had not removed Sobrien's knife. He'd said something about the danger of taking it out and preceded to stabilize it with the supplies from my kit, but it was obvious that she was losing far too much blood. Already the bandages were showing hints of a red stain.

I had done this! I berated myself silently. When Thatcher's voice had unexpectedly sounded through my earpiece, telling me he was in the darkness behind me and had a clear shot at Sobrien, I had not hesitated to tell him to take it. I had been so caught up in my frustration and rage, that I had not taken the time to consider all of the possible outcomes of my call. My carelessness had resulted in Alex's injury and this new threat to her life.

I turned sharply at the sound of running feet; it was Thatcher. He had his rifle in his hands and a worried look on his face. I couldn't imagine how he had found us, but his arrival had been providential.

Thatcher took it all in with a single glance. Alex was unconscious and pale; her breathing was weak. He understood the danger she was in.

"I'll take point," he said simply.

I nodded and turned back to the doctor. "Do yae know how tae use a phase rifle?"

"I'm afraid not." He looked almost regretful. It was just as well. I had left my phase rifle some distance back and I didn't want to waste time sending the doctor for it.

"Let's go then," I said.

We moved as silently as we could. There were others in the cave system with us and, since Sobrien had taken out the rest of our team, anyone we ran into was unlikely to be a friend.

The doctor picked up his light stick so that he could see where he was going, but Thatcher and I relied on our tactical gear. Thatcher led the way, checking his data pad every time there was a branch in the tunnel. In the back of my mind, I wondered again how he had found us, and what was on his data pad that he was checking, but it was a fleeting thought that wasn't nearly as important as my confidence in his ability to guide us out.

We had only been walking for a few minutes when the tunnel we were in opened up into a larger cavern. If I had been there exploring, I might have taken time to appreciate the layered quality of the room's rocks. Either natural formations or man's hands had created handholds that would allow for easy climbing to the top of the cave's thirty-foot height. There were also scattered towers of crumbling rocks randomly placed throughout the cave. They were naturally occurring formations that had been worn somewhat smooth by man's touch over the last several hundred years of use. It was like nature had created the perfect indoor arena for a team battle practice.

Unfortunately, this time we weren't in a practice situation. When a phaser bolt hit the rock formation next to Thatcher's shoulder, we reacted instantly, dropping out of sight as best we could. Thatcher returned fire with well-trained precision, but we were pinned down with insufficient coverage, and one weapon was not likely to be enough to get us out of this one. I suddenly regretted not going back for my rifle.

I set Alex down as gently as I could and reached for the gun in my waistband. It wasn't the best weapon for a situation like this one, but it was better than nothing. A quick glance at the doctor let him know my intentions. He nodded his head, indicating that he would watch over her, then Thatcher laid down a blaze of fire that provided the cover I needed to sprint for a second outcropping some twenty feet away.

As I peered around the edge of the rock formation I had taken shelter behind, I was able to locate our assailant's positioning on a ledge high up on the wall. They had climbed up there and given themselves a bird's eye view of the floor below. The only two things that had saved us from being shot immediately upon entry into the cavern was the angled extension of that particular tunnel's leading edge into the room and that the doctor's light stick had a short glow radius, and he had been sufficiently far back that his glow had not extended into the cavern ahead of us.

Now the only thing that was saving us was the coordinated precision with which Thatcher and I worked to draw out our assailant. We had both been trained for situations like this and we both knew what to do without either one of us having to say a word. My gun proved a slight disadvantage. It didn't have nearly the reach that Thatcher's rifle did, but it was more than sufficient to cause the soldier up on the ledge to duck back each time I fired.

In spite of our coordination, it was a stalemate. The other soldier had the higher ground and the superior positioning.

We were pinned down without sufficient leverage to get a clear shot.

I glanced back at Alex, my frustration growing with each passing moment. We didn't have time to play this back-and-forth game of exchanging shots, especially if the soldier on the ledge was able to call for backup. The bandage on her shoulder was showing more red than white now. The doctor's efforts had slowed the hemorrhaging, but he had not been able to stop it all together. Every minute's delay meant the loss of more precious blood that she couldn't afford to lose.

We needed something to draw the soldier out of his protective shelter, a way to give Thatcher a clear shot. I knew what it would need to be even as my mind raced to find a different option. If I stepped out from the tower of rocks I was crouched behind, I would become the easy target for the sniper, one he wasn't likely to ignore. I would go down, but Thatcher would get a clear shot as well, then he and the doctor could get Alex out.

I closed my eyes as I scrambled for a better choice; nothing came to mind. *So be it!* I locked eyes with Thatcher, signaling with my hand what I was about to do. His eyes widened and he flung his hand in an adamant negative, but I knew we didn't have a choice.

I braced myself for the lunge into the open, determined to take at least one good shot before I was gunned down. Just as I was about to spring, a dark figure surged forward into the open space. The doctor was standing in the area I had planned to move into. He was waving his arms in the air and yelling at the top of his lungs. The sniper reacted as I had predicted and shifted into the open to take the easy shot.

With a grunt, the doctor went down under the spray of phaser fire the sniper released. But even before the man's body hit the ground, both Thatcher and I responded with a return barrage of our own. The assailant's gun went silent, then we watched as it slowly slid forward and off the ledge. The body of the soldier was draped like a rag doll over the rough stone ledge that had made it so hard for us to get a clear shot.

I looked down with a heavy heart at the doctor; his eyes were open, lifelessly staring into the darkness above him. He had understood the sacrifice I had been willing to make and had chosen to take my place instead. Thatcher reached down and closed his open eyes. I was grateful for the man's sacrifice, but sad that it had been made all the same. I sighed heavily, then moved to lift Alex back into my arms.

She didn't stir as I lifted her and shifted her into position against my chest; that worried me. I could feel her breath against my neck which told me she was still alive, but it was far too shallow. We were running out of time. If we didn't get her to medical help soon, I was going to lose her. I instinctively tightened my arms around her, as though doing so somehow ensured that she would stay alive. I knew that it didn't truly do anything for her, but holding her tighter against me helped to ease the anxious spasms in my own heart.

I turned to Thatcher, eager to get moving again. "Which way?" There were two passages leading away from the cavern, besides the one we had entered through. Thatcher checked his data pad then pointed to the tunnel that was to the left. We were halfway into that opening in the wall when a thought occurred to me.

"How do yae have a map of th' cave system?" I asked him as we entered the tunnel. We had not had one when we began the assignment.

Thatcher paused mid-step and turned to look at me with a puzzled expression. "I assumed you sent it to me. It had your callsign at the end of the message."

My callsign? I hadn't sent the message. It was true that any message sent from our data pad automatically attached our callsigns, so the team knew who was sending it, but how could it have been sent from my tactical band, unless...

"Estradé," I muttered under my breath. She must have sent it from my data pad right before she used the chemicals to wake me. That would also explain how Thatcher had found us so easily. I confirmed my thoughts with a question.

"Did th' message also tell yae where tae find me?"

He nodded in the affirmative. "You asked for backup; I'm the only one who answered." His face was grave as he said the last part.

I could piece together what had happened. I was impressed by how thoroughly Estradé had prepared for every contingency in order to ensure that Alex was safe. The more I thought about it, the more it made sense. But now was not the time to explain it all.

"Fine," I said. "Let's keep goin'."

Thatcher looked like he was about to say something more, but then he glanced at Alex and changed his mind. Shaking his head as though to shake away his questions, he turned back and continued to lead the way.

The rest of our journey to the cave's exit was unobstructed. There was one point along the way when we heard faint voices, but they were coming through a tunnel that traveled in the opposite direction from the one we were taking, making them easy to avoid. When we finally reached the opening to the outside world, Thatcher signaled for me to wait in the shadows while he used the scope on his rifle to search for danger; he saw none.

We exited the caves through a different opening than the one the team had originally entered. This opening was about eighty yards to the north, and much more secluded than the other one had been. There were trees around it that further hid our exit from anyone who might have been positioned as a sentinel.

We moved deep into the surrounding trees before we finally paused to catch our breath. Crouching beside the shelter of a large outcropping of rocks, I lowered Alex to the ground so that I could check her bandage; there was no longer any white to be seen. Thatcher saw it as well. Without a word, he pulled the Medi-kit from his pocket and began to apply another layer of bandaging around the one that had become soaked through.

While he did that, I used my tactical band to remove the military cuffs that Sobrien had used to bind Alex's hands. With them off, I could fully see the raw scrapes and cuts, especially on her right wrist, where the cuffs had worn through her skin. Disgusted and angry, I threw the cuffs as far from her as I could get them.

Thatcher glanced up at me sharply, concerned by my momentary lapse in caution. I pointed at her wrists and saw the muscle twitch in his own jaw as he glanced down and took in the lacerations. He was shaking his head when he turned back to finish wrapping the bandage in place.

As I folded her arms across her stomach in preparation for picking her back up, my own hand lingered on hers for just a moment. I was worried for her, but I was also feeling conflicted. What would happen when I got her back to base? Would I still be able to protect her? Would she even want me near her? And how would I keep my heart from being torn apart every time I looked at her?

Deep inside, the roiling, conflicting storm of emotions was still raging its treacherous battle. The desperate urge to protect her was currently winning, but my mind stubbornly continued to connect her to Icarus. The revulsion I felt toward his Alphas was such a deeply ingrained emotion that it refused to be extinguished. At the same time, all the budding emotions that had drawn me to her in the first place were still there every time I looked at her, only now they were tainted by the realization of who she truly was. It was a storm that was silently tearing me apart.

When I finally looked up, I found Thatcher studying me. Thatcher did that a lot, watch people that is. He was the tall, quiet Texan who didn't usually say much out loud, but he did watch. And when he decided action was required, his actions spoke far louder than any words could have.

On the few occasions he spoke, it was obvious that he had carefully thought things through before speaking and that the reason he had spoken was to add to the conversation some important detail that everyone else seemed to have missed. Perhaps that was why General Durnham had so readily respected Thatcher's request to stop referring to Alex as an object.

Now, however, he appeared somewhat confused. "What happened in there?" his deep voice asked seriously.

A lot had happened in there, more than we had time to cover at the moment, but I was pretty sure I could guess which part he was asking about.

"Sobrien turned out tae be workin' for Icarus. He ambushed th' rest of th' team, then came after Alex."

"And Alex?"

"Someone in the UFC thought it was appropriate tae place a nano-explosive in her head when she was a child. They wanted tae guarantee that they could control her, force her tae become their weapon. Estradé made arrangements tae have that explosive removed. She also made sure that I knew th' truth about what had been done tae Alex."

Thatcher's normally passive expression darkened as I spoke. "I see." His voice had a hard edge to it. "Where is Estradé now?"

"She's dead. Sobrien took care of that."

The muscle in his jaw twitched. "And the rest of the team?"

I shook my head uncertainly. "I don't know. Sobrien suggested that he had taken them out, but I don't know where he left them or if any of them managed tae survive."

Thatcher nodded his head in understanding, then he pointed to the southeast. "The transport is a mile that way. Get her to safety."

"What are yae plannin' tae do?" I asked, but I already knew the answer. He was going back for the rest of our team. If anyone was still alive, he would find them and bring them out.

He smiled with bittersweet irony. "No one left behind."

It was the UFC motto, meant to infer that we only progressed as a planet when every country, race, and people were lifted together. But in the military, it had always meant that we never abandoned a team member, no matter how desperate the circumstances.

A part of me longed to go with him. It was a motto we took to heart. But we both knew that I had a more serious responsibility. And then I thought of something that might help him.

"If yae go back tae where yae found us in th' tunnel, and keep walkin' about fifty yards, yae should find me rifle and a small digi-pad. That pad is hooked up tae a system of heat sensors in th' cave. Don't ask me how it works," I intercepted the question he seemed about to ask. "I don't know how it's possible. Estradé gave it tae me right before she died. I only know that it works. It led me straight tae Alex, Sobrien, and th' doctor. If anyone is still alive, th' pad might help yae find them."

"I'll find them," he said simply. Then he glanced down at Alex and said gravely, "Take care of her. I have the feeling she's going to need someone looking out for her."

Then, without waiting for me to respond, he turned and started back toward the caves and the rest of our team. As I watched him go, it occurred to me that there was at least one other man in the UFC whose values were similar to my own; I hoped he made it out of this alive.

Chapter 18: Aiden Haskell

THE JOURNEY BACK to base was mercifully quick and uneventful. Once in the air, the pilot had radioed ahead to tell them we were coming and to advise them of Alex's condition. No sooner had the engines begun to power down at the base's medical facility landing pad then a team of doctors was racing out of the building with their medical equipment. Before I even stepped out of the Daedalus, they had taken her out of my arms and were rushing her into the operating room.

I followed behind them as closely as I could, not about to leave her unguarded until she was strong enough to protect herself, but a burly soldier who had been standing just to the side of the operating room doors stepped in front of me and blocked my way. "Sorry, soldier. Only doctors are permitted past this point." There was the slightest hint of a smirk on the man's lips as his eyes met mine.

My eyes narrowed and I was about to say something when a nasally voice interrupted me. "There you are! If you'll come this way, sir, we'll get your wounds cleaned and stitched." I turned to find a middle-aged doctor with slightly thinning hair hurrying quickly toward me. He was breathing hard as though he had been rushing to catch up to me before I got away from him.

"Me wounds can wait. I'm not goin' anywhere right now except into that room." I indicated the doors they had just wheeled Alex through.

The doctor shook his head. "I assure you that Specialist Jaquette is in the best of care and will be safe in the medical team's hands. Now, if you'll come this way…" He had taken hold of my arm as though to guide me in the other direction; I yanked it back.

"Safe?!" My disbelief was obvious in my voice. "I'll believe that when I'm in there tae make sure it's true." I turned back toward the soldier, intending to step around him, only to have the doctor's next words stop me cold.

"I'm sorry, sir." He seemed somewhat apologetic, but undeterred. "We were given instructions that you were not to go in there."

Instructions? From whom? Why? I looked from the doctor to the still-smirking guard. He had removed his gun from its holster and was now holding it lightly at his side. My eyes narrowed as I suddenly understood. They didn't want me in that surgery room because they didn't want me to stop whatever they were planning to do in there.

I didn't raise the volume of my voice, but there was a new edge to it. "Get out of me way." I shifted my stance, ready to relieve him of his weapon if he didn't do it fast enough. If the man had known me at all, he would have recognized the danger he was in. But it was apparent that he was too stupid to know that his gun was not going to stop me. Instead of moving aside, he raised the weapon so that it was now pointed at my chest.

"What's going on here?" a voice I recognized demanded angrily. I didn't look away from the soldier, but out of the corner of my eye I saw Hadley striding toward us; the expression on his face was as stern as the tone in his voice. The soldier's smirk grew, believing he had backup coming to reinforce his position.

The doctor also seemed to believe that Hadley was coming to back him up and hurried to explain that the hospital director had given orders that they were not to let me into that operating room. He was supposed to instead take me to another room for medical attention. However, I was being resistant to the orders that had been given.

"Aiden?" Hadley turned to me for an explanation.

Still not looking away from the guard, I growled, "She's in danger in there."

Hadley seemed to consider my words, taking in my expression and my stance as he did so. Then he turned to the soldier guarding the door.

"Move," he ordered him simply.

On another occasion, I might have taken pleasure in the soldier's look of shock, but at the moment I was only concerned about getting into that room. Estradé had given her life to make sure Alex was free and I was not about to give the UFC the opportunity to replace the tracking device or the nano-explosive that had been removed.

"Sir?" The soldier questioned the new order, uncertain how he should respond to the unexpected turn of events.

"Soldier," Hadley said with an annoyed tone, "as much as I'd enjoy seeing this man take you down, the doctors in that room don't have time to resuscitate you or mend your broken bones. I suggest you get out of his way like I told you to."

Obviously reluctant to back down, the soldier hesitated just a moment too long for Hadley. Hadley had his own gun out of its holster and against the soldier's head before the man realized it was happening.

"I gave you a direct order, soldier. Now move."

The soldier carefully holstered his own gun and held his hands up to show he was obeying. I didn't waste time thanking Hadley, instead pushed straight through the doors the second the soldier had moved far enough for me to get around him.

What I saw made me glad I had not been delayed any longer than I had been. While one group of doctors was working on Alex's shoulder, another doctor was holding an endoscopic tool in the ready position, about to insert it into Alex's nose.

"No!" I yelled sharply.

The doctor jumped, a startled, guilty expression flashing across his face briefly before he began to bluster at me. "What are you doing in here? You're not supposed to be in here! Who let you in?"

I didn't answer his questions, but instead pulled the gun from my waistband and pointed it at him.

"Get away from her!" I growled. "Yae are not puttin' that back into her."

The doctor's face paled visibly. "Hold on now. There's no need for that."

Most of the other doctors and nurses in the room had frozen in place upon seeing the gun, but one older doctor had not stopped working on Alex's shoulder. In fact, he had barely even glanced up to see who had entered the room.

"Paul," he said in a gruff voice without missing a beat in what he was doing, "you heard the boy. She does not need a tracking device put back in. What she does need though, is for us to stop this bleeding. So, get out of the way and let us work. Sandra, hand me that hemostat." A blonde-haired nurse glanced briefly at me for permission. I nodded my head, and she placed the clamp into the doctor's waiting hand.

Paul, the doctor I was aiming my gun at, shot a look of disgust toward the older surgeon, but he set down the tool he was holding and backed away from Alex as instructed. I followed him with my gun until he was standing against the wall on the opposite side of the room. As he moved, he muttered under his breath, "You'll answer to the director for this."

The older surgeon ignored the threat and addressed me instead. "Boy," he said, still not looking up from his work, "I assume you don't have a problem with me saving her life?" It wasn't really a question; he didn't seem all that concerned with what I thought. But I answered him all the same.

"I'd appreciate it if yae did."

"Good," he said in a matter-of-fact tone. "Then sit over there and stay out of the way." He indicated a stool off to the side of the room with a quick sweep of his finger, then went immediately back to work.

Hadley entered the room seconds later, having first dealt with the guard outside. "Everything okay in here?" His question had been aimed at me, but the old surgeon replied before I could.

"We're fine, thank you. Now get out. This is a surgery room, not a visiting room."

Hadley looked at me, perplexed. I could only smile ruefully and say, "We're good, but his skills," I indicated the man standing against the wall, "are no longer needed in here."

Hadley nodded in understanding then turned to the man standing sullenly by the wall. "Doctor, if you would join me, please."

It was a little over an hour later when the old surgeon pulled off his latex gloves and stepped back from the operating table. "Well, that will do it." He had a satisfied smile on his face as he moved out of the way so that the nurses could clean up Alex and the surrounding area.

He walked casually up to me as he might have an old acquaintance. "I take it you're a friend of hers?" Again, it was more of a statement than it was a question.

"Aye, sir," I replied as I stood up from the chair. I winced slightly as I did so, stiff from the wounds that still needed attention.

"Good," he said simply. "Then you will be glad to hear that the knife wound has been repaired and there was only minor damage done to the Subscapularis muscle and the Clavicle. She's going to be sore for a few weeks while it heals, but she will get back full use of that arm in no time at all." As he talked, he was eyeing the bandage on my arm and the blood-soaked cuts across my ribs.

He nodded his chin toward my arm. "Why don't you let me take a look at those."

I hesitated in answering, glancing toward Alex while I tried to decide if she would be safe if I let my guard down long enough to allow the doctor to look at my injuries.

He noticed my hesitation. "Tell you what, I'll get you fixed up right here where you can keep an eye on her. That work for you?"

I considered the alternatives to his offer and realized that this was likely to be the best offer I would get. Not to mention that over the course of the last hour, I had come to realize that this man was used to being obeyed. "Guess so," I said somewhat resignedly. "I get th' feelin' yer not goin' tae give me a choice anyway."

"Nope." He chuckled lightly at my response as he placed a hand on my shoulder and firmly pressed me back onto the stool. "Take your shirt off while I go get some gloves on."

Forty-two stitches later, my arm, my ribs, my side, and the back of my head had been cleaned, sutured, and bandaged and the raw and torn skin of my wrists and ankles had been likewise cared for. Asking searching questions and gently probing with his fingers, he continued to search for less obvious injuries. I winced when he pushed lightly against my ribs and again when he squeezed my leg just below my left knee. He concluded that, while they were both severely bruised, neither of them was broken. I was to stay off the leg as much as possible for the next few days and give it time to heal but was otherwise good to go.

Hadley had come back into the room while the doctor was assessing my knee. He found a place to stand out of the way and quietly watched while the doctor finished his examination. When the doctor patted me on the shoulder and said, "It looks like you'll survive, young man," Hadley approached at last.

"Thatcher found The Brig and Corporal Callia. He was able to hold their position until Charlie team came in to run off Icarus' soldiers, but the rest of Alpha team didn't make it. The survivors will be in-bound in the next few minutes."

Before I could respond, the doctor asked him, "Any medical emergencies?"

Hadley nodded. "Most likely. The Brig took a phaser shot in the back at close range and Corporal Callia took one in the shoulder."

"Well then, if you boys will excuse me, I'll go make sure the staff is ready to receive them." The old surgeon made it sound like this was all just another day at the office.

"Thank yae, sir," I said as he turned away. He only waved it off and pointed toward Alex. "Make sure she finds a quiet room to recover in, will you? We're going to need this room again soon."

As he left, I limped over to stand next to Alex; Hadley followed me. The doctor had repaired her shoulder and the nurse had cleaned her up and bandaged her wounds, but the nurse had not been able to wipe away the ugly purple bruise on her cheek where Sobrien had struck her, or the raw scrapes and cuts where the cuffs had worn their marks into her wrists.

"She's been through a lot these last two days," I said softly, almost to myself.

"Far too much," Hadley agreed, "but it's not over yet."

I turned sharply to look at him. "What dae yae mean?"

Before Hadley could answer, one of the nurses walked into the room. "Why don't you two boys guide the gurney, and I'll show you to a room where she can recover."

Hadley didn't say anything more as we followed the nurse to the third floor where she led us to a small room that was right next to the nurse's station. It was similar to the room Alex had been in only twelve hours earlier, except that this one had a door that could be closed and two comfortable-looking recliner seats with a much larger sitting area. It was clearly set up for a guest that was intending to stay in the room with the patient.

The nurse deftly hooked Alex up to the monitors and then quietly left the room, closing the door behind her. I didn't even wait for the door to shut before I turned on Hadley.

"What did yae mean, it's not over?"

Hadley took a deep breath, as though not sure where to start, but he finally seemed to come to a decision. "You really care about her, don't you?"

The bluntness of his statement caught me off guard. More than that, I wasn't sure how to respond. I was still being quietly torn apart by the conflicting emotions and didn't know if I should give affirmation to the statement or a denial. Thankfully, I didn't have to make that decision right away because Hadley continued without giving me the chance to answer.

"We received a batch of orders directly from the UFC Directorate about thirty minutes ago. You're being transferred to Fort Hood in Texas effective tomorrow morning."

Stunned, I sat down in the chair behind me. *Tomorrow?!* It was all I could think to say. My mind was momentarily caught in a loop of shock. I had been expecting him to tell me about some new threat I would need to protect Alex from. I had not been prepared for him to tell me that I would not be there to protect her.

An order straight from the Directorate could not be ignored, and there was no one higher that I could appeal to. If I didn't obey the order, I would be thrown into the brig and court-martialed. If I obeyed the order, I would be across the ocean from her. No matter which path I chose, I was going to be forced to leave her unprotected once more.

Hadley sat down in the chair next to me. "There's more, Haskell. Anyone on base that I would consider to be sympathetic toward Alex is being shipped out over the next two days as well. Thatcher. Lance. Rockman. Even me."

I felt my hands slowly clench.

Alex was being purposely stripped of all protection. Was this because I had interfered with the doctor's attempt to reimplant the tracking device? It couldn't be. The doctor would have barely had time to contact anyone, let alone for them to make the arrangements and issue the orders for us to be reassigned. There had not been enough time to find out who they would specifically need to reassign in order to leave her without any allies. Something else was going on.

"Was a reason given for th' transfers?"

Hadley shook his head. "No. Just that the transfers were to be carried out as scheduled and in accordance with the travel instructions that were included."

"Travel instructions? Dae transfers straight from th' Directorate usually come with travel instructions?"

"It's not unheard of, but no. It's not the norm."

"What type of instructions were they?"

"Well, you, for example. You'll be flying out of here at o'five hundred hours with a detachment from 3rd squadron who is headed to Egypt. Once there, you will be transferring to a cargo ship headed for Fort Bragg in North Carolina. The last leg of your trip will be with one of the American military groups that has an overground transport convoy heading toward Fort Hood with military supplies for the base. It's a two-week travel plan."

"Two weeks?" Most transfers took a matter of hours, or a few days at the most. Two weeks was an extremely long time. What was going on?

Hadley was shaking his head, equally bemused. "All of us are scheduled for trips like that. At first glance, I thought the plans had been arranged based on cost savings. But the more I think about it, the more it feels like someone is trying to bog us down in travel time. It's as though they want to keep us isolated. None of our routes place us within easy communication lanes and all of them will tie us down for at least a week."

I slammed my fist down on the arm of the chair. It was easy to see where this was going. She would be all alone with no one to stand up for her.

Alex stirred at the sound, a slight movement of her head. We both glanced up but there was no further movement; she didn't appear to be awake. Laying there, battered and bruised, she looked so vulnerable. I would have given almost anything to ensure that she would never have to face such threats again, but the UFC was effectively stripping me of any ability to help her. I was at a loss. What could I do?

Hadley's thoughts seemed to echo my own. "So, what are you going to do?"

What choice did I have? I laughed bitterly. "I'm followin' orders. I'll be gone before she even wakes up."

Just at that moment, a nurse stepped in through the doorway.

"Is one of you Specialist Haskell?" She asked it in a brusque tone, as though she was annoyed that she even had to ask.

"I am," I said cautiously.

"There's a phone call for you." She said it matter-of-factly, then turned and left, clearly not happy to have been reduced to the role of a messenger.

I only had to glance at Hadley briefly for assurance that he would stay with Alex while I went to answer the phone. When I approached the desk, the nurse didn't even look at me. She just pointed at the phone on her desk and said, "Line 2."

"This is Haskell," I said tersely as I picked up the phone.

"Finally!" the gruff voice on the other end barked back in response. I recognized it at once as Captain Dollard, the base's Chief of Security. "Haskell, you were supposed to report to my office for debriefing the moment the doctor was done with you."

I gritted my teeth, but kept my voice as neutral as I could. "I'm sorry, sir. I didn't get that message. I was a bit busy…"

He cut me off. "I know exactly what you were doing, boy. I'm giving you precisely five minutes to be in my office, so get moving!" He hung up, not waiting for a response.

I hung up the phone too, though somewhat more forcefully than I had intended too. The nurse looked up at me reproachfully. I ignored her and turned back toward Alex's room.

I felt like punching the wall, it was all so frustrating. But instead, I took a deep breath and walked through the doorway. Hadley looked up expectantly.

"I've got tae go," I told him, my voice simmering with frustration.

He nodded, unsurprised. "I'll stay with her."

I thanked him but didn't immediately turn to leave. I glanced at Alex. It was ironic. Less than twelve hours ago, I had wanted to get as far away from her as possible. I had been so angry; felt so betrayed. But now that I was being transferred to the other side of the world, I didn't want to leave her side.

Chapter 19: Alexandria Jaquette

AWARENESS CAME SLOWLY at first. It felt like I was rising upwards through the depths of a silent, cold lake. All around me, the heavily pressing darkness both chilled and alarmed me. But, from within that darkness, memories began to sluggishly stir, drawing my attention away from the darkness.

There was the memory of sitting high up in a tree looking down upon a jungle clearing; it faded quietly back into the darkness before I could fully recall why I was up in the tree. Some moments later, a new memory came floating lazily in and I recalled cuffs that bound me to the chill hardness of the stone floor, though not how I had gotten there. That memory transitioned smoothly into one of Sobrien's arm wrapped harshly around my neck and Aiden stalking out of the darkness, lean and fierce. Then it was the helplessness in Aiden's eyes as his voice told me to keep my eyes on him, followed by warmth and safety as he cradled me in his arms.

And then the rest of my memories came gently floating back in. It was different from the furious rushing memories that I had experienced each time I had woken from my earlier drug-induced sleeps. With this return, it was more like waking from a night's sleep where the knowledge of the previous day was never lost, rather simply waiting for the mind to be alert enough to recall it. And that, I think, was when my mind processed that I had indeed been asleep, and that I was not in fact completely awake yet.

As I lay there, not fully alert enough to appreciate the differences between the opposing experiences of waking, I realized that I had been hearing two voices talking softly not far from me. One of those voices, I recognized with drowsy pleasure, was Aiden's. A gentle warmth filled me as I sleepily listened to the murmuring of his voice; it drove away the panic that had been bubbling in the background of my mind. It also drew me upward from the drowsiness of the sleep and encouraged my mind toward increasing alertness.

I stirred slightly, though I made no effort to sit up or to open my eyes. The voices stopped momentarily, as though they had noticed my movement, but then the talking started back up again. This time I could hear their voices clearly.

The second voice, I was pretty sure I recognized it now as Hadley's, asked, "So, what are you going to do?"

Aiden laughed bitterly. "I'm followin' orders. I'll be gone before she even wakes up."

All hints of the warmth and safety his voice had brought to me only moments before were suddenly gone. They were replaced by an icy chill of panic that threatened to drown me. He was leaving? Why?

But even as I asked the question, another memory surfaced. I remembered the flush of anger on his face when Estradé had told him what I was, and the coldness of his composure as he turned his back on me. Now, I realized with alarm, he was leaving again. But if leaving had been his intent all along, why had he come after me in the caves?

With the painful clarity of that memory in the foreground of my mind, I suddenly saw his actions in the cave with new understanding. He had not gone there to help me; he had gone there to recover stolen UFC property; he had only come to find me because he had been following orders to do so. And now that he had completed his mission and recovered me from my kidnapper, he was glad to be leaving; he wasn't even going to stick around long enough to say goodbye.

With that painful line of thoughts racing through my mind, I heard his voice once more, anger simmering just beneath the surface as though he couldn't handle being around me any longer. "I've got tae go."

I felt a strange sense of loss and pain that I didn't fully understand as I listened to him leave the room. It was like he was taking a piece of me with him. In its place he was leaving behind a hollow emptiness that throbbed in his absence.

I RAPPED MY knuckles sharply on the doorframe of Dollard's office. I think I was hoping he wouldn't answer, but I knew there was no chance of that happening. Sure enough, his voice immediately barked at me from inside the office. "Get in here, Haskell." I set my shoulders and walked in.

Dollard was sitting behind his desk, his attention clearly focused on the display screen in front of him. I took my place in front of the desk and stood at attention, waiting for him to address me. He kept me waiting that way for several minutes.

When he finally looked up, it was with a surly face. "I'm looking at a report from Deputy Director Willard over at the Military Hospital. It says that you pulled a gun on, and threatened, a high-ranking military doctor who was attempting to treat the asset, preventing him from doing his job."

"He wasn't helping her, sir, he was…"

"I didn't ask you what he was doing!" Dollard bellowed sharply.

I had to clench my jaw tightly to keep from saying something I would immediately regret.

Dollard went on angrily, "Willard is calling for your head to be served up on a platter. He's even going so far as to suggest that you be submitted to a full psychological profile, saying that your loyalty to the UFC should be placed into question."

I stiffened, suddenly worried by the ramifications of that threat. I recalled thinking, while watching Alex's body fight for life, that nothing was more important to me than her survival. *But was her freedom just as important? More important to me than my family's survival?* That question burned in my mind as Dollard continued.

"The only thing keeping you out of the brig at this moment is the fact that you were the one who recovered the asset and brought it back in. So," he paused to take a breath and lower his voice back down to a somewhat normal level, "what I have to decide now is just how culpable you were in your actions or whether Willard is barking up the wrong tree. I've also just received orders for your transfer to America." He paused briefly, watching me closely to see my response to this news.

"You don't seem surprised by this."

"Hadley told me, sir," I acknowledged tightly.

"Ah, Hadley. Of course. Yes, he would have seen the orders too. Fine, then. Now to decide whether you will spend the next few years in the brig or in America. We'll start with what happened in the caves."

He kept me standing at attention for over two hours as he grilled me on every detail of what had occurred, who had done what, when, where and how. He especially focused on what Estradé and the doctor had done to Alex, why I had not stopped them, why I thought Estradé had taken me prisoner, and why she had later released me. He downloaded the files from my tactical band and went through them minute-by-minute, requiring me to walk him through each step of the computer's record.

Then he played the videos of the confrontation in front of the surgery room and the one inside of it. He grunted slightly when Hadley came in to the picture and ordered the other soldier to back down but didn't say anything more until I pulled the gun from my waistband. He hit the pause button and looked closer at the screen, then turned to look at me.

"Where did you get that weapon? You were not issued a phase pistol for the recovery assignment."

I swore silently to myself. I had hoped nobody would notice that. I was authorized to carry the weapon, but it wasn't common knowledge, and I definitely had not used it according to the provisions that had been made in order to allow me to carry it.

My permission to have the gun was a deviation from normal protocol, a personal favor if you will, that had been permitted on my mother's behalf. I don't know how she had done it, but the contingency was based on the promise that I would never use it for anything other than self-defense.

"It's a family heirloom, sir." I realized the words sounded a little nervous, so I cleared my throat before continuing. "I uh, have a note of authorization in me file."

He looked at me somewhat skeptically, then typed a command into his computer. I waited nervously as he read what appeared on his screen.

"I see," he said a few minutes later. "However, this provision does not extend to using it against a UFC doctor in the defense of someone else. I think I better confiscate your weapon while I make some inquiries into how the Directorate wants this handled."

He held out his hand for the gun. Reluctantly, I pulled it out of my waistband and placed it into his hand. I had gotten used to having it tucked into my belt; it felt almost uncomfortable to suddenly not have it there.

The remainder of the inquiry went quickly. After seeing the rest of the video, Dollard decided that he wanted to talk to the surgeon who had repaired Alex's shoulder before he made any final conclusions.

"Very well, Haskell," he said at last. "You are confined to quarters until further notice. Vasquez!" he hollered the last word.

The door opened immediately as though the man's hand had already been on the door, just waiting for the Captain to call his name.

"Yes, sir?"

"Escort Specialist Haskell back to the barracks. He is not to leave it until I call for him."

"Yes, sir!"

I had been physically exhausted before the interrogation started; by the time he permitted me to leave, I was mentally exhausted as well. The walk from his office to the barracks was pretty much a blur in my mind. In spite of my exhaustion, sleep was slow in coming; I was frustrated and discouraged. They hadn't even given me the chance to tell her goodbye.

***

MY EYES WERE heavy with grit when a hand on my shoulder woke me five hours later. It was the soldier Dollard had instructed to take me back to the barracks.

"The Captain wants to see you," he said quietly, so as not to wake the other soldiers sleeping nearby. I nodded my head and rolled out of bed.

I was nervous as we walked through the pre-dawn darkness on our way back to the Captain's office. Dollard had said the options were either America or the brig; neither one was all that appealing to me.

Dollard was expecting me when I got there. He was even more surly than he had been the last time I saw him.

"Haskell, you've stirred up a bigger hornet's nest than I thought was physically possible. There's a whole contingent from the Directorate's office on their way here right now to straighten out the mess you made. I've been on the phone with them for the last two hours trying to smooth things over and to get answers on what to do about your gun. The only straight answer I could get from anyone came directly from Director Beckwith's office. He wants you off this base before he gets here. He said, and I quote, 'Send him to America with the rest of the traitors, and good riddance to him.'"

I swallowed hard at the word traitor.

"Seeing as he is expected to be here in thirty minutes, that means you have twenty minutes to be in the air. Vasquez will escort you back to the barracks so you can pack your things and then he will take you straight to the airfield." He looked me straight in the eyes as he said the next part. "If I ever see you on my base again, I will personally shoot you. Now get out!"

Chapter 21: Alexandria Jaquette

I WAS SITTING up in bed, talking quietly with Hadley when they came in. By "they," I mean a loudly arguing group of scientists, doctors and nurses, and men and women in suits. Even before they stormed into the room, I could hear their voices coming down the hall, punctuated by the staccato beat of their rapidly moving feet. There were at least three voices in the mix, speaking over each other.

"...I was promised at least six months..."

"...yes, but unfortunately, we've had to revise the arrangement."

"This is ridiculous! She needs rest, not an angry horde..."

"...that is not fair..."

"...fair or not, it is what is happening!"

"In all my years I have never seen such a circus!"

I looked at Hadley, but he appeared as confused by the commotion as I was. And then they came in, some eight or nine people crowding into the confines of my small room. In spite of having clearly reached their destination, their arguments continued unabated.

Dr. Eris, red faced and clearly upset said, "I demand to know why!"

A man in a pin-striped suit met her demand with a steely gaze of his own. "You can, of course, file a formal complaint with the Directorate's office. Director Beckwith will, I'm sure, look into your complaint at his earliest convenience. However, that will not stop the transfer…"

"Earliest convenience?! By that you mean to say never?"

"You are both being ridiculous. This discussion should be taking place in an office, not in my patient's recovery room."

This last part was spoken by an infuriated-looking old man in doctor's scrubs. He was furiously interjecting himself between the upset group of scientists and the equally stern group of important-looking men and women, all the while being scrupulously ignored by both.

"I did not say that, madame," the man in the suit said in exasperation.

"Of course not," Eris sneered. "Your carefully worded phrases have clearly been calculated to…"

Standing slightly apart from the rest of the group, and yet clearly a part of it, I noticed one old man in an expensive-looking grey suit. He was leaning slightly on an elegant walking stick of the deepest black rosewood, set at the top by an exquisitely carved silver handle that showed a design of lilies and quails. But it wasn't the walking stick that really caught my attention, it was his eyes. His piercing gray eyes were intently studying my face, as though judging me by what he saw there. I raised my chin slightly and met his gaze with a steady look of my own. His wrinkled lips parted into the faintest hint of a smile, and then he looked away from me at last to face the still-bickering group.

His voice, while somewhat weakened by age, still resonated with the strength of authority. "I think I have heard quite enough."

Although the individual parties were clearly still fuming, the arguing stopped immediately, and all eyes turned to look at him.

"Dr. Eris, I assure you that your frustration has been noted, and I will personally ensure that you are appropriately compensated for your lost research time. But," he raised his hand to forestall her when Dr. Eris looked like she might argue back, "you no longer have any say in what is going to happen and you will now leave this room, with your group."

Tight lipped and white faced, Dr. Eris glared at him but said nothing more as she stiffly turned and left the room. The old man didn't waste time watching her leave, and instead turned to the group of suited men and women. "You will all wait for me in the foyer."

Not a single member of that group seemed to be bothered by his instruction. In fact, they all appeared to be well versed in how to respond to his orders. Without a word, that group filed out.

That left the doctor and two other nurses who were suddenly unsure of themselves and what they should do. The old man smiled patiently at them and said, "Doctor, if you would please stay, I would like to have a word with you, but the rest of your staff will need to leave now as well."

The doctor hesitated for just a moment before he turned to his staff with a nod of his head, and they too evaporated out the door. Almost as quickly as they had descended upon my room, the crowd had dispersed. Only five of us remained. Besides Hadley and myself, there was the doctor, the old man, and a tousled haired Asian teenager I had not previously noticed. The old man turned to that boy now. "Harry, if you would be so good."

Without a word, the boy moved over to the counter and opened up the small grey bag he had been carrying. From it he removed an even smaller device, typed a few keystrokes onto the keyboard, and then turned back to the older man. "You're good now, sir."

"Not quite." The old man turned to the doctor. "Would you mind closing and locking that door please."

As the doctor did so, the older gentleman moved to take the seat next to Hadley. Hadley looked somewhat uncomfortable sitting next to him, not sure whether he was intended to be part of this meeting, but wisely keeping his mouth closed in case he had simply been overlooked.

"Now my dear," the old man said looking at me kindly, "there are some things we need to talk about. First, please allow me to apologize for the rudeness of that group. I'm afraid it was inevitable given the circumstances, but that is no excuse for its occurrence. Secondly, I must ask you to forgive an old man's lack of courtesy for not introducing myself as of yet and beg of you to indulge me some few questions before I reveal that information."

"Okay," I said uncertainly, instinctively looking toward Hadley for a second opinion. He shrugged his shoulders ever so slightly, equally confused by the request.

"My first question, my dear, is to ask you your thoughts about being in the military?"

I'm not sure what I had been expecting, but that certainly wasn't it.

"Uh…" I hesitated as I tried to think what I should say.

"Now don't be afraid to be honest, my dear. I know you were not consulted before being brought to this base, but I am curious as to your thoughts about it now that you have spent a few months here."

"I, uh…" I started slowly taking his gentle nod as one of encouragement. "I was frustrated at being sent here to be poked and prodded and forced into a training program I didn't ask for. But at the same time, it's because I came here that I have learned as much as I have."

"And just what is it that you have learned?" he gently encouraged me to go on.

"Well, I learned to do this." I reached out my hand and slowly lifted the empty bag the teenage boy had set on the counter after removing the device from it. The bag floated smoothly across the room to set down gently on the foot of my bed.

Testing that I could once more control gravity had been my first impulse after I had become fully alert, and after the initial sting of Aiden's abandonment had worn away. I had been grateful to find that it had indeed returned.

"Impressive," the old man said, "but we both know you were able to do that before you came here."

I smiled sheepishly. "Yes, but not this as well." Concentrating slightly harder, I lifted myself a few feet above the bed while at the same time lifting the doctor off of his feet and into the air as well.

"That's enough," the doctor said sharply.

As I set him back down, he huffed, "You should not be doing that so soon after your surgery." I had to admit he was right; that little bit of effort was enough to leave me light-headed and breathing hard.

The old man nodded his head toward the doctor. "I'm sorry, Dr. Paxton; you are absolutely correct." Then he turned back to me with a wry smile. "I have seen the reports that show what you are capable of, there is no need to show me. Actually, what I am really looking to understand is your

216

thoughts on the military itself. Whether you would be interested in continuing your career in it?"

"No," I responded emphatically. I didn't need to think about my answer to that question. The military had never been what I wanted, and after what had happened the last few days, I wanted even less to do with it now.

His head tipped quizzically at the forcefulness of my response. "That was a quick answer. Is there a particular reason behind it?"

I sighed, a little surprised by the rapid surge of emotions his question had inspired, but quite certain in my response nonetheless.

"Not everything I have learned here is good. My control of gravity is much stronger than it was before." I hesitated. "Now I can hurt people with what I am able to do, and that frightens me. When my unit was attacked, I responded without thinking. I was angry and afraid. The things I did to those men..." I shuddered, leaving the rest unspoken.

The old man nodded his head as my voice died away. He seemed to understand what was bothering me. "I see. So, it would be safe to assume that you would not be interested in being part of an attack team built to fight against Icarus."

I couldn't meet his eyes, certain he would be disappointed in my answer, but I shook my head. "No."

"Child," he said gently, "there is no shame in your desire to not harm others. In fact, I would have been saddened to find you any other way. The truth is, I came here to offer you another option."

I looked up slowly, a mixture of hopefulness and doubt swirling inside of me. Another option? Was it possible?

"The UFC is building a school in New Los Angeles, on the site of the bombing that started the Regnant War. It is to be a school for all countries in the UFC and will bring together the greatest minds among our children. But it is also likely to be a tempting target for Icarus. As such, we have decided to put together a special team whose job would be to protect that school. We would like you to be part of that team."

"You mean like the teams of specialists that are at Cambridge and Dartmouth?"

"Of a sort," he said hesitantly. "You would technically be employed by the UFC military." He held up his hand to stave off the comment I was about to make. "However, you would answer directly to Captain Marcellus, and he answers directly to me, not the military."

"Marcellus?" I said it slowly. Sergeant Marcellus? The soldier from my school? The one who had watched me leave? Was it possible? I didn't dare to hope, and yet I still did.

The old man smiled conspiratorially at me. "I think you might already know him. In fact, he was the one who brought your situation to my attention. He has been rather insistent that you be given a choice in your future."

A slow smile spread across my face. If it was indeed the same soldier, then my decision was already made; I would be going.

"Now, before you make your decision, I must admit that I have an ulterior motive behind my offer. You are a very special child. Icarus engineered you to be far superior to any other Alphas we have previously created. But these last few days have made it clear that Icarus wants you back.

"By sending you to this new school, I would be surrounding you with state-of-the-art protection and the best team that I have been able to put together. I can think of nowhere safer for you to be. But, in order to keep you safe, I think it would be best that no one knows you are there."

I looked at him quizzically, unsure how that would be possible.

"So," he went on, "if you agree to this arrangement, then we will be making you disappear from off the face of the earth. The only ones who will know who you truly are will be your immediate team. Including, if he will agree to it, Mr. Hadley here."

Hadley seemed to start at the sound of his own name. "Me, sir?" he asked.

The gentleman turned to look him square in the eyes. "Yes, you. If, that is, Miss Jaquette approves." He turned to look back at me. "You see, my dear, the Special Ops Team that you would be part of will be there as much to protect you as they are there to protect the school. It would only seem appropriate that they be a team of individuals that you get along with.

"Mr. Hadley, in particular is not only exceptionally fast in his movements and an expert in hand-to-hand fighting, but a secret little known to his friends is that he graduated from Lexington Military College with top honors last year. He has a keen mind that would make him an excellent choice as your team lead, if you would allow him to tag along with you."

I looked at Hadley questioningly. "What are your thoughts?"

He still looked a little startled that the older gentleman had known his name and addressed him directly. I got the feeling he had been under the impression that his continued presence in the room had been an oversite on the gentleman's part.

"To be honest, I'm not sure what I think. They were sent here by the Directorate, so I feel safe in assuming that this man is working under their direction. But it also appears that he is not working under a coordinated decision of the whole Directorate, or else he wouldn't have asked his tech to disrupt the surveillance equipment in this room."

A broad smile spread across the older man's wrinkled face. "As I said, a keen mind for the observation of details. Well, you indulged this old man's questions and were patient. So now, allow me to introduce myself. I am Director Beckwith." His eyes twinkled as he said the last part, probably in response to the shocked look on our faces.

Director Beckwith was one of the fifteen directors who sat at the head of the UFC. He represented most of the European countries and was one of the most powerful men in the world. I looked at Hadley again, he was clearly as stunned as I was.

"Well, now that we have that part out of the way, what do you say my dear? Shall I let Captain Marcellus know that you will be heading his way?"

His smile was infectious. I found that I was smiling back at him. "I think I would like that, sir."

"Good." He slapped his knees as though that had settled everything then began to stand up before he suddenly seemed to think of something else. "Oh yes, one more thing." He turned to face the doctor who had been standing quietly off to one side.

"I almost forgot, Dr. Paxton. The campus at New Los Angeles has a new hospital that is set to open next month. I have been authorized to offer you the position of hospital director there."

Dr. Paxton raised an eyebrow at this but didn't say anything. It was as though he knew there was more to the story. He wasn't wrong.

Beckwith continued, "There are, however, a few conditions to this offer. You are obviously aware of Miss Jaquette's identity. You would, therefore, be required to keep that secret. You would also be personally responsible for her medical care. Seeing as Miss Jaquette will be leaving this base within the next few minutes…"

At those words, Dr. Paxton began to object. He was clearly not pleased to hear that I would be traveling so soon after my surgery. But Beckwith forestalled his arguments by raising his voice ever so slightly and meeting Paxton's argument with a steely glint in his eyes. It was suddenly very clear that he was much more than just a kindly old man. He was a man who wielded great power and was accustomed to being obeyed.

"That would mean," Beckwith continued firmly, "that you will need to travel with her as well, so that you can continue to monitor her recovery and ensure that she does not overwork herself. Once she is safely off this base, and has been delivered to a secure location, you will then have complete authority regarding when she may continue her journey to the campus."

That seemed to appease the doctor. He thought for a moment, then nodded his head. "I can accept that. But I have one condition of my own."

Beckwith tilted his head slightly, curious as to the doctor's demand.

"As director, I would want full authority over who works in that hospital; meaning that the Directorate will not force any staff on me. I won't put up with an ill-trained nurse who happens to be someone's favorite niece."

Beckwith nodded approvingly. "Fair enough. I will place that authority in your file and ensure that any questions regarding your authority are sent directly to me. Will that satisfy you?"

Dr. Paxton seemed to think about it for a moment then nodded. "That will do."

"Good!" Beckwith said for the second time in as many minutes. "Then I will send Leticia in to explain the arrangement and get things moving."

The plan for getting me to New Los Angeles was not a simple one. What little they explained to me about it involved a lot of disguises and misdirection. I would be leaving the base within the hour, but in order to ensure that no one noticed my disappearance from the base, a decoy had been brought in.

Shortly after Beckwith left the room, a group of three nurses came in with a cart of medical supplies. They quickly shooed Hadley and the teenage boy out of the room, saying that they had been sent in to get me cleaned up.

Dr. Paxton's eyes narrowed as he looked closely at each one of the nurses in turn. "I don't believe we have been introduced," he said to the first one.

"I should think not," the dark-skinned nurse replied with a mischievous smile. "I am Leticia, Director Beckwith's Personal Planner. I take care of the logistics for his "special" events." She emphasized the word special with a sly smile in her eyes. "Now, if you gentlemen will step out of the room, we have some work to do."

By work, she meant the application of makeup and the dying of my hair. All of the work took the three "nurses" approximately 20 minutes. When they were finished, I found myself looking at a stranger in the mirror. My skin and hair had been darkened considerably, the bruise on my cheek was no longer visible, and my clothes were now that of a nurse's scrubs. They had tied my hair up in a tight knot that hid its length and to match the style of the third nurse's hair. That nurse, whose clothes I was now wearing, was in turn sitting patiently in the hospital bed as her hair and makeup was now being done.

Leticia and I left the room while the other two ladies were still working. As we walked, she explained to me that after changing the patient's bedding, the soiled materials were to be taken to the laundry room. The disheveled pile of sheets and blankets I held in my good arm had been carefully positioned to hide the sling.

Still chatting away about the care given to each patient's room while cleaning it, Leticia led me past the nurse's station where Hadley, Dr. Paxton, and the teenage boy were waiting. Not one of them gave us more than a cursory glance before turning their attention back toward the room we had just left. I smiled inwardly to myself at the success of the makeover.

We didn't stop at the laundry room. Instead, Leticia led me to the elevators and down to the hospital basement. There, she directed me to drop the material on the floor and used the data pad on her wrist to text a communication. We only had to wait thirty seconds before a reply came back.

"It's clear now."

There was a moment's worry where it occurred to me that I really had no way to be certain this nurse was truly part of Director Beckwith's team, but all of my doubts disappeared when the door opened from the outside and Marcellus was standing in the opened doorway with a lopsided grin. "Good to see you again, kid. Let's get you out of here."

Chapter 22: Aiden Haskell

------------- — — — —— ——— ————— ———————

THE FIRST LEG of my journey had been fairly short. An hour after we took off, the craft landed at the naval base in Alexandria, Egypt. Alexandria! What irony! I had been forced to leave her, but even the name of the city I had been sent to was intent on reminding me that I had once more abandoned her.

The base was a maelstrom of activity with a constant stream of sailors, ships, and supplies all in motion at the same time, but none of them moving in the same direction. It had taken twenty minutes just to find someone who knew where I was supposed to go and another ten minutes of slow-paced jogging to get there before the ship's scheduled departure with the morning tide. So much for taking it easy on my leg. I was limping heavily by the time I boarded.

Once on board, I had been directed to a small cabin stuffed full of bunks. The crewman who led the way pointed to an empty bunk in the corner and told me it would be mine for the duration of the voyage. He also indicated that I was expected to stay in that room, out of the way, while the crew prepared to cast off. Someone would come to get me, he said, when we had left the major traffic lanes out of the harbor. Only then would it be acceptable for me to leave the cabin.

With nothing more to do, I laid down on the bed and tried to sleep. Sleep, however, turned out to be my enemy. I woke in a cold sweat, my heart racing in panic. I couldn't have told you exactly what had occurred in the dream, but as my eyes shot open, I could still see Alex's frightened face and knew that I had abandoned her to something that had made my own blood run cold.

I sat up on the edge of the bed and rubbed my hands over my eyes, trying to shake the cold chill that lingered from the nightmare. A quick glance at my tactical band told me that less than an hour had passed. I shook my head in silent frustration and laid back down to try and get more sleep; it was a wasted effort. My mind was not interested in returning to the nightmare.

Unable to sleep, I instead allowed my mind to wander toward the conflicting emotions that had harrowed my mind and heart for the past twenty-four hours. Like a storm that couldn't decide which way to blow, my mind alternated between ghosting memories of Alex and haunting images of my brother's murderer.

I would see Alex sitting up in the tree, grinning down at me when I had asked for a lift up, only to have the memory morph into the malicious smirk of Icarus' Alpha as she burned Callen from the inside out. But then, before my anger could ignite from the memory, it switched back to a memory of Alex straining her abilities to help a specialist who had sprained his ankle.

I guess I had thought that not being around her would be enough to calm the storm; it wasn't. Instead, my thoughts began to circle increasingly around the idea that the distance between us was about to become uncrossable. I was slightly surprised by the wave of sadness that thought brought with it. In the end, it was that sadness that finally drowned the storm in my mind.

I realized as I lay there thinking, that at some point in the last few hours my mind had successfully separated Alex from the actions of her siblings. Instead of being the wretched child of Icarus, she had become the victim in my mind; a child that I wanted to protect.

Only she wasn't a child; she was a woman. I sighed as I realized that it wasn't just protecting her from Icarus that my mind had settled on. Even in the midst of my desperation to get her out of the caves, it had felt good to hold her in my arms. Now, I wanted desperately to hold her again. Not just to keep her safe, but this time simply for the sake of holding her.

My heart and mind had finally come into agreement, only it was too late; I would never see her again, let alone ever hold her. It was a bitter realization that kept me occupied until someone finally came to tell me that we had left the traffic lanes and I was now free to leave the cabin.

Anxious to get away from the lingering sadness of my thoughts, I decided to pass my time by exploring the ship. The bulk of the ship consisted of four enormous cargo holds that held row upon row of crates, stacked, in some areas, nearly twenty stories high. A narrow section of the main deck surrounded the cargo holds and provided the closest view of the ocean just over its railings, while the forecastle deck allowed for an impressive view of the wide-open expanse of ocean the ship was sailing into.

I was free to roam the open decks, but there wasn't much to see or do there. Far more interesting was the accommodation structure of the ship and the machinery space below it. In comparison to the rest of the ship, this structure appeared miniscule. But at ten stories above the main deck, and an additional ten stories down into the underbelly of the ship, it was anything but small.

What I found as I roamed the accommodations' structure was a well-laid-out maze of narrow corridors that were connected by even narrower stairwells and a multitude of heavy doors that led to everything from tiny storage lockers to much larger planning rooms. While I wasn't looking for anything in particular, I did find several interesting things along the way.

The engine room, which had drawn me to it by its gentle thrum, held an impressive array of equipment, surprisingly well maintained for the relentless job it did. One of the crewmen, who paused in his duties long enough to talk to me, explained that the twin turbine engines which were housed on either side of the ship never stopped working during the week-long voyage across the ocean. They were constantly in motion and so, were in constant need of observation. In addition to the two engineering officers currently on duty in the engine control room, there were an additional three crewmembers working in the engine room at any given time.

Several decks above the engine room, I found a well-stocked crewman's lounge that had everything from a ping-pong table to a movie screen and projector. The room also had low cabinets built into each wall that opened to reveal items like puzzles and board games, exercise equipment, and a large collection of books.

Back outside, I discovered a landing pad that was big enough for a helio-transport. It was nestled between the ship's bow and the endless rows of crates that lined the ship's deck, but it didn't appear that it had been used very often as the painted lines that outlined the pad and crossed at its center showed little in the way of wear and tear.

In the end, worn down by all the walking and the resultant aching of my injured knee, I returned to the crewman's lounge and chose a well-worn book off the shelf. It wasn't that I was really interested in reading, but anything was better than returning to the bunk room. I took the book and went back outside to the forecastle deck where I found a quiet place to sit in the sun and read. The sun helped to chase away the lingering chills from the nightmare and the book helped to distract my thoughts away from Alex.

When my stomach finally began to grumble from lack of food, I made my way to the mess hall. It was a surprisingly small room for the size of the crew, but it made more sense when someone explained that one third of the crew was asleep at any given time, and those on duty came to meals in shifts. There was also a second mess hall for the officers. So, in reality there were never really more than eight people in the mess hall at the same time.

The woman who explained all of this to me worked on the cooking staff along with two other men. They spent the majority of their days preparing and serving the meals that the rest of us enjoyed. She brought me a fish sandwich, chips, and an apple for lunch with a warm smile and told me to just let her know if I needed seconds, but that I should save room for that night's dinner of steak and potatoes. She said it was the head cook's best recipe and that it was very popular with the crew.

The sailors I shared my lunch with were a varied group of men and women that came from all over the world. The man on my left had been born in Russia. The one across from me had grown up in Brazil. And the woman at the other table had been born at sea. I got to know them just a little bit as we talked and ate.

I learned from them that the cargo ship I was on was named the Argonaut after the group of sailors in Greek mythology that helped Jason find the Golden Fleece. The ship, as I had seen when boarding it, was not a small one. In fact, at 1,500 feet in length and carrying about 200,000 crates worth of materials, it was one of the largest carriers in the world.

And, while this was not a military cargo ship, it was not the first time they had contracted with the military to transport cargo or individuals. It just so happened that on this particular trip, besides me, they were also transporting several crates of military supplies scheduled for delivery to different ports in both North and South America.

Overall, the crew was made up of burly old sailors you wouldn't want to meet alone in a back alley and a few women tough enough to handle their own against them. But they were all proud of their ship and were quick to share with me the tales of their adventures on it. Even so, one by one they drifted back to their duties, eventually leaving me alone in the mess hall.

I spent the rest of the afternoon in a restless combination of alternatingly trying to read the book and wandering the ship. I was stubbornly trying to avoid the thoughts of Alex that kept creeping back into my mind. But near the end of the day, when the sun was setting in a beautiful array of red and gold, I found my mind drifting back toward Alex once more.

Something Estradé had said had managed to creep its way back into my mind and it weighed heavily on me now. At the time she had been taunting me with the information, but that didn't make it any less true: I had sworn to never let a woman into my heart.

I had made that promise to myself when I was thirteen, after seeing the devastating effects of the UFC's mandates on far too many Scottish families as their firstborn sons were forced into the military only to die there. I had decided then and there that I would never have children of my own. At the time, I had believed that love and marriage were necessary parts of having children. While the world had since taught me that neither was truly necessary to bring a child into the world, I had come to the conclusion that it would be easier on me all around if I just kept my heart safely locked up.

In spite of that determination, I finally had to acknowledge to myself that I had failed to protect my heart from Alex, and I wondered just why it was I had failed with her when I had succeeded against so many other women in the past.

Perhaps it was because she had never actively done anything to purposely draw me in. She didn't seem to play the games my sister did. In fact, from everything I had come to know about her, Alex was free from guile and deception; what you saw with her seemed to be what you got.

Or perhaps it was because she was the first person I'd ever met whose comeback to one of my jokes had been so absolutely perfect. Her message on the track board had made me laugh harder than I had laughed in quite some time.

Then there was the fact that being around her made me feel genuinely happy and alive. I found myself drawn to that emotion, like a moth to the flame.

But surely it wasn't just that. I had met other women who had the same traits Alex did. They had been funny, entertaining, smart, kind, even some who were far more beautiful than Alex was. And I had been actively pursued by several of them who had been after my family's money and position, or who simply thought I was a person of interest to them.

In each situation, they had turned on their charm and played their games, and each time I had successfully steeled my heart against them. So why had I failed this time? What made Alex so different from them? I struggled with the question as the sun quietly set in a dazzling display that spread across the vast expanse of the ocean like a fire.

In the end, I couldn't come up with an exact reason that I could put into words. I could only acknowledge that it had happened so gradually that I had missed all the warning signs until it was too late. Now it seemed that the faster I tried to run away from the emotions she stirred in me, the faster I was running back into them.

Eventually, long after the sun had set, I gave up trying to solve the mystery and went to bed. I slept fitfully that night, waking multiple times in a cold sweat of fear, each time to a different variation of my earlier nightmare. Each time, knowing that I had left Alex unprotected and feeling ashamed of myself because I had not had the courage to stay behind and protect her. The sixth time I woke, I gave up on sleep all together and went for a walk on the deck.

The cold ocean breeze chilled me almost as much as the nightmares had, but at least it didn't come with the harrowing images. Instead, the stars in the velvety night sky were putting on a dazzling display. There were even a few shooting stars to accent the scene.

As I leaned against the railing, watching the reflected light of the waxing moon glowing on the water, a faint thrumming reached my ears. It was a familiar sound, though not one I had expected to hear out in the middle of the ocean.

I turned to scan the sky, searching for the approaching craft. There it was: twin lights approaching on the starboard side of the ship. No sooner had I spotted the lights then they dropped behind the rows of crates. If I had not been facing that direction at that moment, I would have missed the lights all together. But then, I knew from my wanderings yesterday that there was a landing pad near the ship's stern, so it made sense that the aircraft would be heading there.

For just a moment I entertained the idea of going to see who had made a trip to the cargo ship at this hour of the night. But the truth was that I was unlikely to make it across the ship to the landing pad before whoever was on it had entered the accommodations building and disappeared into one of its many levels. I decided to just ask one of the sailors about the visitors in the morning.

Thoroughly chilled by the cold night air and having had enough time for the nightmares to begin to fade into the background of my mind and weariness to return, I decided to give sleep another try.

I hadn't quite made it back to the bunk room when a familiar voice called to me from the opposite end of the hall. "Aiden Haskell. Just the man I was coming to see."

"Hadley," I called back with the start of a laugh. The laugh died in my throat as I realized that Hadley wasn't smiling back at me. If anything, his expression was grim, even angry. My eyes narrowed slightly as I took in the group of men who were with him.

One of them was a sailor I didn't recognize; he was the one leading the group toward me. The other two were soldiers whose markings on their uniforms declared them to be connected to the Directorate's office. A sudden sensation of dread settled in the pit of my stomach; something wasn't right.

"What are yae daeing here?" I asked him warily.

"Director Beckwith asked me to deliver a message to you," Hadley said coolly as he closed the distance between us. I looked suspiciously back at him, knowing that any message coming from Beckwith was not likely to be one I wanted to hear.

"What's th' message?" I asked carefully.

I saw the movement of Hadley's arm too late. If it had been anyone else, I still would have been able to block the blow that I knew was coming; but not a blow coming at the speed Hadley could move. I doubled over in pain as his fist connected with my stomach. It was all I could do to choke in enough breath to keep from passing out.

Almost instantly, I felt my arms being harshly grabbed on each side and forcefully yanked behind me; I could do nothing to stop them. Hadley grabbed a handful of my hair and lifted my head up so that I was forced to look him in the eyes. "You should have stayed away from her, traitor." He spit the last word out as he whipped my head back down.

Then he turned to the sailor that stood watching. "We're going to need a room to work in. The Director has a few more things he wants me to tell him." He said it with a malicious grin that did nothing to calm the roiling fear that was suddenly burning inside of me.

The sailor replied back with a grin of his own. "I've got just the place for you."

I was half dragged down the hall as the soldiers restraining my arms in their vice-like grips followed the sailor to a storage room not far from where we had been. The open door in front of us loomed like a dangerous cavern. I knew that if they got me into that room, there was a chance I wouldn't be coming out of it alive. Drawing on all my training, I went suddenly limp, prepping my muscles at the same time for my next move.

The sudden, unexpected full weight of my body caught the soldiers by surprise. The grip of the man on the right loosened just enough for me to slip my arm free; it was all I needed. Surging back up, I jerked my elbow backward and up into his face, catching him full in the nose. Then I spun smoothly and punched the man on my left across the chin, causing him to jerk back in shock and pain. Continuing the counter motion, I stepped back and spun toward Hadley, knowing I had to move the fastest I had ever moved if I was to have a chance against him. It wasn't fast enough! Hadley already had his phase pistol out and was pointing it straight at my chest.

"That will do," he said coldly. I froze, knowing that I had failed. Why? I wanted to ask. Why was he doing this? I had thought he was a friend; someone I could trust to look out for Alex. It was clear that I had misjudged him.

Not looking away from me, Hadley called to the sailor who had taken several steps back the moment I had gone on the attack.

"You, sailor, stand guard outside this door. No one leaves this room unless they leave with my permission. Is that clear?"

"Yes, sir," the man said in a now somewhat nervous voice.

Using his gun to tell me to start moving, Hadley directed me into the storage room without another word. The two soldiers groaned as they got back to their feet, but they both followed us through the door. One thing I knew for certain from the way they looked at me as they came in, they had their own messages to deliver.

Chapter 23: Alexandria Jaquette

MARCELLUS AND LETICIA had taken me straight to the airfield where the pilot had the craft primed and ready for takeoff; we were in the air thirty seconds later. An hour after that we landed at a small landing pad near a secluded cabin in the middle of the Alps. Marcellus told me that this was a temporary, but necessary stop. We would be staying here for a few days while the rest of the team was gathered.

He explained that I would have the opportunity to interview each potential member of the team. Some of them I already knew from the training base; others were being brought in from various locations around the globe and so were likely to be strangers to me. But each one of them had been previously vetted by Director Beckwith's office and himself, and I would have the final say in whether or not they would be joining the team.

The cabin was not a small one. It had been built as a private retreat by a wealthy, eccentric businessman who enjoyed hosting ultra-exclusive events for his closest friends and business partners. However, not all of those events were fully legal. As such, the cabin was kept fully stocked and ready to receive groups at any time, while at the same time being fully secured against prying eyes.

It turned out that Director Beckwith's office had recently been made aware of the man's activities and had come to an arrangement with him. In return for allowing Beckwith to borrow the cabin for two weeks, no questions asked, Beckwith would turn a blind eye to the information he had received and even ensure that the man's activities were discreetly ignored for the next few years.

Everywhere I looked there were discreet signs of the owner's wealth. I say discreet because, although the cabin had clearly been built to the highest standards of quality, none of it was opulent or overdone. In a word, the cabin was exquisite. Its beauty was matched only by the majesty of the snow-capped mountains it had been built among.

The view out of the two-story tall picture window in the cabin's central hall was breathtaking. I would have been happy to spend the rest of the day there, just admiring the mountain views, but Dr. Paxton had radioed ahead that I was to be taken straight to bed, and Marcellus quickly made it clear that he had every intention of following the doctor's orders.

Without pausing, he led me up the grand staircase to a small room on the second floor that was intended to be my room for the duration of our visit. To be honest, small was also relative. It was far larger than any room I'd ever had to myself. The French door entrance led into a formal sitting room with its own fireplace, while yet another set of French doors led to the actual bedroom beyond that. The bed was twice as big, and at least twice as soft, as any I had ever been in. It was made up with a half dozen pillows of varying sizes and a set of matching blankets that were fuzzy and warm. Then there was an oversized bathroom with an attached walk-in closet and dressing room as well.

Perhaps recognizing that I would have liked to stay a little longer in front of the picture windows in the central hall, Captain Marcellus opened the curtains at the side of the room to show me that this room had its own, smaller picture window. The view was perhaps not quite as grand as the downstairs one, but it caught my breath all the same.

While I stood at the window, momentarily lost in the view's beauty, someone else entered the room.

"Alex, this is Lilith." Marcellus introduced us. "She will be working with Doctor Paxton to ensure that your medical needs are met, beginning with getting you into bed."

He said the last part with so much emphasis on the "getting you into bed" part that I automatically rolled my eyes before remembering that he was now my commanding officer. The steely look he gave me in response was a stern reminder. But then his frown softened ever so slightly, and he said, almost kindly, "You haven't changed much, have you?"

Embarrassed by my momentary slip, I didn't have to pretend to be contrite as I replied back, "No, sir."

Lilith didn't bother to hide her own half-smile as she watched our interchange. "Well, now that the two of you have settled that, why don't we get some vitals taken. Captain, if you would shut the door on your way out…"

She didn't have to finish the sentence as the Captain nodded, then turned to leave. He paused briefly at the door and turned back. "Get some rest, kid. There will be plenty to do starting tomorrow," and then he was gone.

Lilith was efficient in her work. She checked my blood pressure, listened to my lungs, and felt my pulse, all the while taking notes on her digi-pad. Unlike some nurses, she didn't try to fill the silent gaps with random prattle, but still managed to say just enough to set me at ease during those moments.

She spoke with a mild Southern American accent that was somehow both stern and friendly at the same time. She gave off the impression that if you did exactly what she told you to, then she would make a great friend. But if you didn't, then you would quickly learn that she was not someone you wanted to mess with.

The way she looked and dressed reinforced that message. Her shoulder length auburn hair was pulled back in a relaxed ponytail, while her medical scrubs were crisply ironed. She also didn't wear any makeup, something that added a touch of severity to her face, while her sparkling hazel eyes and easy smile balanced it out.

After finishing with my vitals, she pulled back the dressing on my injured shoulder to check the wound site. Her eyes tightened briefly as she studied it.

"That's odd." She said it almost under her breath. Then more loudly, "Wasn't this stitched up just a few hours ago?"

"Yes," I said, a little confused. "Why?"

"Well," she said somewhat absently as she ran her fingers along the wound site, "I would have thought just by looking at this, that it had been stitched up several days ago. This wound has already moved well into the proliferative stage, something it shouldn't have done for at least another day or two."

She covered the wound back up with the bandages, her tight eyes smoothing back out into a natural smile as she did so. "I'll let Doctor Paxton know about it, but it looks like you have a very active healing factor that we didn't know about."

"Now," she pointed at the bed, "let's get you settled and see if your body can have that wound healed the rest of the way come morning."

She'd had me sit in one of the armchairs that was positioned near the window while she took my vitals. Now, as I stood to move toward the bed, I realized that I really didn't have the energy to do much more. With the adrenaline rush of the escape wearing off, a slow-moving flood of weariness was creeping in. Sitting down in the chair seemed to have been just the signal my body had been waiting for to shift gears from its flight or fight mode to its rest and recuperate mode.

I was a little surprised by the weariness considering all the time I had been unconscious in the past 48 hours. But when I mentioned it, Lilith explained that the drug-induced sleep I had been put into was not nearly as restful as the real thing, so I had not really gotten all that much sleep in the past two days, especially not when compared to the tremendous amount of stress my body had been put through during that same period of time.

As Lilith closed the curtains, turned off the lights, and shut the door to the room, I thought about all that had happened. Everything had changed so quickly in the last forty-eight hours that I had not really had time to process it all. I had gone from having fun with my team during the orienteering challenge, to watching in horror as friends were attacked and killed. In a moment of panic, I had felt my gifts explode into abilities beyond anything I had thought possible. The power that surged through me in those moments had made me feel alive in a way I had never before felt, but the anger and hatred that had fed that rush of power was not something I was proud of. The things I had done to those soldiers frightened me; I did not want to ever lose control like that again.

What chilled me even more was the way it had felt when I woke up and discovered that I could no longer use my ability at all, even to help those I cared about. Seeing Aiden at Sobrien's mercy, and realizing I could do nothing to protect him, had sent tendrils of horror through my whole being.

Aiden. I closed my eyes as the throbbing emptiness returned. I had felt so safe in his arms, but it had only been an illusion; an illusion that had been painfully dispelled by his own acknowledgment that I was nothing more to him than a set of orders he had to follow.

A slow trickle of tears slid down the side of my cheek and soaked into the pillow under my head. I wasn't sure why his words had hurt so much, but they had. As I silently cried myself to sleep, I took solace in the thought that I had left him and his enmity behind on the base. I would never have to see him again.

THE TWO DIRECTORATE soldiers stared at me with steely gazes as they came into the room and closed the door behind them. I stared back with a hard gaze of my own, not wanting to give any hint of the desperation I was feeling.

One of them took up a position on my right, the other on my left. The soldier on the right looked me up and down, taking careful stock of his target. He nodded his head as though arriving at a satisfactory conclusion, then turned away from me and began stripping off his shirt. He obviously didn't want to get blood on his clean uniform.

At the same time, Hadley turned to the soldier on my left and said with a mirthless laugh, "Told you that you'd need me along for this one."

The man rubbed his chin and shook his head ruefully. "You weren't wrong."

"Alright then," Hadley said as a slow wicked smile spread across his face. "Shall we deliver the rest of Beckwith's message?"

"My favorite part of this job." The soldier smirked back at him. Then he raised his chin slightly to the soldier at my other side. "Let's do this."

I automatically dropped back into a fighting stance, determined to at least try to defend myself. But neither soldier moved toward me. Instead, the smirking soldier removed a small device from his pocket and pressed the button on it.

I was startled to hear the sounds of dull thuds followed by grunts of pain coming from the device. The surprisingly full sound of the device made it sound as though someone in the room was taking a beating. I looked from the device to Hadley thoroughly confused. Hadley's smirk only grew at my bewilderment. Then he said softly, barely loud enough for me to hear over the continuing sounds from the device, "Sorry about the sucker punch, but it needed to look real."

Look real? I thought. It had been real enough. My stomach muscles ached where he had punched me, and I could feel at least one stitch pulling tight. And why was he apologizing to me? Not relaxing my stance, I asked guardedly, "What's goin' on, Hadley?"

"We are delivering a message on behalf of Director Beckwith. And then the three of us are leaving this ship. Scott here, or should I say Aiden Haskell," he pointed at the soldier who was continuing to strip down, "will be staying behind. Though I imagine he is going to be spending the rest of the voyage recovering from Beckwith's message."

Scott grunted softly, seeming to be amused by the idea that he would be doing any recovering. I looked from Hadley to the half-undressed man, even more confused. But as I looked closer at the soldier, I noticed that his hair was the same blue-black shade as mine was, and his lean, muscular body was a similar build to my own.

"Yer not really here tae deliver a message from Beckwith?" I asked it slowly, not thoroughly convinced that this wasn't a ruse.

"Oh, Beckwith does have a message for you," Hadley corrected me, "but not that type of message. He has a job he needs you to do, and he needs you to be untraceable in order to do it."

"What type of job?" I asked, still hesitant. Beckwith wasn't someone I wanted to work for.

"I can't tell you that at this time. But I think it's safe to say that you won't be disappointed by it when you find out what it is." He said the last part with a mischievous smile.

Before I could ask another question Scott walked over to us, a pile of half-folded clothes in his hands. "Enough talking," he said softly, "let's get this over with."

I took the pile, cautiously, not entirely sure what I was supposed to do with it but beginning to get the idea. Scott turned to the other soldier and said, "All right, Everett. Try to not hit me in the eye this time."

Everett grinned at him mischievously then suddenly swung his fist at Scott's face, splitting his lip and bruising his chin.

"Get changed, Haskell," Hadley said to me as Everett took another swing at Scott's face. "We have a flight to catch. Oh," he added, clearly having just remembered something else, "Beckwith asked me to give this back to you and to tell you to take more care with it next time."

Grip first, he held out the gun he had been pointing at me moments before. Only this time I recognized the gun; it was my own phase pistol.

When we opened the door a few minutes later, Scott was lying in a crumpled heap on the floor moaning faintly. He was now wearing my clothes and his face bore multiple cuts and bruises. It had swollen just enough to make it almost impossible to tell it wasn't me.

I, in turn, was now wearing his uniform and kept my face averted from the sailor so that he couldn't get a good look at it. Hadley was rubbing his own fist as though it were a little sore. He hitched his thumb back toward Scott and said, "Get someone to drag him back to his bed. I doubt he'll leave it for a few days. Just make sure he doesn't die; Beckwith wants him alive." He said the last part with a low growl of disgust as we walked past the sailor and headed toward the landing pad.

Chapter 25: Aiden Haskell

THE THREE-HOUR flight away from the ship was mostly a silent one. During that time, Hadley only answered my questions with a mischievous grin and the carefully worded explanation that I would not be disappointed by the mission.

With nothing else to do, I sat back in the transport's seat and watched the sun come up over a terrain that was hilly and green. While I'm not an expert at geography, I did know that Europe had been directly north of the freighter's last position on the Mediterranean Sea and that we had been approaching the boot of Italy when I had gone to bed. We were now traveling almost due north over what I assumed were Italy's hills.

As I watched, I allowed my mind to ponder the question of what the Director could possibly need from me that he couldn't have gotten from any number of the thousands of other soldiers at his disposal. Add to that the fact that a lot of effort was being taken to hide my participation in whatever it was that he had planned. The obvious answer hit me harder than Hadley's sucker punch had: It wasn't Aiden Haskell that was wanted; it was Sir Alistair Buccleuch.

I swallowed hard at this realization. There weren't many reasons that Alistair would be needed by a member of the Directorate's office, and coming from Director Beckwith himself, there were even fewer. Beckwith was no friend to the people of Scotland. In fact, he was one of the few men that I could say I truly hated. He was the man who had signed the death warrants of so many boys, including my own, when he had signed his name to the Scottish Accord and condemned us to our fates in the UFC military.

I wasn't anxious to find out what he wanted from me. In spite of Hadley's veiled hints, I didn't believe for a moment that it would be something I would enjoy. The only comfort that remained to me was the recognition of the obvious effort that had been taken to hide my transition back to my real identity. At least someone was ensuring that the UFC upheld their end of the agreement to keep my identity hidden.

As I pondered this, the terrain outside became increasingly mountainous until we were flying over snow-capped peaks and dazzling displays of fall foliage in the valleys below. Under other circumstances, I might have truly enjoyed the view. It was beautiful undisrupted country. There were virtually no roads or buildings through this region to interrupt the natural landscape, just endless views of nature at its best.

I was slightly surprised when the transport began its descent down into the middle of it. I guess I had been expecting it to continue over the mountains to some place beyond them, maybe even as far as Beckwith's office in England. Instead, we began dropping down right in the middle of the thickly wooded mountains.

We were halfway through the descent before I was finally able to see what the pilot was aiming for; a landing pad nearly hidden by the trees until we were immediately over it. However, there were no other buildings visible to indicate the purpose of the landing pad. Where we were going was still a mystery.

The only thing waiting for us once the transport landed were two Directorate soldiers. They were armed with phase rifles and standing in front of a small cave entrance that had been invisible from above. Hadley greeted the one on the left by name.

"Everything good, Cassie?"

"Yes, sir," she responded crisply. "Candidates Echo and Foxtrot arrived right on schedule about half an hour ago. They are with the Captain right now. Hotel, India, and Juliet are in route and approximately 20 minutes behind you, with the next four arriving at 1100 hours."

"Perfect. Then let's get this one checked in."

By checked in, he meant facial scans and voice IDs on the digi-pad Cassie had waiting for us. Only once the three of us had been cleared, and the pilot was back in the air, did Cassie lead us into the cave.

She led us back about twelve feet, just far enough for the cave's darkness to start closing in around us, but not so far that the darkness was absolute. Following the training I had received in my youth, I focused on the sounds that could be heard, while I gave my eyes the time they needed to adjust to the darkness.

There was the faintest clicking sound, as though a button had been pressed. "Control, this is Mountain Entrance," Cassie's voice came from a few feet in front of me, "I have three incomings to see the Captain."

"Affirmative Mountain Entrance," a male voice responded. "We have you on visual. Their check-in status has been received and they have been cleared to enter. The door will open in 5-4-3-2-1."

Click. Another faint sound proceeded the dimmest outline of movement as a section of the cave wall, or at least I thought it was the wall, swung open. But as we walked through the new opening, I was able to see that it was actually a thick metal door skillfully crafted to appear as a section of the cave wall.

Beyond that door, a well-lit hallway extended some thirty feet in front of us before turning sharply to the right. I quickly dismissed the idea that this was a military facility; the marble tiles on the floor and the crystal light sconces were too decorative for any base I had ever heard of. At the same time, there were carefully hidden cameras and several embellishments that looked suspiciously like openings for phase beams. Wherever we were, it was highly secure.

Beyond the first turn, there were several doors leading off of the hallway at fairly regular intervals. They gave no indication as to what was behind them, but each door had a small silver plaque on it that bore a name: Everest, Kilimanjaro, and Fuji were just a few of the names I was able to read as Hadley led the way. The door Hadley stopped in front of was labeled Matterhorn and was being guarded by two more soldiers.

"Candidate Golf for processing," he said to them.

As he spoke, he held up his tactical band to be scanned by one of the soldiers; Everett did the same.

"Yes, sir." The soldier nodded as his reader beeped approval of their IDs. "He's ready for you."

"Golf?" I asked softly as we waited while the soldier opened the door for us.

"No real names for candidates," Hadley replied under his breath.

The room beyond the door looked as though it had been intended for a use other than the one it was currently being put to. The smoothly arcing wall to the left was lined with wooden shelves, artfully decorated with candles and potted greenery, while the wall on the right was lined with skillfully crafted glass-doored cabinets through which I could see carefully folded piles of white towels and groupings of crystal decanters that held a variety of fluids. The whole of the back wall was a softly tinkling waterfall that gave the room a peaceful feel.

The masseuse table that would have normally been positioned at the center of the room had been moved off to the side. Instead, the center of the room now held a small table and two ornately carved wooden chairs that had been positioned so that they were facing each other. Already seated in the far chair was a smartly dressed old man. His aged, wrinkled hands were folded placidly on top of the walking stick that rested upright between his legs, but his hardened grey eyes hinted at a mind still quick with activity.

He wore no insignia, no indication of who he was; he didn't need any. I knew exactly who he was. Every soldier from Scotland did. It was Director Beckwith. I don't know why it had never crossed my mind that Beckwith would deliver his own message. I guess I had just assumed that he wouldn't demean himself by coming down to my level.

Shocked to find him suddenly in front of me, I froze for the briefest of seconds, waves of hatred racing through me, sudden and fierce. I did not want to be in the same room with him, but it was too late to turn back. Clenching my jaw, I forced myself to take the next step forward and enter the room.

With a voice that was closer to a command than an invitation, Beckwith indicated the seat across from him and said to me, "Please, have a seat."

Then, turning to Hadley and Everette he said, "Thank you, gentlemen; that will be all for now. I'd like to speak with this particular candidate alone."

Hadley looked slightly confused at this request, as though it were a variant from some previously established pattern, but he only nodded his head in recognition of the order before closing the door behind them on their way out.

Inwardly I was buzzing with adrenaline. From a young age, I had daydreamed about what I would do if I ever had the opportunity to be alone in a room with this man. Yet now that he was actually in front of me, none of those daydreams felt right. Maybe it was the look in his eyes, or maybe it was just my curiosity as to why he wanted to see me. Whatever the reason, I stiffly moved to the chair and sat down.

"Well," Sir Beckwith said. "It seems we owe you some thanks for recovering our asset."

Inwardly, I bristled even further at his reference to Alex as an asset, but outwardly I managed to keep my mouth shut and simply nod an acknowledgement of his thanks.

"It also seems," he continued, "that you are uniquely positioned to help me with a second task. You see, it recently came to my attention that a breech in security has necessitated the relocation of one of our assets. Unfortunately, due to the situation surrounding this particular asset, it would be unwise to move it through any of our normal channels. As a result, I am putting together a handpicked team of specialists who will be tasked with the movement and care of this asset."

"Now," he leaned forward ever so slightly as though to add weight to what he was about to tell me, "each candidate for this team has been vetted by my office based on their skill sets and their service record, and I am personally interviewing each candidate before they are permitted to move on to the next step in the selection process. But you are in a slightly different situation than the other candidates."

Instinctively, I understood that whether or not I was placed on this team depended on the opinion he formed of me in the next few minutes. What I didn't know was whether I wanted to be on this team. My first instinct was to avoid anything he was connected to. But something he had said was tugging at the back of my mind. I couldn't quite place my finger on what it had been, yet it seemed to be countering my instinctive desire to steer clear of this man's team.

Guardedly, I asked, "Different in what way, sir?"

"You're Scottish. Worse, you are the progeny of a traitor." He said it with such frigid force that it came across as a punch to the gut.

My jaw clenched in bitter anger. A traitor? Who was the traitor? The one who tried to overthrow the government that was suppressing millions or the one who murdered tens of thousands of innocent boys by signing his name to the Accord? I didn't say what I was thinking out loud. Instead, I did what I had learned to do early on in my life in order to keep myself out of trouble: I quickly smoothed my clenched jaw into a half-smile and laughed lightly instead. "You'll have tae forgive me for that, sir. I wasn't given a choice in who me parents would be."

His eyes glinted darkly at my attempt at humor, and he waited a split second for my half-smile to slide nervously away before he continued. "I've made no secret of my distrust for the Scottish people. And no one can deny that I have had good reason to hate them. However," he paused slightly, as though carefully thinking through what he was going to say next, "I also recognize that my reasons for hating them occurred long before you were born, and that it would be ignoble of me to hold you accountable for the faults of those now dead. Instead, my sense of fairness requires that I hold you accountable for your own actions. So, let's take a look at those instead."

He removed a small digi-pad from the pocket of his jacket and appeared to be scanning through it, though I suspected that he was already familiar with what was written there.

"It says here that you were drafted into the UFC military at the age of fifteen. In spite of your youth at that time, you came very close to being awarded the Honor Graduate Ribbon and being named the top of your graduating class. Yet, instead of placing in the top three as you were on track to do, you failed to even complete the final test course, dropping your graduating position down to fourth in your class, and out of the immediate line of commendations."

"Interesting," he murmured, seemingly to himself as though noting an oddness in the report, but not having a desire to discuss it at that moment.

"Then, after graduation, you applied for, tested for, and were accepted into the Special Forces Division." He glanced up briefly from his digi-pad. "Not bad for someone who failed to complete the final testing course."

Not giving me a chance to respond, he continued reading, "While serving in the Special Forces, you served multiple tours throughout the world including two duty tours in Iraq, one in Iran, one in Saudi Arabia, and another in Egypt. You have one hundred eighty-two successful direct-action missions with your unit and an additional sixty-four special reconnaissance missions that resulted in the information needed for successful military strikes. On two different occasions, your direct commanders even recommended you for medals of honor related to acts of bravery in the field of combat. But, and now here is the interesting part, it says that each of those recommendations was followed up shortly by some act of foolishness on your part that insured the recommendation was denied."

Straining hard to keep my laughter light in spite of the feeling that he was closing the exits of some unseen trap, I responded, "I guess I just didn't dae a good enough job. I'll have tae dae better next time."

Beckwith didn't smile back at me. Instead, he continued to study my record with his cool grey eyes and replied almost absently, "Oh, I think you have done a very careful job at being just good enough without being so good as to attract attention. What I want to know is why. And why you suddenly decided to change tactics when you broke the speed record. That is the mystery that I need solved before I decide whether or not you are going to be given the opportunity to join this team."

He sat back, folding his hands in his lap. "So, Sir Buccleuch, kindly explain to me why."

My chest tightened as I realized this old man had seen far more of the truth than I was comfortable with. I had been careful in my military service to stay below the radar. Always performing a few steps behind others so that they were the focus of attention and I was mostly ignored as the one who just wasn't quite as good. I had learned early that those in the spotlight were exposed to the most scrutiny. It was attention I didn't want. Yet, in spite of my carefully calculated choices, I had somehow managed to place myself directly in the focus of one of the UFC's most powerful men.

How was I supposed to answer him? Tell him that my father had broken the law by ensuring that I received the best combat training from the best private instructors available the moment I had been old enough to know one end of a gun from the other? Tell him that I had not even been running my fastest the day I broke the speed record? Or that I didn't trust the UFC any more than he trusted Scotland, which is why I had always carefully guarded the true level of my abilities from anyone but my family? No. I couldn't tell him the truth about any of those things. Instead, I chose a halfway truth, hoping it would be enough to satisfy him.

"I, uhm," I cleared my throat uncomfortably but didn't back down from his cold gaze. "I guess I was tryin' tae avoid trouble."

"Trouble? How so?" He raised one eyebrow as though challenging my answer.

"Well, sir, you aren't th' only one who doesn't like Scotsmen, and th' men in me graduatin' class were even less fond of bein' shown up by a fifteen-year-old Scottish boy." That much was true. He could fact check that and would find that I had indeed been reprimanded for getting into a fight the day before the final field test.

"I was informed, uhm, rather roughly, that it would be better for me health if I didn't show up for th' final test. When I did show up, a few of them decided tae ensure that I wasn't able tae finish the course." I paused, swallowing my discomfort, and instead allowing my lips to form into a slow

256

wicked grin. "But I wasn't th' only one who didn't finish th' field test that day."

"I imagine they weren't in too good of shape after that either." He smiled slightly, almost as though he were trying not to.

I allowed my smile to grow. "No, sir. I don't believe they were. But after that experience, I decided tae be more cautious about showin' off me abilities."

"Then why break the speed record?"

My grin slowly faded. I had fleetingly hoped that my bravado would have sidetracked him from that part of his question, but it was clear he wasn't going to be derailed. And somehow, I felt sure that a half-truth wouldn't work here; it was all or nothing on this one.

"That was actually an accident, sir."

"You accidentally broke the record?" His voice was thick with disbelief. "How do you accidentally break a speed record?"

I didn't have to feign embarrassment this time as I shrugged. "I, uhm, got distracted by a pretty face with a quick wit."

"Go on."

"I, uhm, had already run a few five-minute warm-up laps when the girl came on tae the track looking like she was intent on outrunnin' a rough day. So, I decided tae help her out by makin' her smile."

"And just how did you do that?"

I felt a slight flush rising in my cheeks. "I ran backwards, crossed me eyes, and stuck me tongue out at her."

Beckwith stared at me for a moment, surprise crossing his face, and then he began to laugh a deep guttural laugh.

257

"And did it work?" he asked when his laughter calmed down.

"Aye, sir; she was smilin' when we parted ways. But then she did somethin' that caught me off guard. I had cheekily told her that she must be part of th' ABC unit that was stationed at th' base."

"The ABC unit?" he asked, obviously confused.

I ducked my head slightly in embarrassment; it really had been a stupid thing to say. "The, uhm, Absolutely Beautiful, Crazily Delicious, Entirely Female Group."

"I see." His half-smile was back. "And how did she respond to that?"

"She posted a scrollin' message across th' bottom of th' track's board. It said that th' ABC unit also included Adorably Bonkers, Clearly Desperate, Engagingly Funny Guys. Her response was th' most perfect comeback I'd ever received tae one of me jokes. It left me grinnin' like a fool and thinkin' about her more than me runnin'. The next thing I knew, alarms were going off and scientists were comin' onto th' track wantin' tae congratulate me on breakin' th' record."

Beckwith's smile was gone as he steepled his fingers under his chin and leaned back in his chair. He was silent for a moment before he finally spoke.

"Am I to understand that you knew you were capable of breaking the speed record before that time, but you purposely held back to avoid attention?"

I was hesitant to confirm a truth I had purposely kept secret, but it was clear that his question was only a formality; he already knew the truth.

"Aye, sir."

"And am I to also understand that this young lady is the reason you decided to accept the offer to join the base's Specialist Core?"

Again, I was hesitant to admit that truth, but he had clearly discerned what I had only recently admitted to myself. "Aye."

"And now that you are being transferred away from this young lady, what are your intentions?"

I knew the answer I was supposed to give. My father had raised me with the knowledge that my life belonged to the UFC to do with as they pleased, and I was to be ready at all times to serve with honor wherever they sent me. But at this moment, I desperately wished I had been permitted to stay on the base, to protect Alex from the UFC.

I wondered if Beckwith sensed the truth; he had read me correctly on everything else so far.

"I would've been happier tae stay on th' base with her, sir," I said slowly, meeting his gaze resolutely, "but I will serve, with honor, anywhere yae send me."

"I see. Very well then." He slapped his knees, seeming to come to a decision. "Sir Buccleuch, I am going to send you home for a few days."

That caught me off guard. "Home? Sir?"

His lips twitched into an almost smile that vanished just as quickly as it had formed. "Yes, soldier. Home. You're not opposed to that I assume?"

"Uh…no, sir. Just a little confused. I thought yae said yae needed help movin' an asset. How is sendin' me home goin' tae accomplish that?"

This time he really did smile. "Why, you are going to take it with you, of course. Who in the world would expect me to entrust you, a son of Scotland, with the movement of such a valuable asset?"

Of course not! No one would believe for a moment that the UFC leadership had entrusted a Scotsman with anything of value, because it was well known that they didn't. We were forced to serve in the UFC's military, but we were not trusted with anything more than fighting on the front lines where we could kill the UFC's enemies for them and, more often than not, be killed ourselves.

That brief flash of bitter anger must have crossed my face because Beckwith held up his hands as though telling me to hold off on my anger until I had heard him out.

"Now, I am not an unreasonable man. I recognize that a lot has been required of you as the firstborn son of the Duke of Buccleuch. And up to this point you have performed your duties admirably. So, allow me to make you an offer in exchange for your services."

I waited cautiously, not trusting his intent.

"Upon the successful delivery of this asset to its new destination, I will offer you a choice: You may choose to continue your service with a permanent assignment to the team tasked with the care of that asset, or I will personally sign your discharge forms, bringing an end to your required military service. You will be free to move on with your life in whatever way you see fit."

I was stunned. No Scotsman had ever been released from service while he was still young and fit to serve. Was it possible?

Skeptically I asked, "Why are yae givin' me a choice?"

His eyes were twinkling with mischief. "Let's just say that it's an added incentive to ensure the asset is safely delivered."

"Now," he continued without pause, "Hadley will take you to meet Captain Marcellus next. There will be the brief formality of a final interview, but I see no reason you won't be accepted onto the team. And then, later this evening he will fill you and the rest of the team in on the logistics of how this is all going to take place."

Beckwith had stood as he said the last part. He held out his hand to me now. "Congratulations, Sir Buccleuch. And my best wishes for a quick, successful mission."

IT HAD BEEN a busy morning, but Lilith had insured that I carefully paced myself, even to the point of lecturing the Captain when he failed to follow her instructions as to how much time I was allowed to be in meetings before I was required to take a break. In spite of that, I had already met with some fifteen candidates.

They were brief meetings, not more than twenty minutes each with only a short break between each one so that we could discuss the pros and cons of each of them before moving on to the next person.

I had been pleased to find Thatcher, Rockman, and Lance among the candidates. They were easy picks for me, and Hadley had readily agreed to each of them. Then there had been four others from the Ghana Base that I recognized and liked, though none of them had been in my training group; so, I was only somewhat acquainted with them before today's meeting.

Ginerva was an Italian Beta who could both see and hear across great distances. She had been on base a whole year before I got there but had remained on base instead of transferring out because she was working closely with the scientists there to narrow her hearing accuracy down to quiet conversations at distances of up to half a mile away.

Absko was a Kenyon Charlie with the incredible ability to throw objects great distances with uncanny accuracy. I had once seen him flick a bottle cap and hit a fly that was droning in the air twenty feet across the room from him.

Dontre was a Canadian Beta whose body was capable of adapting to extremes in temperature. Frozen icebergs and blazing deserts were not a problem for him. He had done a display of fire walking during a recent class, even holding a live coal in his hand for almost two whole minutes without so much as a blister or scorch mark.

Dupré was French, like me, only she had actually grown up in France so she had that rich, romantic accent that was common among the French. Having never lived in France, I had never developed a similar accent. But I had studied the language in school for five years, so I at least understood what they were saying when Captain Marcellus started talking to her in French.

"Dans quelle branche de la force armée avez-vous servi?"

"Armée de Terre."

"Pourquoi avez-vous choisi celui-là?"

"J'ai peur des hauteurs donc l'Armée de l'Air était sortie, et je n'aime pas nager, alors j'ai pensé que je devrais éviter la marine."

I translated for Hadley who was looking lost as he listened to their interchange. "What branch of the military did you serve in? The Army. Why did you choose that branch? I don't like heights, so the Air Force was not the best choice, and I don't swim so the Navy was a bad choice."

"Good translation, Alex." Captain Marcellus nodded to me. "I am glad to see that you were paying attention in your language classes. However, she said that she doesn't like to swim, not that she couldn't swim."

I was slightly annoyed that I had missed the translation, and even more annoyed that Marcellus had called me out on it, but I didn't have time to dwell on my annoyance as Marcellus returned back to his conversation with Dupré.

It turned out that Dupré had served in the canine division. She had been assigned a service dog named Gamine which was the French word for kid. He was a Golden Labrador who had a knack for knowing when an enemy was nearby. Whether the enemy was hidden in the bushes or hunkered down in a building a hundred yards away, he seemed to have a sixth sense that warned him when trouble was around and he in turn would warn her.

Dupré's Beta abilities were to hear sounds outside of the normal range of hearing and to smell scents that were nearly undetectable to others. Combined with the unusually strong bond the two seemed to have that allowed them to understand each other without words, they had proven a very effective team in the field.

She and Gamine had been transferred to Ghana Base two months ago under the auspice of a brief period of rest between deployments. But the base's scientists had quickly made it clear that the opportunity to study how she and Gamine worked together had been a major factor in the decision to have their break scheduled at Ghana Base.

The final eight candidates had been soldiers from all over the world. They brought with them a wide variety of skills and backgrounds. With one exception, I had enjoyed getting to know them all and was looking forward to working with them. The one exception had been an American from California who had been a little too pushy with his suggestions and ideas. Even Hadley had been clearly annoyed with him by the time the interview was over.

When we had delayed lunch for the second time because we wanted to keep talking to candidates, Lilith ordered the guards at the door out of her way with a steely gaze and then informed us that if we didn't stop for lunch immediately, she would pull rank and send me back to bed.

To tell the truth, I was glad for the forced break. As much as I hated the idea of being treated like an invalid, the fact was, this was proving to be more tiring than I had thought it would be.

As I walked out onto the balcony where lunch had been set out for us, I took a deep breath of the afternoon mountain air. It had a clean crispness to it that was both refreshing and rejuvenating. I could smell the musky scent of the spruce trees, the rich earthiness of the soil, and just a hint of the sweet-smelling edelweiss that grew wild in the area.

Moving to lean against the balcony's railing, I found myself captivated by the peaceful tranquility of the forest around me. A gentle breeze stirred the vibrant green branches of the forest's numerous trees while the sun's golden rays created a dappled pattern of shadows and lights. Not far away, a small blue chested bird trilled from its perch on a tree branch while a second bird flared its wings to land at its side.

I smiled to myself as I watched the two of them begin to prance back and forth along the branch in a ritualistic courting dance. In the dappled streams of light that shone through the branches, the two birds' chests shone in brilliant flashes of blue that brought to memory the way Aiden's hair had shone in the sunlight when he had been sitting in the tree branch grinning at me and teasing me about the backpack that was in charge of the enemy soldiers.

My smile faded suddenly at the memory and the sun no longer felt warm. I wrapped my arms around myself as a tremulous shiver shook through me.

"You okay?" I jumped slightly at Hadley's words. He had come out onto the balcony to stand beside me, but I had been more focused on the view in front of me than the people behind me.

I forced my smile back into place. "Yea, I'm good; just lost in thought."

His head was tipped in slight concern. "Anything you want to talk about? It's been a crazy few days."

"Crazy?" I didn't have to force my smile this time. "Is that what we're calling all this?"

He shrugged with a grin of his own. "Well, I'm sure I could come up with a few more creatively descriptive words if you'd like."

I chuckled lightly. "No, actually, I think crazy works rather well. If someone had told me two days ago what was going to happen and where I'd be now, I would have told them that they were crazy."

"Speaking of crazy events, has Captain Marcellus told you the plan yet for spiriting you away to this new school?" There was a mischievous glint in his eyes that indicated he knew what the plan was and knew equally well that I did not.

I shook my head with an exasperated laugh. "You know very well that he hasn't." Hadley had been dropping veiled hints all morning that it was something I would find especially enjoyable but had thus far refused to give me any actual facts as to what the plan was.

The twinkle in his eyes sparkled and shone as he held up his hands to ward off my exasperation. "Ok, ok. Just asking."

I rolled my eyes and turned away. "I'm going to get some lunch while you keep your secrets to yourself."

The first candidate after lunch wasn't particularly impressive. He was a career soldier from South America who had recently rotated back from the front lines after completing his fourth tour in the field. His fine motor skills made him exceptionally good at controlling drones, but his gruff military bearing and short curtness in answering questions made him seem unapproachable and more of a loner than a group player. While his MER sheet, Military Experience Report, was impressive to look at on the screen, in real life he wasn't someone I wanted to work with.

The next candidate to come through the door was the same tousled haired Asian teenager who had been with Director Beckwith in my hospital room. He came in with a lopsided grin and a relaxed wave of hello. Captain Marcellus greeted him as Candidate Alpha.

All of the candidates had been given code names that were being used until the team was formally chosen and each had officially accepted their new position. They weren't coming to me in alphabetical order, so I could only guess that the names had been assigned through some other system, perhaps the order Beckwith had decided to make them candidates. If that was true, then this boy was one of Beckwith's first picks for my team.

Captain Marcellus invited him to take a seat and then preceded to review his credentials out loud. Surprisingly, this candidate's MER sheet had his real name on it, not the moniker that had been assigned to him.

"Huang Zhaohui," the Captain read the name from the MER on his screen. Well, actually, that's the way his name was written on the report I had in front of me, not the way Captain Marcellus pronounced it.

The boy winced as Marcellus butchered the pronunciation. "Just call me Harry, please."

Marcellus grimaced slightly in embarrassment. "Sorry about that. Harry it is. Your records indicate that you graduated at the top of your class three years ago at the age of fifteen from Peking University in China with five concurrent doctorate degrees in Cyber Information Technology, Neuro Networking Science, Integrated Systems Architecture, Cybersecurity Systems, and finally in Digital Structure Editing.

"However, your total work experience consists of an entry-level technology position at the UFC Directorate Building in Greece that lasted for a mere two weeks before you were terminated for attempting to 'hack' into the UFC mainframe."

While his collegiate success was quite impressive, his listed work experience looked odd to me. Beckwith didn't seem like the type who permitted less than the best into his inner circle. So why was Harry working for Beckwith if he had been terminated, and why didn't his MER sheet include his current employment with Beckwith?

Marcellus seemed to be thinking along the same lines. "Care to explain why a teenager with no previous military service and almost no real work experience, who was fired for attempting to hack into an unhackable system has been recommended by Director Beckwith himself for our military team's position as Lead Technology Expert?"

Harry leaned forward, his confident grin not wavering one bit as a result of Marcellus' doubtful tone. "Because I didn't fail."

"You didn't fail what?" Marcellus asked, with a frown.

"I didn't fail to hack into the system. In fact, I got in so deep and so cleanly that I had access to everything, and no alarms had been triggered. No one had even realized that the system had been hacked until I took over all of the computers in the Directorate Building and left my calling card."

"Your calling card?" I asked, slightly hesitant to admit that I had no idea what a calling card was, but curious as to what benefit it gave Harry to leave one on Beckwith's computer.

"It was a 19th century practice." Harry turned to talk directly to me, actually seeming to be excited for the opportunity to share what he knew. His gestures, as he explained the term to me, were full of energy.

"It was a piece of paper with your name on it to let someone know you had stopped by their house or business. In my case it was a hundred locked, blank screens with my name and contact info displayed on them. After two days of their best technicians trying to get me out of their system, Beckwith himself called me and offered me a job. I've been working with him now for the past three years as one of his personal assistants."

"I see," Captain Marcellus said with a slight frown. "You successfully hacked into a single system and were offered a top position. But how does that qualify you for…"

While he had been talking, Harry had been fiddling with his tactical band. He wasn't really looking at it as he fiddled, so I thought that he was just absently fidgeting with it. But before Captain Marcellus finished his sentence, the screen of the digi-pad in my hands suddenly changed to show an ariel image of a lodge in the mountains. The moving image began to zoom in closer on a single window. Continuing to zoom in, I could now see a meeting room with four individuals sitting at a conference table. I recognized the faces of those individuals. In shock, I glanced up at the window across the room from me. There was a small drone, silently hovering at its center. It waggled in a sudden lopsided up-down motion as though waving to me.

I began to laugh in surprise. This lodge had a highly sophisticated defense system that was supposed to be able to identify and eliminate drones that attempted to approach the building. Captain Marcellus had explained the impressive defense setup the lodge's owner had put in place which allowed him to guard his and his guests' secrets. Yet Harry had managed to somehow bypass the system while holding a conversation with us and had flown a drone right up to our conference room.

Startled by my laughter, Hadley and the Captain looked at me in concern. I showed them my screen. Hadley's eyes narrowed and he began to scan the room for the camera before finally catching sight of the drone behind the window. Marcellus seemed to not be concerned about the actual location of the camera, and instead focused on Harry.

"Are you behind this?" he asked gruffly. His tone made it difficult for me to tell whether he was angry about the drone or amused by it.

Harry, who had now relaxed back into his chair with his arms folded while beaming from ear to ear responded confidently, "Captain, I know I'm young and my record is not much to look at, but there is no system I can't get into. I am the best you will find when it comes to technology."

"I'm not bragging," he hurried to assure the Captain when a frown appeared on his face, "it's simply the truth. You won't have to worry about someone infiltrating the school's system because I will be there to make sure that they can't."

Seriousness replaced his smile for just a moment as Harry looked directly at me. "Beckwith wants you to have the best protection available. He was willing to give me up as his Personal Aide to ensure that you would have it."

I smiled softly at him, not just comforted by his assurance that Beckwith cared about more than my abilities, but also pleasantly surprised by Harry's obvious willingness to fill the position of my digital guardian. I looked to the Captain and Hadley and nodded my head. Hadley nodded back with the slightest of movements.

"Very well," Marcellus said, standing up and holding out his hand to Harry, "welcome to the team."

As Hadley showed Harry out of the room and went to get the next candidate, I forwarded my screen to the next MER sheet. Beckwith's team had set up the MER sheets in a specific format. The candidate's code name was typed in large, bold letters across the top. This one read GOLF.

The next section gave a brief outline of their military expertise. Candidate Golf was a five-year veteran of the UFC's Special Forces Reconnaissance and Recovery Division. He or she, the form didn't specify which at this point, had specialist rankings as an expert in both Hand-to-Hand Combat and Tactical Reconnaissance.

The third section went into more detail about their military career. Candidate Golf had one hundred eighty-two successful reconnaissance missions and ninety-six direct-action missions. I stopped and read that twice. Two hundred and seventy-eight missions in five years?! That was a lot of missions! More than double what I had seen from any other candidate so far. Whoever this candidate was, the military had kept them busy.

I continued reading. They had graduated from basic training fourth in their class, scored a ninety-one percent on the Special Forces Test, had a respectable firing range score of ninety-two percent, and an impressive two-minute, forty-three-second time on the outdoor obstacle course.

They spoke Basic, English, and Scottish Gaelic fluently and had some minimal fluency in Arabic. While the MER sheet didn't tell me where the candidate originated from, with that combination of languages they were probably from the English Islands at the bare minimum and more likely from the Scottish North specifically. If I had to guess, I would say that the Arabic had been learned as part of their Special Forces Reconnaissance training.

Out in the hall, I could hear twin sets of footsteps approaching, their measured staccato echoing off the tile floors. The next candidate would be here any moment. I took the last few seconds before they arrived to scan through the final section of the report, where the candidate's Alpha Ranking and any data relevant to that ranking were listed.

They were a Charlie…their ability was listed as running… they had been officially clocked at speeds of up to forty-two miles-per-hour bursts during the fifty-meter dash…their most recently tested mile speed was one minute fifty-eight seconds…

I dropped the digi-pad with a clatter onto the table, my trembling fingers suddenly unable to maintain their grip. Aiden! The next candidate was Aiden! The throbbing emptiness of the night before raced back in with a vengeance; painful and harsh.

"You okay?" Marcellus asked softly, looking up at me with sudden concern. Hesitantly, I nodded my head as much to assure him as I did to convince myself. But as the door opened, I wasn't so sure.

Following our previously set pattern, Hadley stood just outside the door and announced the next candidate by their assigned moniker. "Captain Marcellus, this is candidate Golf for your consideration." He then stepped back and allowed the candidate to enter the room.

Afraid to have my fears confirmed, I kept my eyes on the digi-pad I had dropped. However, the edges of my vision couldn't escape the vibrant shock of blue hair or the crisp edges of the Directorate soldier's uniform that showed off his lean form as he came through the doorway; it was Aiden.

My heart skipped a beat, leaving me even more confused and lost. He had rejected me; I wanted nothing more to do with him. So why did his sudden appearance stir emotions that were so completely opposite what I wanted?

Aiden's normally fluid movements were likewise interrupted by a missed step and an audible gasp, "Alex!" But being the absolute professional he was, he quickly recovered and continued into the room.

"I see you already know each other." Marcellus said it with a hint of curiosity.

"We dae," Aiden said with his normal dazzling smile. A slight gruffness in his voice was the only sign of his quick recovery from the shock of seeing me.

"I should say they do." Hadley chuckled, somehow amused by the situation, though I couldn't imagine why. As he moved to take his normal seat on the opposite side of Marcellus he explained, "These two have become somewhat of an iconic pair on base. Except that they haven't figured out what everyone else can so clearly see."

Out of the corner of my eye, I saw Marcellus turn to look at me, his eyebrow slightly raised in question, but my mind was screaming too loudly for me to fully register his look. *I hadn't figured it out?! Hadley was wrong! I knew exactly how Aiden felt about me because I had heard him say it: he hated everything about me!* The bitter disappointment I had felt at Aiden's changed behavior toward me in the hospital came creeping back in like a painfully sharp dagger that threatened to split me open from the inside out.

Oblivious to the pain Aiden's presence was causing me, Hadley went on, "Aiden is also the one who carried Alex out of the caves and brought her safely back to base."

"So, you're the one," Marcellus said solemnly, then stood up and extended his hand. "Thank you. I am in your debt."

Startled, I looked up at the Captain. *In his debt? He considered himself to be in Aiden's debt? Why?* If anyone was in Aiden's debt for coming after me in the caves, it was me, not the Captain. Except that I knew the truth: the only repayment Aiden wanted was for me to stay as far away from him as he could get me.

Aiden stepped forward to accept the Captain's proffered hand. "No debt, sir. I'm just glad I was able tae be there for her." There was a tone in his voice that caught me off guard. I couldn't think exactly what that tone meant, but without intending to, I looked over at him.

I found his brilliant blue eyes staring right at me, as though he were studying me intently. Then his eyes locked with mine and, for the briefest of seconds, I felt myself being drawn in and nearly lost myself to the surge of raw emotion that roared through me. The only thing that saved me was his voice as his lips parted and I heard him begin to say, "Alex, I'm sorry…" In that moment, I realized with painful clarity that

I couldn't bear to hear a second rejection from him. What small thread of dignity and self-composure I was desperately hanging on to would be torn apart if he spoke.

I stood suddenly, knocking my chair backward. "I need to go!" I hurried around the table in an attempt to escape before any of their shocked faces could clear and they had a chance to respond. Aiden, however, recovered before I had even rounded the table. He took a step toward me, reaching for my free hand as though to stop me. "Alex?"

"Don't," I said tremulously as I sidestepped out of his reach. The shaking fingers of my unslung arm fumbled briefly on the door handle, and then I was through it and practically running down the hall. I didn't slow when I heard the door open and Hadley's concerned voice calling, "Alex. What's wrong?"

I just shook my head, not trusting myself to speak without also releasing the tears of embarrassment and frustration I was barely holding back. I didn't stop moving until I suddenly found Hadley in front of me, his hands on my shoulders forcing me to stop. He looked at me intently, taking in the paleness of my face and the shuddering draws of my breath as I fought back the tears that were brimming in my eyes.

"Alex," he asked searchingly, "did something happen between the two of you?"

I shook my head adamantly, not wanting to admit that Aiden had rejected me for what I was, or that I still desperately wanted him near me in spite of it. I finally forced myself to say, "I'm just tired. I've pushed too far for one day."

He nodded his head slightly as though considering that it was possible, though his expression clearly showed that he didn't believe that was all it was. Regardless of what he believed or not, he touched the com button on his tactical band. "Nurse Alcott," that was Lilith's last name, "Alex is coming your way. Would you please meet her and make sure she gets to bed?"

Lilith's response was immediate. "I'm on my way."

I made to go around him, but Hadley stopped me once more. "Alex," he said earnestly, forcing my attention momentarily away from my desperate need to flee. "If Aiden has done something wrong, I need you to tell me right now."

Something wrong? You mean besides hating me? Or besides showing up after I had already cried myself to sleep with my only comfort being the certainty that I would never have to see him again? Those answers were screaming so loudly in my mind that I didn't see how Hadley wouldn't be able to hear them.

But when he continued to search my face, waiting for an answer, I finally managed to choke out, "He did his job. Nothing more." Hadley's expression clearly showed that he didn't understand my answer, but before he could question me further, Lilith's light steps could be heard moving rapidly in our direction.

Realizing he didn't have much time before she was within hearing range, Hadley lowered his voice and asked a question I had been hoping he wouldn't ask. "Are you okay with Aiden being on the team?"

I shook my head, not wanting to answer. No! I wasn't okay with him being on the team. At the same time, I desperately wanted him to be. As much as I wanted to never see Aiden again, just being in the same room with him had rekindled the draw I felt toward him. I didn't want him to leave; I didn't want him to stay. The contradiction was both emotionally and physically painful. It felt as though my heart was being pressed between a vice.

Hadley squeezed my shoulders. I think he meant it as a reassurance, but instead, it felt like a trap closing in on me. "Alex, I need your answer on this one."

I didn't want to choose, to be the one who decided whether he would stay or go. I just wanted to escape the pain of the question, to escape the intensity of Hadley's searching gaze. Gathering all of my strength, I raised my eyes to his and lied softly, "I don't care. You make the decision on this one." Then, not giving him a chance to push me any further, I pulled free of his hands and fled.

Chapter 27: Aiden Haskell

HADLEY CAME BACK into the room a few moments later, a look of intense contemplation on his face. Whatever Alex had said to him, it had given him a lot to think about. For my part, I was stunned almost beyond thinking. The shock of seeing Alex and realizing that she was the asset Beckwith had been referring to had caught me completely off guard. I had been so stunned that I had even stumbled my step.

Less than twenty-four hours ago, when I had left her side, she had been unconscious in a hospital bed, battered and bruised; it had torn me apart to leave her like that, knowing that I could do nothing more to protect her. Seeing her now, still bruised but conscious and safe, and knowing that I was being offered a second chance to protect her, had sent a rush of euphoria through me that had left me grinning like a fool.

But then she met my eyes. There had been so much pain and fear in that look. And when I reached for her hand, the way she had drawn back and the trembling of her hand as she fled the room, it was as though she was terrified of me. All of my instincts to protect her were screaming at me that something was very wrong. At the same time, the realization that I was somehow the source of that wrongness sent tendrils of ice racing through my heart, constricting my chest and making it hard to breathe. What could have happened to cause Alex to react that way? What had I done that made her so afraid of me?

The Captain's deep voice mirrored my thoughts. "What was that about?" He asked it firmly, with a tone that suggested he was not at all pleased with Alex's sudden departure.

Hadley, somewhat distracted, answered, "She said she wasn't feeling well and needed to go lay down. I had Lilith meet her and take her to her room. But there is clearly something else going on."

Then Hadley turned on me, his thought process seeming to focus in on a suspected answer. "Aiden, did something happen in those caves that we don't know about?"

I hesitated in my answer, racking my brain for something to explain her behavior, but nothing came. "No," I finally answered with a weak shrug.

The Captain, who was watching me through thoughtfully narrowed eyes, sat back in his chair and folded his arms across his broad chest. "Kid, I've read Dollard's report about the mission and the incidents that followed, but I think I'd like to hear about it from you. Why don't we start with what happened during the orienteering challenge?"

"Aye, sir," I replied automatically. As I gave the report for the second time in as many days, my voice was mechanical and empty. My mind was only halfway on what I was saying. The rest of it was scrutinizing every moment that I had been with Alex.

The Captain and Hadley poured over everything I told them as well. They were especially interested in why I had left Alex alone with Estradé, though neither condemned me for

279

my action. Their interest seemed to be more on what had caused me to change my mind and whether she knew my reasons.

Finally, Hadley sat back, his mind clearly calculating through everything I had said, studying every angle a second and third time, searching for something we had missed. At last, he shook his head, clearly having not reached any solid conclusions. "Well, I'll go see her in the morning and see if I can get her to talk about it. In the meantime," he looked at the Captain, "if it's all right with you, I suggest we move forward with the other preparations."

Marcellus nodded his approval, but he had one piece of unfinished business. "And this candidate here?" His expression was stern and cold, as though suggesting that he thought I should be sent back to the ship instead of being permitted to stay.

My heart sank. For the first time since entering the room, it occurred to me that I might not be permitted to join this team after all. A sinking feeling of desperation exploded inside my chest, warning me that the nightmares of the previous night were all about to become a reality.

I opened my mouth to argue that I should be permitted to stay, but Hadley raised his hand to cut me off.

"He needs to be part of the team," he said simply, as though it were obvious. "Alex told me to make the decision on this candidate, and everything I know tells me he's the key to getting her safely to that school. We can work through what is bothering her later."

The Captain muttered something under his breath, shaking his head in exasperation. But then he squared his shoulders and turned on me with a steely gaze. "If I find out, boy, that there is something you are hiding from me, or that you did anything to hurt her, there will not be a dark hole deep enough in this world for you to hide in. Do I make myself clear?"

"Aye, sir." I swallowed hard, not doubting for a moment that he meant it.

"Good," he barked. "Now, Hadley will show you to your room."

***

I SLEPT A sleepless night alternating between sitting in the over-plump blue armchair that complemented the room's still-made bed and pacing back and forth between the room's other furnishings, wracking my brain for what I might have done wrong to upset Alex. But by the time the first rays of morning light began to peak through the window, I still had no answers. I was also still dressed in the same Directorate soldier uniform I had borrowed the previous day, though it was no longer crisply ironed.

A knock at my door drew me away from my fruitless thoughts. I opened the door to find Hadley patiently waiting. He took one look at the dark circles under my eyes and said with a wry smile, "You didn't sleep, did you?"

"No," I said with a shake of my head as I opened the door wider to let him in. "I just don't get it. What happened?"

"Not sure yet. Alex is up, but that nurse of hers is pretty strict about visitors. She won't let me talk to her until after breakfast."

Hadley handed me a black bag that had my name on it. "New uniforms for the team. Beckwith had one made up for each potential candidate," he explained as I looked from the bag to him.

"Why don't you get showered and changed, then join me in the common room for some food."

Fifteen minutes later I walked into the common area to find a buffet of breakfast foods that had been arranged for the ten or so candidates who were gathered there. A quick glance told me that I knew a surprising number of those men and women, including Thatcher and Rockman.

I grabbed a plate of food and made my way over to the table where Thatcher, Rockman, and a few others from Ghana Base that I recognized, but didn't know the names of, were sitting.

"Mornin'," I said as I joined the group.

Rockman looked up sharply, saw me, and then swore softly. Still grumbling, he pulled his wallet out of his back pocket, removed a bill, and handed it to Thatcher who was smiling mysteriously. Several of the others around the table were grinning as well.

"Glad you could make it," Thatcher drawled as he put the bill into his pocket and then took another bite of his food.

Before I could ask what that was all about, Hadley and Captain Marcellus came into the room. Everyone quickly stood up at attention.

"As you were." The Captain's voice carried easily through the room. The two of them then began to circulate, talking to the candidates and generally checking on how everyone was doing.

"So, what happened last night?" the girl next to Rockman asked curiously as she deftly fed a piece of bacon to the dog waiting patiently at her side. "I thought we were supposed to have a briefing at nineteen hundred hours?"

"We were," one of the other candidates responded, "but something must have happened during one of the interviews.

I saw Alex and her nurse leaving the interview area and heading toward the North wing yesterday afternoon. Alex looked pretty shaken."

"Does anyone know who they were interviewing?" someone else asked.

"No idea. They've done a pretty good job of keeping the candidates separated until after we signed the contracts."

I busied myself with cutting a piece of food, hoping no one would think to ask me if I knew anything; I wasn't sure what I would say if they did.

Hadley must have overheard the conversation because he stopped what he was doing and came over to our table to respond to it before the questions could go any further. "I heard you talking about Alex. You all know that she's been through a lot in the last few days, both physically and mentally."

There were nods from several of those around the table who had either been part of the previous few days' events, or who had heard about it from those who had been.

"Unfortunately," Hadley went on, "she pushed herself too hard yesterday. We had to call an early halt to the interviews and send her to bed. Doctor Paxton wasn't too happy with us." Hadley grinned sheepishly. "He gave us a tongue lashing and then placed Alex under strict orders to sleep in this morning. He threatened the Captain and I with a court martial if either one of us disturbed her before she was ready."

Thatcher, who never seemed to miss anything, and who had been watching me push my food around my plate while Hadley told the half-truth, seemed to understand more than was being said. His eyes narrowed slightly, but, in his usual way, he kept what he suspected to himself.

Instead, he turned to Hadley. "How's your shoulder doing this morning?"

I had forgotten about the phaser shot Hadley had taken through the shoulder. He had clearly ditched the sling the first chance he had gotten, but now that I looked closer, I could just make out the added bulk of the bandages that were under his uniform. He glanced toward the shoulder and laughed. "It's fine. The doctor said I'm healing like a pro and should be good to go in another week."

"How about you? How are your wounds doing?"

Thatcher had to tap me on the shoulder before I looked up and realized Hadley was talking to me. Everyone around the table was looking at me as well.

"Uh, they're fine."

"I didn't tear any of your stitches when I punched you, did I?" He asked it with a mischievous grin.

"What's this?" Rockman asked with more than a hint of amusement.

Hadley proceeded to entertain the group by telling them how they had engineered my removal from the cargo vessel. He seemed to take especially great pleasure in emphasizing the look on my face when I thought they were there to 'deliver a message' from Beckwith.

It turned out that all of the Ghana Base candidates had gone through a similar experience. Each had started out their transfers according to the orders sent by the Directorate's office only to be spirited away at some point in their journey by a team of individuals who had been sent to ensure that their leaving went unnoticed.

Hadley's recollection sparked a round of storytelling as they each took turns telling how they had been brought to the lodge. While the group continued to share their experiences, Hadley quietly turned to me. "In all seriousness, how are your stitches?"

"They're holdin' up," I answered just as quietly. The truth was, one or two of them had been stressed by his punch, but none of them had been torn. I had been careful in showering to keep them dry, not an easy feat considering I had stitches on my head, arm, ribs, and side. But I had managed well enough and rebandaged them afterwards with the medical kit that I had found waiting for me on the bathroom counter when I arrived.

"Good," Hadley said. "Dr. Paxton asked me to check on you for him. He also said to remind you that if you get any redness or tenderness at any of the sites, you are to go see him at once."

"I'll dae that," I assured him.

Across the room, Captain Marcellus stood up from where he had been eating his breakfast and talking with another group of candidates. He looked at Hadley and then nodded toward the door.

"Well, that's my cue." He stood up, walked to the front of the room, and raised his voice loud enough to be heard by everyone. "Ladies and gentlemen, while we finish up with the last few interviews, you are welcome to take advantage of the facility's entertainment areas and spend some time getting to know each other. Lunch will be served on the West Deck, just as it was yesterday, and we will reconvene in this room at fifteen hundred hours for the briefing that was promised yesterday. Until that time, enjoy the rest of your day off. There won't be many of those in the future."

Several people laughed, all too familiar with the military's idea of a day off. While the conversations began to resume around the room, my mind kept me from becoming an active

285

participant in the one happening at my table. Instead, I quickly finished my food and then excused myself from the group.

When I left the common room, I hadn't really had any intention of going anywhere in particular. I figured I'd just sort of explore the lodge and see what I found. But it wasn't long before I found myself in a garage filled with four-wheeling vehicles and other modes of outdoor entertainment. I considered taking one of the vehicles out for a drive, then decided that probably wouldn't be a good idea without getting authorization first.

Just as I turned to leave and take my explorations in another direction, I noticed that one of the vehicles had been partially dismantled with replacement parts and tools arranged neatly on the cart beside it. The vehicle was a Bradley Jeep style, similar to the one I had at home. I was more than a little familiar with the repair work necessary to keep that particular vehicle operating. I had spent many hours under my own after my off-roading expeditions had led to a broken suspension or a bent stabilizing bar. Working on my jeep had always been relaxing for me, often becoming a means of clearing my head when I returned home for one of my semi-annual leaves of absence.

Without really deciding to, I found myself next to the cart mentally cataloging the replacement parts and the type of repairs they indicated needed to be done. Absently, I picked up one of the spanners and a portable light and crawled under the vehicle.

Because I allowed my mind to let go of my other problems and simply focus on the task at hand whenever I was tinkering with mechanisms, I couldn't have said how long I had been working on the vehicle. But I had already succeeded in replacing the stabilizing brackets and the connecting lateral ties when I heard the garage door open and a set of footsteps approaching the vehicle I was under.

Wiping my greasy hands on one of the rags I had nearby for that purpose, I rolled the crawler out from under the vehicle and sat up to find Thatcher leaning casually against a nearby support column, silently watching me.

"Get bored of watchin' everyone else have fun?" I asked with a smile.

He scoffed lightly and indicated my greasy hands. "You found something to distract your mind."

"Aye," I replied, no longer smiling.

Getting straight to the point, he asked me, "What happened with Alex?"

I considered brushing off his question and pretending I didn't know anything, which actually wouldn't have been very far from the truth, but somehow that didn't seem like the right choice with him.

"I'm not really sure," I finally answered him. "I showed up for th' interview and was surprised tae find her a part of it. But when her eyes met mine, it was with a look of fear and desperation, like she couldn't handle being in th' same room with me. Then she practically ran out of th' room without a word of explanation. I spent th' whole night tryin' tae figure out what happened, but I'm at a loss. Do yae have any idea what's goin' on?" I didn't really expect him to have any answers either, but I was grasping for straws at this point.

He shook his head. "No."

Not sure what else to say on the subject, I decided to change it. "What happened in th' caves when yae went back for th' rest of th' team?" I knew about The Brig and Corporal Callia, but not the hows of it.

Thatcher shrugged. "Sobrien shot The Brig point blank in the back. Fused his spine together with the blast and fried his nerves from the chest down; he probably won't ever walk again. Sobrien left him to die and relayed the team's gathering point to Icarus' soldiers, then went after Alex.

"By the time I found the team, Gallagher and Finley were already dead and Corporal Callia was barely hanging on. In the end, we had to carry most of our team out in body bags, but at least we were able to bring them home." He said the last part solemnly. We both knew he had done all he could, but anytime you lost team members, you always dwelt on what more you could have, or should have, done.

"I'm sorry," I said simply; there wasn't much more I could have said.

He nodded curtly in acceptance.

"I heard a rumor that you just about got yourself court-martialed over her care in the surgery room," he finally said.

"One of th' doctors thought he would try puttin' another tracking device back in," I growled. "Wasn't goin' tae let that happen."

"I see."

After that we didn't talk much. Thatcher stuck around and handed me parts and tools as I needed them to finish the repair work, but otherwise we worked in silence.

By the time we finished, it was well after fourteen hundred hours. We had missed lunch and only had an hour before the scheduled briefing, but the vehicle was back together and ready to roll the next time someone wanted to take it out for a ride. More importantly, my mind had finally cleared enough that I was able to bring its focus back to Alex and our current situation.

"Thanks for yer help," I told Thatcher as I finished putting all of the tools back in their places. "...and for th' silence," I added as an afterthought.

He smiled knowingly, seeming to have understood that silence had been exactly what I had needed.

As we walked toward our rooms to clean up, my mind was able to at last identify and categorize several facts that had been jumbled together with everything else that had happened in the last few days.

First, Beckwith had set up a team specifically for the purpose of protecting Alex from future attacks. Almost everyone Hadley had previously identified from the Ghana Base as being sympathetic to Alex, and who were being systematically transferred away from her, had in truth been brought here to be part of that team. He was surrounding Alex with a group of men and women who were both trained for the job and willing to do it.

Second, I had been permitted to join the team even though Alex had developed an unexplained revulsion to my presence. In Hadley's words: I needed to be part of the team...I was the key to getting her safely to the school. They already knew how they were getting Alex to the school, and I was somehow a key player in making that happen.

Finally, something had happened to Alex that I didn't know about. She was afraid of me, or angry with me. I wasn't sure which, and I had no way of knowing unless she chose to tell me. But because I was the key to keeping her safe at this time, I was going to have to tread carefully to ensure that I didn't mess things up accidentally. That meant that for the time being I was going to have to find a way to do my job while staying out of Alex's way. I decided that, in order to do that, I was going to have to set aside my uncertainty and return to being the professional soldier I had been trained to be while trusting Hadley to piece together what was bothering her.

I didn't have to like the current situation, I just had to make sure the plan, whatever it was, played out correctly. It was a scenario I was familiar with. The military had never been in the practice of telling me its reasons, it had only ever told me what it expected me to do, and I had always made sure to do it with exactness. I would make sure Alex arrived safely at the school. And then I would decide whether or not to take Beckwith up on his offer to sign my release papers.

Until then, I would continue as I had always done, hiding my true emotions behind the façade of joking relaxation. I knew how to do my job, and I would do what was required of me. No one would ever know how much pain was actually being hidden behind the mask.

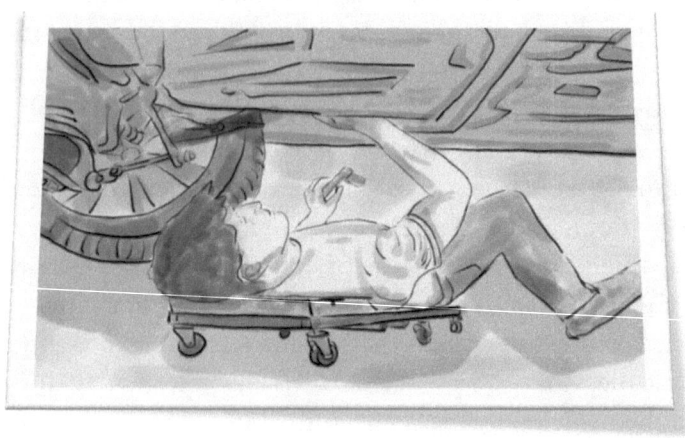

Chapter 28: Alexandria Jaquette

HADLEY CAME BY shortly after breakfast. He was obviously concerned with my behavior during Aiden's interview and wanted to know what was wrong. But after spending a mostly sleepless night struggling to get my emotions under control, I was in no condition to reopen the raw emotions I had barely succeeded in stitching together during the long night.

Lilith seemed to recognize that it wasn't my shoulder that was bothering me but didn't push me to find out what was wrong. Instead, she told Hadley that I wasn't up and about yet and that he would have to wait to talk to me. She would let him know when I was ready to start the interviews and that he would just have to be patient until that time.

I was pleased to learn when she checked my shoulder that the stitches were ready to come out. It was several days ahead of schedule, but the skin was obviously healed and there was no reason to leave them in. After moving my arm through several mobility checks, she also declared that the muscles had stitched back together sufficiently that I could remove the sling as well.

Dr. Paxton, who was watching the whole check-up via a video conference, commented that it was an impressive healing factor someone had given me. It explained why I had woken up so soon after the surgery to repair my shoulder and why the anesthesia Estradé had given me had worn off so quickly.

He said that when he got to the lodge around lunch time, he wanted to take a closer look at everything to make sure it had truly healed as well as it appeared to have. But if everything was still looking good, he would clear me to continue the journey to the school the next day.

When I was finally ready to continue with the interviews again, Lilith 'accidently' forgot to warn Hadley I was on my way. That insured that he didn't have an opportunity to corner me before we got started. Allowing myself to ignore the fact that I had no idea whether Aiden was still in the lodge, I turned my attention to the interviews. We added eight more members to the team before lunch and then I slipped back to my room while Hadley was showing the last candidate to the common room, ensuring that he was once more unable to talk to me privately.

I knew I was being childish, avoiding talking with him, but I just wasn't ready to allow myself to think about Aiden yet. After lunch, Lilith turned him away once more as Dr. Paxton had finally arrived and was taking the opportunity to fully examine my shoulder. It was nearly fourteen hundred hours by the time he declared me fit to travel and by then, the lack of sleep from the previous night had finally caught up with me. I couldn't have told you if Hadley came by again during that time because this time, I truly was sound asleep in my bed.

I felt a gentle hand on my shoulder pulling me from peaceful dreams of walking along wooded mountain trails and opened my eyes to find Lilith patiently waiting for me to be alert enough to listen. She smiled gently. "I'm sorry to wake you up, but it's time to get ready for the briefing."

When we entered the briefing room half an hour later, I saw several sets of curious eyes watching me walk to the front; one set, however, did not. Aiden had glanced at me briefly and nodded his head in greeting, but then had immediately turned back to face the front as though I were nothing more than a fellow soldier. So, Hadley had decided to invite him to stay and, for some reason I couldn't fathom, he had taken them up on the offer.

Determined to not let it bother me, I squared my shoulders and continued to my place next to Captain Marcellus. But walking past Aiden, I couldn't help noticing how the new uniform snugged his broad shoulders and set off his strong jaw line. Nor could I help but feel hurt by the way he had once more turned away from me.

As I took my place, the Captain smiled kindly at me, then stood to address the team. There were some twenty-three team members, men and women in addition to Hadley, Captain Marcellus, and myself, assembled throughout the room, plus Lilith and Dr. Paxton. Some were in chairs, some were leaning against the walls, but all of them gave the Captain their immediate attention, curious to hear what he had to say.

"Well," he began, "now that the interviews are complete, and you have all signed on to be part of this Special Ops Team, I can finally fill you in on some of the finer details of our job.

"Over the next few days, we will be continuing our journey to the new school we have been assigned to protect. For reasons I'm about to explain, none of your journeys will be quick or direct. They are designed to ensure that no one is able to follow you or track you to your intended destination.

"In addition to guarding the school, we have been assigned to protect an unspecified asset that will be housed on the campus of this new school. It's above your pay grade and clearance levels to know exactly what that asset is. However, in order for us to protect the movement of this asset, we will be breaking into travel squads."

Travel squads were teams of four to six soldiers assigned to work together to reach a particular destination. I had been assured that it was not an uncommon practice in the UFC military, and that nearly all of the other candidates were already familiar with how they operated.

"Each squad will be transporting an identical case, but only one of those cases will carry the actual asset, and no one but me will know which group is carrying the real one. So, assume that your group is carrying the real deal and defend it appropriately. Because you probably are!"

I thought it was an interesting decision to make it appear as though there was a separate asset we were transporting. The truth was that none of those cases had anything of value in them. But Beckwith had decided that it was too dangerous for the members of our Special Ops Team to know that I was the real asset being protected. As far as I knew, the only members of the team who knew the truth were the Captain, Harry, Hadley, Dr. Paxton, and myself. And as far as everybody else knew, I was just another member of the team who happened to have been placed in a position of leadership as Hadley had.

Marcellus continued, "I will be calling teams to the conference room throughout the next few hours to discuss the actual carrying out of each group's journey and then you will be on your way. Once all teams have finally assembled at the school, we will get into the nitty-gritty of how we will be doing our job to defend the school and the asset. But for now, I'll turn the time over to Hadley to deliver the team groupings and then we'll set you free to get to know your group a little better before you start your journey."

As Marcellus sat down, Hadley took his place at the rostrum and opened the screen of his digi-pad. His voice was crisp and clear. "Alright then. Squad One will consist of Lance, Borrek, Gantry, Solé, and Rockman. You will be assembling in the conference room immediately after this meeting.

"Squad Two will consist of Absko, Dupré, O'Connell, Felix, Smith, and Cox. Squad Three will be Haskell, Thatcher, McLagan, Jaquette, and Wren."

My heart skipped a beat as Hadley read the names for my team. Aiden was going to be on my team? I felt my heart sink. Why had Hadley put us in the same team? I found myself looking in Aiden's direction to see what his response was to the announcement, but if he had physically reacted in any way, I had missed it.

Hadley continued, oblivious to my discomfort. "Squad Four will consist of myself, Saunder, Ginevra, Asher, and Trebeck. And finally, Squad Five will be made up of Captain Marcellus, Harry, Dontre, Garret, and Baryshnikov."

True to the professional training many of them had, no one had said a word while Hadley was announcing the groups. But when Hadley asked if there were any questions before he dismissed everyone, several hands shot up.

"Dontre?" He called on the first hand to go up.

"Do we have any reason to believe that information related to the asset has already been compromised?"

Hadley didn't hesitate in his answer, clearly having expected that such a question would be asked. "We learned the hard way a few days ago that Ghana Base, where the asset was previously being stored, had at least one leak. While the asset itself was not stolen, and we can't say for certain that the enemy is even aware of its existence yet, top secret information about Specialist Jaquette was leaked. That means Icarus' forces had access to classified information and we have no way of knowing how much, if anything, they discovered or disclosed about the asset in the process. So yes, you should proceed with the assumption that information related to the asset has been compromised."

That brought a general murmur of voices. Out of that murmuring, someone, it sounded like it might have been Rockman, didn't wait for Hadley to call on them next. "Is this related to Alex's kidnapping?"

My heart tightened at that question. Perhaps I shouldn't have been surprised by it, but I hadn't been expecting it. Thankfully, Hadley was clearly ready.

"Are you asking about the mission or the asset?"

"Both," the voice replied.

"Rockman, you could probably have answered your own question if you had paused to think through what you already know about the situation. Specialist Jaquette is an Alpha. You should already know that the information on all Alphas is registered as top secret. Information about her should not have been readily available to Icarus, and yet someone did leak it. So, as for why she was kidnapped, we suspect it had to do with the fact that Alex is one of the strongest Alphas of her generation and that Estradé was working for Icarus with the intent of turning her over to them, effectively stripping the UFC of a potentially strong weapon. But, since

Estradé is dead, we can't ask her directly. So instead of guessing how much information was leaked on either the asset or Alex, Director Beckwith decided to have Alex disappear at the same time as the asset, effectively taking both of them back off of the grid."

"Won't Icarus be able to follow her to the new location by her name?"

"Not likely. None of the classified data on Alphas is linked directly to their names in the computer systems. But just to be safe, Alex's name in the records has been altered. As far as the UFC is concerned, there is no Alexandria Jaquette serving at the school."

That was news to me. I looked over at Marcellus, but he wasn't looking back at me. What name were they planning on me going by? I liked my name just fine and wasn't really excited about taking on a new one.

"Alright then," Hadley said before any more questions could be asked. "Group One, head straight to the conference room. The rest of you are dismissed until we send for you."

I stood up to go, not wanting to be in the same room with Aiden any longer than I absolutely had to. Unfortunately, I wasn't fast enough. Hadley intercepted me before I could escape once more. "We need to talk." He said it simply and without accusation, but with every indication that he wasn't going to take no for an answer; I was stuck.

Just at that moment one of the career soldiers approached us. His name, if I remembered it right, was O'Connell. He was an Irishman in his thirties, who had an impressive record as a military scout. He also had a darling Irish accent and a lively way of talking that made him quite entertaining to listen to. He had been one of the final interviews today and so had

had very little time to become familiar with the rest of the team members.

"Beggin' yer pardon," he said, coming to a stop right in front of Hadley. "But I have de wee problem of not knowin' me squad members. Do you mind helpin' me tae find dem?"

Hadley looked for just a moment as though he was going to tell the man no. But not really ready to talk to Hadley and explain how much I had been hurt by Aiden's change in attitude toward me, I decided to take advantage of the situation. I smiled sweetly and replied for him, "Why of course the Team Leader would be happy to help you find your team." I had emphasized Hadley's new title on purpose.

Hadley frowned at me for the briefest of seconds, just long enough for O'Connell's smile to begin to fade. Then Hadley seemed to change his mind. "Of course. They're right over here."

As he placed his hand on O'Connell's shoulder to show him the way, he said softly to me, "Don't disappear; we really do need to talk."

Yea right, I thought. Like that was going to happen. Unfortunately, as I turned to leave, I quite literally smacked into the back of someone. I looked up to realize it was Aiden. As he turned around to see who had bumped into him, I found myself unable to move. I was face to face with his brilliant blue eyes once more, freezing me in place like a deer caught in the headlights. They were twin pools of liquid azure; they drew me in and trapped me there. Lost in the depths of his gaze, I was suddenly trembling from head to foot: desperate to escape; unable to make my legs move.

"Pardon me." He said it as though he were the one who had bumped into me. "I'll try tae be more careful where I stand next time." His voice had the same light, joking tone that I had become familiar with before his sudden change toward me, though his previously bright smile seemed slightly dimmed now. He gracefully stepped back out of my way so that I could continue.

The spell broken, though still trembling, I muttered a nearly incoherent apology and then turned and fled. This time, I could feel his eyes on me all the way to the door. *Why?* I thought desperately as I ran. *Why couldn't he have stayed at the base?*

***

I WAS SITTING quietly in the armchair by the window, absently watching the tree line slowly darken while the sun set without really seeing any of it. A firm knock on the door drew me out of the silent emptiness I had sunk into. Lilith, who had been methodically packing her medical supplies for transport, paused in what she was doing to see who it was.

I recognized Thatcher's deep Texan drawl as he softly said, "Sorry to bother you, ma'am, but Captain Marcellus has called our squad to meet in the conference room. I was sent to ask Alex to join us."

Not waiting for Lilith to relay the message to me, I slowly stood up and walked to the door. I had cried myself empty more than an hour ago. I was emotionally drained and physically weary. Lilith looked at me with concern. She knew that I had been crying; I had made no attempt to hide the tears' streaks when she had returned to my room. But she didn't know why and had not pushed me for answers; I appreciated that about her.

"I'm okay," I said simply as I walked past her and out into the hall. Out of the corner of my eye I caught her glance toward the tall Texan, and his face, likewise drawn in concern as he watched me go.

"Don't worry, ma'am," I heard him say quietly as I continued walking. "I'll keep an eye on her."

"Thank you," Lilith replied just as softly.

Then I heard his long strides catching up with me until he was walking by my side. He didn't say anything as we traveled through the long halls, but he did step forward to get the door for me when we reached the conference room. I nodded my head slightly in thanks and then went in to take a seat.

Haskell, McLagan, and Wren were already there. Captain Marcellus was there as well. They all looked at me with varying degrees of concern, but I met each of their gazes with straight-faced emptiness until they finally looked away. Captain Marcellus cleared his throat. "Thank you for coming," he said to me. I nodded my head in acknowledgment.

Clearing his throat again, he indicated the case on the table. "This is your squad's case. Wren, you are specifically charged with carrying it during the transport. The rest of the team will cover you if necessary.

"Haskell, you are the lead for this squad. You will ensure that the team follows the plan that has been set up for you. You will also be the only member of your group who has your complete travel plans." He handed Aiden a digi-pad. "Once you are in the air, the digi-pad will unlock, and you will be able to view your travel plans. You can then decide how much to let the rest of your team know about where you are going."

"Aye, sir," Haskell replied as he tucked the pad into his shirt pocket.

"Supplies are being loaded for you on your transport as we speak. You will each find a bag with your name on it with sufficient clothes and toiletries to get you to the school. Thatcher, your rifle is being delivered directly to the school and will be waiting for you there.

"In the meantime," he opened a second case that was sitting on the counter behind him, "you are each being issued a phase rifle and a phase pistol to be used only for emergencies during your trip. Harry has installed a special transponder unit onto each of your weapons. If it is fired, it will send an alarm through the satellite system, and we will know that you are under attack. Forces will be sent immediately to back you up. Any questions before you head to your transport?"

No one said anything.

"Very well. Hadley is waiting for you in the hall and will lead you out to the transport."

We all stood to leave, but Captain Marcellus called my name before I had taken more than two steps. "A moment please." I stopped and turned to face him. There was obvious concern in his eyes, but he waited until everyone else had left the room before he continued. When the door closed behind the last person out, he put his hands on my shoulders and looked me straight in the eyes.

"Kid, something is obviously wrong. Will you please tell me what is going on?"

I smiled an empty smile that was meant to be reassuring. "It's not important…" I started to say, but his face fell into an unimpressed frown at my attempt to brush it off. That frown touched me in a way nothing else could have.

The Captain had always been there for me. He had held me in his arms when I was three, something I couldn't remember anyone else ever having done. He had quietly watched me from the background throughout my life and had stepped in when necessary to keep me safe. He was the only one who had argued against the military taking me away. But I suddenly wondered if he would have done those things if he had known who I really was.

On an impulse I asked him, "Did you know that I was created in Icarus' lab; that I'm one of his Alphas?"

I was afraid to meet his eyes; afraid his response would be like Aiden's had been. And when his hands tensed on my shoulders, I felt I had my answer. But then he let go and lifted my chin so that I had to meet his eyes.

"Kid, I don't care if you are Icarus' child himself. I will always be there for you when you need me."

The conviction with which he said it made me smile for the first time in days.

"That's the smile I've been looking for," he said softly in response, his own face breaking into a gentle smile.

As he walked me to the transport, I felt the emptiness begin to fade away. I wasn't alone; I never had been. I still wasn't sure how I was going to handle several days of travel with Aiden so close. But for the first time, I knew that I would manage it.

The Captain stood outside watching the transport take me away from him, just as he had done so many months ago at Dartmouth. Only this time, there was no uncertainty about where I was going. When I reached the end of this journey, I knew he would be waiting there for me.

Chapter 29: Aiden Haskell

I DISCREETLY WATCHED Alex for the first several minutes of the flight. She was smiling softly as she looked out the transport's window. I had no idea what the Captain said to her in the few minutes before they joined us, but I was grateful to him that he had. The emptiness in her face when she had walked into that conference room had been more painful for me than the lack of understanding her change toward me had been. I found myself hoping that, just maybe, that smile meant that something had changed and that there would be a chance for me to fix whatever I had done wrong.

In the meantime, it was time to find out where we were going. As I opened the digi-pad and read the plans, I sucked in a sharp breath. Seriously? This was where they were sending us? When Beckwith had said that he was sending me home, I had assumed he didn't mean with a team of people who would find out in the process who I really was, especially not Alex.

Thatcher asked softly, "Something wrong?"

I looked at him, not quite sure how to explain. He waited with a raised eyebrow while I worked it out in my mind. By then Wren and McLagan were also watching me curiously. Alex was the only one who appeared to have no interest in what I had discovered. Knowing that Beckwith was probably laughing impishly to himself somewhere, thinking about how he was manipulating and using me once more, I muttered a few choice words under my breath. *Fine!* I thought. *So be it!*

"Our first stop is in Scotland," I announced to the team. "I'll be takin' yae tae me parents' home for a few days before we move on. Accordin' to th' plan, me parents have requested me presence for a matter of family business. Yae are just a couple of me friends who decided tae tag along for the visit while enjoyin' yer own leave time."

"Where is de concern in dat?" McLagan asked it innocently, having no idea that my situation could possibly be any different from his own. Like me, McLagan was a Scotsman. Like me, he had been forced into the UFC military when he was fifteen. As a result, we had both seen far too many battles and lost far too many friends to enemy fire. They were shared experiences that under normal circumstances could have led to a bond of camaraderie between us. But, unlike me, he didn't have any secrets to guard. And the secret I had been so carefully protecting these past five years was the reason we had both lost so many friends.

Aware that there was no way I was going to be able to keep my secret from him after we arrived at my parents' home, I met his question the only way I could think of. "Are yae familiar with th' Buccleuch family?"

"Of course, why wouldn't I be..." He said it automatically as though everyone should be familiar with them, but then he stopped mid-sentence and took in a sharp breath of his own. "...Oh." He said it tersely, his mind suddenly connecting the dots I had laid out for him. "I see."

Thatcher and Wren looked between the two of us, all the more confused by McLagan's abruptly tense reaction. Alex was the only one who seemed to not be interested. She was still looking out the window into the night's darkness, giving no indication that she had heard anything that had been said, or was even the least bit interested. At least, I hoped she wasn't listening.

"So what?" Wren finally said. "What's the big deal?"

"De big deal," McLagan said with clear bitterness, "is dat he isn't who yae think he is."

I winced at the way McLagan said it, knowing that the rest of the team had heard it as well.

"Who are you then?" Alex's soft voice startled me. I realized with a heavy heart that she had been listening after all.

I sighed deeply before finally answering, "Me name is Alistair Buccleuch."

She stared at me for a long moment, then shook her head slightly and turned back away to look out the window. I'm not sure what I had hoped for, but her brief exchange left me with the feeling that she was not the least bit surprised to learn that I had been lying to her about who I was; just disappointed.

The rest of the flight to Scotland was uncomfortably long. McLagan scowled at me the whole way, Thatcher studied me, and Alex ignored me.

Fortunately, the travel plans moving forward were fairly ordinary and standard. It turned out that the transport was also carrying a full load of military supplies scheduled for delivery to the UFC base just outside of London. As we unloaded from the transport in the early morning hours, we looked like any other group of soldiers on leave who had been granted space on a transport because its scheduled delivery had left enough room for a few extra passengers.

From that base, we took a train north to Carlisle and then finally a cabby for the final few miles to Drumlanrig where we were stopped at the gate to my family's land holdings by an armed guard. This particular guard was unfamiliar to me; he must have been hired since my last visit home.

"IDs please," he stated gruffly when I told him we were expected at the house.

McLagan scoffed, "Yer secret identity so good that even yer staff doesn't know who yae are?"

I ignored him and handed my military ID to the guard. "You'll find me name on th' guest roster with authorization tae bring four friends with me."

"Their IDs?" The guard held out his hand.

I shook my head. "Go check th' roster please. Yae'll find that me guests aren't required tae show IDs."

The guard looked doubtful, but he seemed to know how to do his job. He returned less than three minutes later, he demeanor dramatically changed. "Welcome home, sir. I'll get th' gate open for yae right away."

I nodded heavily, wishing to myself that he would have left the 'sir' off. The cabby was now looking at me strangely in his review mirror, clearly having strong suspicions about who he was transporting.

At the house, I paid the cabby's fee and thanked him for driving us while the others unloaded our bags from the trunk.

"Sir Buccleuch, huh?" he asked.

"Yeah," I said hesitantly, deciding to discreetly pass him a hefty bonus. "I'd appreciate it if yae kept that fact between us. I don't need everyone knowin' I'm home."

He grunted his acknowledgement of my request, but I noticed that he didn't verbally promise. I sighed as I watched him drive off. All I could do now was hope that the extra amount I had paid him would buy his silence long enough for us to move on before anyone else realized we were here.

Speaking of someone realizing we were here: the front door opened as a stunningly beautiful woman came out to pose gracefully at the top of the stairs. Her long, auburn red hair had been gently curled to frame her porcelain pale face, while her cream-colored pants and white blouse had been artfully chosen to accentuate the slender curves of her lithe figure.

"Alistair Buccleuch," she said playfully, "aren't yae just a sight for sore eyes. An' look at all those strapping muscles yae brought home with yae." She looked appreciatively at each of my companions in turn.

"Hello, Roisin," I replied with a laugh. My sister knew how to catch a man's eyes, and she was clearly starting her games early. McLagan seemed especially caught under her spell as he stared up at her. I noticed that, in spite of his clearly displayed dislike for my family, his jaw had dropped, leaving his mouth slightly agape. Not wanting to let her win her games that easily, I leapt up the stairs and spun her around, effectively ruining the sophisticated grace she had been exuding only moments before.

"Well?" She giggled as I set her back down.

"Well, what?"

"Are yae goin' to introduce me tae yer friends, or not?"

With a laugh of my own, I led her back down the stairs. There was something magical about coming home. No matter how dark my circumstances had been in the days and months prior to my arrival, just walking up the front stairs had a way of lifting my spirit and easing some of that load. I was grinning easily as we approached the rest of my team.

"I'd like yae tae meet me sister, the Lady Roisin Buccleuch. Roisin, this is Specialist Cody Thatcher…"

Thatcher tipped his head slightly. "Ma'am."

"…Specialist Lakota Wren…"

Wren nodded his head but said nothing.

"…Specialist Logan McLagan…"

McLagan finally succeeded in closing his mouth. He swallowed hard, then mumbled something that sounded suspiciously like, "Me' Lady."

"…and finally, Specialist Alexandria Jaquette."

Before Alex could say anything in greeting, Roisin smiled sweetly at her. "Well, it's about time me brother brought a girl home with him; and a pretty one at that."

The color drained from my face and my smile disappeared. "Uh, Roisin…" I choked.

At the same time, Alex's shoulders tensed, and she said stiffly, "We're not together."

But Roisin acted as though she hadn't heard our protestations and quickly turned around to proclaim, "Well now that the introductions are finished, why don't I show yae where yae can store yer things."

She hooked her arms playfully through Thatcher's and Wren's, drawing them toward the house as she moved away. McLagan followed immediately after, leaving Alex and I momentarily alone on the driveway. Alex's eyes had narrowed and her countenance darkened. I searched desperately for a way to apologize.

"Alex…"

"Don't!" she said sharply. Then, without another word, she turned and followed the rest of the team up the stairs and into the house. All I could do was follow after her, the happiness of coming home momentarily dispelled.

Chapter 30: Alexandria Jaquette

I WASN'T SURE who I was more annoyed with at the moment, Aiden or his sister Roisin. Roe-sheen, as Aiden had pronounced it, appeared to be every bit the master that Aiden had warned me she was. We hadn't even been here for five minutes and already she had half the team wrapped around her finger, hanging on her every word.

As she guided us through the halls, she continued to hold on tightly to Thatcher's arm, clearly marking him as the primary target of her interest. At the same time, she would regularly find opportunities to lightly stroke McLagan's and Wren's arms so that they never reached the point of feeling left out of her attention.

Aiden followed at the back of the group, obviously aware of her games, but making no effort to put a stop to them. If anything, he appeared slightly amused, occasionally shaking his head with silent mirth when McLagan seemed especially caught in by something she was saying.

I was also more than a little annoyed because the family home that Aiden had said he was taking us to was not a home; it was a palace! Roisin explained that it was officially titled Drumlanrig Castle and had been in their family since roughly the seventeenth century AD.

Its five storied, four towered, pink sandstone design held more than one hundred rooms including a grand reception room, an extensive library, and an art collection that was second to none in the country. The castle had housed such guests as King James VI in the seventeenth century, Bonnie Prince Charlie in the eighteenth century, Neil Armstrong the American Astronaut in the twentieth century, and the Duke of Cornwall, Prince of England, during the fallout of the Pernicious Bellum War.

Roisin took obvious pride in her ancestral home and, while I wasn't that impressed with Roisin herself, I had to grudgingly admit that her home was both beautiful and impressive. At the same time, as she continued to guide us through the many halls, I found myself spending more time watching Aiden then I was spending admiring the structures and the artwork she was pointing out.

With each step Aiden took inside his ancestral home, his stature seemed to straighten, and his head seemed to raise ever more slightly. The change that was gradually coming over him added a touch of nobility to his features that I had never noticed before. Aiden had grown up within these halls and their strength clearly resonated within him.

Alistair, not Aiden, I reminded myself! He had lied to me about who he was. And not just to me, he had lied to everyone else as well; even his own countrymen had not known him for who he was. It was just one more deception. I shook my head, determined to force my thoughts away from him.

The suite of rooms Roisin led us to were on the third floor at the front of the house. They were attractively appointed rooms with a common sitting area centrally located in the middle of them. Two of the rooms had views of the grand driveway we had come in on while the other two rooms had views of the interior courtyard.

"Now for a few housekeepin' items," Roisin declared after assigning each of us to a particular room. "The maids will come by each afternoon at about one tae make up yer beds and do yer laundry. Breakfast and lunch will be available at yer convenience in th' breakfast room on the second floor, but dinner is always a formal affair and is served in th' first floor dining hall at six o'clock sharp. Yae will be expected tae dress appropriately."

Appropriately? I thought to myself. I wondered if they had included an 'appropriate' dress in the bag of supplies that had been packed for me.

"The grounds are at yer disposal while yae are here. I recommend takin' the horses for a stroll through th' countryside, but if there is somethin' else yae would like tae do, yae only need tae ask. Th' staff has been instructed tae help yae in any way they can.

"Now, Alistair and I will leave yae tae get settled in while we attend tae some family matters. We've kept our parents waiting quite long enough tae see their son," she concluded with a brilliant smile that was very much like Aiden's.

"An' jus' where is Aiden here stayin'?" McLagan asked curiously, noting that Roisin had not assigned Aiden to a room near ours.

"Why, he'll be staying in his own room of course; in the family wing," Roisin answered with mild surprise at McLagan's lack of recognizing the obvious.

"Of course," McLagan grumbled, his earlier terseness abruptly returning.

Personally, I was glad he wasn't staying near us. It meant I would see a lot less of him while we were here. In fact, the sooner I could escape from him, the happier I'd be. Yet, after an awkward moment of silence, no one had moved to leave. Realizing that Roisin was still playing her game, and that none of the men were going to take the first step, I rolled my eyes at all of them and decided to take Thatcher's arm away from Roisin to ease their separation. Surprisingly, Thatcher didn't hesitate to let go of her arm and take mine instead. As I guided him away from her, I said curtly, "Well, we won't keep you any longer. Thank you for your time."

Roisin laughed it off gracefully and said goodbye with classic style. But as they left the room, I thought I saw Aiden glance back at me, as though there was something more he wanted to say. I decided it was my imagination, but just to be safe, I released Thatcher's arm and walked into my room, shutting the door behind me.

I tossed my duffle bag into the closet, deciding I would unpack it later, then went to lay down on the bed. I intended to only lay there for a moment while I decided what I should do next, but when a knock came at the door, I opened my eyes to find that the lighting in the room had dramatically shifted. The waning light told me that it was late in the afternoon.

The knock came again, a little louder this time. "Just a moment," I said as I slid off the bed and reached for the handle. Thatcher was standing at the door in a dress uniform.

"Dinner will be served in thirty minutes. I thought you might want a little time to get cleaned up."

"Thank you," I said appreciatively. "I'll go get ready."

I quickly unpacked the duffle bag, looking for something 'appropriate' to wear. I didn't find any dresses, but the same dress uniform that Thatcher was wearing had been packed for me. The uniform hugged my hips, my waist, and my shoulders while still giving me just the right amount of room to freely move in it. It had obviously been tailored to my specific measurements. Even better, the black base of the uniform accentuated my creamy complexion while the violet stripes at the shoulders made the violet of my own eyes shine all the brighter. It wasn't a dress, but it was far from a disaster.

To give it the finishing touch, I tied my long hair up into a braided twist that kept it off my neck while giving it a slightly classy look that I hoped would be appropriate for dinner. When I exited the room, Thatcher gave me an approving nod.

We walked down to the dining hall in silence, with Thatcher taking a quick step forward to get the door for me each time there was one to be opened. At the door to the parlor, he stepped forward once more.

"You do know that I can open my own doors?" I teased him as I walked past.

He gave me a crooked half-smile but didn't say anything in response. Not that I had really expected him to. In all of the times I had interacted with him back on the base, I had never heard him say more than a few words strung together at any given time; he obviously wasn't much of a talker. He did, however, have a reputation for being one of the more gentlemanly soldiers on base. I doubt he would have been capable of letting me open my own doors even if The Brig had given him a direct order to do so.

The dining hall we were led to by a smartly dressed servant was nearly as large as the one on base had been. At its center, and running almost the entire length of the room, was the largest table I had ever seen; it was also one of the most beautiful. The highly polished rosewood had been artfully carved with delicate vines and tiny birds along its edges.

Evenly spaced around it were more than forty hand carved, high-backed chairs. For just a moment I wondered if they would be filling all of those chairs this evening, but then I noticed that only perhaps ten of the seats had place settings in front of them.

The place settings consisted of carefully stacked, finely crafted china plates, each edged with delicately stamped gold leafing and crowned with a linen napkin cleverly folded into the shape of a swan. They were further accented by the two sparkling crystal goblets and gleaming silverware that framed each set of dishes.

"There yae are," Roisin's voice exclaimed from the far side of the room, interrupting my examination of the table. She had been talking to two older men at the other end of the room when we came in, but upon seeing us she excused herself from them and, with a flirtatious smile, approached Thatcher to loop her arm through his. "I was starting tae wonder if I should send someone tae look for yae," she teased him playfully.

Roisin had traded her cream-colored pant and blouse outfit for a sleeveless, sage-green gown that complimented the porcelain smoothness of her skin and the deep auburn red of her perfectly styled hair. If she had been beautiful earlier, she was breathtaking now; and she knew it.

As she coyly leaned into him and whispered something only he could hear, I had to bite my tongue to keep from saying something I might regret. It wasn't that I was interested in Thatcher myself, or that I was worried about Thatcher falling under her spell; I thought I knew him well enough to be certain he was just being polite to her. No, it was the game itself. I had never been impressed by the games, and Aiden had warned me that his sister was a master at them.

315

No one deserved to be the target of someone else's game, least of all Thatcher. It was just one more reason I was glad we weren't staying long.

Turning away from Roisin and her games, my eyes happened on one of the mirrors that adorned the far wall of the room. Staring back at me from within the silvery glass was a tall lithe figure, smartly dressed in an attractive uniform but otherwise nothing special to look at. I stared at my reflection for a long moment, utterly unimpressed by what I saw. Then, shaking my head, I turned away and walked to where McLagan and Wren were standing by themselves, sullenly watching Roisin laugh coyly at something Thatcher had said.

Only when I came to a stop in front of them, did the two men seem to finally notice me. McLagan spoke first, the frown on his face suddenly giving way to a smile. "Well hello there las. Yer lookin much better this evenin', like yer finally ready tae take on th' world."

"I'll settle for making it through this dinner," I grunted back.

He laughed dryly. "I know what yae mean. But don't yae worry las. We'll have our own little dinner party on our side of th' table."

It turned out that while I had been sleeping, McLagan and Wren had decided to explore the castle and its grounds. They shared with me what they had learned while we waited for dinner to be announced.

The castle, as it turned out, had been fitted with the latest technology including a home entertainment center, a gaming room, and a garage filled with a variety of adventure-seeking equipment. For those wanting to get away from technology, there was a stable filled with thoroughbred horses, an extensive garden filled with pathways for walking, and a nearby lake for fishing, swimming, or boating.

McLagan excitedly told me about a large fish he had seen jumping in the lake. I could only laugh along with his antics as he excitedly described his plans to go back and catch it in the morning. In stark contrast, Wren reverentially described the horses he had found in the stable. It turned out that he knew quite a bit about horse breeding, and the horses he had found in the stable were some of the finest he had ever seen.

Wren had just started explaining to me the unique characteristics of different horse breeds when the dining room door opened and a new couple came into the room. They were a handsome pair that could have walked straight out of some guidebook to local royalty. They had clearly taken great care to be matched in every way from the style of their clothes to the gait of their step. Except for the slight limp in the man's step, they walked in sync. The lady didn't appear to be much older than me, yet she had a delicate beauty that was accentuated by the graceful glide of her step and the regal poise with which she carried herself into the room. Like Roisin, she was wearing an exquisitely designed dinner gown with jewels that were far fancier than anything I owned or had ever seen for that matter, reminding me once more just how underdressed I was.

Feeling slightly annoyed, I started to look away from the couple, but something familiar about the handsome man on her arm caught my attention and drew my eyes back to his face. I did a double take; it was Aiden!

He wasn't wearing the dress uniform that the rest of the team was, or any other style of uniform for that matter. Instead, he was wearing a smartly cut, dark blue designer suit that showed off his lean figure and perfectly accented his hair and eyes. In the back of my mind, it registered that this was the first time I had seen him dressed in anything other than military fatigues; he looked good.

That stir of emotions that seemed to keep coming back to haunt me every time he came into the room was swirling now. I wished whatever part of my heart it was that couldn't take the hint would just shrivel up and die. I forced my eyes away from him as a second couple followed them into the room a moment later.

The man looked like an older version of Aiden. He had the same unruly blue hair, though with distinguished-looking streaks of silver at his temples, the same strong jawline that was accented around the lips by slightly wrinkled smile lines, and even the same measured gait in his step that had Aiden's unique slight hitch to it.

The woman on the man's arm had Roisin's alabaster skin, long auburn hair, and gracefully lithe figure. I might have thought her to be Roisin's sister if it weren't for the delicate crow's feet wrinkles at her eyes and lips that suggested she was older than she first appeared. Her eyes, however, did not match Roisin's green ones. Instead, they were identical to Aiden's brilliant blue eyes, even down to the almost indistinguishable tightness around them that suggested they weren't entirely pleased with something that was going on. I hadn't noticed it right away in Aiden's eyes, lost as I had been in the sudden realization that it was indeed him I was seeing, but glancing from his mother back to him, it was easy for me to see now. It was the same tightness that had been in his eyes when he had turned and walked away from me in the hospital.

My curiosity was peaked. What had happened to cause that tightness now? I didn't think this was a continuation of

Aiden's response at the hospital. I had seen no hint of that tightness during our few days at the cabin. Besides, the woman's gaze wasn't aimed at me; it was focused on the young woman in front of her instead, the one on Aiden's arm.

I turned my attention back to the girl, seriously wondering for the first time who she was. How was it that she had come to be on Aiden's arm for the evening? No one should have known that Aiden was coming home today. With the care that was taken to conceal our travel plans, no one should have been able to anticipate our arrival.

And yet, Roisin's reaction to our arrival had been a little too well scripted for it to have been a spur-of-the-moment response to a surprise revelation that her brother had returned home. And here was this girl, with a self-satisfied smile, possessively grasping Aiden's arm in a way that suggested he was a prize she had won. Somehow, Aiden's family had known he was coming home.

Something Aiden had said stirred in the back of my mind. "According to the scripted plan, you are friends joining me on a trip home while I take care of some family business…" Was this girl the family business that he was coming home to take care of?

Aiden stepped forward to pull out a chair for her near the head of the table. As she sat down, she reached up to gently touch his cheek. "Thank you, my dear." She said it with a purr that was just loud enough for everyone to hear. I saw the muscle in Aiden's jaw clench for the briefest of seconds in response to her touch, then smooth back into a smile as though it had never happened.

Now that was interesting. If I had not spent so much time watching Aiden back on the base, I might have missed the clench. It was a quirk of his, to absently tighten the muscles in his jaw whenever he was frustrated. Granted, that hadn't been very often, but I had seen it often enough to recognize it now. Clearly, he wasn't impressed.

Another thought crossed my mind. *Why had she been seated first and not Aiden's parents? Shouldn't the Lord and Lady of the house have been seated first?* Then again, what did I know about formal dinners? Maybe they seated the guest of honor first.

Aiden's father held the chair for his wife next, followed by Thatcher who stepped forward to hold a chair for Roisin. But then, in spite of the women now being seated, no one else moved to take their own seats. I wondered curiously what we were waiting for when I suddenly realized that everyone was now looking at me. With a start, I realized that the men were waiting for all of the women in the room to be seated before they took their own seats; they were waiting for me.

"Well," the young lady said archly to no one in particular, "I guess it's true what they say, that the women in the military lose their femininity. This one doesn't even seem to realize anymore that she is a woman." She followed her words with a delicate peal of laughter.

Behind her, Aiden's face darkened in response, as though he were embarrassed by my obvious lack of culture; just one more way I had failed him. Next to him, his mother's back stiffened and her smile faded to a frown as well, equally unimpressed by my failing.

Standing at the far end of the room, one of the older men smiled patiently at me, but addressed the young lady. "Now, now, my dear. I'm sure she is just unfamiliar with our customs. You can't expect every woman to have been raised with your breeding."

"No," she sniffed lightly, "I suppose I can't." Then, turning to me, she spoke with the air of an adult addressing a child. "Come, my dear, join us at the table."

I felt a hot flush rising up my neck but determined to not let any embarrassment show. A small voice in the back of my head noted that no one had offered to get my chair. Not waiting to see if anyone would, I strode forward with more confidence than I felt and pulled out my own chair. The moment I was seated, the rest of the men in the room moved forward to take theirs.

Dinner was a five-course meal interspersed with scattered, halting conversations that were primarily led by the woman next to Aiden. It quickly became apparent that she had a strong set of opinions and no qualms about voicing them. If anyone disagreed with her, she would politely laugh as though they had spoken with childlike foolishness and then arrogantly correct their error.

"Why, Sir Darlough," she said at one point, responding to something one of the other guests had said, "you can't possibly be under the impression that she was in the right. It would have been far better that she had stood by her husband's side and supported him. I know that I will never make that mistake." She emphasized the word 'I.' "I will always stand by my husband's side, supporting him through better and worse, through sickness and health." She said the last part with a suggestive glance at Aiden.

I rolled my eyes and turned away from her, more than a little disgusted with her personal opinions and obvious self-importance. Beside me, Wren was just setting down his cup of wine. His stony expression suggesting that he had also heard enough.

"Tell me, Wren," I decided to start up that party on our side of the table that McLagan had suggested we would have, "how did you learn so much about horses?"

He smiled one of his brief smiles at the question; it didn't surprise me. I had chosen the topic on purpose, fairly certain that he would be willing to continue the conversation we had been unable to finish earlier.

"My family breeds Appaloosas and trains them for western riding shows." He started slowly but sped up ever so slightly as he warmed to the subject. "I have worked with horses since I was old enough to sit on their backs and my father insured that I knew not just our horses, but all of the breeds that went into strengthening the Appaloosa line and all of the breeds that were strengthened with Appaloosa blood. I have worked with Thoroughbreds, American Quarter Horses, Arabians, Nez Perce Horses, and many more breeds."

"You obviously liked working with horses. Why did you leave them for the military?"

Wren gave me a wry smile. "My family breeds horses. My mother says I breed trouble. She decided the military would force their discipline and obedience into me far better than her wooden spoon would."

"And has it?" I asked, laughing.

He shrugged sheepishly. "She was right about the obedience."

"What about you?" I turned to ask McLagan.

He cocked his head ever so slightly, as though unsure if I was teasing him. "I'm th' firstborn son of a Scottish family, me dear. It was a military uniform or a prison one."

Thoroughly embarrassed by the lapse of memory that had led me to ask the question, I shook my head and quickly apologized.

"Oh, no need for that, me dear. I can't complain too much. Military life has been good tae me. After all, it brought me tae this entertainin' little dinner party with yae and Wren."

I had to laugh at that. "Well, I for one am glad you decided to join us. I would have been ever so bored in the military without you."

His grin widened. "Pleasure tae be at yer service."

"So, you're in the military." The woman next to Aiden said it loudly and with a hint of sarcasm as she studied me over the crystal goblet she was absently swirling. "I've always been of the opinion that women don't belong in the military. Don't you agree, Alistair?"

When Aiden didn't immediately respond, her eyes narrowed slightly and she turned to look at him as though reprimanding him for not immediately agreeing with her. He had paused with his fork mid-way to his mouth, but now he slowly set the fork back down, clearly thinking through what he was going to say.

"I have worked with many women in th' military," he finally said, "and I will admit that some of them dae not belong there." He glanced briefly at me as he said the last part, as though suggesting that I was one of those women, but then his next words seemed to contradict what he had just said. "But, if Alex had not joined the military, I would be dead right now instead of sittin' at this table with yae. I owe me life to her."

He thought he owed his life to me?! Is that why he had come after me in the caves and then joined this team? If that was the case, then I would be glad to disabuse him of that notion.

But before I could respond, the woman's amused laughter began to reverberate sharply through the room.

"Alex?! Oh, this is just too much. She even has the name of a man."

All around the table, people stopped their conversations and looked our way. I felt a flush rise to my cheeks and had to fight hard to not reach out for the gravity around her and use it to rip that cup of wine out of her hand and bring it slamming back down on top of her perfect hair.

Taking a deep breath, I instead sat back in my chair and met her sparkling eyes with a cool gaze of my own. I waited until her laughter had begun to slow, then said softly, "You only think women don't belong in the military because you yourself wouldn't have the strength to survive it."

Her laughter stopped abruptly as my insult sunk in and a faint pink flush rose to her own cheeks. But I didn't give her the chance to respond before I followed up with, "I have found that a woman who is not strong enough to stand with a man will never be strong enough to stand next to one."

I'd had enough of this dinner and its company. Not pausing to consider whether my actions were appropriate, or even caring whether or not they would be viewed as offensive, I pushed my chair back from the table and stood up. "I believe I've had enough dinner."

As an afterthought, I paused at the end of the table and turned back toward Aiden's parents. "Thank you for the meal." And then I left the room, shutting the door behind me only slightly more firmly than I probably should have.

As I walked away, a small corner of my mind considered something that I had seen, but not fully processed in the moment. While I was putting the woman in her place, I had expected the same dark anger in Aiden's face that he had shown during my earlier 'lack of culture.' But instead of anger, Aiden's lips had twitched into the slightest hint of an approving smile before quickly returning to their set frown; it was not the reaction that I had been expecting.

Chapter 31: Aiden Haskell

I YANKED THE tie off and unbuttoned the top few buttons of my shirt as I sat down heavily on my bed. Dinner had been an absolute disaster. It had been a relief when Lord Remington and his daughter Collette had finally excused themselves and retired for the night.

Their presence in the house had been an unpleasant surprise, one I had walked into at a moment that should have otherwise been a happy one. I had opened the door to the family parlor looking forward to a private family reunion only to stop short at the realization that my parents were not alone in the room.

Lord Remington, as I soon discovered, was traveling through on business. He was the UFC's Secretary over the Department of Policy and Compliance. While his job included everything from drafting international policies and procedures to issuing fines against those countries that failed to follow them, he was also responsible for ensuring that Scotland was obeying the demands laid out in the Scottish Accords.

Part of that responsibility brought him to Scotland annually to tour our country and to meet with the Scottish representative, my father. He and Collette had often stayed at our home while traveling through the region on their annual survey. I had seen them many times over the years. With Collette only a few years younger than me, it had always been my job to entertain her while our fathers were in the study conducting business.

That had all been well and good when we were younger, but as she got older, she developed the frustrating habit of telling people what to do and threatening them with abuses when they failed to do exactly as she had instructed. On her last visit, at the tender age of seventeen, she had told me that she intended to marry me and join our two great houses together. I had laughed at the suggestion thinking at first that it had been a joke, but the fury in her face had quickly wiped away any humor on my part. I had then preceded to earnestly explain to her that marriage was not something I was interested in, whether to her or to anyone else. I had also reminded her that, as the firstborn son of a Scottish family, I was condemned to the war effort and that any son we had would be condemned to the same. But she had dismissed all of my arguments with a flippant wave of her hand and told me that she was sure her father could arrange for it all if she asked him to; he always gave her what she wanted.

In the end, I had been forced to brutally tell her that I did not love her, would never love her, and had no interest in marrying her. I had left her sitting on the bench in the garden, red faced and furious because I had refused to let her have her way. Then, not waiting to give her a chance to retaliate against me, I had cut my visit home short and left that very night. That was two years ago.

I had assumed that the lack of anything more being said on the subject over the past two years had meant that she had abandoned the idea. But when I had entered the family parlor

327

to find Lord Remington and his daughter there, there had been a distinct shine of victory in her eyes.

It turned out that the family business I had been called home to attend to was the well-advanced discussion of a union between our two families. My father and Lord Remington had already hashed out all of the major details and come to a gentleman's agreement regarding the matter. All that remained was for me to formally propose to Collette. They would, of course, give me the evening to consider the obvious benefits of the union and anticipated that the proposal would be made the following day.

To sweeten the pot, as an early wedding gift, Lord Remington had further arranged with Director Beckwith for me to be released from my military service at the end of my current mission. I would be free to take my place in the political arena, with the view of one day taking my father's place at the head of Scotland, and Collette would be at my side to support me in my transition.

I rubbed my hands over my eyes. What a mess. At the very least, it would be a loveless marriage. At the worst, it could lead to far more pain and suffering for Scotland than they were already being forced to endure. The worst part was that I didn't see any way out. She had neatly tied the box she had trapped me in.

I thought back bitterly on Director Beckwith's unexpected offer, particularly the mischievous grin he had worn when he made me the offer. What amusement it must have given to realize the quandary he would be placing me in. I could choose to stay near Alex, but remain trapped in my military service, or I could choose to be released from the UFC's service and be trapped into a marriage I didn't want, never to see Alex again. I suspected he had known very well what he was really offering me. It was just one more reason to hate the man.

A soft knock at the door interrupted my thoughts. I didn't need to ask who it was.

"Come in, Ro," I said wearily.

Roisin smiled at me sympathetically as she came in. She knew me better than anyone in the world did, better even than my parents did; she always had. I had once heard it said that it was not uncommon for some siblings, especially twins, to have a shared emotional or mental connection. Ro and I weren't twins, but I imagine that our connection was the closest thing you could come to without being one; she had always been able to read me like an open book.

"Some night." She said it with a weak smile as she crossed the room and sat down cross-legged on the bed next to me.

"Yeah." It was all I could bring myself to say.

"Alli…" she started hesitantly, as though worried I would not want to hear what she had to say. "If I had known what they were plannin', I would never have led yae into that lion's den. I'm so sorry."

I smiled weakly back at her. "I don't think there was any way yae could have stopped it."

"Probably not. But I'm still sorry for it all the same."

"I know." I sighed.

Roisin had always looked out for me, doing her best to buffer me from the pain of what we both knew would be a part of the life I would be forced to live. It wasn't much; there was very little that anyone could have done. But here in our home, her interference had often softened a blow that would have otherwise been far sharper. Knowing this, it didn't surprise me that she had been kept in the dark regarding their plans for me.

"So, what dae we dae about it?" There was a hint of challenge back in Ro's voice, as though she were trying to prod me into some action. "How dae we get yae out of this mess?"

"Is there a way out?" I laughed bitterly.

"There's always a way out!" She said it with a determined intensity that brought a fleeting smile to my face. Ro had always been good at finding the chinks in other women's games and turning them to her advantage. I suppose if a way existed, she would be the one to find it. That is, if there was enough time for her to find it.

We spent several minutes bantering around possibilities, but none of them held much promise. Frustrated, I fell back on my old habit of hiding behind the jokes.

Teasingly, I suggested, "I suppose I could ask Thatcher to propose tae yae first thing tomorrow. Maybe an announcement like that would throw them all off balance just long enough tae let me escape."

Ro threw a pillow at me in protest, but then she sat back thoughtfully. "Yae know, that might not be such a bad idea, an earlier proposal that is."

"What dae yae mean?"

"What if…" She paused thoughtfully, taking her time to thoroughly examine the idea that had come to her. I didn't say anything that might interrupt her thought process. I knew from our time growing up that Roisin's mind was quite capable of formulating intricate plans that were almost always successful. I just had to stay out of her way and watch her work her magic. As the seconds slowly stretched into minutes, her frown began to transform into a smile. "Yes," she said at last, with an air of satisfaction. "That should dae it."

"What should?" I asked with a raised eyebrow.

"Why, yer being already engaged, of course. It just happened a few days ago and yae haven't had a chance to tell yer parents. It truly is sad that yae didn't have a chance to tell them earlier. It would have saved a lot of confusion and heartache." She practically purred as she explained. "Of course, yae were plannin' to tell them about it this evenin' when yae came home, but they surprised yae with the marriage arrangements tae Collette and yae didn't want tae embarrass the Lady in front of everyone, so yae held yer tongue through dinner. But now yae feel the need tae straighten things out with everyone. Yae aren't free tae make a proposal tae Collette because yae have already given yer word and yer heart tae another woman."

I was laughing with mirth and shaking my head before she had even finished explaining her plan. The audacity of it was a little too much. "And just who dae yae suggest it is I've proposed tae? They'll want tae see her and talk tae her before they even begin tae believe me. They'll demand the opportunity tae try tae convince her tae release me from me word and I can't exactly pull a fiancé out of me suitcase."

"What about the one yae brought with yae?"

Confused, I asked, "The one I brought with…" and then I stopped cold. Alex. She meant Alex.

"Uh, Ro…" I said, no longer laughing. "That's not goin' tae work."

"Why ever not? I saw the way yae looked at that woman over dinner, especially when she so competently put Collette in her place. You can't tell me yae don't like her." She said that last part with a mischievous smile.

"It's not that easy." I hesitated, partly from embarrassment and partly from the coldness that had suddenly sunk into the pit of my stomach at the reminder of where I stood in Alex's eyes.

"Ro, she hates me."

Ro's eyebrow rose, the way it did anytime she didn't believe something she was being told. But as the moment continued in silence and she came to realize that I wasn't joking about this, the momentary triumph slid off her face and her lips formed into an almost silent, "Oh."

I had tried very hard during dinner to keep my face emotionless. I knew that I had not been completely successful, but I had hoped that the momentary flash of irritation at the things Collette had flippantly said and the surge of pride when Alex had fought back had been brief enough to be missed by those at the table. I should have known that Ro would not have missed it; she had keen eyes for things like that.

Gently, she asked, "Yae goin' tae tell me how that happened?"

"I don't really know," I admitted with a shrug. I told her what I did know; how I had met Alex, about her perfect comeback to my joke, and how I had been so distracted by her that I accidentally broke the speed record. Ro laughed at that last part, chiding me for letting a girl I had just met get under my skin that way. But as I told her about the times we had hung out together and how Alex made me feel, her smile faded once more.

"Yae lost the game, didn't yae?" she interrupted me softly, asking it without accusation or condemnation, but with a measure of certainty.

I didn't have to ask what game she meant. It had always been a topic of amused discussion between the two of us anytime I came home on leave. She would ask about the women I had met over the past few months; I would tell her in great detail about the games they had played trying to capture my interest. We would laugh together over their failures and discuss amusing ways to handle them in the future. Only this time, it was different. This time, I hadn't won the game and Ro knew me too well for me to be able to deny it.

Abashed, I admitted, "I lost the game tae her before I even knew it had begun."

Ro smiled gently. "She must be somethin' special for yae tae have lost the game so early on."

"She is." I smiled sadly, partially in agreement with her observation, and partially in remorse for the loss of what might have been.

"Then what happened tae cause her tae dislike yae so much?"

I wanted desperately to tell Ro everything; we had always been completely open and honest with each other in the past. At the same time, if Roisin knew the complete truth, it was quite likely that she would turn on Alex, just as I had done at first. I didn't want that; Alex didn't deserve that.

"Ro, I can't tell yae everything. There's a lot about what we've been doin' these last few weeks that is classified. But I can tell yae that there is more tae Alex than bein' just another soldier, and she's not like any other woman I've ever met either. She's different."

"Well, she'd have tae be tae win the game against yae. I trained yae tae well tae lose tae any ordinary woman." Ro said it gently, no hint of sarcasm or reproof in her voice. "But yae still haven't answered me question. Why does she dislike yae so much?"

"That's just it." I shrugged my shoulders, at a loss for the answer. "I don't know. I wish I did, but that's the part I haven't figured out yet."

"All right then." Ro's eyebrows furrowed thoughtfully. "If yae don't know the why, then perhaps we should start with the when. When did her behavior toward yae change?"

I had to close my eyes and think back. When had it changed? "I suppose it was after I was transferred off base. At least, I didn't notice any changes before that. But when I saw her next, she took one look at me and fled the room. I tried tae stop her, tae ask her what was wrong, but she pulled back like I was a deadly viper. Ro, the look in her eyes, it was like she was terrified of me."

Ro sat up suddenly. "Wait. I thought yae said she hated yae? Hate and fear aren't the same thing for a woman. Does she hate yae or is she afraid of yae?"

I shook my head; not sure I understood her question. Of course, I knew they were different things, but for Alex they seemed to be interchangeable emotions when she looked at me. What difference did it make?

"She avoids me and won't talk tae me. When yae suggested we might be together, she was angry. What else could it be?"

A slow smile spread across Ro's lips. "Alistair, me dear brother, yae need tae go get that pen and paper. Yer goin' tae write an apology letter tae Collette and explain that yae are already engaged."

"Ro," I said with exasperation, "they're not goin' tae believe me, and I am not goin' tae pull Alex in tae me problems."

"Hush, little brother," she said with an imperious smirk that suggested I was too young to understand her ways. "Yae just write that letter and let me handle the rest."

Shaking my head, I stood to get the paper and pen. Whatever idea had suddenly popped into her head, it wasn't going to work if it involved Alex, but I knew better than to contradict Roisin when she had settled on a plan of action. For better or for worse, I was about to dive head long into a roiling kettle of trouble. I'd just have to trust that my older sister really did know a way to get me out of this.

Chapter 32: Alexandria Jaquette

SLEEP HAD COME...eventually, though it had taken far longer than I would have liked, and it had not been nearly as restful as I had needed it to be. My dreams had mostly been disjointed images of Collette and Aiden, side by side, alternatingly mocking me and then condemning me for being one of Icarus' Alphas. When I finally woke, it had almost been with relief that the dreams had stayed behind and were not my reality; at least, I didn't think they were. Collette had certainly seemed on track to make it my reality, and Aiden clearly didn't care for me any more than she did. Then again, the look on his face when I had left the dining hall had me more than a little confused, unsure what to think.

Yawning, I checked the digi-pad I had left sitting on the nightstand next to the bed. O'six hundred hours. Right on schedule according to the military routine I had been living for the past several months, but too soon for a body that was worn out and tired. On the other hand, tired and awake seemed to me the better option at that moment than enduring more of those dreams.

Climbing out of bed, I headed for the shower. Ten minutes later, with my damp hair pulled into a low ponytail, I left the suite of rooms we had been given and headed for the breakfast room. I had to ask directions of an older woman who was carrying a basket of freshly pressed linens. She was all too happy to help me, mentioning as well that two of my companions were already there eating breakfast.

I found Thatcher and Wren seated at the table, quietly talking over their plates of eggs, bacon, and some type of potato pancake that I was unfamiliar with. Looking up and seeing me, they stopped their conversation mid-sentence. I had caught just a snatch of what they had been saying: "…you take care of her, I've got him…" That had been Thatcher's voice.

Curious, I asked, "And just what are the two of you planning with your heads so tightly together?"

Wren looked at Thatcher for the briefest of seconds, but it was Thatcher who answered my question.

"Just discussin' schedules, ma'am. Thought I would keep an eye on Aiden this mornin'."

"Oh? Why would he need watching?"

A slow smile crept across Thatcher's face.

"Why, to protect him."

Protect him from what? I was about to ask, but Wren interrupted my thought.

"I will go riding this morning. Perhaps you would join me, if you do not have other plans."

There was the faintest hint of anxiousness in his voice. As though he were worried that I might decline his offer. But as tired as I was, the recognition of that emotion was fleeting before it slipped away to a stifled yawn. I didn't have any plans, and horseback riding was as good as anything else. It would also give me a chance to get to know Wren a little better. I had selected him to be on the team, but the ten-minute interviews had only allowed me to scratch the surface of who these men and women were. I liked the idea of getting to know them a little better.

"Sure," I replied as I pulled out a seat and sat down. In the back of my mind, I noticed that Wren seemed relieved by my answer, but again, I was too tired to really wonder why.

McLagan joined us a short time later, a huge grin across his face. His shirt had the faint outlines of splashed water that had air dried, and he had the faint smell of fish about him. It didn't take much to guess what he had been doing this morning.

"Early start?" I asked him with a raised eyebrow.

"Early worm gets th' fish," he replied with a roughish grin. "And catch him I did. He was a fifteen-pound beauty, and cook says it will be fish stew fer lunch today." His childish delight at his success was so catching that I couldn't help but smile as well. He proceeded to excitedly share his adventure with so much gusto that we were all laughing and congratulating him on his cleverness. It was an enjoyable way to start the day.

After breakfast, I followed Wren down to the stable. In my mind I had pictured a medium sized, basic structure with ten to twenty horse stalls, similar to what I had known at the college I had grown up at. What I had not expected was a massive structure that looked more like a small country estate than it did a stable. It was a two-story building that had been built with cobble stoned walls and a sloping wooden shake roof. Inside, the brick floor was laid out in a herringbone pattern while the stalls themselves had been built of redwood slats framed by black wrought iron. Each horse's tack and gear were hanging neatly on racks in front of their stalls. The lighting was provided by several wrought iron chandeliers that hung at even spacing above the walkway. We hadn't gone ten feet down the hall before we were met by a sharply dressed groom.

"How can I help yae?"

Wren answered, "We would like to go riding."

"What type of horse and saddle would you like?"

"Appaloosas if you have them; with western saddles."

"Actually," I interjected, "I'd prefer an English saddle, if that's all right."

"Certainly, madame."

Wren looked at me curiously as the groom walked away from us.

I shrugged. "I've never used a western saddle."

"But you have ridden before?"

I shrugged again. "It was a required course for years 8 and 9 at my school."

While it was indeed a required course for the 8th and 9th years, the truth was that I had been riding horses since I was ten and had continued doing so right up until I had been transferred to the military base. I would never win any competitions, but I most definitely knew how to ride a horse. When the groom returned a short time later with two spotted horses, I double-checked the tightness of the girth strap before climbing up.

Wren led the way, away from the stable and the house, and along a trail that led off toward the wooded area to the south. The ribbed, woody leaves of the Alders and the distinctively flowing branches of the Oaks in those woods reminded me of the trees I had been reprimanded for climbing more than once when I was younger.

As we rode, Wren told me more about his family and the people he belonged to. His people, he explained to me, were the Nimíipuu. They were American Indians who had worked with horses since early in the eighteenth century. They had survived both the American encroachment of their lands and the fallout following the Pernicious Bellum War that had devastated so many other tribes.

"We are the people of the coyote," he said simply, as though that explained everything. "We have never been a large people, but we have always been mighty."

Curious to know more, I asked him, "Wren, you said that your mother is the reason you are in the UFC military. Why did she send you here?"

I thought for a moment he wouldn't answer as the silence stretched on, but then he said, "Among my people, when we are ready to enter the world of the adults, we must first seek the tutelary spirit that is to be our guide into adulthood. This spirit usually takes the form of an animal that speaks to us, but may occasionally take the form of a man. When I went on my quest, I took my knife, my bow, and a waterskin with me into the mountains as many before me had done. For three days I waited patiently on the edge of the highest cliff I could climb. From there I saw great soaring eagles, but they did not speak to me. I saw mighty, lumbering bears, but they did not approach me. I even saw majestic, hunting wolves, but they did not acknowledge my presence. I despaired and began to believe that my ancestors had not found me worthy enough to send one to be my guide.

"But on the morning of the fourth day, as the sun was just coming over the peaks, two forms approached me from opposite sides. On my right, a great grey coyote strode purposely forward until he was nearly within my reach. Then he sat down on his haunches and waited. On my left, a UFC soldier approached. He too moved forward until he was almost within my reach. Both were so close that I could see the mist of their breaths in the early morning air, yet neither seemed to look at me. Instead, the two of them were looking at each other as though a silent conversation was passing between them. At long last, the coyote bowed his head to the man and said simply, 'So it shall be. This boy is yours.' The coyote faded before my eyes, but when I turned to ask the man what was meant by the coyote, he too had disappeared.

"I returned home to my family, discouraged and confused. I had not received the vision that I had expected. Yet when I told our shaman of my vision, he said that I had had my vision and would have to reason out for myself what was meant by it. Two days later, a UFC representative came onto our lands, seeking to buy horses for the military's use. My mother, in her wisdom, went to talk to the man. When he left our lands, I went with him."

A vision guided him? Well, I'd heard of stranger things. I shrugged mentally, dismissing the thought as unimportant.

"I suppose the man was glad to have someone join him who knew how to handle the horses," I mused out loud.

Wren looked at me, slightly amused. "I do not work with horses in the military."

Curiously cocking my head, I asked, "Why not? Wouldn't that be the obvious place for someone who knows horses?"

He shrugged. "That is not where the military needed me."

"Where is it that the military needed you?"

He looked at me as though I had asked a ridiculous question. "I am needed here." He said it simply; matter-of-factly.

I was about to ask him what he meant by that, but the whicker of a horse coming from the path ahead of us startled me. I glanced toward the sound to find Roisin sitting gracefully astride the most beautiful horse I had ever seen.

The smoothly shining coat of her bay-colored mare was accented by a lustrous black mane and tail, and long lashes framing big brown eyes. Roisin and her horse were poised perfectly in the middle of the pathway as though posing for the cover of an equestrian magazine. I rolled my eyes. And…now she was back to posing.

"Lady Roisin." Wren greeted her with a soft nod, the slightest hint in his voice to suggest that he, at least, was not surprised to find her there. *Had the two of them planned to meet here?* I thought in irritation. *If so, then why had Wren invited me along?*

But before I could vocalize the question, Roisin startled me by saying, "Thank yae for bringing her."

For bringing me? My eyes narrowed as I turned away from her to look back at Wren.

"What's going on?" I asked him coldly.

He met my eyes without even a hint of abashment. "The Lady Roisin needed to talk to you in private. You," he said with quiet emphasis, "are now where you need to be. I will leave you here to talk."

Not waiting for me to respond, Wren turned his horse around and headed back down the trail at a trot. For a long moment, I considered turning my horse around as well and following him, but the tone in his voice had suggested that he thought I needed to stay and hear what Roisin had to say to me. Fine! I would stay for now, but I was not at all pleased with the situation.

"He rides th' horse very well." Roisin's voice had a slight purr to it as she watched him go.

I turned back to look at her in annoyance. "What do you want from me?"

Her lips twisted with the hint of an amused smile. "You don't waste time, dae yae?"

"I've never had much to waste."

She laughed with a short, musical burst of sound, but the laughter didn't reach her eyes. Whatever she had to tell me, it wasn't something she found amusing. "All right, then. I'll get straight tae th' point. The woman at dinner last night, Collette Remington, is threatening me brother and I need yer help tae put an end tae her threat."

Aiden was in danger?! A sudden rush of adrenaline jolted through me, startling me with its ferocity. It was as though my body was instinctively preparing to race to his aid. I had to force myself to hold still, my breathing to remain slow and even. He wanted nothing to do with me; I wanted nothing to do with him. So, why was my body responding this way? I didn't understand it. Worse, I couldn't seem to control it. My hands were trembling ever so slightly from the sudden adrenaline spike. Shaking my head as though doing so would shake away the unwanted emotions, I stared at her through narrowed eyes.

"Why should I care what happens to your brother?"

"Because yae love him."

My heart froze mid-beat at her accusation. I wasn't sure what I had been expecting her to say, but that most certainly had not been it. What was worse, she had said it with a hint of sympathy, as though she recognized the conflicting emotions that seemed to battle inside of me every time I thought of him, and somehow understood it. A sudden flare of anger coursed through me. What did she know about me or how I felt?

"Love him?" I spat back bitterly. "I don't even know him! Is his name Aiden or Ali—whatever you called him? Is he a soldier or a prince? Why did he agree to join this team when he so obviously wants nothing to do with me? He found it so easy to leave before, why couldn't he have done it again?"

As my angry tirade continued, her expression remained calm, seemingly waiting for my frustration to run its course. Only when I paused to take a breath did she softly interject, "He's just a man, tryin' tae protect his family."

Once more caught off guard, I froze. Protect his family? Hesitantly, I asked, "Protect them from what?"

Instead of giving me a straight answer, she asked a question of her own. "What dae yae know about th' Scottish Accords or th' reason they were written?"

Not much. I thought to myself. But so what? What did that have to do with Aiden or the danger she has just suggested he was in?

As though reading my mind, or somehow seeing my mental shrug, Roisin didn't wait for me to give an answer out loud. Instead, she continued, "I see. Yae know about as much as th' average person outside of Scotland does. Which is tae say, almost nothin'."

She raised her chin with a haughty expression. "You were probably taught in school that Scotland attempted tae overthrow the' UFC leadership in 152 PB. But I sincerely doubt that yae were taught about th' real reasons we rebelled, or how many of our sons and brothers th' UFC continues tae murder each year because our grandfathers dared tae stand up tae them." She spat out that last part with a sense of acrid bitterness. "They are not in such a hurry tae remind others about the injustices they meet out tae those who don't fall in line with their propaganda and lies."

I raised an eyebrow, challenging her charges against the UFC, but let her continue speaking without interruption.

"Me grandfather was the leader of Scotland during th' Scottish Rebellion. He could see the cancer growing inside of th' UFC leadership as they increasingly ignored th' constitution that outlined what they were supposed tae be doin' for th' countries they represented and what they were not allowed tae do. He watched as the leaders at that time were orderin' their military into countries that had not yet joined th' UFC and were forcing them tae join at gunpoint. And for those that resisted? Well, the UFC quietly ordered th' execution of their leaders, in the name of world security. Switzerland, a country that had remained neutral and independent for over 400 years, was th' first tae fall tae their imperialism. South Africa, Guatemala, Iran, and Kosovo all came shortly thereafter.

"Scotland alone, was willing tae stand up tae them. We fought back. But we weren't strong enough tae stand alone, and those who had promised tae stand with us, betrayed us. For our efforts tae correct th' wrongs that were so blatantly evident, every firstborn male of Scotland since that time has been condemned tae servitude in the UFC military. We fight, bleed, and die for a government that is more corrupt than a boilin' cesspool."

As she spat out that last part with clear disgust, I decided that I needed to reassess this woman. There was no hint of the flirtatiously playful girl that she had seemed only moments before. Roisin had a glint in her eyes that hinted instead at something dangerous just below the surface.

"Lord Remington is the UFC's guard dog, ensurin' that Scotland does not step out of line. For us, a misstep does not result in a slap on th' wrist, it results in th' death of yer whole family."

I scoffed in disbelief, not believing that claim for even a moment.

"You think I'm lyin'? I have seen th' UFC's retribution with me own eyes. I can still hear th' screams of the McLean family and th' desperate sobs of their teenage son. I knew him, their son. He had been a childhood friend. He had always been one tae choose books and learnin' over play and rough housin'. So, it didn't surprise me to learn that he had fled instead of joinin' the UFC military when he came of age. But when they caught up tae him, Remington decided tae make an example of him. He had th' boy chained tae a pole and forced tae watch while they torched his home, with his family locked inside of it. He was only fifteen years old!" The fury in her voice had given way near the end so that her last words were spoken with little more than a horrified whisper.

She drew a shuddering breath before continuing. "After that night, he was emotionally broken. No one was surprised when we heard rumors of his death three months later, in his first battle out of boot camp."

Recounting the memory left a haunted glow in her eyes that left little room for me to doubt the truth of her testimony. Exhaling slowly, she closed her eyes; the fire was back when she opened them again.

"Now Lord Remington has added a new demand on Alistair. It's not enough that Ali has served in th' UFC military honorably these past five years, or that he would have continued servin' in that same way for th' next forty. No. Because his daughter Collette has taken a fancy to Alistair, Remington is forcin' Ali into a marriage that he doesn't want. Collette is tryin' tae collect him like she would a butterfly. She will dangle him on a golden chain and bring him out tae show off like her other pretty things, but she doesn't love him. She will tire of him eventually, and when she does, she will dispose of him; cast him off as a thing no longer valued. Alistair doesn't deserve tae be treated that way." She met my eyes, pleading. "Please, don't let her dae that tae him."

"And just how am I supposed to stop this?" I asked skeptically. It was no longer a question of doubt or frustration on my part, the raw emotion in her voice had been too real. But I didn't see what I could possibly do to help. I had no power over the decisions of the UFC, and certainly no influence with Lord Remington.

"There is one way tae force Lord Remington tae withdraw his request: if Alistair has already given his word tae another, if he were already engaged, then Scottish custom demands that he is not free tae issue another proposal until the first woman has released him from his vow."

I laughed as I suddenly understood what it was she wanted from me. It was ridiculous, but in a twisted sort of way, it made sense. I was the last person in the world Aiden would want to be engaged to. By asking me to pretend to be engaged to him, he could escape Collette's trap without fear of being caught in another one, though I was surprised he was willing to even pretend such affection toward me. Then it occurred to me to ask, "Does he know you're asking me to do this?"

She nodded hesitantly. "He knows, though he doesn't think yae will help him."

"No, I don't suppose he would." I laughed bitterly. "Did he at least tell you why?"

"Not exactly," she admitted. "He suggested yae weren't the average soldier but said he couldn't tell me about yer time together; somethin' about it being classified."

I laughed sharply. Classified? Which part? The part that I was an Alpha or the fact that he hated me for it? Well, I suppose I was classified, but I was under no obligation to keep who I was a secret. Would she still want my help if she knew? I decided to find out.

"He doesn't think I will help him because I am an Alpha, one of Icarus' Alphas to be precise. Aiden turned on me the moment he found out what I was; he left me without so much as a backwards glance. And now that you know, can you really tell me that you want the help of a monster created by Icarus?" The words came out more bitterly than I had intended, surprising me with their ferocity, but the emotions didn't seem to rattle Roisin.

She studied me in silence for a long moment, her lips drawn in a tight line, as though she were waiting to see if I had more to say. When I didn't, she said dismissively, "Is that all? I knew who and what yae were before yae arrived."

My forehead furrowed in confusion. *How was that possible?* No one should have known I was coming. But the thought had not finished processing before she was continuing.

"Yae misjudge Ali. I've seen th' way he looks at yae, and he doesn't see yae as a monster, and he most certainly doesn't hate yae."

Wait. What did she just say?

Confused and caught off guard once more, I retaliated. "Your brother made it very clear back at the base what he thought of me. It was very obvious that he wants nothing to do with me."

A satisfied glint flashed through her eyes and then was gone just as quickly, leaving me to wonder if it had truly been there at all. Instead, she shrugged again, dismissing my argument out of hand. "As I said, yae misjudge him."

I sat in stunned silence, unsure what to think or say. She gave me a moment to try and process her words before going on. "Tell yae what. Before yae make yer decision, why don't you go talk tae him; he's in th' garage on the west side of th' house."

I automatically shook my head. No. I was not about to set myself up for another rejection from him. But she ignored my response as though the matter had been settled. "He deserves th' chance tae explain, and yae deserve th' chance tae learn th' truth."

Then she turned her horse away from me, clearly done with our conversation. She had only gone a few paces though, when she paused and turned back to look at me over her shoulder. "Please consider carefully. Alistair will dae whatever it takes tae protect his family, even tae th' point of sacrificin' himself. Collette's demands will break his spirit and destroy him. I don't think me family would survive th' loss of another son." And then she heeled her horse into a gallop and was gone.

Another son? What had happened to the first? I sat there for several minutes thinking through what I had just learned. Beneath me, the horse pawed the ground impatiently, wanting to be on the move. Was it possible that I had misunderstood Aiden? A small shiver raced through me. What if she was wrong, or playing one of her games? I had finally gotten to a place where I could look at Aiden without feeling the crippling pain of loss and disappointment; I had no desire to spiral backwards. But I also didn't want to let fear itself cripple me. And if he really was in danger? I sighed in resignation; I was going to have to talk to him.

When I approached the garage twenty minutes later, I did so hesitantly. I think I was halfway hoping he wouldn't be there. But as I quietly opened the door and stepped through, I could hear his muffled voice drifting out from under one of the vehicles. There was a discouraged quality to it that seemed to echo Roisin's earlier words.

"The thing I don't get, is why Hadley seems tae think that I'm th' key tae getting her safely tae th' school. I can't imagine they would purposely send Alex in tae any situation without a full knowledge of what was goin' to be occurring. So, they must have known about me situation. Why then, would they send her into th' middle of it?" The clicking sound of a ratchet interspersed his words. He was obviously working on something under the vehicle while he was talking. "It just doesn't make sense."

Thatcher, who was leaning forward with his arms crossed on the top of a black toolbox watched me as I came in. I put my finger to my lips, telling him not to say anything; he nodded his head ever so slightly and stayed where he was. Unaware of my entry, Aiden's voice continued.

"But whatever is goin' on, she doesn't need tae be caught up in me troubles. Now, instead of keepin' her out of it, Roisin wants me tae ask Alex tae step right smack dab in tae th' middle of this whole explosive situation. Aside from th' fact that Alex wants nothin' tae dae with me, for reasons I still haven't figured out..." He paused as there was a loud clunking sound from under the vehicle. "Would yae hand me th' larger ratchet?"

Thatcher's lips spread into a slow, roguish grin. He pointed to the tool Aiden needed but didn't make a move to pick it up.

No! I shook my head adamantly, not ready to make my presence known. Thatcher seemed to have a different plan. His grin grew even bigger as he held up his hands and stepped away from the toolbox, then leaned back lazily against the wall behind him and folded his arms across his chest.

Shaking my head in exasperation, I picked up the tool he had pointed to and bent down to place it into Aiden's waiting hand. Aiden's voice stopped mid-word and his hand stiffened in response as he recognized that Thatcher was not the one who had handed the tool to him. Moving slowly, he rolled the cart he was laying on out from under the vehicle. His expression was guarded and I could see the apprehension in his eyes as they met mine.

"Hi," I said hesitantly.

"Hi," he replied back, the same hesitancy in his own voice. "How long have yae been here?"

He was nervous about what I might have heard him say and what I will think about it. In spite of my own nervousness, I found myself smirking at him with a hint of mischievousness. "Long enough to hear that you've gotten yourself into more women trouble..." But then I took a deep breath and continued with what I had truly come for. "...and long enough to realize that we need to talk."

He set the tool down on the ground and stood to grab a rag to wipe his hands on. The whole time, his eyes never left mine. It was as though he were gauging whether I was a dangerous animal about to pounce. To be honest, I was probably looking back at him the same way. I was terrified that he would say or do something to crush the tiny ember of hope that had faintly begun to glow. Absently, I noted that Thatcher was no longer in the garage with us. He had slipped silently out, leaving the two of us alone.

"What did yae want tae talk about?" Aiden finally asked, his voice still guarded.

There were a lot of things I wanted to ask him, but I quickly settled on the one question I had been silently asking myself ever since I had watched his angry retreat from my room in the hospital.

"Why did you leave when you found out who I was?" As though voicing the question that had been haunting me for the past week broke down the flood gates, several more questions followed rapidly through before he could even answer the first. "Why did it change the way you looked at me? And if you hated me so much for who I am, why did you come after me in the caves or agree to join the team? Why didn't you just stay away if I am so abhorrent to you?"

His mouth opened several times as though to answer my questions, but nothing seemed to come out. He finally closed it again, instead just looking at me. It was as though he were fighting a battle within himself; a war between wanting to answer my questions and an internal restraint that kept him from being able to. My own sense of dread grew as the silence dragged on. But then he seemed to reach a decision. "I think there is someone yae need tae meet before I answer yer questions."

Did he think his answers would be so hard for me to accept? Yes, he probably did. But I'd committed myself this far. "All right." I nodded my head for him to show the way. I followed him out of the garage and up into the house. He led me to the family wing, coming to a stop in front of a closed door. He hesitated for the briefest of seconds, studying me with an expression I couldn't read before he pushed the door open at last. Who was he taking me to meet?

I was surprised to find the room empty; there was no one in it. No, that wasn't quite true. The room we entered was lined with shelves full of pictures situated artfully among a scattering of toys, folded clothes, a variety of musical instruments, and other seemingly random items. All of the pictures were of the same individual, though they reflected a range of ages from infant to teenager. The boy in the pictures had Aiden's same chiseled face and brilliant blue eyes, though his hair was the deep auburn color of Roisin's. With startled understanding, I realized that this must be the brother Roisin had mentioned, the one that had been lost. Looking with greater interest, I also realized that the seemingly random items were not random at all; they must have been his belongings. The whole room had been turned into a shrine for him.

As if confirming my realization, my eyes were drawn to the shiny, black grand piano that had been situated in the center of the room and the large portrait of the boy in his mid-teens dressed in a tuxedo and proudly standing next to that same piano while holding a large championship trophy. While the keyboard was open and the piano's top was raised as though ready for someone to sit down and play, I noticed that there was a thin layer of dust on the keys; the piano had not been touched in some time.

Aiden walked over to the portrait and reached up to tenderly touch the rich dark wood of its frame. "This is me brother, Callen." He said it almost reverentially. "He was th' baby of th' family, and we all adored him. He was also th' musician in th' family. This was his piano. He would play th' most beautiful music on it."

"What happened to him?" I asked hesitantly, remembering Roisin's reference to a lost son.

"Do yae remember th' July Massacres a few years ago?"

I nodded my head. It had been all over the news: a coordinated attack aimed at several private schools in multiple countries. Icarus had purposely targeted smaller schools that did not have any Alphas or Betas, reminding the

353

world that no one was safe from him. His soldiers had left behind more than three hundred dead students; the youngest of which had been a five-year-old girl who was in her first week at the school. But the biggest shock had been the wanton atrocities committed by his Alphas during the attacks. They had used their gifts to torture, maim, and murder. The fact that even the news sites had been unwilling to show images of the destruction those Alphas left behind had been a testimony to their brutality.

"Callen was studyin' at th' Royal Conservatory of Music in England on th' day th' attacks happened. He stood between one of Icarus' Alphas and a group of younger kids she was targetin'. For standin' in her way she burned him alive, from the inside out."

I looked at him in horror. "She did what?"

Aiden turned away from his brother's portrait to face me. "I wasn't supposed tae see it, but I called in some favors and got hold of th' video from th' attack. I watched him die, Alex." He choked on the words. "The Alpha was a teenage girl not much younger than yae. I saw th' rapture in her eyes, th' pleasure she took from th' pain she was causin' him. He was sixteen years old, and she murdered him." His voice hardened as he said the last part.

"For two weeks after seeing th' video, all I could think of was me hatred for Icarus and his children. I vowed tae meself that I would avenge his death. For more than a year, I requested every mission that even hinted at somethin' tae dae with one of th' Alphas. I was determined tae help hunt them down and eliminate them, tae remove their threat from th' face of th' earth. But then I met yae, and for th' first time, somethin' distracted me from me hatred; yae made me smile again."

I didn't need him to tell me the rest. Now I understood why he had reacted the way he had in the hospital. To find out in that way that I was one of Icarus' Alphas, no different than those who had killed his brother? He would have felt betrayed by that knowledge. And then to be forced to rescue me in the caves? It would have gone against everything that had driven him for the past year. Now I was in his family's home, adding insult to injury.

Part of me wished I could just fade away; quietly remove myself from the situation, to spare him the pain that I finally understood I was causing him and his family. But I wouldn't leave just yet. Collette was a threat to his safety and security, and I was in a position to do something about it. It was a bitter paradox, yet I would not abandon him to face that threat alone. And perhaps, by doing as Roisin had asked, it might atone in some small way for what I had been putting him through.

"I'm so sorry, Aiden." It came out barely more than a whisper. "I will help you with Collette, and then I will leave. Perhaps that way…well…" I wasn't sure how to say what I wanted to say; nothing I could think of sounded right. The ember of hope was truly dead. Then, realizing that there really was nothing more to say after all, I turned away from him and quickly left the room before he could see the tears that had started to form in the corner of my eyes.

I was halfway down the hall when his voice called after me. "Alex, wait!"

Wait? Why? The questions reverberated loudly in my head. I understood now, painfully and completely, exactly what I had done to him. Roisin had been wrong; the damage was too great. He would never be able to look at me and see anything other than the one who had murdered his brother.

355

You are a child of Icarus. You are one of them! The thoughts seemed to scream in my head. *You will never be able to escape that!* I walked faster, trying to outrun the accusations.

"Alex!" He called louder, his steps echoing down the hall as he ran after me. In seconds he had closed the distance between us and forced me to turn around. He was suddenly so close to me that I could feel the warmth of his skin; smell his heady scent. It was a painful contrast to the swirling emotional storm of loss. All I wanted was to turn and run, but his fingers clenched tighter on my shoulders, stopping me from fleeing while his eyes searched my face as though they were searching for answers of their own. Then, without warning, he pulled me forward into a kiss. I was so startled that I didn't pull back.

The accusations in my head went silent, drowned out by my shock and the rush of euphoria that suddenly raced through me. The tension in my muscles melted away and I found myself leaning into his kiss, not wanting it to end.

A gasp from the end of the hallway made us both look up sharply. Collette was standing there, all color drained from her face.

I felt a flash of anxiety and started to pull back, but Aiden's hands didn't let me go or push me away. Instead, they held me tighter to him as though he meant to shield me from her. *He was shielding me? I was not the one who needed protecting.* My whole body was tingling; I felt like I could have lifted the whole castle if that was what it would take to protect him from her. Realizing this, a slow smile began to spread across my lips and I raised my head in challenge. Reacting, more than thinking through what I was doing, I reached up to touch Aiden's cheek, intently staring into those brilliant blue eyes of his, then said just loud enough to be sure that Collette would hear, "I'm sorry, but I will not release you from your promise. You asked me first, and I will hold you to your word."

Then I pulled away from him and strode up to Collette. I stood defiantly in front of her, looking her up and down. The tone in my voice surprised even myself. It had a feral snarl to it that was both warning and challenge. "I will not step aside and let you have him!"

Then I left her standing there, her mouth moving without a sound, perhaps for the first time in her life at a loss for what to say. As for myself, I was glowing inside. Even if it could only be for a short time, his kiss had set me on fire.

Chapter 33: Aiden Haskell

I WATCHED ALEX leave, a silent thrill racing through me. *Had that really just happened? Was it possible?* The look in her eyes when she finally pulled back from the kiss, the way she had laid claim to me in front of Collette? The possibility that the tension between us had been washed away with that kiss left my mind racing with relief. But the relief was short-lived as Collette seemed to suddenly come back to herself.

The color returned to her cheeks with burning fury. Her fists clenched and she strode up to me waving a crumpled piece of paper in my face; it was the letter I had written the night before.

"You proposed to someone else first? To that whore?! How dare you! You are mine!"

"Collette," I fought to keep my voice even and calm, "I don't belong tae you. I told yae two years ago that I did not love yae and that I would not marry yae."

"You also told me that you would never marry anyone else either," she spat back.

"Two years ago, I had no intention of ever being married. But then I met Alex and discovered that there was someone I could love."

"Love?!" She scoffed at my explanation. "What does love have to do with it? Scots don't deserve love. But I'm offering you a way out, a way to help your country. A marriage between us will give Scotland back some of its respect."

I was suddenly furious, unable to stop the anger that surged into my voice. "A way out? The only thing you're offerin' me is th' chance tae trade one form of slavery for another. And Scotland would only gain dishonor from a union with yer family; yer father has brought nothin' but pain tae me country. Why would I ever want tae join with that?!"

My fury burning hot, I towered over her as she cowered away from me. Then, shaking my head, too angry to register the steely glint in her eyes as I turned away, I stormed past her and left.

***

ROISIN FOUND ME an hour later in the training room, beating out my frustration against a sparring bag. I grunted with each punch and kick that I lashed out. The room was a little-known secret in the basement of our home. The Scottish Accords had made it illegal for Scotsmen to be trained to fight unless they were already in the UFC military, but my parents had quietly arranged for specialists to come to this room and train me from a young age. They had wanted to make sure that my name would not be added to Scotland's long list of war casualties. When I had left to fulfill my required draft, they had chosen to leave the room set up for me in case I ever wanted to use it during one of my shore leaves.

Roisin found a stack of floor mats to climb on top of, the same way she had done when we were younger, and waited patiently until I was ready. With a final swing, I punched the bag one last time. Then, wiping the sweat off my forehead with a towel, I walked over to lean against the wall next to her.

"Collette was not very happy with th' letter I wrote," I said with a disgusted shake of my head.

"I should say not." Ro laughed musically. "She and Lord Remington left a few minutes ago lookin' like they had eaten somethin' sour. Father was not very happy either, hearin' about it from Remington th' way he did. It would have been better if yae had gone tae talk tae him first thin' this mornin' th' way we had planned, but at least I'd had a chance tae talk tae mother first."

I grunted in dismissal. "I tried talkin' tae him first thing, but he was sequestered in his office with Remington all mornin'. It didn't exactly go th' way we had planned it."

"It rarely does," Ro shrugged, "but mother managed tae smooth things over between them pretty well. She reminded them all that yae are bound by yer honor until Alexandria releases yae. She'd like tae speak with yae and Alexandria, by th' way."

I looked up in surprise. "Yae did tell her that this is only a pretense, didn't yae?"

"Oh, I told her," Roisin said with a sly smile, "but she still wants tae talk tae the two of yae."

Grande. "Well at least they're gone." I sighed in what should have been relief, but really seemed more a sense of resignation. "Let's just hope that Collette accepts defeat on this issue and that nothin' more comes of this."

Ro studied me intently for a moment before finally speaking. "How is it that yae attract so much trouble? First Collette, and then one of Icarus' Alphas?"

361

I looked back at her sharply. "How did yae…?"

Roisin raised an eyebrow as though to suggest that I shouldn't be surprised she knew about Alex and answered before I could finish the question. "She told me, Ali. She seemed tae be under th' impression that her being one of his Alphas was th' reason yae hated her. Is it?"

"Hate her? Why would she think I…" As though the electrical discharge of a lightning bolt had struck into my very being, the answer coursed through me sharply and I swore in sudden self-disgust. *Of course it was that!* It was so obvious now that it was staring me right in the face. *Alex thought I hated her!* And no wonder. The last thing she had seen from me before being kidnapped was my cold, furious rejection. I had turned my back on her!

The tension I had been working off came back with the ferocity of a snarling tiger. I pushed off the wall and stormed back to the sparring bag, putting all of my force into a roundhouse swing. I followed it up with an undercut that had the full power of my shoulder behind it. Again! Again! Again! The heavy bag creaked loudly as it absorbed my fury.

The pain in her eyes every time she looked at me?! She must have still thought that I was disgusted by who she was and that I wanted nothing to do with her! She'd had no way of knowing the emotional battle I had gone through while bound to that chair, helpless to protect her. Or the soul-searching struggle I had endured on the ship when I thought that I would never see her again. How could she have known that she had won the game; that she held my heart in her hands? I had never told her!

I swung at the bag again, over and over, hitting it hard enough to split the skin on my knuckles, and still I kept swinging. I was startled when Ro gently touched my shoulder between swings. Lost as I was in my anger with myself, I had forgotten she was there. When I paused to look at her, she reached forward to take my hands in hers and gently ran her fingers over the torn, bruised skin.

"Ali," her voice carried a gentle reproof in it, "yae can't fix the past by beatin' yerself up over yer mistakes. Yae can only move forward and work tae ensure yae never make th' same ones again." She looked up at me, intently holding my gaze. "Tell her how yae feel. It'll work out." She didn't release my hand until I finally nodded my head, acknowledging what she had said. Then, smiling encouragingly, she released my hands with a final squeeze and turned to leave the room. Just before closing the door, she called back over her shoulder. "Don't stay down here tae much longer. Oh, and take a shower; yae reek."

I stood there for several moments after she left. Part of me still wanted to punch the bag over and over until it broke, but her words had managed to soften my tension and frustration just enough to take their edge away. She was right. Punching the bag until either it broke, or my hands did, was not going to fix what I had done to Alex.

I looked down at my hands and sighed; they were going to hurt tomorrow. But as frustrated as I was, I could have done far more damage to them if Ro had not stepped in when she had. She had a way of doing that for me, soothing my pain and softening my anger. It was one of Ro's many skills. Just as blindness seemed to be one of mine. Shaking my head, I turned away from the sparring bag.

At the same time, I wasn't really ready to leave the security of this secret room and face the reality of my situation again. In the afterglow of the moment, I had hoped that a single kiss would have been enough to wash away the tension between Alex and I. But now I wasn't so certain. When I had walked away from her in the hospital, I had left her with doubts and pain that would not be so easily wiped away. Healing took time. Ro was right. I needed to talk to Alex, to tell her how I felt. She needed to know.

And what would happen if Collette came back to challenge the pretense that Alex had agreed to? Ro's plan was tenuous at best. Collette rarely gave up easily when she set her mind to something. And while the protection of a prior proposal was sound based on tradition, it was not binding by law. Lord Remington had it in his power to force the marriage my father had agreed to, just as he had it in his power to order my execution. What then?

I glanced around the training room and the equipment my parents had put in place to ensure that I was prepared for what was to come. It had been a hard, difficult path, growing up knowing that what I learned here would very likely be my only chance for survival. I had worked hard and listened studiously to those who trained me. Yet for all my training, the real battle for my life and freedom seemed to have come down to something that nothing in this room could have prepared me for.

I sighed heavily, finally admitting that the room had done all it could for me; it truly was time for me to leave. As I locked the door behind me, the unexpected thought flashed through my mind that I was saying goodbye to the room I had practically grown up in; I would not be going back in there. It was a ridiculous notion, and I dismissed it as quickly as it came. This room would be here for me the next time I needed it; my parents would make sure of that. And, even if I found myself forced into Collette's marriage, this estate would one day be mine. I would come here again, when next

I needed to battle the demons that carried the world's demands. I left the hall, confident that I would come back to it again. Some day.

Chapter 34: Alexandria Jaquette

AFTER LEAVING AIDEN and Collette, I made my way back to the common area that adjoined the guest rooms we had been assigned. With the rest of the team out and about, it was a quiet place that I could sit and think. My mind was still spinning from the exhilaration of Aiden's kiss, but at the same time, there was a dark corner of my mind that had begun sinuously taunting me with whispered thoughts: *You think that a single kiss changes anything? You are a fool! He's only using you to escape Collette! And when her threat is gone, he'll be gone too. He will not hesitate to turn his back on you again, just like he did before.*

I rubbed my hands against my forehead, as though doing so could push the voice out of my head. I didn't want the doubt. I wanted to hold on to the warmth that had rushed through me when he had pulled me protectively against him. I wanted to trust that his searching gaze had been a desperate hope on his part that I felt for him what he felt for me. But, in spite of what I wanted, the exhilaration was slowly being replaced by the anxiety of doubt.

The soft rap of knuckles on wood interrupted my thoughts. I looked up to see Thatcher standing in the doorframe. He was studying me with a look somewhere between concern and sympathy.

"You doin' okay?" he asked.

"Yea, I'm fine." I smiled feebly.

His eyebrow rose doubtfully, and he studied me for a moment longer before seeming to come to a decision. He came into the room and sat down in the chair across from me, leaning forward with his arms folded across his knees.

"Seems to me you could use someone to talk to." He said it softly, but firmly, the set of his mouth suggesting that he would brook no argument on his suggestion.

"And you're the one I should talk to?" I laughed doubtfully.

I wasn't really one to share my thoughts with others, especially others I didn't know very well. But he only shrugged dismissively at my laugh and sat back into the chair. "Ma always said I was good at listening. Why don't you give me a try?"

I almost laughed again and told him no thanks, but something about the set to his jaw, or maybe it was the way he had folded his arms across his chest, either way, something about him made me realize that he was not going to just let me get up and walk away. I sighed inwardly, wondering how much he already knew.

I shrugged my shoulders resignedly. "Okay then. What should we talk about?"

Thatcher didn't respond to my question, but the corners of his mouth twitched up in a knowing smile.

I rolled my eyes and laughed. "Fine. We'll talk about Aiden." No sooner had I said his name then my own smile disappeared.

"Thatcher," the words came out hesitantly, "why did he join this team?"

It wasn't really the question I had intended to ask, but it was the one I needed to ask.

Thatcher cocked his head, confused by the question. "Why do you ask?"

"In the hospital...after the caves...I overheard Aiden talking to Hadley." I spoke haltingly, like I was afraid to get to the point of my question. In truth, I was. I was afraid of what I might discover about Aiden's true intentions. "They thought I was still unconscious, but I was just starting to wake up and I heard what they were saying. He told Hadley...he said..." I took a deep breath before saying the rest in a rush. "...He said that he wanted to leave before I woke up. He sounded so angry about being delayed, like he couldn't wait to get away from me."

Thatcher's face was expressionless except for a faint tightening of the skin around his eyes, but he didn't say anything, so I kept going.

"And then, when he came into the conference room at the lodge, he was startled to find me there. He obviously hadn't planned on me being part of his next adventure. I think he tried to offer an excuse, but I couldn't handle another rejection from him, so...I ran." I admitted the last part with more than a hint of embarrassment.

"I think I expected him to leave again after that, but he didn't and I don't understand why? Why did he stay?"

Thatcher remained quiet for a moment more, seeming to carefully consider what I had said. But when he finally spoke, he didn't answer my question. Instead, he seemed to change the subject with a question of his own. "Have you seen Aiden's wrists?"

"What?" I asked confused. "What about his wrists?"

"When Aiden carried you out of the caves, his wrists were chaffed, raw, and bloodied."

"And?" I asked, not seeing what this had to do with anything.

"There was a chair in the room where Estradé took you. A chair with leather straps that had fresh blood on them."

A vague image of Aiden bound to a chair stirred in the back of my mind. It was a fuzzy memory, but I was certain that it was a true one.

"The recovery team identified the blood as Aiden's. They said that Estradé must have made him watch whatever they were doing to you in that surgery room, and he had clearly fought like a lion trying to get out of that chair." Thatcher said the last part as though it were the answer to my question.

"Anyone would have fought to get out of that chair." I still didn't get it. How was this an answer to my question?

Thatcher shook his head slowly. "Someone who hated you, and didn't care what happened to you, would not have done that type of damage to themselves trying to get to you."

My mouth formed a silent "oh" as understanding dawned on me at last. "You're suggesting that he cared more about me than about what happened to himself."

Thatcher nodded.

"Then why was he in such a hurry to leave me in the hospital afterwards?"

He shrugged uncommittedly, though the steady tone of his voice suggested he already knew the answer. "Maybe that is the question you should really be asking."

Footsteps coming down the hall interrupted our conversation. I looked up to see a square-faced man dressed in the brocaded blue and yellow clothes that seemed to be the uniform of those who worked in the castle. He bowed slightly and spoke with a gravelly voice. "Begging yer pardon, miss. Th' Lady of the house, Duchess Eithne Buccleuch, sent me tae ask if yae would dae her the honor of joinin' her for tea in her sittin' room."

I looked to Thatcher, not entirely certain how to respond. Why would she want to meet with me? He only smiled with the slightest hint of amusement and said simply, "Best not keep her waiting."

"Um, sure," I muttered uncertainly as I stood up.

"Very good then." He nodded, as though there had not been any doubt in his mind as to how I would respond. "If yae will follow me, miss."

The room he led me to was bigger than the one I had left; it was also much more elegant. As I glanced around the room, I had to admit that Aiden's mother had excellent taste. The room's cream-colored furniture was the perfect combination of form and function with smooth lines that flowed just short of being overly simple, while at the same time having diminutive design details that suggested they had been built by a master of their trade.

Complementing the cream-colored furniture were occasional dark wood pieces that kept the room's light colors from becoming overbearing while giving the room a sophisticated feel. The two-toned paint of the wall's wainscoting added hints of pale sage green that were further carried throughout the room in the occasional throw pillow and the simple floral arrangements that had been placed on several of the side tables. The room's central piece was a wooden table that was as simple in its form as it was elegant; it perfectly suited the woman seated next to it.

Eithne Buccleuch was a portrait of simple elegance. Her rich auburn hair was pulled up into an uncomplicated French twist and her makeup was little more than hints of shading on her eyes and cheeks. At the same time, her beauty was not the type that existed because of how she did her makeup or coifed her hair. Instead, it was the type of beauty that came from her gentle smile and the warmth of her eyes. It was obvious which parent Aiden had gotten his eyes from; hers were the same brilliant shade of blue his were. But unlike Aiden's, there was a depth to them that suggested wisdom her son had yet to gain.

A girl not much older than myself carried in a silver tray bearing a gently steaming teapot and several other matching pieces of delicate bone china. The pink and sage floral design of the cream-colored tea set was the finishing touch to the room's setting.

"Thank you, Sylvie." Lady Buccleuch smiled appreciatively as the girl placed the tray on the table in the midst of a variety of sweet breads that were already there. The breads included everything from scones and tarts to some doughy confection that I was unfamiliar with.

Aiden's mother picked up the teapot and gracefully filled two cups with the aromatic black tea. "Sugar and milk?" She glanced toward me for my answer.

"Yes, please."

Then she handed one of the cups to me before taking a sip from her own.

"So, tell me about yourself, Alexandria?" She had the faintest hint of Aiden's lyrical accent, but it was mild enough to suggest that rather than growing up with it, it had been acquired as a result of living among others who spoke with it.

"There's not much to tell." I shrugged uncomfortably. "I'm eighteen, I grew up in England, and now I'm a specialist in the UFC military."

Lady Buccleuch smiled indulgently. "Forgive me, I didn't ask quite what I meant. Roisin has already told me that much about you." My heart skipped a beat as she paused to take another sip of her tea. What else would Roisin have told her mother? Would she have told her that I was one of Icarus' Alphas, or would she have left that part out to avoid trouble?

"And yet, you are quite different from how I imagined one such as yourself to be. Last night you showed a level of self-possession coupled with self-restraint that is not often found in one such as yourself; let alone the delicate grace you carry yourself with. It makes me curious to know more about your upbringing."

Rather than clarifying her intentions, or assuring me that Roisin had not told her what I was afraid she might have, her words left me even more uncertain than I had been before.

"Well…" I hesitated, my mind racing to decide how best to respond. "I'm not sure that I can agree with your assessment of me. To be honest, I was more possessed by anger than any self-restraint last night when I reacted the way I did."

"Oh, quite understandable." The lady nodded with the hint of a sly smile. "Collette's opinions were not very gracious, and should have been kept to herself. Had it been me she was speaking to that way, I might have considered turning a bowl of soup overhead, not just using words."

Was she hinting at my ability to control things with gravity? Aside from the slyness, which I wasn't even positive I was interpreting correctly, her face was a picture of innocence.

"Perhaps, then, you could start by telling me about your parents. Was it your father who drove you to the military? What kind of man is he?" She raised her cup to take another sip, seemingly oblivious as I choked on the sip I had just taken.

"My father?" I cleared my throat.

"Oh, dear. Forgive me. Have I touched on a tender subject?" Aiden's mother hurriedly set her cup down and handed me a linen napkin.

"Uh, no," I lied as I used it to wipe the few drops of tea that had spilled onto the front of my uniform. "It's just that there isn't much I can tell you about my parents. My mother died when I was born, and I never knew my father. I'm afraid I didn't have the advantage of a family the way your son did."

"Oh, my dear, I'm so sorry. That must have been very hard for you." Her voice sounded as though she truly was. At the same time, there was a gleam of challenge in her eyes, as though to say that she knew I wasn't telling her everything and that she was disappointed by what I had left out.

I was suddenly discouraged; discouraged, but at the same time annoyed. There were very few people in my life that I cared one way or another what they thought about me. A psychiatrist might have diagnosed me as having built an emotional wall around myself. It didn't stop me from making friends, but it protected me when they later abandoned me, as they always seemed to do when they found out what I was. Captain Marcellus was one of the few I had allowed inside of that wall; this woman was not. *So why did her expression bother me so much?* I shouldn't have cared what she thought about me. Yet for some inexplicable reason, I did. I wanted her to believe me. I wanted her trust, even while knowing that the truth would likely prevent me from ever having it.

I almost laughed at the whiplash irony of my thoughts. Moments ago, I had been worried about whether Roisin had told her who I was. Now I was weighing what it would most certainly cost me if I told her myself against what it might cost me if I didn't.

Sighing, I set back down the cup I had just picked up. "Actually, nothing about my life has ever been easy, or simple. The truth is that I was born as a result of one of Icarus' experiments. My mother was one of his prisoners. She escaped from him before I was born, but that doesn't change who or what I am."

Her back stiffened noticeably, and her eyes narrowed as she studied me for what seemed like an eternity before she finally set down her own cup and asked, "And just what are you?"

"I am…" I hesitated nervously as her gaze seemed to harden, but I wouldn't turn back now. If there was any chance of earning her trust, it could only happen on the other side of the truth. "I am one of Icarus' Alphas, just like the one who killed your son." I couldn't meet her eyes as I said the last part, shame pulling my gaze down. I braced myself for the rejection that I knew must follow; just as it had from Aiden when he had been told the same thing. How could it not?

I heard her move from her seat and halfway expected to feel the sharp sting of a slap across my face. It was no less than I deserved for the pain I had brought into her home. I flinched when her hand did touch my face, but it was not the slap I had been expecting. Her fingers were gentle as she firmly lifted my chin so that I had to meet her eyes. The hardness was gone, replaced by a motherly tenderness.

"No, child," she said gently, "you are not anything like the girl that killed my son."

That was not what I had been expecting her to say. She ignored my startled expression and continued with a tone that now took on a pragmatic quality. "Thank you for being honest with me. Now allow me to be so in return." She released my chin as she stepped back to sit in her own chair once more. All hints of the earlier indulgence, slyness, and challenge were gone. She was still the same woman, but now her calm composure radiated undercurrents of power and authority that had not been there moments before. I realized with slight surprise that this woman was not simply Aiden's mother, this was a woman who was familiar with command and was comfortable in it.

"I asked you here to find out for myself what kind of woman you are. My son is placing a tremendous amount of trust in you. I needed to know for myself whether his trust was wisely placed, and whether I can trust you with my son's life as well. Because it is indeed his life we are balancing in the scales of what we are attempting to do."

"And what have you decided?" I asked nervously.

Her lips twisted ever so slightly into the hint of a mischievous smile. "My son is more of a fool than he realizes to have gotten himself into the situation he did with you; he clearly has far too much of his father in him for his own good."

A situation with me? Well, yes, I had to admit that being dependent on one of Icarus' Alphas for help would be considered a troubling situation by most people.

"However," she continued without pause, "I believe his trust is well placed. If you are willing to put up with his faults, and help him despite his bullheadedness, he just might walk away from here with more intact than his life. On the other hand, I suspect that your trust is a little more difficult to earn than his is. So, allow me to share some details with you that I don't believe you are yet aware of.

"My children, in spite of their cleverness, have only identified one aspect of the danger facing Alistair. You see, although she is the more visible danger at this moment, Collette is not the real threat in this game. She will, of course, throw her tantrums and spit out threats against you, but she herself cannot carry out any of those threats. Lord Remington, on the other hand, has considerable actual power over life and death here in Scotland. But, while he pampers his daughter and indulges nearly all of her whims, he will not permit her to make a fool out of him or to maneuver him into a position he himself does not wish to be placed in.

"He is the real threat to Alistair, and to Scotland, and the real problem that we are facing. While the UFC has effectively stripped away much of the power behind my husband's title, it is not all gone. Up to this point, I have been able to carefully guide my husband around the worst of Remington's suggestions, the ones that would have harmed the people of Scotland most. But I believe that Remington has designs on the power that remains to the Buccleuch family name and was encouraging his daughter's behavior in order to gain that power. He will see your claim on my son as a threat to his designs.

"So, the question that faces us now is how far he will take his challenge to your claim, and how far you are willing to take your claim in order to stop his challenge. If I know Remington as well as I think I do, he will come at us with every weapon he has in his arsenal to force Alistair's hand. And Alistair will do whatever he believes necessary to protect his family, even surrendering himself if he thinks that is what it will take to ensure our safety. That leaves only the question of you. How far are you willing to take this engagement to ensure Alistair's safety, how far will you trust Alistair to guard your back in this, and how far will you trust me to guide you in your actions?"

I sat in quiet consideration for a moment. I had been so worried about gaining her trust that I had not paused to consider whether or not I should be trusting her in return. But now that the question had been asked, I realized that I had already made my decision. Whether or not I should, I did trust her. The rational part of my brain was screaming that I was being foolish to trust someone I had only just met, but I would trust her in this nonetheless. And I wanted to trust Aiden. But with or without that trust, I would do what I could to keep him safe.

"I will trust your guidance," I said it slowly, not out of doubt, but because I was a little shocked to realize that it was true, "and I will not leave Aiden unprotected, whether or not he will do the same for me."

Her head cocked curiously at the last part, but she only said, "Thank you, that will be enough."

Then she raised her voice slightly and called toward the door. "Come in please, Sylvie."

The door opened quickly enough that it was obvious the girl had been waiting there for just such a call.

"Yes, m'lady?"

"Would you ask my son to join us."

"Of course, m'lady."

As the door closed behind the girl, Lady Buccleuch picked up her cup of tea once more.

"From a young age, Alistair has shown a remarkable ability to judge people. He seems to instinctively know who can be trusted and who should not be. Unfortunately, that skill has rarely been coupled with the ability to control his emotions toward them. He thinks he does a good job of hiding it, but his face is an open book to everyone who knows how to read it. Perhaps you have noticed this?"

I wasn't really sure whether she was asking a question or making a statement, but the image of Aiden's clenched jaw flashed through my mind; it did that when he was angry.

"He has also never been a very successful liar; the muscles around his eyes tighten when he tries."

I had never noticed that. But was it because he had never lied to me or because I had simply failed to notice that particular tick?

"Lord Remington knows Alistair too well for him to get away with a deception. So it will fall on you to carry this story when Remington begins to ask questions. I think simple will be best," she mused softly over the top of her still-steaming cup. I wasn't entirely certain whether she was talking to herself or to me.

"Alright, then." She set her cup down and faced me directly. There was no doubt that she was talking to me now. "This is how we are going to do it."

By the time a soft knock came at the door, I was feeling a little wild eyed. I had agreed to follow her guidance, but this? I swallowed hard. Just how far was I willing to take this to ensure that Aiden was safe? As far as she had just suggested?

Before I could answer my own question, the door opened and Sylvie said lightly, "Your son, m'lady."

I closed my eyes and took a slow, steady breath, trying to regain control over the bubbling sense of panic that

378

threatened to drown me. The air that filled my lungs carried the faint scent of the cologne that I was coming to associate with the stranger Aiden had become; he had never worn cologne back on base.

I opened my eyes to see his lean form gliding past. He passed me with only the briefest of glances in my direction before he bent forward to give his mother a kiss on the cheek. If he had been surprised to find me here, his expression had given no indication of it. But then, neither had he given any indication that he was pleased to see me either. If anything, it was guardedly neutral, leaving me, if it was possible, even more anxious than I had been before he walked through the door.

Lady Buccleuch smiled warmly up at Aiden. "Thank you for joining us, Alistair. I was just telling Alexandria about our plans for this evening."

"Our plans?" Aiden froze.

"Our plans for tonight's engagement party, where you will formally present your lovely fiancé to the people of Scotland." She said it as though she were reprimanding Aiden for being forgetful.

He glanced nervously in my direction. "Uh, mother, that was not part of th' plan."

"But of course it was, Alistair dear." Her voice sounded slightly amused as she addressed him, but it was an amusement that didn't reach her eyes. "Surely you must have realized that a quickly written note would not be sufficient to dissuade Lord Remington from his plans for you? You did realize that it was Remington's plans you were attempting to counter, didn't you? Or did you manage to fool yourself into thinking that Collette was behind all of this?" She said the last part with a much more direct gaze.

Aiden's face drained of color and his back stiffened.

All pretenses of amusement were gone from Lady Buccleuch's face, a sad smile having taken its place. "Alistair, you and Roisin should have come to me with your plans before putting them into action. I could have helped you side step some of the trouble that you have created. But what's done is done. Now we can only move forward and patch this situation as best we can."

She reached up to gently squeeze his hand. "Please sit down. We have more to talk about and you will be better prepared to receive it if you are sitting."

Lady Buccleuch went on to retell most of what she had already told me. It was no less alarming to hear the second time around, but having already heard it once, my mind found it easier to analyze what she was saying and spent less time hyperventilating from the near panic her words caused. It really wasn't that complicated of a plan. Each step logically progressed forward, driven by the necessity created during the previous steps. It had begun with the letter Aiden had written and delivered under Collette's door early this morning. It ended one year from now with the two of us married.

And that was what shocked me most. Marriage had not been an immediate part of any of my plans. It had, of course, always been an aspiration for some later date, maybe when I was in my late twenties and had graduated from college. But with the development of my abilities, and my forced entry into the military, such considerations had become so diluted by the reality that the UFC had other plans for me that they no longer seemed probable.

What was more, it was not a marriage for love as I had always hoped I would one day have, it was a marriage of necessity. It was definitely not something I would have chosen for myself, but was it something I would do to secure Aiden's safety? Lady Buccleuch had made it very clear to me that for Aiden, there was no other choice. His letter to Collette, and her subsequently seeing us in the hall, had insured that. He would either marry me or he would suffer the bitter consequences of his deception; Remington would make sure of that.

"Do you finally understand your situation?" his mother asked gently, yet firmly as she finished her explanation.

Aiden seemed too stunned to speak. He only managed a slight nod.

She smiled sympathetically, but spoke no less firmly. "Good. Now, here is what is going to happen next. I am going to step out of the room for a few minutes to gather the others we will need in order to make this work. When I return, this will be on Alexandria's finger."

She reached for Aiden's hand and turned it over so that she could place a small blue velvet box into it. I'm not sure where she had been keeping it; I hadn't noticed it before it was suddenly in her hand. But Aiden's hand began to tremble ever so slightly as he stared down at the box with an expression somewhere between shock and fear.

Lady Buccleuch, ignoring her son's unease, rose gracefully from her chair and placed her hand gently on his shoulder. "You chose a remarkable young woman, Alistair. Be certain you are worthy of what she is doing for you." Then, not waiting for his response, she strode from the room and closed the door behind her.

The click of the door handle seemed to pull Aiden from his shock. His head snapped up and he met my eyes with a look of desperation. His words came out in a jumble. "Alex,

I am so sorry. This was not what I had intended. I had no right tae dae this tae yae. I had no idea…I didn't expect…I…" His voice trailed off miserably. "It wasn't supposed tae go like this."

Part of me wanted to assure him that I knew this was not what he had intended, but the rest of me was still too stunned to speak. The questions reverberating through my head seemed to block out all other coherent thoughts. Just how far was I willing to take this? Was there really any choice?

I'm not sure how long I made him wait in his silent misery, but eventually my numbness began to fade and my thoughts began to coalesce around an answer to at least one of the questions: I did have a choice. I could still walk away, but he could not. He no longer had control of his situation. He knew that his fate was in my hands, and he was clearly afraid that I might leave. And why shouldn't he wonder? After all, he had already walked away from me twice, hadn't he?

Thatcher's words floated through my head: *Someone who hated you…would not have done that type of damage to themselves trying to get to you.*

Almost not realizing I was doing it, I reached for his free hand and gently pushed up the sleeve to reveal the wounds on his wrist. Aiden was startled, but he didn't pull away. Instead, he watched uncertainly as I ran my fingers lightly over the three-inch-wide band of torn and scarred skin that the shirt had been hiding. Blisters had begun to form over the second-degree friction burns, but the skin was still chafed and raw around the edges.

Hesitantly, I asked him, "How did this happen?"

For a moment, I was afraid he might not answer the question as his expression became hard and he started to pull his hand away from mine.

"Aiden, please," I stopped him, tightening my grip so that he couldn't easily pull away.

He froze, looking at me nervously before seeming to suddenly collapse in on himself. He sighed heavily. "When we went into th' cave system tae find yae, Estradé had set a trap for me. She wanted me tae see what th' UFC had done tae yae, only I was still tae angry tae think rationally. I think she knew I would be, because she bound me in a chair and forced me tae watch th' procedure as they removed th' trackin' device and th' nano-explosive."

My eyes narrowed in momentary confusion as ghosting memories of Estradé and the caves swirled with his words. He must have taken my expression for skepticism because he hurried on to explain. "Alex, I was a fool. I can't apologize enough for leaving yae in the hospital. If I had just stayed, yae would have never been hurt. I knew it was me fault. And then, when I saw yae on that table, all I could think about was gettin' tae yae…" He looked down at the wrist I was holding. "But I wasn't strong enough."

The last part came out as though it were an apology, as though he believed that his efforts had not been enough. Not enough? He'd known what I was, yet he had still done this to himself trying to help me! My hands instinctively squeezed his, offering encouragement.

I think I finally understood why he had been in such a hurry to leave me in the hospital. He didn't hate me. In fact, he had done all he could to make sure I was safe. But in rescuing me, he had betrayed the memory of his brother. He had not been strong enough to retain his anger against an enemy he had become friends with. What that must have cost him emotionally I couldn't imagine, but I could understand that it would have been painfully conflicting for him.

"You came after me; it was enough."

He smiled weakly, clearly unconvinced. "Alex, there's somethin' more I need tae tell yae."

I shook my head with a reassuring smile. "It's okay. I understand…"

He interrupted me. "No, Alex, yae don't, but I need yae tae. I need you tae know what yae mean tae me. I had tae be forced tae leave yae before I understood it for meself, and fear made me hold me tongue when I should have told yae long before this." He took a breath to steady himself, then reached out to take my hands with his. "Alex, me heart is yers, wholly and completely. Wherever yae are, that is where I want tae be. But th' truth is that I never intended tae marry. Not Collette, not yae, not anyone. This is not what I meant tae have happen."

His heart was mine? How was that possible? When had that happened? And when had he been forced to leave me? How had he been forced? It couldn't have been the first time he had turned his back on me; he had just apologized for that one. But the second time, when he had thought I was unconscious? Had I misunderstood his reason for wanting to leave? Was it possible it hadn't been his choice at all?

For the space of a heartbeat, I felt a thrill of excitement, but then reality returned to dampen the feeling. No matter what he felt about me now, there was no guarantee it would always be that way. He had to be conflicted between his hatred for his brother's murderer and the love he thought he was developing for me. *How long could his heart possibly remain mine in that situation? Until he found someone less painful? Someone who didn't remind him of his brother's killer?*

And then the second part of what he had said caught up with my thoughts. *Not get married? But, wasn't that what this was all about?*

"Aiden, why were you not planning on marriage?"

His eyes dropped and his voice sounded defeated. "I am a son of Scotland; I'm bound by th' Scottish Accords. Any child I have will be bound by it as well, and I refuse tae bring a child intae this world who will be forced tae go through what I have. I'm not goin' tae let that happen, even accidentally. The Buccleuch family name will end with me."

Reluctantly, he let go of my hands. "It's okay for yae tae go. I'll let Thatcher know th' change in plans. He and th' others will see yae safely tae th' school, but I'll need tae stay behind, I have…duties I need tae attend tae here."

I sat in stunned silence, waiting for the punch line; it never came. *He's serious! He's avoiding marriage and trying to send me away, not because he doesn't like me or doesn't want to marry me, but because he doesn't want to have kids?* I stared at him; shock etched on my face for the span of a heartbeat. And then I began to laugh, a deep bitter laugh.

Aiden looked up in startled confusion. "Alex?"

I had to wipe tears from the corner of my eyes. *Of all the reasons he thought I would walk out of the room and abandon him, he thought it was because he wouldn't give me a child?*

"Aiden," I finally managed to get out between laughs, "I am an Alpha. I can't have children."

It was his turn to be shocked as the truth dawned on him. My laughter became real watching his shocked expression morph into a sheepish grin.

"Well, I guess I make a better lady's fool than I dae a lady's knight," he said self-mockingly.

Still laughing, I nodded in agreement. But something more had just occurred to me as I watched his expression change: the smile on his face and the twinkle in his eyes was not the look of someone who was conflicted about his situation, it was the look of someone who had just had a great weight lifted from his shoulders. Even as I laughed, my mind processed this realization. Maybe, just maybe, the conflict he felt was no longer about who and what I was. But how could I be sure?

Wiping another tear away, I asked, "Do you have any other objections to your mother's plan?"

His smile faded again. "This isn't your fight, Alex, and I had no right tae ask yae tae become part of it. Yae shouldn't be part of this situation. We really dae need to go talk tae Thatcher about takin' yae on tae th' school."

I studied him for a long moment, not saying anything. It had been made clear to me that Remington would not allow Aiden to walk away from this unscathed. If I left now, he would face that man's wrath alone. His only real hope of escape was the plan his mother had proposed. More than that, I realized that I didn't want to abandon him, not just because of the situation it would leave him in, but because of how much it had hurt me when I thought he had been the one abandoning me. Something else had occurred to me as well, a truth that startled me as much as it assured me; there was another reason I couldn't walk away from him.

"No," I finally responded, "I don't think so. You said that you had to leave me before you understood how you felt about me. Well, I figured something out for myself when you walked away: you already owned a piece of my heart. You took it with you when you left and it very nearly tore me apart. I don't think I could handle going through that again right now, so I'm not going anywhere."

Aiden looked shocked at first, clearly not having expected me to say any of that, but then his grin slowly returned. "Yae dae realize that we're a little unbalanced here. Yae own all of me heart, but I only have a piece of yers."

I felt the heat rising in my cheeks as I replied, "Then I suppose it's a good thing you'll have a year to prove to me whether or not you deserve the rest of it."

I couldn't help the smile that came to my own lips when he laughed in response.

"Very well, then." He was still grinning.

Opening the box and turning it around, he knelt down in front of me. His voice was somehow both solemn and playful at the same time. "Alexandria Jaquette, will yae accept a humble fool as yer husband with th' promise that he will dae everythin' in his power tae become th' knight in shinin' armor that yae deserve?"

Laughing in return, I nodded my head. "Yes, Aiden Haskell..." Then I paused, suddenly unsure of myself. "Or is it Allestare Bugelow?" I laughed again, this time in embarrassment as I butchered his name, then I shrugged with a faint smile. "Well, whoever you are, humble fool or Lord of Scotland, I wouldn't have it any other way!"

THIRTY MINUTES LATER, I sat in agitated silence, twisting the delicate ring on my finger. The ring, as it turned out, was a family heirloom. Aiden had explained that his grandfather had commissioned it to be made from four different metals with the thought that each of its intricately woven strands would represent a different side of his love for Aiden's grandmother. The silver represented the purity of his love, the platinum was for the strength of his love, the gold represented the passion of his love, and the rose gold represented his hope that she would return his love in equal measure. He'd had it styled after the Celtic sailor's knot, an unbroken weave that was supposed to represent a bond that could not be broken. It was beautiful in its simplicity and its meaning, but right now the only thing I noticed about it was how smoothly it was twisting around my finger.

Around me, several voices were speaking all at once.

"Yae have gone tae far…"

"…goin' tae start another war with this!"

"We are already at war…"

"We don't have authority for this!"

"What were yae thinking?"

"…no right to put Alex in danger…"

"She's not th' one in danger…"

"…the mess yae two created…"

"Your bloody family is th' reason for all of Scotland's problems…"

"Remington has left us no other choice…"

"…yae should have talked tae me first…"

"…we would not have helped if we'd known…"

Their words were a tangled weave of dissenting opinions. Lord Buccleuch's voice was the loudest as he scolded his children for what they had done, but he was far from being the angriest. Wren's quiet tone, icy cold in its delivery, had that honor as he accused Roisin of misleading him and insisted that our team did not have the authority to get involved in this situation. McLagan's enraged mutters added a steady staccato of swear words and accusations that punctuated the first two voices while the rich timbre of Roisin's voice added the final weave as she unapologetically argued the necessity of their actions.

Aiden had tried early on to defend his actions, arguing that the marriage to Collette would have hurt Scotland. But a few angry words and a stern look from his father had made him close his mouth and hang his head. He had been quiet ever since.

Thatcher's voice was also absent from the argument. He had not spoken a single word since the eruption of voices had begun. Instead, his piercing gaze had moved from me to Aiden and back again with a stony expression that seemed to speak louder than all the other voices combined; he was not at all pleased with the situation.

Aiden had not been able to meet his eyes for more than a few seconds, but I returned Thatcher's stony gaze stubbornly, if not a little uncomfortably. I believed that I had made the right decision in not abandoning Aiden. So why did his gaze make me feel like I had done something wrong? Half of me wanted to shrink back into my chair under his stare, the other half bristled with frustration. As a result, I was agitatedly twisting the ring on my finger.

Realizing what I was doing, I let it go and purposely folded my arms across my chest. I was not a little kid and I had made the right decision. Everyone else was just going to have to deal with it.

"Enough," Thatcher said suddenly, his deep voice rumbling. Almost as one, every head swiveled toward him.

Looking squarely at Aiden he said, cold and hard, "Whether you intended to or not, you have placed our mission in jeopardy. We cannot safely guard the asset under these circumstances and you clearly cannot continue with us. We have no choice but to continue on without you."

I expected Aiden to argue back. To my surprise, he only nodded his head dispiritedly. My eyes narrowed.

Thatcher grunted, as though Aiden's response had settled the matter. Then he turned to face Lady Buccleuch and said gruffly, "I'm sorry we can't be of more help, ma'am. Thank you for your hospitality, but we will be leaving within the hour…"

"No, Thatcher," I interrupted firmly. "I am not leaving here without Aiden, and he can't leave without this problem resolved. The rest of you are welcome to go, but I will not."

Thatcher's jaw clenched as he slowly turned to face me. "Do you not understand that Captain Marcellus will have our hides if anything happens to you?"

I knew that the whole purpose of sending us out in small groups with decoy assets had been to keep me safely hidden while we made our way to the school; Marcellus' team had gone to great lengths to ensure my anonymity. But what did my own safety mean to me if Aiden's was in jeopardy? I would not trade his for mine! Besides, what danger was I really in?

"Do you not understand that I can't leave? I will not go through that again." I didn't say what 'that' was, but I was pretty sure Thatcher would understand. His brows seemed to crease, considering what I had said.

Finally, he growled in frustration, "You know very well that we can't leave here without you."

"I'm sorry," I apologized, and I truly was, but that wasn't going to change my decision.

Out of the corner of my eye I noticed a slight tightening around Wren's eyes as he looked back and forth between Thatcher and me, contemplating our exchange.

With an angry grunt and an exasperated shake of his head, Thatcher finally growled, "Fine, we stay."

Wren's eyes widened in surprise, then narrowed once more as though he suddenly understood something that had previously escaped him. McLagan's jaw simply dropped.

Rounding on Lady Buccleuch, Thatcher snarled, "But no one can know who she really is! If I think for even a moment that her safety is compromised, I will take her out of here by force if needs be and Aiden be damned!"

I was about to argue with him that he didn't get to make that decision for me, but Aiden's head had come up during the interchange and he cut me off with a hard edge to his own voice. "If her safety becomes compromised, I will help yae dae it."

My head swung to glare at him. "You will do no such thing!"

He met my anger with steely resolve. "I didn't carry yae out of those caves just tae put yae right back into danger. I will only allow yae tae remain here so long as I am certain yae can dae so safely."

"You won't allow?! What makes you think…"

Aiden cut me off as he turned back to Thatcher. "Cody Thatcher, I am officially relinquishin' me position as team lead tae yae. I will bring the command pad tae yer quarters as soon as we finish here. Yae will be callin' th' shots from here on out."

"Now hold on a minute…" I tried again, but this time it was Thatcher who cut me off.

"So be it," he said ominously, ignoring my angry glare. Turning back to Lady Buccleuch he went right on, "As of this moment, Alexandria Jaquette does not exist. You will have to choose a new name for Aiden's fiancé and come up with an appropriate background story that hides who she is."

Lady Buccleuch, who had been calmly silent up to this point said simply, "Arrangements have already been made for that. She is the Lady Claire DuCain. Daughter of Lord and Lady DuCain of Sussex, England. They will both be present tonight to support this claim."

My jaw dropped. What? I wasn't the only one whose face showed surprise.

"How is it that these arrangements have already been made? Why did yae not talk tae me about this first?" Aiden's father asked angrily.

Her eyebrow arched as she turned to meet his angry gaze and countered coldly, "The way you talked to me before arranging for our son to marry Remington's daughter?"

He was clearly abashed as he looked down at his hands. "Well, no, but I thought…"

Her face softened and she patted him on his hand. "My dear, we'll talk more about our mutual failures when we are in private. For now, let us focus on the problem at hand."

Turning back to the group she continued, "Director Beckwith's secretary reached out to me a few days ago. She said that Alistair would be returning home soon with a group of friends and asked if I would assist his office with a unique situation regarding one of them. It was to be a top-secret effort that I was to tell no one about. In return for my assistance, Director Beckwith would see to it that Alistair was released from his military service."

Roisin gasped. McLagan hissed. She ignored them both and went right on talking.

"But it would seem that the situation has changed somewhat. It is not safe for Alistair to leave his military service at this time. Besides," she smiled sadly, "if I'm not mistaken, he won't leave it anyway."

"No, I won't," Aiden replied softly, apologetically.

I looked at him incredulously. "What? Why not?"

He shrugged. "I told yae. Where yae are, I want tae be. And there is no chance the military is lettin' go of yae."

"Hold on!" McLagan demanded. "Why won't they let her go?"

Wren answered him matter-of-factly. "Because she's the real asset, isn't she? That case is just a decoy."

"Yes, she is," Lady Buccleuch confirmed. "The real reason your team came here was so that I could help her disappear, or rather, so that I could help her become someone new. Beckwith's team made the arrangements, I was asked to ensure that they are carried out."

McLagan appeared to be in a state of shock as he turned from Wren, to me, to Aiden, to Lady Buccleuch and then finally back to me. Somewhat warily he asked, "Just what type of asset are yae that th' UFC is goin' through all this trouble?"

I rolled my eyes then glared at Aiden and Thatcher. "The type that gets annoyed by people who think they can tell me what to do."

Aiden didn't flinch from my angry glare, but he also didn't rise to my challenge. Instead, he asked his mother, "What exactly dae yae mean about turning Alex intae someone else?"

Lady Buccleuch shrugged as though it were unimportant. "As I said, Alexandria is going to become Claire DuCain. That is all you need to know for now. Far more important for you to hear is the explanation of what is needed from each of you in order to make this work."

She went on to outline what she expected from each person sitting in the room. It was as though she believed each of them was going to do exactly what she told them to do without question or complaint. The truly shocking part was that they did. I'm not sure if it was her way of telling them with the obvious expectation that they would do it or if it was something more. But, thirty minutes later, they all left the room to take care of the things she had instructed them on.

"And now, my dear, for you." She smiled cryptically as she stood. "Come along."

I hesitated for just a moment. I had no desire to change who I was, but I was following her out the door and down the hall before I fully realized that I had even stood up. I began twisting the ring again as I walked. Just how far was I willing to take this? Apparently, as far as she tells me to. I shook my head in frustration but continued to follow.

The room she led me to was not that far away. In truth, it was literally just around the corner. It had a similar feel to her sitting room; decorated with the same elegant taste, but for a clearly different purpose. The large room held several pieces of furniture. Against one wall there was a simple dressing table with the same evident touch of a master woodworker's hand. On another wall, there was a smoothly elegant dress rack that held several gowns, displayed for easy viewing. In the center of the room was an arrangement of armchairs and chaise lounges surrounding a central table that held several photo frames with images of her children. I smiled in spite of myself at the image of a young teenage Aiden standing next to an even younger boy. Both were grinning proudly while holding a large, freshly caught fish between them.

Directly across the room from the door we entered were two other doors, one of which was currently open. Through it, I could see what appeared to be a wall of shelving and cabinets designed to hold small items. An older woman in servant's livery came through that open door carrying a strand of cultured pearls in one hand and a pair of drop pearl earrings in the other, suggesting exactly what those small drawers were meant to store.

"My lady." She curtsied briefly upon seeing us then went on with what she had been doing. In a tone that suggested more of a woman who believed she was in charge than that of a servant, she spoke over her shoulder as she placed the jewelry onto a black display bodice that appeared to be for that purpose. "I thought the pearls would go best with your gown this evening. Now which would you prefer, the

Luckenbach broach or the Glendevon for the gown's cascade belt?"

Lady Buccleuch smiled tolerantly. "The Glendevon, please. And Celeste, it is time to begin."

The woman only paused for a brief moment. She looked me up and down with a critical eye that didn't seem to miss anything. Then, with the tone of one reading from a shopping list, she quickly catalogued what she saw. "Tall, lithe figure with well-balanced hips and bust, though perhaps a bit too thin at the waist and not quite enough of a derrière. Fine bone structure, with a delicate collar bone and long, slender neck, delicate fingers and wrists, but strong muscles beneath it all." Then she nodded her head firmly as though having reached a conclusion. "I think we'll want to go with the pale rose gown. It will show off her lithe form and creamy skin to its best. And I'd suggest the Thistle Flower set to finish it all off." Not really waiting for approval, she nodded her head to herself and then left the room without a backward glance.

Too thin? Not enough of a bottom? I rolled my eyes.

Lady Buccleuch's lips twisted into a knowing smile. "Celeste has been my lady's maid since I was sixteen. She has never had much in the way of a filter when it comes to her opinion of what a healthy figure should look like. In spite of that, she has never led me wrong in her suggestions for what would look best on me or in a given situation and I don't believe she'll make a mistake in dressing you either. Now, please, sit down." She indicated one of the chaise lounges, but didn't sit down herself. Instead, she walked over to the dressing table and opened its drawer. When she walked back, she was holding a small dig-pad.

"I have something for you. Estradé requested that this be given to you if anything should happen that prevented her from being here herself. It was brought to me so that I could give it to you now."

I looked up in startled surprise. "Estradé?"

She handed me the digi-pad with a sad smile. "I think she would have preferred to be able to tell you all of this herself, but what we wish for is not always possible."

Then, touching me lightly on the shoulder, "Alexandria, I know that your life has never been easy, and that a lot of unexpected and unasked for things have been happening to you recently. But please know that you are not alone in all of this. You have unseen friends, watching over you and working in the shadows to make sure that you are safe and secure."

She squeezed my shoulder with the last part. "Now, I will leave you alone for a few minutes so that you can read her words. When I come back, we will get started."

As the door closed behind her, I looked down at the digi-pad in my hands. Why would Estradé write me a letter? It had been a shock to learn that she had died in the caves. A dishonorable end for a dishonorable woman, they had told me. But something in the back of my mind insisted on disagreeing with that view of her. It's not that I had forgotten that she had drugged me and kidnapped me; there were big gaps in my memory from the caves, but I remembered that much of it. It was more that I couldn't shake the nagging feeling that there had been more to it than a malicious kidnapping.

> Alexandria,
> As we make plans for what is going to happen in the next few days, I realize that even the best laid plans often go awry. I

397

decided that I needed to write this letter and make arrangements for it to be given to you at the appropriate time should I not be able to share this information myself.

First, I want to explain how impressed I have been as I have watched you these last few weeks. I came to this base expecting to find a child of Icarus who was as selfish and cruel as all the rest of her siblings; a youth who was a danger to others and who did not deserve to live. What I found instead is that your separation from his influence, or perhaps you would have been this way even if you were not, has allowed you to grow into a kind, caring young lady who often places the needs of others before her own. It was not what I was expecting.

As I continued to watch you, I began to dig into your records and learned more about the UFC's plans for you. I discovered that there are things going on in the UFC that are troubling, and that you would need help if you were going to retain the innocence and purity that you have developed. In my search for solutions, I crossed the paths of a few very powerful people who were likewise becoming aware of your position and who were themselves in a position to potentially provide the help you needed. I reached out to them and together we began to develop a plan that would ensure your safety.

We realized that the first thing you would need is the freedom to continue to choose who and what you will be. The UFC had implanted a tracking device and a nano-explosive into the base of your skull when you were very young. They intended to use those things to control you, to give them the ability to force you into the weapon that they want you to become. If all has gone well, those have been removed. With them gone, no one will have the power to force you into anything you do not wish to do.

The second thing you would need is a way to escape from those who would force you to become a weapon. To this end, I was put in contact with Captain Marcellus. I believe you already know him; you certainly made quite an impression on him in your youth. I learned that he has his own reasons for helping you and will tell you them in his own time. But he was more than willing to be part of your escape and protecting you thereafter. He will tell you the plans for that when it is time.

There is one arrangement, however, that I wanted to tell you about personally. It involves a couple that has agreed to become a major player in transitioning you away from UFC control.

I met John and Esther DuCain a few years ago, a short time after their daughter, Claire DuCain, had been seriously injured during an attack on her school by one of Icarus' children.

It was a brutally cruel attack that left Claire broken in both body and spirit. The physical damage to her body was well known, as were the efforts they made to repair it. Her emotional injuries, on the other hand, were not at all publicized. I was quietly brought in to help her with those.

Over the course of the next eighteen months, she appeared to be moving forward emotionally. So much so, that when I was asked by the Directorate's office to go on a special mission, I felt comfortable ending my sessions with her.

Unfortunately, I had misjudged the level of her progress. Upon my return from the mission, I learned that she had suffered a relapse and had recently taken her own life. Her parents were distraught. They could have blamed me for my failure to accurately diagnose her state of mind, but they didn't. Instead, they placed the blame for their daughter's death squarely on Icarus and his children.

As sad as their daughter's death was, it presented an opportunity to help you that was undeniably providential. You see, during Claire's struggles, the family had drawn into seclusion, rarely venturing out among others so that very few have seen the repairs to Claire's body or were even aware that she was struggling emotionally. And no one but her parents and a few select others are even aware that she is no longer alive. This is where you come in.

You see, Alexandria Jaquette belongs to the UFC; Claire DuCain does not. When I explained your situation to the DuCains and what you needed, they saw in you a chance to help someone where they had been unable to help their daughter. Therefore, you will become Claire DuCain. Removing the UFC's tracker and nano-explosive were only the first step in this process. The DuCains will guide you through the next few necessary steps.

The final thing you will need in order to remain free of both the UFC's control and Icarus' influence is a safety net of friends who will watch over you and protect you. To that end, I have worked with someone I will not name, but one who had it in their power to contrive a situation where you would be both safe and surrounded by capable friends. It is my hope that, in this setting, you will be able to find peace and contentment as you choose the direction your life will move in.

Mijá, I'm sorry for all that you have had to go through, especially for what I put you through in my ignorance. I wish that I could have done more to protect you and can only hope that what we have set in motion will be enough.

I wish you the best in your new life and pray to the Virgin Mary that it will be a life filled with the joy that you deserve.

-Estradé

I had a hard time reading the last few paragraphs; my eyes had begun to blur with unshed tears. As I read, flashes of forgotten memories began to appear in my mind. I saw Estradé in the clearing, leading the enemy soldiers astray with her carefully chosen words. I saw her again in the hospital, telling me what she had done and asking my forgiveness. I saw her in the cave, holding me as she lowered me to the ground, wiping the hair from my face and promising that everything would be okay.

Now I knew the truth. All that had been done for me in the past few days had been her doing. More than that, it appeared that there was something going on with the UFC that I didn't yet know about, but which posed a threat to me. She had taken steps to protect me from whatever that threat was and to ensure that I had choices in my life. Those steps included making arrangements to change who I was.

Now, I could choose to continue down the path she had set me on, or I could choose a different one and hope that I would be successful on my own at avoiding the dangers I didn't yet see. It all came down to whether or not I really trusted her.

I sighed in resignation; I knew the answer to that: I did trust her. If my becoming Claire was what she wanted, then I would do it. She had gone through far too much effort for me to scorn her plans now. When the door opened sometime later, I didn't resist the changes that it brought with it.

***

THREE HOURS LATER, my hair had been lightened to a golden gleam and then lightly layered into a shoulder-blade-length style that was currently popular. I had been given contacts that hid my violet eyes and made them a warm brown instead. My ears, which I had never chosen to pierce before, now bore a pair of dangling diamonds. The nails that the military had never really given me time to take care of had been manicured and painted. Finally, my eyebrows were shaped, and makeup was applied, with the stylist taking time to explain to me how to perform the applications so that I could do it on my own later. The soldier I had seen in the dining room mirror, and been so thoroughly unimpressed by the night before, was gone. The woman in the mirror in front of me now was someone I didn't recognize. Someone who could have just as easily come out of that magazine on local royalty as Collette could have.

Yet, for all that, the physical transformation itself was surprisingly simple; the changes yet to come were not. Lady Buccleuch began instructing me on the most salient points in Claire's life. She, I, had been born on April the fourth of 169 in Sussex, England. I had no siblings, though I had had a long line of pets including dogs, cats, birds, and fish. My current pet was a singularly unique long-haired male calico cat named Osiris.

Surprisingly, I had attended Dartmouth College up until my sixteenth year. That would be easy enough to remember since it was the same school I had actually attended, though Claire had been two years ahead of me. Shortly before my sixteenth birthday, I had transferred to The Lady of Grace Finishing School, a private college for girls, where I had been when the attack had occurred. My best friends, Monique and Joy, had been killed at that time, tortured in front of me.

I was a Beta with gifts in music and languages. I had focused my training on the harp and my voice, though I had stopped playing music after the attack, and I was fluent in Basic, English, French, Mandarin, and Russian. I had been working on adding Arabic to that list when the attack had occurred. I thought ruefully that I could at least pull off the first three languages, but if anyone tried talking to me in Russian or Mandarin, I was in trouble.

Once the initial changes were completed, and I had been dressed in an appropriate pant outfit, we moved from the dressing room to a garden patio for lunch. As we ate, Lady Buccleuch instructed me in the finer points of etiquette including how to sit with my ankles crossed, how to hold my fork at meals, and how to hold conversations with people of importance. Before she was done, I had begun to feel a little panicked. I had a good memory, but it was far from perfect. I doubted that tomorrow I would remember even half of what I had been told today.

Lady Buccleuch must have sensed my growing panic because she smiled knowingly as she reached over to gently squeeze my hand. "It will be all right, Claire. I know it's a lot to take in, but you can do this."

I smiled back weakly; certain she was only saying it to be kind.

After lunch, she took me for a short stroll among the fall colors and falling leaves of the trees just down the lane from the castle. As we walked, her instructions changed to focus on the cover story that had been woven to explain my presence at the new school. As my physical situation resulting from the attacks was somewhat well known, they had decided to build on that. The idea was that I had come out of the trauma with the determination to fight back. I had focused on building my physical strength and then applied to join the UFC's Educational Facilities Defense Division. I wanted to protect others from going through what I had.

About that time, Roisin joined us. She shared with us the backstory that had been devised to explain how Aiden and I, no, not Aiden, Alistair—I would need to call him by that name tonight—had become engaged. It turned out that, while I had been undergoing my physical transformation, Alistair, Thatcher, Wren, McLagan, and Roisin had put their heads together to create the story.

As the son of Duke Buccleuch, and the future heir to the Scottish title, his military service record was confidential. Only his sealed military records could say for certain where he had actually served, so it was easy for them to weave his story to match mine.

They decided that Alistair and I had met six months ago during my training. He had been rotated off the front lines shortly before my arrival to the training base and was being utilized as a trainer there before his scheduled rotation back to his team. While there were several bases they could have chosen from for my training, they concluded that keeping their spun tale as close to the truth as possible would allow for us to give more realistic details if it ever became necessary.

So, I had trained on Ghana Base as part of the base's primary unit, specializing in my language skills, and had met Alistair on the training mats where he had been one of my trainers. While relationships between trainers and trainees are highly discouraged in the military, we had bumped into each other off of the mats enough times that we had begun to develop a friendship. When he transferred back to his field team, we continued to exchange communiques, leading to an even stronger friendship.

At the completion of my training, during my week-long leave, I had gone home and been surprised to find Alistair there. He had used his shore leave to visit with my father and, following a centuries-old practice, had asked his permission to pursue marriage with me.

For the next few months, while I was continuing with my specialized training, we had maintained our long-distance relationship, meeting up any time our schedules permitted. His formal proposal had been made only a few days ago. It had been a private moment between the two of us, but he had brought me home yesterday to introduce me to his parents, though it had not gone quite the way he had hoped.

It felt odd as I listened to her explain the backstory; they were recreating the last few months of my life. Absently, I wondered how much of it Aiden, no I corrected myself again, how much of it Alistair, had contributed. Had he made suggestions to this story based on how he wished it could have gone? "Yae own all of me heart..." he had said. I still wasn't entirely certain how that had happened, but it made me smile to think about it.

An hour later my smile was gone. We were back in Lady Buccleuch's sitting room and had just finished discussing the arrangements for the evening's event, but that was not what had me twisting the ring nervously once more: the DuCains had arrived and were on their way up.

Lady Buccleuch, who was reading something on her digi-pad while we waited, didn't say anything as she absently lifted my hand away from the ring and set it back down on my wrist.

It was a struggle for me to keep my hand where she had placed it, as it was already taking almost everything I had simply to stay in my seat. I was fighting a growing sense of panic that left me unsure whether I wanted to huddle into a ball or to jump up and run for all I was worth.

I knew what the feeling stemmed from. A large part of my emotional stability in a world that often didn't like who and what I was had developed around the belief that I was strong enough to keep out anyone who could hurt me. Yet Aiden had proven just how fragile that strength actually was when he had walked away from me. His leaving had been a painful lesson in the reality of my own weakness.

Worse, I had never intentionally let him inside. I had always carefully guarded who was allowed inside my circle of trust and who was not. Yet, in spite of my caution, he had somehow gotten through the barriers that should have kept him out. I might have been okay with that small crack in my defenses as it appeared now that things might work out after all. But Aiden had not been the only one to slip through; Estradé had found a way in as well. While she had not caused the kind of damage that Aiden had, now that I knew she was there, I felt obliged to honor her unspoken request to allow the DuCains in as well.

It was that last part that was the real source of my panic. If I let the DuCains in, I was purposefully opening myself up to the pain of rejection that would come when they eventually left. Perhaps if I had not been torn apart so badly by Aiden, I might have been secure in my ability to handle them. But I was still feeling raw and battered. I doubted that I would be up to the rejection that I felt certain to be only a matter of time in coming.

The door opened, heightening my panic.

"Lord and Lady DuCain, m'lady." Sylvie stepped back to allow them to enter the room. Lady Buccleuch and I rose from our seats to greet them.

Lady DuCain was a plump little woman with rosy cheeks and a warm smile. Her dark brown hair was pulled back into a softly sweeping bun that gave her a grandmotherly look, though the smooth skin of her face suggested she was too young yet for that title. As she came in, her warm brown eyes swept the room with an excited expression of anticipation that came to settle on me. Not waiting to be introduced, she glided forward to embrace me.

"Oh, my dear, just look at you," she said fondly as she stepped back to study my face. "John," she continued almost without a breath, "do come over here and see what a lovely young lady she is."

"I can see just fine from here, thank you," he muttered darkly.

She looked back at him disapprovingly. "Oh, quit worrying about it and be happy for her. So, she's engaged?! So what?"

Not giving him a chance to respond, she turned to Lady Buccleuch. "John is just bitter that he is barely getting to meet his new daughter before some young man has swept in to whisk her away from us."

Lord DuCain harrumphed loudly but didn't contradict her. Standing stiffly off to the side, he appeared to be quite the opposite of his wife. Where she was short and round, he was tall and thin. His perfectly combed, golden-blonde hair had hints of silver blended into it and his pale, ice-blue eyes scowled darkly, giving him the appearance of a rancorous old man who was ready to bite off the head of anyone who crossed his path.

Her voice light, but laced ever so slightly with a hint of reproval, Lady DuCain asked, "Eithine, why didn't you tell us yourself that she was engaged?"

Lady Buccleuch smiled apologetically. "I'm afraid it was a last-minute change in the plans. There wasn't time to tell you before you arrived."

"Ah well," she waved it off as a thing of no concern, "no harm done." Laughing brightly, she moved over to one of the bench seats and sat down. Tapping the seat next to her expectantly, she said warmly, "I want to hear all about this young man who has won your heart."

I looked to Lady Buccleuch for permission. She nodded her head ever so slightly before moving back to her own seat.

"Uhm…sure." I sat down nervously at Lady DuCain's side. "What would you like to know?"

"His name for starters," she laughed warmly, "and then you can tell us how the two of you met."

Lord DuCain remained where he was standing, his back stiff, but I thought I saw his head tip slightly in our direction as though he were listening in to hear what I would say.

I cleared my throat, my mind racing for how to answer her, nervous that I would say the wrong thing. "Well, it was a bit of a surprise for me as well, but I believe you may already be familiar with him, or at least with his name and family. It's Aid…I mean Alistair Buccleuch." Lady Buccleuch had helped me with the pronunciation so that I was no longer butchering it.

Lord DuCain's eyebrows lifted in surprise; Lady DuCain looked delighted.

"Oh, that's wonderful," she exclaimed. "How long have the two of you known each other?"

I looked to Lady Buccleuch for guidance, not sure whether I should be telling the real situation or the backstory that had been created, but her expression gave no hints as to what she wanted me to say; only a suggestion of watchful curiosity as to how I would handle the question.

"It's, uhm, well, it's a little complicated," I finally said, turning back to face Lady DuCain.

"Complicated?" She laughed in amusement. "Well, that is certainly a good description for any relationship, but what is the complication in this one?"

Inwardly, I groaned; complicated really didn't begin to describe this relationship. Outwardly I smiled back nervously.

410

"I guess the complication is in the dual nature of our relationship."

Her eyebrows lifted curiously, but she didn't interrupt me, so I went on. "The story that everyone else will be told is that we met during my UFC training about six months ago and became friends. When Alistair was transferred back to the front lines, we continued our relationship via communiques and occasional outings when both of our leave times happened to correspond. Alistair even followed the traditional path of asking for your permission before proposing to me last week."

"He did, did he?" Lord DuCain grunted under his breath. Lady DuCain shushed him and told me to go on.

"In reality, we did meet during my training at Ghana Base. In fact, the first time we met, it was on the base's track and he used a rather unique pickup line."

I told them what he had said and what my response had been. Lady DuCain laughed heartily; even Lord DuCain cracked a small smile.

"The next day, he stepped in to save me from getting into hot water with one of the senior officers on the base and our friendship began to grow from there."

I considered leaving the story at that; it would have been easier to do, but I decided that if they were going to be playing the part my parents, and before I allowed them in too deeply, they should know what they were getting into, so I told them the rest. I told them about the attack in the clearing and Aiden's subsequent abandonment after discovering that I was one of Icarus' Alphas. I told them about being kidnapped and the things I had been told had taken place in the caves. I told them about Aiden carrying me to safety and then leaving me once more. I held nothing back, expressing

411

my sense of loss when he had abandoned me and the pain his return had caused. I described the offer Director Beckwith had made to me and the plan that had brought our team here. Finally, I told them about last night's dinner, the position Aiden had found himself in, his request, and the plan we had come up with to counter the threat from Lord Remington.

All the while, I watched their reactions, waiting for them to decide that this was more than they wanted to be part of. So, it didn't surprise me, by the time I was done, that neither of them was smiling any longer.

"Is this true?" Lord DuCain's voice demanded suddenly of Lady Buccleuch.

Seemingly unfazed by his rancor, she responded calmly, "It is. Remington will not willingly let this challenge to his power go unpunished. Alexandria is Alistair's only chance of survival now."

"And you expected us to approve of this?" His face was growing redder by the second, and he seemed to be shaking with fury as he took a step forward. This was the part I had dreaded; I may have been expecting it, but that didn't stop it from hurting. I felt my shoulders slump. I knew what would come next. Why had I even allowed myself to think that it was possible they would want me as their daughter, even as a pretend daughter?!

I was startled when Lady DuCain's hand came to rest protectively on my shoulder. "So you thought that gave you the right to put our daughter into danger as well?"

Our daughter? I looked up in confusion. Lord DuCain was at his wife's side, his face a mask of fury, though not one that was aimed at me. "We did not agree to this arrangement just so we could watch a second daughter be drawn into an unwinnable battle."

I was stunned as I suddenly understood that it wasn't me they were angry with; it was the danger they feared I was in. That didn't seem possible to me. I think my jaw must have dropped visibly because Lady Buccleuch ignored their anger for the moment and instead addressed me. "Don't look so surprised, Alexandria. I told you; you are not alone anymore."

Lady DuCain's breath caught. "Goodness, no child. We're not angry with you. We…"

I interrupted her timidly, "How can you not be? I'm a child of Icarus, just like the one that hurt your daughter. How can you stand to be near me?"

"Child," her tone was equal parts assuring and soothing, "you are not the one that hurt Claire. In fact, you are quite the opposite of the one who did."

"How can you know that?" I wanted to believe her, but I knew better; I knew what I was. I looked down, unable to meet her eyes any longer.

Lady DuCain cupped my chin to lift my head back up. She held my gaze as she said firmly, "Estradé showed us who and what you are. She showed us your psyche eval. She showed us your school reports since you started primary school. She showed us your military training reports. We have read the comments your teachers and trainers made. How you always do your best on every assignment and yet always seem to think what you have done is not good enough. How you readily accept criticism and then try to improve on your perceived faults. How you befriend the outcast and friendless and find ways to help even those who have been unkind to you. One and all, they reported that you are a sweet, kind, caring young lady. You could not be less like a child of Icarus than if I had actually given birth to you. I know who you are,

413

Alexandria Jaquette, and I could not be more proud to have you as my daughter."

"But…" I started to argue only to have Lord DuCain cut me off.

He knelt down at my side, his face hard but his voice gruff with emotion. "I don't know what others have told you in the past, but hear this now: Who and what you were yesterday is not nearly as important as who and what you are today, or who and what you will be tomorrow. And who you are now is my daughter, if you will have us as your parents."

They knew everything, and yet they still thought I was worth having as their daughter! It didn't seem possible, and yet, there it was. I felt a tear slide down my cheek and had to reach around Lady DuCain's hands to brush it away. She smiled warmly as she brushed another tear from my other cheek and asked gently, "Will you allow us to be your parents?"

Parents! The word made me smile. "Yes," I said softly, the faintest hint of a hopeful smile on my lips. "I think I would like that."

Her smile broadened. "Then it is done."

Lord DuCain's lips twitched upwards ever so slightly as well. Rocking back on his heels, he stood up, squeezed my shoulder briefly with a slight nod of his head, then returned to his position near the door.

"Very good." Lady Buccleuch nodded curtly in satisfaction. "But I believe you still have the concern of Alexandria's participation in my son's engagement." Lady DuCain suddenly appeared to transition back to the angry-bear mom.

"That matter is settled, Eithine. You cannot use our daughter as a pawn in this dangerous battle you have started."

I expected Lady Buccleuch to come back with a string of counter arguments as to why I should be permitted to participate, but instead all she said was, "If that is what she wants."

If that was what I wanted? I looked down at the ring Aiden had placed on my finger and thought of the promise that had come with it; I wanted the chance to find out if he had meant what he had said. But there was more to it than that. Whether he had come after me in the caves because of an order or not, he had come. And in doing so, he had quite likely saved my life. At the bare minimum, he had preserved my freedom. I owed him a debt that I was not going to walk away from, even for parents.

I sighed heavily. "It's not that simple. Alistair came after me when I needed help. I won't return that service by abandoning him now. Besides, he made a promise to me that I think I would like him to keep, and he won't be able to do that if he is married to Collette."

The DuCains looked at each other anxiously before Lady DuCain asked hesitantly, "What promise did he make you?"

I blushed brightly but answered, "He promised that if I accepted his proposal, he would become the knight in shining armor that I deserve."

I was startled when Lord DuCain barked a laugh that was half amused, half fierce. "He did, did he? If we decide to allow you to go through with this, I will hold him to that promise."

Lady DuCain's voice was cautiously thoughtful. "Alexandria, I need you to answer a question for me, and I need you to be completely honest in your answer. Why did you agree to be part of this engagement? Is it because you feel you owe him a debt, or is there more to it than that?"

While she had not come out and asked it directly, I knew what she really wanted to know; it was the same question I had been asking myself for the last few hours. I had already accepted one part of the answer: in spite of the pain he had caused me, or perhaps the pain had been a result of it, he held a piece of my heart in his hand. But the rest of what I had not yet admitted to anyone, not even to myself, had become a growing knot of suspicion in the back of my mind. To speak the words out loud was to accept them as true, a choice that frightened me because it meant accepting that my defenses were well and truly shattered. But I forced myself to speak the words now, finally accepting that I could not keep running from their truth.

"I love him."

They looked at each other once more, a silent exchange passing between them. Lady DuCain's eyes were imploring; Lord DuCain's were fierce. It was a soundless communication that spoke volumes. Finally, Lord DuCain growled in frustration as he turned away from his wife. "Fine! But if he hurts her again, I will kill him."

Behind me Lady Buccleuch snorted, the first unladylike thing I had heard come from her. "I'm afraid, Lord DuCain, that you will have to wait in line. If I find that he has treated her that way again, I will personally skin him alive. He was taught better than that."

Lady DuCain was not exactly smiling, but there was a slight twinkle in her eyes as she laughed lightly. "Oh, I don't think you will need to do any such thing. Something tells me that he has learned his lesson already."

The next few hours were a blur of information and preparations. If I had thought that Lady Buccleuch had given me a lot of information to assimilate before the DuCains arrived, it paled in comparison to what we discussed now. We covered everything from holiday schedules, campus housing, expectations for weekly communications, and care for Osiris, to Claire's medical records, reconstructive surgeries, recovery periods, old habits, and how to communicate with school friends who were trying to reach out to her.

They gave me a digi-pad full of information that was intended to be a reference guide for me. It had everything from a family tree with pictures and stories to detailed medical records and even old school papers that Claire had written. I felt a sense of smallness as I accepted the pad with my nervous hands. That tiny piece of metal, circuit boards, and wires held the summation of her life; all that she was, everything she had been, boiled down into digitized data. *Was that all there was to life? All that would be left of me someday when I died?* It was a humbling thought, but I didn't have time to dwell on it for long. At some point during the discussion, Lady Buccleuch had slipped out to attend to other necessary arrangements. She returned now with Celeste in tow, carrying a dress bag and several boxes.

Once more, I was transformed into something I had never before been. With my hair pulled up into a pile of curls that was allowed to gently cascade off to one side and my makeup redone in a more dramatic style, the woman staring back at me from the mirror's reflection was as alien as she was beautiful. The dress that Celeste brought in and helped me put on was a long, slimming creation of pale rose-colored chiffon that swirled gently in the slightest breeze. The open-slit sleeves draped breezily from my shoulders to my wrists while the tightly fitted bodice flowed into an artfully folded waterfall that swished softly around my ankles. The shoes on my feet were a pair of matching-colored heels with straps that artfully wrapped around my feet and up my ankles to securely hold them in place. The finishing touch was a delicate set of interlocking thistle flowers, chained together around my neck and a matching pair dangling from each ear. Accenting each of the flowers were tiny rose-colored gemstones that sparkled brightly in the rays of the setting sun. I had never worn anything so fine before, and seriously doubted that I ever would again.

Celeste took a step back to admire her work and nodded with a satisfied smile. "You're ready."

Ready?! Her words echoed in my head and were answered by my own thoughts. *No; I'm anything but ready. How am I supposed to pull this off?*

I closed my eyes and took a deep breath, trying to get control of my nerves. In truth, whether or not I was ready mattered very little. Ready or not, it was time to walk out the door and become someone I had never been.

The touch of a hand on my shoulder made me open my eyes and look up. Lady Buccleuch was standing next to me, studying my reflection in the mirror.

"It's okay to be nervous," she smiled encouragingly, "but the woman in that mirror has nothing to fear. She is stronger than she knows and I suspect she will surprise everyone this evening, including herself."

Strong? Once I might have agreed with her, at least I had always thought of myself as strong. But the protective barriers that Aiden had gotten through were no longer intact and self-doubt had begun to seep in. Still, I didn't tell her my fears. Instead, I just nodded my head and forced a small smile onto my lips.

"Much better." She nodded approvingly. "Now, let's go see if we can save my son."

Chapter 36: Aiden Haskell

BUTTONING THE CUFFLINK on my sleeve, I happened to glance down at my wrist. The shirt sleeve did a good job of hiding it, but the skin there, as Alex had reminded me, was far from healed. In truth, much of my body ached. It was only three days since the caves; just long enough for the bruised muscles, torn skin, and stitched wounds to start the healing process, but not long enough for the nerve endings to let up on their constant screams for relief. I was able to ignore the aching for the most part, though I suspected the injured knee would need more medical attention before it fully healed; my knee throbbed even when I was holding still. Unfortunately, holding still had not been an option for the past several hours. The tasks my mother had set us to had kept me moving.

Shortly after leaving her sitting room, I had claimed the command pad from my room and taken it to Thatcher. He had only grunted when I gave the commands that released myself as group lead and gave him control of the mission.

My next task had been to finish the repair work on my jeep. My mother had explained that its climbing ability would be necessary to take us to our next location, though she had not as yet revealed where that was. I had been in the middle of replacing the jeep's broken suspension components when Alex had come to talk to me; that at bare minimum had needed to be finished. But the tires themselves had also begun to show considerable wear on their outside edges, a result of my past climbing expeditions. So, I planned to balance and rotate them as well.

Wren and McLagan, who had been dispatched to gather the team's gear along with a list of additional supplies, began showing up when I was just about finished replacing the broken parts. They brought everything from tents and sleeping bags to food and a medical kit. We loaded and strapped it all down before taking a break in our current assignments to head back to the main house for lunch.

During lunch, we had tackled our next assignment, establishing a backstory for how Claire and I had met and become engaged. Roisin and Thatcher joined us partway through and were very helpful in ironing out some key points. However, the whole situation held a strong sense of irony for me. Knowing that I would never marry, I had never spent much time thinking about how I might go about it. As a result, there I was, with the opportunity to rewrite how I had proposed to Alex, to make it far more romantic than the reality had been, and I couldn't think of the first thing I would have done to make it so. In the end, my only real contribution to the final story was to suggest that we kept Ghana Base as the place we had met because we both had sufficient knowledge of the location and the base's routines to back it up.

After lunch, I had returned to do a final systems' check of the jeep. I was fairly certain that I would find the systems to be in good, working order, but I hadn't wanted to take any chances. It was well into the afternoon when I put the last tool away, satisfied that the jeep was finally ready to go.

What remained of the afternoon had been spent with my father. It was an expectation of his that whenever I came home on leave, I would spend time reviewing the state of affairs in Scotland. As his firstborn son, if I survived my mandatory service, I would eventually take his place as the leader of Scotland. If I didn't survive, well...there was Roisin. But, until the day I died, he would continue to expect me to visit him in his study. Seeing as we would be leaving in the morning, he had made it clear that that visit would have to be fit in today.

Although he used some of the time to berate me once more for my actions, he had spent the majority of it bringing me up to speed on current events that he felt I was unlikely to be aware of. In truth, I had already known the majority of what he had to tell me, but there were a few surprises. Among the most startling was to hear that in the past three months, one hundred and twenty-eight boys who had come of age, and were due for enlistment, had never shown up at the UFC's Enlistment Center. More than that, their families had disappeared right along with them.

One hundred and twenty-eight out of some ten thousand boys eligible to start their service during that time doesn't seem like much, but it was a far larger number than had been seen since the forced draft had begun. There was a search underway for each of the boys and their families, but if they weren't found soon, and if that news got out, there were likely to be severe repercussions.

Even so, my father had delayed reporting the numbers to Remington, hoping in part that the marriage arrangements between Collette and I would have resulted in a situation where the quarterly enlistment report would have been overlooked by Remington as his time and focus would have been spent on the engagement instead. Unfortunately, because of my actions, continued delay was no longer an option. Remington would return at some point to complete his annual review and it was certain to include the quarterly enlistment report. Even more unfortunately, given his mood when he left this morning, it was unlikely that he would be feeling lenient toward the people of Scotland.

I sighed as I pulled the jacket sleeve down to fully cover my wrist. I had made a fine mess of things, but what had the alternative been? Would I have willingly sacrificed myself to Collette if I had known it would have appeased Remington and spared Scotland some small measure of pain? Would my sacrifice have even made a difference? Somehow, I didn't think it would have. I had given my life thus far in service to my country, and yet, as far as I could see, I only seemed to have made things worse.

At least with Alex I had finally gotten something right, even if I had made a lot of wrong turns getting there. I had been terrified that she would leave; terrified that I had hurt her too deeply. It had been such a relief when she had agreed to stay and help. But my mother was right. She deserved better than me, better than to be caught up in my troubles. *My troubles!* If Lord Remington came back tonight, how was I going to keep her safe? *I shouldn't have let her stay!*

It was frustrating. Put me in the middle of a pitched battle and I was completely at ease. I could face an enemy soldier with nothing more than my bare hands and still be confident that I would successfully complete the mission. Tell me that I was to protect a particular asset and I knew I could do it. But the moment I had realized that Alex was the asset I would be giving my life to protect, all of my confidence had begun to evaporate. All of my training, all of my experience, and none if it had prepared me for her. If she had just said no, if I had just had the strength to make her leave, she would have already been safely away. It would have killed me to see her go, but at least then I could have been certain that she wasn't being placed into more danger.

A knock at the door interrupted my thoughts. I sighed in resignation.

"Come in, Ro."

Roisin glided through the door. She was, as always, resplendent in her evening dress, but she had chosen one that was particularly curve fitting with a long slit up one leg. I shook my head in exasperation. "Which of me teammates are yae aiming tae charm into submission with that dress?" I asked it only half teasing, the other half very much serious.

She smiled impishly but didn't answer my question. Instead, she reached up to brush a piece of dust off of my shoulder; a piece I very much doubted was really there. Her voice was playful. "The guests have started arrivin' and I'm already dressed. But as I suspected, yae are not quite ready."

"Is it possible tae be ready for this?"

She laughed in amusement. "Of course it's not. Everythin' has changed so much in the last twenty-four hours that none of us could have seen this comin'. But it's goin' to be all right, Ali; everythin' will work out. Just look at yae, after all. Yae didn't even think she would be willing tae help yae, and now here we are: me little brother is goin' tae be gettin' married tae th' woman who stole his heart."

I shook my head ruefully. "She stole me heart sure enough, but the weddin' will only happen if I can convince

423

her that I am worthy of her love in return, and I am anythin' but certain how I am supposed tae accomplish that."

Ro's smile took on a hint of mischievousness. "Oh, I have no doubt how this is goin' tae end. But don't yae let that worry yae tonight. Tonight, yae just put on that roguish smile of yers and go show off yer fiancé to everyone. Leave no doubt in Collette's mind that yae belong tae someone else."

Fifteen minutes later, I was pacing back and forth in the family lounge. It felt a little like déjà vu. Just last night I had been in this same room, agitatedly doing the exact same thing, though for a completely different reason.

I looked up sharply as the door opened.

To my disappointment, it was only our chief of security. He was a grizzled old war veteran with a scarred cheek and a sour disposition, but he was good at his job and had been with us for as long as I could remember. He nodded curtly to my father before getting straight to the point. "There was a power surge a few minutes ago at th' South fence. I've already had a team check it out and there doesn't appear tae be anythin' out of order, but yae asked me tae let yae know if there was anythin' unusual tonight."

My eyes narrowed slightly. A power surge was not unheard of; it happened periodically. A bird flying into the electrified fence or a tree branch falling onto it could cause the surge. But it could have also been triggered by someone trying to get onto the property. The castle's security equipment was top of the line, but there have always been ways to get through even the best equipment. I should know; I had been trained to do so. For nerves that were already on edge, it was not a comfortable thought. However, my father didn't seem to be concerned by the news.

"Thank yae, Erik. Let me know if there is anythin' else."

424

Erik nodded curtly once again then turned to leave the room. He had just stepped through the door when I saw him step aside to hold the door open. "Beggin' yer pardon, ma'am," he said with a slight bow.

"Thank you, Erik," my mother said formally with a nod of her own as she glided past him. Behind her a trio of unfamiliar people came in; two women, one younger and one older, and a man. I looked beyond them for Alex, expecting that she must be following behind them, but there was no one else. Confused, I looked to my mother; she only smiled back mysteriously then turned away from me to speak to my father.

"My dear, allow me to introduce to you the Lord and Lady DuCain of Sussex, England, and their daughter Claire."

Claire? Wasn't that the name… I looked back sharply at the younger woman and my breath caught. "Oh, wow!" I whispered, not quite loud enough to be heard. It was Alex, and yet it wasn't. The delicate fingers that were nervously twisting the ring on her left hand, the willowy figure that somehow portrayed both confidence and uncertainty at the same time, even the shy smile that I had fallen for; all of those things about her were the same, but everything else had been changed. I was so stunned that my mother had to call my name multiple times before I realized she was talking to me.

"Alistair," she said in an amused tone when I finally glanced over to her. "I will admit that your fiancé is breathtaking, but if you have recovered your wits sufficiently, perhaps you would care to come over here and meet her parents."

Alex looked my way, her nervous expression giving way to a timid smile as she met my eyes. I felt my breath catch again; to say that she was breathtaking was an understatement. She had worn very little makeup, if any, prior to today; in truth, she had never needed it to look beautiful. But the coloring and contouring that had been applied to her face this evening accented her cheekbones, narrow nose, and the almond shape of her eyes in a way that was undeniably stunning on her. Combined with the changed hair and eye coloring, the curled hair that had been pulled up, and the formal gown that clung to her in all the right places, it was quite probable that I would not be the only one caught staring at her tonight.

Still, that was no excuse for allowing myself to be so fully distracted that I had not been aware of what was happening around me. Embarrassed, I shook myself mentally and crossed the room to join them. I bowed formally and tried to cover my lapse with lightheartedness. "Forgive me for me distractedness, but tae be fair, yer daughter," I emphasized the word, "seems tae have stolen more than just me heart. I shall have tae carefully guard me wits in her presence if I am tae be permitted tae retain any sense of decorum this evenin'."

Alex blushed delicately and looked down at her hands, clearly self-conscious from the compliment; it made my grin grow.

"But of course." Lady DuCain laughed warmly. "I would have been disappointed had your reaction been otherwise."

"Nicely done, Alistair," my mother said with an amused smile. "And you are certainly going to need those wits about you right now, because Lord DuCain has requested a few minutes of time to speak with you alone. So, in order to ensure that you are not distracted, we will leave the two of you to have your little talk."

A talk? About what? I glanced over at the man who was claiming to be Alex's father. He was staring straight back at me with a steady, piercing gaze. Meeting his eyes, I suddenly felt like a caged animal at the mercy of a stronger predator. I swallowed hard.

Lady DuCain saw my nervousness and smiled conspiratorially at my mother just before she took Alex by the arm to guide her from the room. They paused briefly in front of Lord DuCain so that she could place a hand softly on his chest. "Now dear," her voice carried the faintest hint of amusement, "don't be too hard on him. We really would like to keep him in one piece."

He only harrumphed in reply, his steely gaze never leaving me. I swallowed again as the door clicked shut behind them. I didn't think my mother would have left me alone with him if I was in any real danger, but that thought didn't do much to soothe the sudden, fierce pounding of my heart. Unconsciously, I took a step back, altering my stance to a more defensive one.

He grunted again, as though amused, then waved his hand toward the chairs. "Take a seat."

I hesitated, not sure I wanted to; standing was an easier position to defend from than sitting was. He raised his eyebrow when I delayed, but otherwise gave no indication that he was bothered by my hesitation. Finally, he shrugged and took a seat of his own; he was no less imposing sitting down than he had been while standing.

"Eighteen!" he said suddenly with a harsh edge to his voice.

I cocked my head, uncertain where he was leading with the word. "Eighteen what?"

"That's how old this girl is that you are putting into a position of danger so that you can be safe."

So that I could be safe? I bristled unconsciously at the accusation. Did this man have any idea how many times I had placed myself in danger to help others? Whether or not I was safe mattered very little to me. I had known for a long time that I was unlikely to survive my time in the military; it had never been about keeping myself safe. It had always been about those I could protect, especially Alex. In my sudden ire, I successfully ignored the fact that only a short time before this I had been feeling guilty that I hadn't sent her away.

I responded angrily, "I've spent the last week gettin' her out of danger. I'm not about tae put her back intae it!"

He barked a skeptical laugh. "You're not?" His expression suggested that he knew the truth, and knew that, in spite of my denial, I did as well. But he allowed me to dig my own hole. "And just what are you planning to do when Remington shows up with soldiers to force you to bend to his plans. How will you keep her safe then? You won't even be able to protect yourself in that situation."

I growled, "Me safety is not yer concern."

"But hers is!" he retorted sharply. Then continuing on slightly less sharply, "The truth, boy, is that I don't think you have what it takes to care for her."

I couldn't take care of her? Who did this man think he was; deciding what I was and was not capable of? I took an angry step forward, my hands balled into fists, my voice trembling with anger. "Alex means everythin' tae me. I would give me life tae keep her safe."

I expected him to stand up, to meet my challenge with his own. Instead, I was startled to see him lean back into his chair, a smile of satisfaction slowly spreading across his lips. "You can't take care of her if you're dead, boy." His voice was ice cold. "I don't want you to die for her; I want you to live for her."

My eyes narrowed as I tried to figure out what he meant. Live for her? Warily, I said, "I don't understand."

He barked a bitter laugh. "Of course you don't. You think love is about being willing to die for someone. But it's the living for the other person that is the real sign of your love, and the much harder part. Sit down, boy, and I'll explain."

There was something in his tone that suggested that this time he would not take my continued standing lightly. I moved cautiously to the seat across from him and sat down stiffly, my back ram-rod straight. He nodded his head once in satisfaction before continuing.

"Dying is the easy way out. You get yourself killed and your problems are over. Not so for the people you leave behind. You get peace; they get holes in their hearts. Living for someone, on the other hand, means that you spend your life making sure their needs are met. Everything you do from here on out will be about Claire. You stay alive so that you can take care of her. You give up what you want so that you can give her what she needs. If you can't do that, then you do not truly love her, and you can get up and walk out that door right now, knowing that there will be no wedding and I will be taking her away from here and from you immediately."

While part of my mind had heard everything he had said, and recognized the wisdom in it, it was the implied threat in his last line that redoubled the hot fury surging through me. He was threatening to take her by force? That was not going to happen again! My muscles tensed, ready for the fight. My own words came out ice cold. "The last person who tried tae take her by force is dead. Yae don't get tae…"

He cut me off with a harsh, cold snarl of his own. "Boy, I can and I will. You made her a promise that you are going to keep. You probably made it in a moment of passion and have not thought about it again, but it seems to have impressed her enough to give her hope. So, let me make you a promise of my own. If you do not become that knight in shining armor that she deserves, or if you ever raise a hand to her or otherwise abuse her, I will contact my friends at Adskaya and you will quietly disappear."

I felt the blood suddenly drain from my face and my fury evaporate into cold shock. I swallowed hard. Adskaya Dyra was a political prison in the frozen wastelands of Russia. It was not a place people talked about except in hushed whispers and no one ever willingly admitted to having friends there. *Who was this man?* I thought again. His iceberg cold eyes met mine without any hint of softness. There was a gleam in them as well, something that warned me he meant what he said and he had the ability to follow through with his threat. A shiver ran through me.

"Claire is my daughter," he said coldly, with all of the weight that simple line implied. "So, what's it going to be? Will you choose to die for her or to live?"

Chapter 37: Alexandria Jaquette

THE LAST TWO hours had been a whirlwind of names and faces that there was little chance I would be able to recall in the morning. Aiden, on the other hand, had expertly greeted each person by name, casually recalling facts about each of them that included such things as where their children were currently attending school or what type of pet they owned and what that pet was named. He had an impressive way of talking with the individuals that gave the impression that they were the most important thing in the world to him at that moment. Well, perhaps the second most important thing to him.

The whole time we circled the courtyard, he kept his hand securely wrapped around mine, his face lighting up in a brilliantly satisfied smile each time he introduced me as his fiancé. For my part, I shyly nodded my head at each introduction and exchanged the pleasantries that Lady Buccleuch had instructed me on. I wish I could say that I had been more confident, but the truth was that I was still reeling from the whirlwind changes that I had been experiencing since morning. There was the slight sensation of panic, quietly bubbling beneath the surface, that had started with the decision to let the DuCains in and had only grown with each new revelation in the plan for what would be expected of me in the coming days. It had been threatening to catch up with me all afternoon if I slowed down long enough to allow myself to dwell on everything I was supposed to do and remember.

Only what Ethine had said about Aiden's inability to tell a lie without revealing his deception in his expression overrode that panic for the moment. He may not be able to hide his deception from others, but I could. So, anytime someone asked how we met, I intervened with a soft laugh and explained to them that Aiden had literally swept me off my feet on the training mats and then carried my heart away with him when he had transferred off the base. But mostly I just stood back and let him lead the conversations, watching the magic of the man that Aiden had transformed into.

In this way, the evening had been passing reasonably smoothly. There had been one small interruption some time ago, when one of the Buccleuch's stony-faced security guards had wound his way through the guests to report something to Aiden's father. Seeing it, Aiden had excused himself from me briefly, but had not seen fit to share what he had learned when he returned moments later. I was left to wonder what his suddenly thoughtful expression might indicate, but no time to ask questions before we were caught up in yet another introduction to some important dignitary from one European country or another.

There were a surprising number of guests to be introduced to for an event on such short notice. It turned out, as Ethine had explained to me in the dressing room, that Collette and her father had arranged for the evening's festivities, including sending out a considerable number of invitations, back when they were certain that Alistair would be unable to refuse the arranged marriage.

While Lady Buccleuch had initially been unaware of the event's planning, she had smoothly taken everything in stride and turned it to our advantage when the event planner had arrived unexpectedly to coordinate the evening's preparations shortly before lunch. I guess no one had thought to tell the planner or the guests that the plans had changed.

As a result, the castle had effectively been transformed from its normal daily family routine into an elegant setting ready to receive several hundred guests. The courtyard, where we had been positioned by the planner to mingle with and greet the guests, had undergone the greatest transformation. It was normally a rather plain space that, while well cared for, was little more than an enclosed area of grass and granite tiles. This evening it was a garden of twinkling lights strung in and among the hundreds of potted trees and bushes that had been brought in for the purpose, and interspersed by tall cocktail tables with delicate silver candelabras bearing tall tapered white candles that flickered gaily in the evening's gentle breeze. Off to one side, a string quartet was playing soft, lively music that seemed to float in the air just below the din of conversation. There was even a photographer deftly moving in and out of the crowd to expertly capture it all.

"Look this way," the photographer called, intending to snap yet another handshake between Aiden and the next guest who had approached us. But the older gentleman, his sun-darkened face creased by wrinkles and dominated by a nose that had been broken several times, ignored the photographer's instruction and instead shifted his stance ever so subtly so that he was effectively blocking any image of his face that the camera might have otherwise been able to get.

"Fix your stance there, lad." His voice, though a low growl, carried a surprising mixture of sternness and warmth. "Even at rest, you must be ready for action, especially with such a lady as this on your arm."

"Knox!" Aiden released my hand and surged forward to embrace the old man. It was the first time he had done so with anyone this evening. "What are yae daeing here?"

The man's tough expression broke into the faintest hint of a smile as Aiden stepped back.

"Checking on my star pupil to make sure he's not getting sloppy. And more than a little curious to learn what type of woman this is that you are willing to break your promise to me for."

To my surprise, Aiden blushed deeply, causing the man to raise his eyebrow.

"Interesting. Well then, are you going to introduce me or are you going to drop and give me fifty."

Still blushing, Aiden turned to me.

"Claire, allow me tae introduce yae tae an old bodach who is as frighteningly dangerous as he is perceptive. This is Knox."

The man snorted at the introduction but reached forward to take my hand with an expertly executed bow. As I dipped into the slight curtsy that Ethine had instructed me on, the man suddenly lost his balance, his grip on my hand tightened and started to pull me down with him. We might have both gone down had I not instinctively shifted the gravity under both of us before I thought about what I was doing.

His steel grey eyes met mine and his lips twitched upward into a knowing smile. The sudden realization of what I had done sent a cold chill through me. The look in his eyes left no doubt that he also knew exactly what had just happened; he had been testing me.

"So," he said slowly, almost inaudibly, "you're an Alpha."

Aiden had seen though the pretense as well. No longer smiling, he stepped forward protectively, taking my hand away from him.

"No one here knows that," he said quietly, a dangerous edge to his voice. "And we are going to keep it that way."

Knox didn't flinch at the implied threat.

"You know me, lad; I'll keep your secrets just as I always have." Their voices were barely loud enough to be heard beyond the three of us.

The tension between the two was almost palpable as Aiden seemed to consider his statement. Finally, he nodded in acceptance. "I do know yae, Knox. And now yae know the answer tae yer questions as well. Me promise still stands and yours had better as well."

"What promise?" I started to ask, only to have my question interrupted by a loud crashing sound coming from the direction of the main hall. Both men's heads shot up, their expressions becoming guarded watchfulness. Then, in the space of a heartbeat, that watchfulness became cold, determined hardness.

"Go!" Knox hissed, not looking away from whatever had triggered the hardness. "Get her out of here!"

Aiden didn't hesitate. Without a word, he suddenly surged forward, pulling me behind him as he rapidly moved us away from the courtyard's entrance. I had to quicken my steps to keep up with him, something that wasn't easy to do in the unfamiliar heels I was wearing.

"Aiden," confused by what was happening, I forgot to call him by the correct name, "what's wrong?"

He didn't answer me or even look back. Thatcher, who only seconds before had been near the string quartet with Roisin, Wren, and McLagan, had begun running toward us as well, the same cold expression on his face. In a small corner of my mind, I noted that McLagan and Wren had moved to position themselves in front of Roisin, as though to protect her from something. Their faces were equally hard and they had phase guns in their hands, held at the ready. *They had brought their phase guns to the party? What was going on?*

A familiar hissing whoosh made me look back sharply. *Phaser fire?!* Through the windows at the end of the courtyard, I could see several bright flashes of glowing lines of light. One of those blasts had ripped through a window, melting and shattering it into shards before leaving a darkened hole in the pink sandstone wall opposite it. Screams began to fill the air as people started to panic, pushing and shoving through each other to get away from the entrance hall where the blasts were coming from.

Aiden, who hadn't bothered to glance behind him at the sounds, didn't stop moving until Thatcher met up with us. Only then did he look down at me for the briefest of seconds, a flash of regret in his eyes before he released my hand and pushed me toward Thatcher. "Go," he hissed sharply, then turned away from me and ran back toward the panicking crowd.

"Wait…" I started to say, but Thatcher was already moving. He grabbed my arm and began to pull me in the opposite direction. Less concerned with where Thatcher was leading than with where Aiden had gone, I looked back over my shoulder, searching for him. He had already disappeared.

He had left me! Stunned, I didn't resist as Thatcher guided me between the plants and tables and toward a doorway in one of the castle's central, cylinder-shaped stairwells. We were through the door and into the hall beyond in a matter of heartbeats. Even with the door shut behind us, I could still hear the screams of terror coming from the courtyard, though they were much more muted.

We passed a startled man who had been carrying a tray of hors d'oeuvres from the kitchen, nearly knocking the tray from his hands as we rushed by.

"What's going on?" he called after us. Thatcher didn't bother to answer. At the corner, he paused only long enough to carefully glance around it and ensure that the way was clear. Then we were moving again, down another hall before descending a flight of service stairs and entering into a long, stark hallway. We were several yards into the tunnel when the stunned fog in my mind finally began to clear. *What was I doing? No!* I thought angrily. *I'm not leaving Aiden behind!*

I pulled my arm free of Thatcher's hand and started to turn. With a curse, Thatcher grabbed my arm back.

"We have to keep moving," he said firmly as he tried to force me forward.

"No!" I growled, setting my feet and resisting his pull so that he was left with the choice of either stopping or letting me go. "I'm not running away."

He stopped, turning back to look at me, disbelief on his face. His voice was low, but insistent. "Your safety is the only thing that matters right now. We have to get you away from this."

"This what?" I countered angrily. "We don't even know what this is. And regardless of what it is, I'm not going to abandon my team…"

"Your team," he interrupted with a quiet hiss, "only exists to keep you safe. That, back there, was the start of a military raid and every member of the team recognized the danger that placed you in. They stayed behind to ensure that you could escape. Let your team do their job."

"If it's a raid, then Aiden will need help..."

"Aiden does not want your help! He does not want you there," he said harshly. "He can take care of himself, but if you go back, he'll put your safety in front of his own and that will put him at greater risk."

His cold, quiet words felt like a slap in the face as the truth of them hit me. I felt my cheeks reddening in response. He paused, making sure they had sunk in. Then, more gently, he continued, "He needs to know that you are safe. Give him that strength by getting clear of the danger."

That last part did it. I felt the fight go back out of me and I hung my head in defeat. Oh, how I hated it, but he was right. If I went back, I would be a distraction that could get Aiden killed. Reluctantly, I nodded, not trusting myself to speak.

"Good," he grunted, "let's move."

He didn't try to take my arm again. I think he knew that there was no longer any danger of me turning back. But we hadn't gone more than twenty yards when Thatcher stopped suddenly, holding up his hand in a "hold" signal. From ahead of us I caught the faint sound of multiple boots thumping on the hard floor.

"Where does this tunnel lead?" I whispered just loud enough for him to hear.

"To the garage," he whispered back, "but there shouldn't be anyone in it. It was supposed to remain empty tonight in case we needed to leave suddenly." He listened for a moment longer, then swore under his breath, shaking his head in frustration; the footsteps were coming our direction.

"Turn back, we'll try another way."

We doubled back, pausing only long enough at the bottom of the stairs to listen for noise coming from above. Hearing none, Thatcher crept carefully up the stairs, peeking over the floor ledge.

"Clear," he whispered, waving me forward. "We'll try the back doors and see if we can go out that way."

I went first, with Thatcher following right behind me. In spite of the tenseness of the moment, I almost laughed when Thatcher lengthened his stride to reach the door before I did. The laughter died with us still several steps away from the door as it suddenly swung open, an armed soldier coming through it.

Thatcher side-stepped the swinging door, twisting as he did so to slam his fist into the man's face. The soldier dropped like a rock, out cold. Outside, a voice was raised in alarm and several others responded to it. We were not going to be able to escape that way. Reacting on instinct, I rammed my shoulder into the door, slamming it closed on the arm of a second soldier who had been trying to come through. The soldier howled in pain then yanked his arm free of the door allowing the latch to click shut. I slammed the lock into place. Voices yelled and the door shuttered as something outside rammed into it. It was a sturdy door, unlikely to break any time soon, but I wouldn't make any bets if they remembered their phase guns and turned those on it.

"What now?" I asked nervously.

Thatcher was already moving; he grabbed my arm as he passed.

"We go upstairs!"

Thatcher took the stairs two at a time. I was slower in the dress and heals but he never let me fall more than a few feet behind him before he would slow enough to allow me to catch up. At the third floor landing he eased up to the door, pausing this time to listen for sounds on the other side. Hearing none, he carefully pushed the door open and guardedly went through it. We cautiously made our way down the halls, working toward our quarters. Thatcher closed the door to the sitting room behind us and barricaded it, then moved to do the same with the door on the opposite side.

"Get your guns," he called over his shoulder as he worked.

I didn't wait for him to finish. I grabbed the rifle first; I had left it on top of the shelf of the closet within easy reach. The pistol was in the nightstand drawer on the far side of the bed, within reach when I was sleeping. I glanced out the window as I went around the bed and froze.

Soldiers had begun rounding up the guests onto the grassy area at the front of the house. They were herding the group into a tight knot near its center. I could easily see their frightened faces in the sharp light of the flood lamps that someone had set up.

Off to the left side, another group of soldiers were pushing several men forward; the men's arms were bound behind them. Those men walked with an air of defiance, but they had clearly taken a beating.

I could just make out the trickle of blood running down the side of the first man's face from a large cut above his eye. The second man limped heavily with each step; there was a large gash in his pant leg and a dark red stain blooming outward from it. But it was the blue hair on the third man that froze the blood in my veins. Aiden stumbled to his knees as a soldier shoved him from behind, and he had to struggle heavily to regain his feet again before being able to continue on. That meant the other two men were McLagan and Wren. My team had been caught! Stunned by the realization, I watched as the three of them were led to a set of five low posts that had been recently driven into the ground; I was certain those posts had not been there when we had arrived yesterday. My team was forced into kneeling positions as their hands were bound to the posts by short lengths of chain.

"People of Scotland…" A teasingly familiar voice carried faintly through the closed window as the soldiers worked. I thought I recognized the voice, but I couldn't quite put a name or a face to it. I needed to hear it better. I cracked the window open ever so slightly, letting in a rush of sounds: women crying, men muttering angrily, soldiers shouting commands, and on top of it all, the hauntingly familiar man's solemn voice. I knew he must be standing at the top of the stairs two stories below my window, in the same place Roisin had posed for our arrival, but I couldn't see him without pressing my face to the window. What I could see were the heads of several soldiers fanned out against the stairs' balustrades, their weapons held at the ready.

"I am saddened to say that your leaders have betrayed you. The Buccleuch family, sworn to uphold your honor, to defend the UFC and its partners, has instead turned on us once again."

As he spoke, soldiers pushed three people forward to the edge of the stair railing where I could see them. The deep auburn hair of the two ladies and the dark blue hair of the man left no doubt in my mind who they were. I cautiously leaned closer to the window and could just make out that their hands had been bound behind them. In spite of the

441

bonds, they stood stiffly regal, ignoring the guns that were pointed at their backs.

"These three conspired to steal an object of power from the UFC, sending their son and his companions to infiltrate the UFC base where it was being studied and…"

"Liar!" Roisin spun, her face furious. "We haven't stolen anything! It's you that has stolen our young men…" Roisin's voice cut off with a gasp as one of the soldiers stepped forward and slapped her sharply across the cheek followed quickly by a second soldier who roughly shoved a gag into her mouth. The soldiers appeared to have been expecting an outburst and had come prepared to silence it. An angry murmur rose from the crowd, but it was likewise quickly silenced by the threatening step forward of several of the armed soldiers around them.

"Now, now, my dear. You know very well that your young men were the cost of your grandfather's betrayal. If only you had learned from his mistake we would not be here today."

Suddenly I knew the speaker; it was Lord Remington, the man whom Ethine and Roisin had warned me would not let Aiden walk away without retribution for interfering with his plans. I felt myself grow cold, ice settling into my chest. This was his retribution.

"As I was saying," he went on, "stealing the object was their first step toward the coup they planned against the UFC, but it was not their only step. They have been gathering an army of young men, withholding them from their required enlistment in the UFC army so that they can instead raise an army of their own against the very government they were sworn to defend. This bitter betrayal has not just been against your government, it has been against you, the loyal people of the UFC. It is a betrayal that cannot be permitted to stand, that cannot be permitted to stain the name of the good people of Scotland. Justice must be dealt out in your name. And so, in an effort to restore the honor they stole from you through their actions, it is with a heavy heart that I must pass judgement on this family; these leaders who should have represented you with dignity, but instead dragged you through the dirt with their actions. The judgement that their betrayal forces me to declare is that the Buccleuch family will be executed for their crimes."

"No!" Aiden tried to surge to his feet only to have the chain pull him up short. Desperation showed in every inch of him as he begged, "It's me you want. Let them..." The soldier closest to him stepped forward and rammed the butt of his phase rifle into Aiden's face, cutting off his words and sending him sprawling awkwardly back to the ground.

Enraged, I furiously began searching out the flows of gravity around that soldier and started to reach for them, intending to send the man flying into the nearest stone wall with enough force to break every bone in his body. But before I could lift the gravity, a hand on my shoulder wrenched me backwards, breaking my concentration and my hold on the fields. Thatcher's voice hissed in my ear as he pulled me deeper into the room. "What are you doing?!" Shock at unexpectedly being pulled back caused my instincts to kick in. I spun on him, lashing out with a blow that he only barely reacted in time to block. He grabbed my wrists to stop me from swinging again. I growled at him ferally, not immediately registering who had my wrists.

"Alex!" he said sharply.

With stunned recognition, I immediately stopped fighting. "Thatcher," I whispered his name apologetically, "I..." Then

I desperately looked from him to the window. "We have to stop them. They're going to kill them!"

Outside, Remington, oblivious to what was occurring just above his head, continued as though Aiden's outburst had been his cue to turn his attention to the three men bound in shackles.

"Alistair Buccleuch, and those soldiers who assisted him in the stealing of the object will not escape their own punishments."

Still holding my wrists, Thatcher stiffened as he listened.

"The judgment I declare for them is that Alistair will be required to watch his family's execution, and then he and his companions will be shipped to the front lines of the battle against the enemies of the UFC where they will be required to fight for their government without reprieve until the day they die. I will not permit Scotland's good name to be tarnished by these few who would betray the UFC and all that it stands for. By my orders, Scotland will be cleansed of this dark blight."

As Remington continued, Thatcher's eyes grew wider before finally narrowing into a steely glint. He slowly released my wrists.

"What we have to do is get you out of here." It was all he said as he turned to pick up the rifle I had left lying on the bed.

Desperately, I started to argue, "We can't just abandon them…"

I was interrupted by a crashing sound coming from the sitting room. Thatcher spun, automatically raising the rifle into position as soldiers came rushing through the sitting room's now shattered door. They spread out as they came, searching for signs of resistance. Thatcher gave it to them as he began firing the rifle. I threw myself back against the wall, dodging their return shots.

"Can you get to your gun?" he asked between shots.

"It's inside the nightstand."

Thatcher took the briefest of seconds to glance behind him toward the bed and the piece of furniture beside it before turning back for another shot.

"That's a no then," he muttered; the nightstand was in clear view of the door and the soldiers beyond it. The room gave us barely enough cover to stay just out of their immediate line of sight so long as we hugged the wall.

The room around us was starting to look like a war zone. Several phaser shots had burned through the bedding. One had even shattered the far window. I could hear the startled shouts of the people below as the broken shards of glass rained down on them.

Thatcher swore under his breath as he glanced at me; there was a frustration in his eyes that told me all I needed to know. "We're pinned down," he finally admitted.

I sighed, somewhat surprised by how calm I suddenly felt given the situation. I gave him a small smile. "I'm sorry for getting you into this."

He cracked the faintest hint of his own smile and nodded ever so slightly. "Been a pleasure, ma'am." Then, without another word, he turned back and fired several more shots.

I closed my eyes and leaned my head back against the wall. Without being able to see the room outside, there was little I could do to help; I had to see the gravity fields to be able to manipulate them. My eyes shot open seconds later as Thatcher grunted and dropped the rifle. He fell back heavily against the wall, his hand pressed firmly against his arm where a trickle of blood was starting to ooze from between his fingers. I looked from him to the rifle he had dropped, considering using the gravity under it to bring it to my hands. From the corner of my eye, I saw movement in the sitting room; there was a soldier cautiously approaching the room's entrance. I made my decision, and the gun flew into my hands.

I aimed, my finger on the trigger, at the same time registering the soldier's startled expression from having seen the gun fly through the air. But I hadn't even pulled the trigger before the man's expression changed from shock to horror, and then to slackness. The soldier slowly toppled forward, the handle of a knife sticking out of his back. Behind him, a startled cry of alarm cut off with a gurgle, followed immediately by two other cries of pain elsewhere in the sitting room. A single phaser blast hit the ceiling just outside the door; it wasn't followed by any others.

Confused by what was happening, I looked to Thatcher for an answer. He appeared just as confused as I was. In the room outside the doorframe, there were several louder thuds intermingled with the sounds of scuffling and shouts of alarm, and then there was silence. I had allowed the rifle's nose to drop slightly with my confusion over what I was hearing. I brought it back up now as I nervously searched the stillness beyond the open doorframe for the soldiers that had been shooting at us only moments before.

"Claire?" a deep voice called cautiously from the stillness.

DuCain?! I thought in shock.

"Claire," he said again, "don't shoot. I'm coming out into the open."

I held the rifle nervously, but steadily, unwilling to let down my guard in case this was some type of trick.

DuCain stepped carefully into the space in front of the door so that I could easily see him. There was a dangerous, predatory edge to his stance, like a viper ready to strike. But upon seeing me, some of the tension left him. He breathed a sigh of relief. "She's okay, Esther," he called back over his shoulder.

A relieved voice answered from somewhere behind him, "Oh, thank goodness."

Continuing soothingly, he took a cautious step toward me. "You can put the gun down now, Alex. There is no one left out here that you need to shoot."

I searched his eyes, looking for any hint that he was deceiving me; there was none, just the same gruff expression he had worn earlier when he had told me I was his daughter, if I wanted to be. A wave of relief suddenly flooded through me and I let go of the breath I had not even realized I had been holding. I practically threw the rifle onto the bed, relieved that I had not been required to fire it. I thought that I would have done so to protect Thatcher, but it would have been the first time I had ever fired a weapon for more than just target practice. I had been trained to use it to kill, but in the back of my mind, I had always harbored the hope that I would never have to actually use it for that purpose.

Lord DuCain nodded in satisfaction then waved for someone to come forward. Lady DuCain rushed past him and into the room, sweeping me into a tight hug without any hesitation. "Oh, my child," she murmured, "we were so worried about you." I only hesitated for a moment before returning her hug. As I did so, I was surprised to hear the faint sob of relief that escaped my lips. She hugged me tighter in response. "It's okay now; we're here."

Lord DuCain cleared his throat. "I'm sorry to rush you, Esther," he said gently, "but in just a few minutes there are going to be more soldiers arriving to check on what that fighting was about. We need to be moving before they get here."

Lady DuCain nodded her head in understanding and released her tight hold on me, but then her eyes came to rest on Thatcher. At DuCain's words, he had begun to push himself back up into a standing position, determined to be ready to move. But his jaw was tightly clenched in pain and the black sleeve of his dress uniform glistened with the blood that his hand's pressure had been unable to fully stop.

"I think, John," she said thoughtfully, "that you had better go take care of them. This one needs some attention before we can move."

I expected him to tell her that that wasn't an option and that we needed to be moving in spite of Thatcher's injury. I was surprised when he smiled fondly in response to her instructions, then simply turned and walked away, as though he were going to fetch something for her from the other room. He paused only long enough to reclaim his knife from the fallen soldier's back.

Seeing my startled expression, Lady DuCain laughed lightly and assured me, "Oh, don't you worry about him. He's quite capable of handling the soldiers who are coming. Now, let's see to this young man's arm."

I didn't see how one man would be able to hold off a team of trained soldiers. Yet, at the same time, I was strangely comforted by her confidence in her husband's unusual abilities. Thatcher's eyes were thoughtful as he watched DuCain leave. Esther worked quickly, with steady hands that seemed to know exactly what they were doing. She ripped the shirt sleeve back so that his wound was exposed and began to gently probe it with her fingers, searching for the extent of the damage.

Thatcher stiffened with a sharp intake of breath when her fingers touched a particularly tender spot, but he didn't try to pull away. Then, almost as a way to distract himself from the pain, he asked with a strained voice, "SIS or ex-military?"

Lady DuCain smiled, though she didn't stop probing the damaged flesh. "You're a very perceptive young man," she finally acknowledged. "Yes, John was SIS. He retired officially when our daughter was injured during the attacks a few years ago, but I don't believe one can ever fully retire from the type of training he was given during his time serving the crown."

"And you?" Thatcher asked, surprising me with the suggestion that she might also be similarly trained.

Esther laughed out loud this time, pausing to meet his eyes and nod her head in approval. "Very perceptive indeed." Then she turned to me. "Claire, would you please get me a damp cloth from the bathroom?"

As I moved away to get it, I heard her continue to explain, "Yes, I was also SIS, though from a completely different department than John's, and I had retired many years before he did so that we could start our family."

Thatcher nodded, clearly far less surprised by her answer than I was. SIS? If I remembered correctly from the classes I had been required to attend on base, that was England's Secret Intelligence Service. They were composed of a group of highly trained agents who specialized in gathering information and combatting terrorism in one-to-one settings as opposed to the military's large group approach.

I handed her the cloth I had found and she began to wipe away the blood around the wound.

"Now, dear, if you would be so good as to take the sheet off of the bed and tear a three-inch wide strip for me." She didn't look at me as she said it, but it was obvious she wasn't asking Thatcher to do it. "I believe we can bind this wound up and he'll be ready to move. It's an ugly one, and it's going to hurt like the dickens, but it's not life-threatening and there is little more I can do for it here."

Thatcher didn't cry out when she tightened the bandage, though his jaw clenched tightly in an effort to manage the pain.

"Thank you, ma'am," he said through still-gritted teeth when she finished.

Lady DuCain smiled back and patted him on the shoulder. "Thank you for watching out for my daughter."

In between the shock of Lady DuCain's answers, I had been considering the situation outside. I was not about to abandon Aiden, his family, or my team to Remington, no matter what Thatcher had said about the need to get me to safety. It had been one thing when my presence might have distracted Aiden, but now it was obvious that my presence could not put him in any more danger than he was already in. Of course, neither would my presence alone be sufficient to resolve the situation.

I considered and discarded several plans for how I could rescue them; unfortunately, the truth was that I was not a strategist. My skill was with gravity. I could manipulate a limited number of gravity fields simultaneously, and I could use those fields to disarm some of the soldiers out there. But, beyond that, there wasn't much more I could do alone. I couldn't break the restraints on my team's hands and I didn't have the strength to hold off more than eight or nine soldiers at once; certainly not the dozens I had seen out there. I would need the help of Thatcher and the DuCains at the bare minimum, neither of which I felt confident were going to be willing to allow me to put myself into danger, no matter who else it might help. Nor did I think they would support anything that made a display of my use of gravity.

I was still sifting through arguments for how to convince them when Lord DuCain returned. He had someone with him. I recognized the man's sun-darkened face and crooked nose as the man Aiden had been speaking with in the seconds before the attack had begun.

"I found an old friend," Lord DuCain said simply.

"An old friend?" Lady DuCain's words seemed more of an amused phrase than an actual question. And at first it appeared that her husband intended to leave his statement at that, but the slight lifting of her chin that followed the silence must have made him think twice.

"Yes," he said finally with a mischievous smile. "An old friend who speaks with an awful English accent and who doesn't know that trainers are a pair of shoes."

"American." Lady DuCain rolled her eyes in mild disgust.

Knox seemed to find amusement in her response. His mouth twisted into a wry smile, and he offered a slight bow with an arrogant flare. "How can I be of service?"

"You can wipe that cocky grin off your face for starters, and then you can go check the hall and make sure we're clear to go through it. We're just about ready here." She may not have been impressed that he was American, but she had no problem putting him to work. His grin broadened as he bowed once more before turning away to go check the hall.

Lady DuCain huffed slightly under her breath but wasted no further time before she began issuing more orders. "John, gather some of those shooters laying around the room. Claire, if there is anything you absolutely need to bring with you, now is the time to grab it. And now for you, my dear." She turned to help Thatcher to his feet. He grunted, but didn't reject the steadying arm she offered.

Anything I absolutely needed to bring with me? Her words repeated in my mind, becoming a mantra. *Yes! I need to take my team away from the danger they're in.* But how could I accomplish that? I had taken on ten in the clearing and passed out because of it. There were ten times that here. There would be little support from the others. So, what did that leave me with? Not much I had to admit. I shook my head, frustrated by my lack of clear answers.

"Start with what you can do." The words were from an old memory. It was something Captain Marcellus had told me when I was ten and frustrated over an assignment I didn't know how to complete. He'd seen me sitting in the school's courtyard, my textbooks and notes spread out in front of me, but me with my head down on my arms as I tried to hide the tears that were seeping from the corner of my eyes. I had forgotten what the teacher had said about how to solve the algebraic formula and was too stubborn to ask anyone for help. I hadn't known he was nearby until I had heard and felt someone sit down on the bench next to me.

"Hey kid," he'd said softly. "What's got you so upset?"

I didn't raise my head; I'd known him by his voice. It wasn't the first time he'd come to sit next to me when I was doing homework; he'd shown up randomly on multiple other occasions to check in on how I was doing and to give me a hand when I needed one. But at that moment I was so frustrated that instead of admitting I needed help, I just pointed at the digi-pad and the problem on it. "I don't remember how." I'd said it with a murmur of frustration.

He'd sat silent for a moment, then asked, "Did you check your notes?"

"I'm supposed to know how to do this without the notes," I'd grumbled back.

"You silly goose." He'd said it kindly, but there had been just the slightest hint of a reprimand in his words as well. "You'll never know how to do everything and you'll certainly never master it all on your first try. When you find yourself in a situation like this, and you don't know what to do, start with what you can do. You can go back to your notes and re-read them. Chances are, it will help you think of what to do next."

At the time I'd thought he had only been referring to math problems. Now I realized that he had been referring to anything I was having trouble with. It was good counsel. I needed to look at this impossible situation from the perspective of what I could do. Well, I could start by taking steps to protect myself and the team I was currently with.

A weapon. I wanted a weapon in my hand. The drawer to the nightstand slid open easily. The cool metal of the gun fit perfectly into my hand, yet it felt so wrong. I wanted it, but I didn't like it. I almost set it back down. No! I don't have to like it. I just have to be willing to use it if that is what is required to help my team. I moved to put the gun into its holster only to realize I wasn't wearing one. I looked down at the flowing material of the dress. This was not going to work. I needed something I could move more easily in. My uniform was in the closet; I would change into that next.

A long, drawn-out scream of agony tore through the air outside the window, startling me. My body stiffened, immediately knowing whose throat that cry was being torn from. All thoughts of my team and self-preservation were seared away in that instant as I rushed to the shattered opening, terrified by what I would find, praying I was wrong. That prayer evaporated like water on hot sand. Aiden's tortured form was writhing on the ground.

His screams continued unbroken as I desperately searched for the source of his pain, intent on destroying whatever it was, but there was nothing there; nothing that was capable of causing such obvious agony. There were soldiers standing guard around him, but they were more focused on preventing McLagan, Wren, or anyone else from interfering than they were on the tortured figure at their feet.

Aiden's hands were still bound behind him, still connected to the low post. But then, so were McLagan's and Wren's. And while both of them were straining against their own bonds, trying to reach Aiden, neither of them was suffering as he was. Could it be the posts? Tentatively, I reached for the waves of gravity around the post and tugged on them. There was a sense of heft from the mass of the post, and drag from the dirt and roots that locked its positioning spikes into place several feet under the ground, but there was no sense of a power source within it or connected to it.

Identifying an active power source connected to an object was something I had learned to do when I was in my early teens. It wasn't the same as lifting gravity fields, but I had to be lifting them to notice it. It was a faint buzzing sensation that tickled the edges of the object I was lifting. The scientist working with me at the time had concluded that it had to do with the way the electrons flowed and how they interacted with the gravity fields. I could feel the buzz with all living organisms and most any object that had even a small battery causing power to flow through it, but I had never been able to do more with that ability than to recognize that some form of electrical impulse was present. There was no electricity actively flowing through the post. The post couldn't be the cause then. And while I could possibly still yank it out of the ground, what then? I didn't have any way to disconnect it from Aiden. Reluctantly, I released the fields around the post and kept searching.

Remington? Surely, he was responsible for this, so he must have a way to control it. Remington had moved to a position where I could now see him, but he wasn't looking at Aiden or even his direction. Instead, he was standing imperiously in front of Aiden's father, sneering as Lord Buccleuch pled for his son's life. Off to the side, Lady Buccleuch had tears streaming down her face even as she stood ram-rod straight, glaring at Remington with pure hatred and Roisin struggled wildly against the two soldiers that restrained her. But I couldn't identify any type of control box in Remington's hands or any of the soldiers around him for that matter. Remington wasn't even wearing a tactical band or a watch. If he was controlling whatever was causing Aiden's pain, he wasn't doing it directly.

My desperation grew as I continued to search without success, all the while Aiden's screams haunted and tormented me. I couldn't see anything touching him beyond the chains. No weapons, no soldier, no nothing. There wasn't anything I could send flying away from him; nothing I could crush. I couldn't even bring him to safety. How could I stop his torment if I couldn't find what was causing it?

A low sob escaped my lips as his screams kept going; they were becoming increasingly ragged. He was getting weaker and there was nothing I could do but watch. I felt so helpless. Numbness began to creep over me; a dizzying, vertigo-filled emptiness that made it feel as though I were viewing the scene through somebody else's body. Only, their eyes could see nothing but his agony and their ears could hear nothing but his cries. How long could this possibly go on for? How much strength did he have left?

Behind me, a voice swore, though I barely registered it through the numbness. Someone was pulling me away from the window. I didn't resist. I was unable to think coherently beyond the agonized cries that were echoing in my mind. The door, or what was left of it, was pulled closed as we passed through it. It dulled the sound of Aiden's cries but didn't stop them completely.

"Claire!?" Lady DuCain's worried face floated in front of my eyes. Her voice was a dull, empty sound compared to the raw, ragged screams that continued to echo in my head. A hand moved from side to side in front of my eyes, just beyond the ghost of the scene that haunted my vision. *Oh, Aiden!* I groaned inwardly as his ragged screams finally began to taper off. Fading, not because his pain had stopped, but because the muscles of his throat couldn't physically continue to maintain the hoarse cries that were being ripped from him.

Fingers snapped in front of my eyes. I looked up slowly, uncertain how the movement fit in with the images in my mind.

"John, she's in shock." Esther's voice sounded like it was coming through a long tunnel.

From somewhere outside of that tunnel, other voices drifted to me.

456

"They're torturing Alistair."

"Why?"

"Something about a stolen asset."

"We've got to get her away from this."

"I'll go check the hall…"

"I couldn't stop it." My words came out in a horrified whisper, cutting off their voices as effectively as if I had yelled at them.

There was silence for a brief moment before Lord DuCain's face came into focus in front of me. "Alexandria, look at me." A small part of my mind noted that he had used my real name. It seemed to draw my focus in a way the other name had not. He waited until my eyes met his, then he said slowly and steadily, "What they are doing to him, there is nothing you can do to stop it."

"But…"

"No; keep your eyes on me." I had started to look back toward Aiden; his hand on my cheek prevented me from turning away. "The tool they are using to cause his pain is not something you have the ability to remove from here."

"When will it stop?"

"It already has."

That confused me. I could still hear Aiden's screams in my head, but at the same time, I trusted DuCain. If he said the torture had already stopped, then why was Aiden still screaming? Or…was he? Uncertainly, I looked away from him and back toward the closed bedroom door; he didn't stop me this time. It was silent. No one was talking; no one was screaming.

DuCain's voice drew my attention back to him. "Alexandria, we are going to start moving. Can you do that?"

"I…" *What had I been about to say?* My mind was caught in a loop of confusion. *The screams had stopped? When had they stopped? Was he still alive? Could I move? Yes. Yes, I could move.* I focused on that single thought. I stood up.

"Good girl. Now…"

DuCain was still talking to me, saying something about staying next to Esther, but a different voice had broken through the haze and drew my focus to it instead. "They want something his father has; a weapon, I think. I overheard one of those soldiers say something about it. They're using Alistair to force Buccleuch to reveal where it is."

"What weapon?" That was Thatcher's voice.

"Something you lot supposedly stole and brought back here with you. A silver case of some sort."

"The case?" He sounded confused for just a moment, then his voice turned hard. "It's not a case they're looking for, it's a person. They want her."

Their voices trailed off as they moved away from me and toward the hall, but I had stopped listening anyway. Something he had said was churning over and over in the emptiness of my mind. *The case. They want the case.* Slowly, that thought was beginning to coalesce into something cold and hard. *Why the case? No, not the case; he wanted what he thought was in the case. He wanted power, only he didn't know that I was the power. He thought it was in the silver case.*

Deep inside of me, a cold fury ignited. It began to burn away the fog and numbness. He had invaded the Buccleuch's home, taken prisoners, and tortured Aiden, all for something he thought would give him more power than he already had. My eyes narrowed and a low growl formed in the back of my throat. *If he wanted power, then I would give him power like he had never known!* At some point, my body had begun to buzz with adrenaline. I could feel it coursing through me, sharpening my mind and preparing my muscles to fight.

"Enough!" I hadn't really intended to say it out loud, but as my head came up, my mind clear at last, it was obvious that I had said the word loud enough to stop everyone in their tracks.

"Alex…" DuCain started hesitantly, not sure what to make of the sudden change in my behavior. His voice trailed off as I met his eyes.

"Remington wants the asset." I said it slowly holding each of their eyes in turn. "So we are going to give it to him."

The DuCains and Knox shared concerned looks, but Thatcher's face only hardened.

"Whatever it is you're thinking, Jaquette, forget about it. The best thing we can do right now is to get you to safety."

I moved across the room until I was standing directly in front of him. I met his scowl with a cold, feral smile.

"I'm done running, Thatcher." My voice sounded cold even to my own ears. I'd had enough. I was done feeling helpless. A cold, angry fire had been kindled inside of me and that flame was growing hotter by the moment. I would set my team free and then Remington would pay for hurting Aiden.

Chapter 38: Aiden Haskell

I CURSED MYSELF for not seeing that one coming. I had reacted without thinking, crying out in response to Remington's declaration that my family was to be executed, but I should have known better. He wasn't going to allow me to defend myself or my family; he had already made his decision. The guard's weapon swinging at my head had not really been a surprise.

Now the side of my head was throbbing; a just reward for allowing my emotions to control my actions. Stubbornly, I rolled forward and forced myself back to my knees. I knew the chain wouldn't let me stand, but even so, my pride required me to get up; I would not remain on my back. I would not give Remington that satisfaction.

The fight in the courtyard had been so short. We'd been outnumbered and outgunned. In truth, I'd known from the moment I'd left her with Thatcher that our resistance would be little more than a delaying tactic designed to give him enough time to get her to safety. And to that end, it had been successful. She, at least, was safe. What I'd never seen coming was Remington's accusations and threats against my family.

Traitors?! He knew it wasn't true. He must know it. So why make this accusation? Why threaten to kill them? If I had thought for even a moment that turning down Collette would result in this, I would have gladly agreed to the marriage. I could have lived with the consequences if I had known it would mean their safety. Instead, I'd failed again.

The misery of my failure only served to compound the horror of what Remington had declared their punishment to be. Their deaths would be on my shoulders; my actions had brought us to this. My own punishment mattered little to me after that realization. What did I care if I was sent back to the front lines? I'd always known I would die there. But my family? They were supposed to live! They weren't traitors, and they certainly weren't thieves who...

Wait! All of my thoughts about my failure and my family came to a screeching halt. *What exactly was the accusation he had made? That we'd stolen an asset?* The blood drained from my face as the pieces fell into place. I felt so stupid for not seeing it before. This wasn't about my family. It wasn't about me. This was about getting his hands on more power. He wanted...*Oh Light!* The horror I'd felt at hearing his judgment on my family was nothing compared to the dread that flared through my mind now. *Alex! He wanted Alex! Please...* I pled desperately in my mind. *Please let Thatcher have gotten her to safety.*

It was McLagan's sudden oath that pulled me back to what was happening around us. He was looking toward the house where a newly shattered window was allowing the sounds of a battle to carry into the night. Phaser fire flashed again and again in staccato bursts of bright light that gave the appearance of a strobe light in the room. It was clear that someone was putting up stiff resistance. But that was the third-floor guest suites. Who would be up there fighting...*No. NO. NO!* "NO!" At some point, the word had moved from my mind to my lips. I surged back to my feet,

461

straining against the bonds that held me down, desperate to pull free of them. *That's Alex's room!*

Outside of the raging storm that flared into my mind, I could hear people shouting. A command to get back on my knees. A cry for help as I kicked out and sent the soldier closest to me to the ground. Arms that wrapped around me, only to go flying over me as I swung my shoulders with a hard twist. More people shouting. The slickness of blood trickling down my wrists from where the cuffs were cutting into the unhealed, raw skin. Burning pain in my side as a fist connected below my ribs followed by another across my chin. It didn't matter; nothing mattered but getting to her. Sharp pain in my injured knee as a foot kicked it from behind. And then the weight of three men as they forced me down, restraining me with their combined mass. I continued to struggle, wild desperation drowning out coherent thought. *NO!* My mind kept screaming over and over as I fought to break free of them. And then there was nothing but wave upon wave of pain as electrical jolts coursed through my body. I screamed in agony. I hadn't felt the shock collar being snapped around my neck, but I felt its effects with excruciating clarity.

Time stretched out endlessly, painfully as the jolts continued to wash through me. Some small part of my mind knew how the collar worked, though it was a detail that failed to extend beyond its mere existence. The military had developed shock collars more than ten years ago. They were considered a socially acceptable form of torture by the UFC, if any form of torture could be socially accepted. They tapped into the spinal column and targeted pain receptors throughout the body, inflicting intense amounts of physical pain, but little actual physical damage. A prisoner could be tortured for days, weeks, or even months on end with only minor physical repercussions.

But none of that crossed my mind as I screamed until I could no longer breathe. Only when I had nearly passed out did the lightning-hot pain abruptly come to a stop. It was designed to do that. It read the prisoner's biometrics and took their pain right up to the threshold of their body's ability to handle it. Then it automatically shut off. I would have a thirty-minute reprieve, and then it would start up again. Pain upon pain upon pain, until I broke. For now, I was left gasping on the grass, my throat raw from screaming.

My eyes were squeezed shut and I was breathing hard as my muscles continued to spasm, but I could hear the commotion all around me through the ringing in my ears. Angry shouts, interspersed by commands coming from the direction of the corralled guests. Remington speaking again, though exactly what he was saying I didn't care. I hated that man. Hated him for what he was doing; hated him for everything he had done. I hated him for what he represented to Scotland. He wanted my people to grovel at his feet? Well, I refused to give him that satisfaction.

I gritted my teeth and forced myself to roll over in spite of the pain; my muscles protested, but they obeyed. Getting to my knees was much harder than it had been last time. Still, I managed to get upright, holding myself as proudly as I could while kneeling shakily. From the corner of my eye, I saw McLagan watching me. He didn't say anything, but his head nodded slightly in approval.

Alex's room was still. There were no more bright flashes. No more sounds of battle. What had happened? Was she okay? Was she alive? Why hadn't Thatcher gotten her away like he was supposed to? Cold, awful dread filled my chest. If she was hurt up there, there was nothing I could do to help her.

Below the window, my family was watching me. I could see the concern on their faces. I realized that as worried as I was for Alex, they'd just been forced to watch me being tortured. How that must have hurt them. Tears were streaming down my mother's face leaving little doubt in my mind as to how it had affected her. Roisin, who had always tried so hard to protect me, wore an expression of horror mixed with fury. My father's expression was one of shock, as though he couldn't reconcile what was happening. No, he probably couldn't. He had been raised to believe that if he did everything the UFC asked of him, then they would take care of him. Years of certainty in that belief were being stripped away by Remington's actions tonight. I wished, for their sakes, that I could do or say something to ease their burden. But the truth was that even if I had been allowed to, there was no comfort I could give. They would be forced to watch again and again for as long as Remington saw fit to allow this to continue. And, from the satisfied look on his face as his eyes met mine, he wasn't going to remove this collar any time soon.

How much time had passed? How long did I have until it started up again? I didn't know. Strangely, the knowledge that the excruciating cycle of pain would be starting up again soon didn't frighten me. I was furious about it, but not scared of it. I was strong enough to survive this ordeal. I was sure of it. At least...I hoped I was. *Everyone breaks eventually.* The thought echoed in the back of my mind making me shiver. What would I eventually give away when I couldn't take it anymore? How long could I resist?

Movement at the top of the stairs drew my eyes away from my family. Two soldiers were exiting the house, dragging something limp between them. My heart sank; it was Thatcher. His arm was bandaged and he appeared to be only half conscious. Another soldier followed them, carrying the silver case that had been in Wren's room. I searched desperately for Alex, but no one else came through the door. What did that mean? Had Thatcher hidden her somewhere before he was caught? Was she still safe? Or...no! I refused to consider any other possibility. She had to be okay!

One of the soldiers delivered the case up for Remington to examine. He hungrily stroked it while searching for a way to open it. I knew he wouldn't succeed. The case was biometrically set to open only to the team lead's touch. I barked a sudden, sharp laugh as it occurred to me that we had forgotten to reset it to Thatcher's touch. It was still set to only open for me. Remington glanced my way, scornful consideration in his look. As he stared at me, I could almost see the corroded gears of his mind turning over the problem of the locked case. I shuddered as a cold smile suddenly spread across his lips. He turned from me and crouched down in front of Thatcher.

"How do you open this, boy."

Thatcher looked up slowly, wearily. He was clearly beaten down, but his voice carried the sound of the resistance that remained in him. "You don't."

"Come now. I'm sure you could tell me how to open it if you had the proper motivation. Perhaps a shock collar for you as well?"

Thatcher's jaw clenched tightly, the muscle in his jaw twitching in anger, but he remained silent. Remington studied him for a moment longer, then shrugged and stood back up.

"So be it. Stand him up." Thatcher wobbled unsteadily as they hauled him to his feet, their strong grips on his arms keeping him from collapsing or trying to escape.

Remington gave him one last chance as a soldier approached with another collar. "If you value your life, boy, you'll tell me exactly how it can be opened."

For a moment, Thatcher looked like he wasn't going to answer Remington, but his eyes locked on the collar coming toward him and he seemed to change his mind. "Wait." He licked his lips, making an effort to look away from the collar. I had never seen this side of Thatcher before. It made my heart sink.

"The case is coded to Alistair," he said nervously. "He was training with the asset back on the base. Only he can open and operate it."

Wait! What? That wasn't true. I mean, yes, I was the only one who could open the case, but training with the object? What was Thatcher saying?

"I see," Remington said, glancing in my direction once more. Then he seemed to have an idea that amused him. "Tell me," he began with an almost gleeful air, "what happened to that pretty young lady that was with your team? The one who was part of the fake engagement?"

Thatcher's face hardened, and his jaw clenched. This time he didn't answer the question. Remington's eyebrow raised as he waited. When it became obvious that Thatcher wasn't going to say anything more, he shrugged and turned instead to one of the soldiers for an answer. The stern-faced man on Thatcher's far side replied, "The girl that was with him is dead, sir. She was caught in the crossfire."

I heard those words as though they had come from a great distance; a distance that was covered in seconds by the wall

466

of horror that slammed into me. "No!" The word was torn from me just as the torture had torn the screams. My breath became ragged gasps once more as I surged to my feet, desperate to make them say it wasn't so. She couldn't be dead...she couldn't...only...Thatcher's head was hanging in defeat. He was injured and barely alive himself. *But he wouldn't have let her be killed... He wouldn't...he...* The thought broke off, as the truth sunk in. A heartbroken cry of agony escaped as I collapsed back to my knees. *Oh, Alex. What have I done?*

From somewhere beyond my grief, I heard Remington's callous voice. "Oh that's too bad. Collette really wanted to have a talk with her. Well, what's done is done. But all is not lost. Let's go see how this item works, shall we? Bring those two along."

His words couldn't touch me any longer. I was lost in the numbness of my grief. How many times could I fail? How many ways could I hurt the people I loved? *Alex!* My heart ached as I thought her name. *Why didn't I make you leave? Why did I allow you to become a part of this? Oh, Alex. I am so sorry.*

I squeezed my eyes shut against the pain, tears pooling at their edges. I wanted nothing more than to sink into the pain, but the sound of Remington's footsteps approaching wouldn't let me slide away. *Remington!* I felt a low growl of anger well up inside of me. He had done this! My grief began to kindle the flame of hatred like fuel poured onto a fire. Only this time, it wasn't a wild and uncontrolled rage. This time it was driven by a single thought: I was going to kill that man. I lifted my head to glare at him. A smile of satisfaction was on his lips. He thought he was in perfect control, but he had no idea what he had started.

"Unbind his hands," Remington commanded imperiously. "Let's see what he can show us." A cold smile of my own crept onto my lips; that would be his last mistake.

As I felt the soldier reach behind me to enter the release code, I braced myself to lunge. Every muscle was coiled like a spring ready to strike. Hatred was searing through me. I no longer cared if they killed me. If my last act was to rid Scotland of this monster, then it would be worth it. But, at the last second, just before the shackles slipped off, the soldier at my side leaned close to my ear and I heard his deep voice, barely louder than a whisper. "Keep it together, boy. You promised to live for her."

I looked over sharply. *DuCain?!* The soldier had already stepped back, turning away from me so that I couldn't make out his features. I shook my head, certain that the words and the voice must have been my imagination. But, as I turned back to Remington a second later, the opportunity to strike was gone. He was holding Roisin in front of him, a knife against her throat. I cursed myself for becoming distracted.

"Your hands on the case, if you will." Remington practically crooned with excitement. When I hesitated, he pulled the knife harder against her, causing her to wince.

My fury flared higher. But, despite my determination to kill the man, I found myself unable to make a move that would lead to more pain for Roisin. I growled in frustration, torn between the nearly unbearable pain of losing Alex, the furious drive to kill the man who had caused her death, and my inborn desperation to protect the ones I loved, even when it conflicted with the other emotions that sought for control of my actions. All for an empty case. *He had killed Alex for an empty case!* I thought in fury. *Fine, then. He can have it. And may he choke on the realization that he will get nothing in the end!* Angrily,

I turned to the case and placed my hands on it. Almost immediately, I felt the locking mechanism begin to whir followed by a click as the locks came undone in response to my touch.

I expected to find it empty; it had been a decoy after all. But inside of it lay a dull black disk about twelve inches in diameter and three inches thick. To my complete shock, the disk smoothly lifted out of the case to hover in front of me as though it were responding to a familiar friend. Stunned, I stared at it. How was this possible? And then I felt it, a faint floating sensation as though I were about to be lifted off the ground. The thrill of recognition raced through me. I knew this sensation and its source. *Alex!* They had been wrong. Somehow, Alex was alive. It had to be her controlling the gravity under the disk and under me. Relief coursed through me even as my head shot up searching for her. *Where is she?*

Remington's suspicious voice pulled me up short. "What are you looking for, boy?"

Fool! I thought. Don't give her away. Annoyed with myself for being so careless, I slowly turned to look at him, thinking to cover my carelessness with bravado. "I'm looking to see what it would take to destroy this force you brought with you. After all, you just handed me the means to do so."

He barked a sharp laugh, obviously not believing me for a moment. "You have boldness, boy, I'll give you that. But just remember that I am the one holding the knife to your sister's throat, and I have no scruples against using it. You've already lost one woman tonight. One foolish move on your part and you will watch this one bleed out in front of you. Now, the disk, if you don't mind. You will explain what it does in detail and teach me how to use it."

My fists clenched tightly in response. I didn't doubt that he would carry through with his threats. But still, I hesitated as something more occurred to me. If the shock collar went off during this, it would immediately be obvious that I was not the one controlling the gravity. I had no idea how much time was left until it started its next torture session, but I thought that it must be getting close. Should I take hold of the disk now, or delay until the collar's next session ran its course so that I was less likely to give her away?

I looked from Remington, to the disk, to Thatcher, as desperation drove me to make a decision. It was the look in Thatcher's eyes that made the final decision. All suggestions that he was on the verge of collapse had faded, replaced by a coiled readiness. I knew in that instant that his defeated, worn-down appearance had been a deception. His hard brown eyes looked from me to the disk and he nodded his head ever so slightly. That was all I needed. I reached out and grasped the disk with both hands.

Instantly, I felt the gravity underneath me shift so that my feet left the ground. Alex had only been waiting for me to touch the disk. She didn't lift me very high, maybe only two or three feet off the ground, but it was enough to elicit a startled gasp from several of the guests and guards. In that moment, several things clicked together in my mind.

First: *Alex is alive!* The words repeated themselves over and over in my mind with reassuring certainty. She was controlling the gravity under me right now, so she must be somewhere that she could see me even if I had been unable to locate her. The relief that washed through me was as intense as the torture had been painful. Whatever had really happened up in the rooms, Alex had survived it.

Second: Remington had known we were transporting an asset of power. No one should have known about that, but he had. Despite all our precautions, there was still a leak.

Third: Alex had shown her hand the moment she had lifted the disk out of the case. If I didn't successfully reinforce the appearance that I was controlling the disk, Remington might begin to suspect that it was not the real source of the power. I didn't want him to consider for even a moment that there might be a different asset he should be searching for.

Finally: Thatcher had set my path in motion when he told Remington that I had been training with the object back on the base. Whatever they were planning, they intended for me to be the decoy that would keep all suspicion away from Alex so that she would remain safe. Well, I could do that. I would be her decoy.

I lifted my chin and stared down at Remington. My voice, despite its raspy edge, came out hard and angry. I tried to make sure it was loud enough that Alex could hear it wherever she was hiding. "You want to know how this works? Then let me show you."

Everything erupted into chaos. In front of me, Remington's knife arm dropped away from Roisin's neck as though the knife's weight had suddenly increased a hundred-fold. It was wrenched from his grasp and thrust into the ground blade first, sinking into the dirt up to its hilt. The startled look on Remington's face was intensely satisfying. In the same instant, Thatcher surged up and wrapped his arms around Roisin, pulling her out of Remington's grasp as his momentum carried them out of reach.

In quick succession, the weapons of the soldiers closest to us were ripped from their hands and sent flying up into the air even as several of the guards themselves were thrust down, gravity's increased pull on them grinding them into the ground. They cried out in pain as the pressure continued to build.

Moving in near tandem with the start of Alex's assault, two soldiers dressed in UFC uniforms turned on their companions and began to attack as well. These two were particularly good at hand-to-hand combat as they took down soldier after soldier. My eyes narrowed as I watched the one on the left. His style was familiar; the way he stepped into his attacks and broke through his opponent's defenses. I had struggled against it many times when I was younger. With a start, I realized that I recognized not just him, but the other man as well. The first was Knox, the other was DuCain. I hadn't been mistaken about the voice telling me to keep it under control. My cold grin grew in satisfaction. Alex and Thatcher weren't trying to do this alone; they had allies.

It was the uniforms that had caused me to overlook them before this. That also must have been what had allowed them to get so close without raising suspicion. Was Alex wearing one of those as well? Was that why I had not been able to find her? I started to scan the area a second time, but a yelp from Remington as he was suddenly elevated some twenty feet into the air drew my attention back to him. I berated myself for getting distracted again. I couldn't afford to appear caught off guard by something Alex did. So, I watched with a stony, cold expression as he dangled in the air, suspended like a monkey caught in a vine and flailing for something to grab onto.

Still supporting the gravity fields she had already set in motion, Alex reached out next for the soldiers closest to my parents. I had to admit I was impressed as she continued, one by one, to systematically either strip the soldiers of their weapons or to send them flying over the balustrades to lie in a crumpled heap on the ground below. She was almost single-handedly turning the tides against Remington's army.

Unfortunately, Remington chose that moment to regain control of his fear. He had stopped flailing and was instead yelling furiously at his soldiers.

"Shoot him! Shoot him!"

Soldiers trained to respond to commands in an instant, brought their weapons to bear on me. Time came to a standstill in my mind as I watched the brilliant lights streaking toward me. There was no time to get out of their way, and it would be impossible for all of them to miss. I felt a bitter moment of loss for what could have been as I closed my eyes, waiting for the shots to tear my body apart; they never arrived.

After several seconds without the anticipated pain of the blast's arrival, I finally opened my eyes. I was stunned to see some thirty dark streaks on the ground below me where the phaser bolts had struck the earth instead of me, though I carefully kept my face expressionless. How had Alex managed to catch all of them? Several well-trained soldiers, not driven to inaction by the odd behavior of their phaser bolts, attempted to fire again. I watched in amazement as the trajectory of those phaser bolts arched suddenly and inexplicably down into the ground. Over and over, each time a soldier fired a shot at me, the corresponding bolt would arc down as though bent by an unseen force. It seemed impossible. The speed and accuracy with which Alex was reacting to make this happen was incredible. This was far above and beyond all that she had managed in the clearing only last week. I was in awe and a little worried. Her strength had limits. Surely this must be pushing those limits.

Several of the soldiers had lowered their weapons, uncertain of what to do. But those who continued to try shooting me were the next to be rewarded with an unexpected flight into the air followed by a ten-foot drop to the ground below. Those soldiers that Alex didn't personally attend to were taken down by the return fire of my teammates who had taken up weapons of their own. Thatcher's gun, to no real surprise, fired with extreme accuracy taking down soldier after soldier until there were none left who were willing to attempt another shot. Though I did note that his jaw was more tightly clenched than was normal for him. I wondered if that bandage on his arm had anything to do with it.

The guests who had previously been kept in a tight knot at the center of the lawn had begun to resist as well. Several were engaged in altercations with the soldiers closest to them. A few others stood with shocked expressions, watching events unfold. But most had taken the distraction Alex had created as their cue to flee. *Good!* I thought. *They should have never been made a part of this in the first place.*

Throughout it all, Remington remained helplessly suspended in the air. His face was red from swearing and yelling orders that no one was obeying. "What's wrong, Remington?" I asked sarcastically. "Isn't this what you asked me for?" He responded with several choice curse words that brought a smug smile of satisfaction to my lips.

Slowly, gently, I felt myself being lowered back to the ground. Thatcher was waiting for me there with another soldier held at gunpoint. That soldier nervously reached up and unlocked the shock collar from around my neck. I shuddered as I felt its micro-thin filaments retracting from

474

my skin. Its removal came with a wave of relief; I would not be subjected to a second torture session after all.

All around us, Remington's soldiers were being rounded up and led to the center of the lawn where the guests had previously been. A surprisingly large number of weapons were now in the hands of older men dressed in evening wear. As I listened to one of them issuing commands in a strong Scottish accent, I realized that these were likely Scotsmen who had previously served their time in the UFC military and then been summarily released after being injured. Some were amputees, others walked with a limp, but every one of them had joined our resistance without hesitation, taking their stand against Remington.

Speaking of Remington, I turned back in time to see the beginning of his rough descent back to the ground; Alex didn't take the care with him that she had taken with me. His return to Earth was awaited by Knox and several other armed men. It was done; Remington had lost. I lowered the disk to my side, not consciously thinking it through, but instinctively knowing that Alex would not be doing any more lifting of gravity tonight.

Knox slapped a pair of cuffs onto Remington's wrists and started to lead him away. Remington was still threatening retributions, but he stopped as Roisin stalked up to him, blocking his way.

He eyed her coldly and snarled, "You and your family will pay for this."

"I think we have paid quite enough already," she snapped back. The fury in her voice was cold and harsh. "We have given yae our sons and brothers for more than forty years, and all we have received in return is the pain of watching them bleed and die for yae. The generation yae claim betrayed the UFC is dead, but it was never going tae be enough for yae, was it? We have kept our honor. But yae, Remington, have not. Tonight, yae've shown everyone just how corrupt yae are."

"Honor?!" Remington sneered at her. "You think Scotland could ever have honor again? Scotland will never be able to pay enough to cleanse its name."

She had opened her mouth to reply, only to close it again as something that glinted silver in the darkness flew through the air to bump her in the shoulder before falling to the ground. I realized with a start that the object's flight had been sloppy, without the control that Alex had been exhibiting up to this point. She was getting tired.

Roisin bent down curiously to pick the object up. As she stood again, her expression changed to one of wicked delight. What was she holding? I was suddenly suspicious. Alex, what are you up to? Before I could say anything, Roisin was speaking again, her voice loud enough that everyone could hear her clearly.

"Remington, for yer crimes against Scotland, I sentence yae tae the same punishment yae subjected me brother tae."

What punishment? *No!* I thought in horror as I realized what she was holding. Surely not. I hated Remington and had been ready to kill him only minutes ago, but he didn't deserve this; no one did. I had to stop her.

"Roisin!" I shouted and started toward her, only to be stopped in my tracks as the gravity under my feet increased just enough that I could no longer lift them. Alex?! She was stopping me? Stunned, I looked up, searching for her again. Just visible through the now thinned ranks of soldiers was a willowy form dressed in a UFC uniform that swayed, appearing to be on the verge of collapse. I was certain it was

476

her. She met my eyes and shook her head ever so slightly. "Don't interfere," her expression seemed to say. Then, just as suddenly as it had started, the gravity under me returned to normal and I stumbled forward. She had released me, too late to stop Roisin. Remington's sputters of protest were cut off in a sudden howl of pain as the collar began its work.

Desperately I looked around for the soldier who had unlocked the collar when it was on me. He knew the code; he could stop this. My eyes fell on his prone figure, eyes opened sightlessly to the darkness above. The knife that Remington had used to threaten Roisin had been driven into his throat. I stared at the knife in horror. *Oh, Alex. What have you done?!* Remington's screams continued to fill the air. I looked back at her just in time to see her stumble backward and slump down against the wall. Everything else was forgotten as I dropped the disk and ran to her.

Chapter 39: Alexandria Jaquette

I REALIZED BELATEDLY that I didn't have the strength to keep myself standing. Everything was spinning around me and my muscles were on fire from the strain of doing so much. With the rush of adrenaline fading away, there was nothing more to keep the weariness at bay and I felt drained. But it was Remington's screams that suddenly stripped all remaining strength from me. They tore through the air, shredding my thoughts as his cries of pain filled my head. I stumbled back against the wall, sliding down it to keep from simply collapsing.

My eyes were wide open, but it was Aiden's body, not Remington's, that I suddenly saw lying on the ground, the tortured screams being torn from his throat once more. I pressed my hands against my ears to block the sound out; it wasn't enough. I felt a sob escape my throat. What had I done? I remembered wanting Remington to pay for the pain he had caused Aiden. Sending the shock collar to Roisin had seemed so right in the moment, such poetic justice. But I had been wrong; I could see that so easily now that the fury was gone. *Please, someone, take it off of him!* The thought silently begged in my mind as I began to rock back and forth.

I was so lost in the darkness of Remington's screams that I almost didn't notice when strong arms swept me off the ground. A deep voice whispered words of comfort as the voice's owner carried me swiftly away from the screams. A small piece of my mind registered that the voice belonged to Lord DuCain; he was the one carrying me. At his side, I could hear Esther's concerned voice. "She's going back into shock, John. Remington's screams must have triggered her mind into an emotional relapse. Eithne," she called more loudly, "we need some place where she can't hear the screams."

The screams dimmed somewhat as we moved inside. But, like the last time, the distance didn't really matter. It was in my head now, and distance couldn't dim the echoes there. If I had been able to think straight, I would have felt foolish for allowing Remington's screams to send me into this tailspin. Unfortunately, thinking straight was not something I was capable of right now. I kept seeing Aiden in my head, his body wracked with pain. This time it was my fault; I had given the collar to Roisin. I whimpered softly, "Please, let it stop."

DuCain's voice came again. "It's okay, Alexandria. I've got you."

I clung to the strength of his voice, even as the screams threatened to pull me deeper. I think there was a part of my mind that knew what was happening. It knew that those screams were not really Aiden's and it knew that we had been successful in setting him free. But it also knew that I was the reason Remington was screaming, and that realization terrified me even more than the images in my head. What was I becoming?

DuCain gently lowered me into a chair as strong fingers began softly, but firmly prying my hands away from my ears. At the same time, DuCain's steady, calming voice kept trying to break through the fog. "Alexandria, the screaming has stopped. It's over. It's okay to let go now."

"I can still hear him." I whispered the words in an unsteady voice, even as I weakly resisted the hands that were holding mine, keeping me from being able to cover my ears again.

"No, Alexandria, you can't. It's all in your head now. Listen to the silence."

The part of my mind that knew what was really happening was screaming at me to open my eyes and see the reality. The rest was screaming in horror at what I had done. I was no better than Icarus' other children. *I really am one of them!*

"I did this to him," I groaned.

"No, you didn't, Alexandria. You are not responsible for what happened out there. Remington did this to himself."

I felt a tear slide down my cheek. "But...I..."

"No, Alex. He's right. This is not yer fault."

The screams in my mind faltered as those words and the voice that had spoken them sunk in. *Aiden? But, how?* If he was speaking to me, then whose screams was I fighting so hard to block out?

"Come on, Alex. Open yer eyes and look at us, please." The image in my mind flickered again, as though struggling to maintain dominance against the voice that was speaking. There was a desperation in that voice that drew me away from the images in my head and toward him. At the same time, the screams seemed to echo even louder in my mind, as though they, like the image, were fighting to pull my attention back to them.

"Please, Alex."

Those last two words were filled with pain more real than the screams in my head. Slowly, I opened my eyes, looking

480

up to see Aiden kneeling in front of me. It was his strong hands that were holding mine away from my ears. I could see his eyes frantically searching my face, but I could only stare back blankly. Numbness had slowly begun replacing the horror in my mind, like a cushioned padding that deadened the sound of the screams. But like thick layers of mismatched padding that were not quite right for the job they were applied to, it not only failed to completely eliminate the screams, it muffled my ability to think. I couldn't seem to put two thoughts together.

"Keep talking to her," Esther's soft voice instructed from somewhere nearby. "Talk about anything but what happened out there." Aiden nodded.

"I, uh, never did get tae tell yae about what happened after I left yae on the base. I had gotten orders, from the Directorate's office, transferrin' me tae America. They had me scheduled tae be on a cargo ship leavin' out of Alexandria, Egypt." He chuckled nervously. "Can you imagine the irony? They forced me tae abandon yae, only tae send me tae a city that shared yer name. It felt like a kick in the gut. I spent the better part of th' day feelin' frustrated because me heart had fallen in love with yae, but me head still was still fightin' acceptin' it. I would see yae in me dreams anytime I tried tae sleep, but I also knew that th' transfer meant I would likely never see yae again. It was tearin' me apart."

I blinked, hearing his words, but not truly comprehending them. *America... Alexandria... love... dreams... never...* The words repeated in my head, a disjointed collection whose only value was in the voice that spoke them.

"And then Hadley showed up. He was there tae bring me back, only Beckwith's team had set it up tae make it look like he was really there tae give me a message. There was a man with him who was about me height and build, with blue hair like mine. He'd come along so he could take the beatin' for me that was Beckwith's message and then stay behind pretending' tae be me, recuperatin' so that no one would know I was gone. I'm goin' tae have tae find a way tae thank that man someday." He chuckled again; it sounded forced. "When I told Roisin about it, she suggested I…"

Roisin! I startled him as I suddenly yanked my hands away to press them back against the renewed pounding in my head. Emotions had come raging back in with the mention of her name.

"The collar…Roisin…I sent it…I…" The words came out in a horrified, disjointed muddle as what I had done came crashing back in on me once more, threatening to draw me back down. I squeezed my eyes shut, trying to block out the visions of Aiden thrashing on the ground and the screams that had flared back to life, once more dominating my mind. I started shivering uncontrollably. "What have I done?" I whispered in horror.

"No, don't close yer eyes." The desperation was back in Aiden's voice as he reached up to cup my face in his hands. "Come on, Alex, keep lookin' at me. I'm right here." His voice was like a lifeline that refused to let me sink; it kept drawing me back from the edge of the abyss. "Yer goin' tae be okay." He paused, seeming to be thinking through what to say next. "Tell me, have yae ever been tae America?"

It worked. I found myself focusing on him again, trying to reason out what he had just asked me. *America? Had I ever been there? I…no. I had never been there.* It was hard to shake my head through the shivering, but he seemed to understand.

"I haven't either." He forced a laugh. "So tomorrow will be th' first time for both of us, then. I've heard that America has some neat things tae see. I even heard that they have th' tallest trees in th' world up in th' mountains of California. Maybe we could go…" His voice drifted to a stop as my shivering suddenly grew stronger.

A random thought had crossed my mind: *The ice of Icarus runs in your veins!* I had wanted to scream in horror at the thought, but then it had drifted back out of my mind as quickly as it had come. All I was left with was the memory of ice and the feeling of dread to match the screaming in my head. I was freezing from the inside out!

"I'm so cold," I whispered through chattering teeth.

Aiden was moving, almost before I had finished speaking. He picked me up and pulled me into his arms. The warmth of his body and the steady rhythm of his heartbeat as my head settled onto his shoulder had a calming effect on the shivering, though it did not stop it completely. Nearby, a door opened and closed again. Someone approached to lay a blanket on me. Aiden only loosened his arms enough to allow the blanket to be wrapped around me; he retightened his hold the moment it was in place.

"Alexandria," DuCain's warm, deep voice drifted in from beside me. "Why don't you close your eyes and rest for a little bit? You must be very tired. We can talk more in the morning."

Tired? No…I'm not… The thought didn't make it any further as a yawn interrupted it. His words and tone had an almost hypnotic, suggestive quality to them. I was suddenly struggling to keep my eyes open.

"It's okay to close your eyes, Alexandria. You're safe now. We'll watch over you while you sleep."

Aiden softly echoed his suggestion. "I've got yae. I won't let anythin' happen tae yae while yae sleep."

With another slow blink, I tried to hold his gaze for several heartbeats longer, but my eyes fluttered closed of their own accord and darkness came. With the darkness, the screams finally faded to nothingness, replaced by the silence of the room; the silence…and Aiden's heartbeat.

Chapter 40: Aiden Haskell

SHE WAS ASLEEP. I looked down at her face, peaceful for the first time since she had collapsed. I had reached the top of the stairs only seconds after DuCain had swept her up and rushed her inside. So, I'd followed them to the library at the back of the house. As I followed, it quickly became obvious that something more than exhaustion was affecting her. The horror in her voice when she whispered those few words and the haunted look in her eyes were not things I had been prepared for, but years of battle experience had taught me to keep my voice calm and my expression neutral; even when I was panicking inside.

"What was that?" I was careful to whisper so that I didn't wake her.

DuCain ran his hand over his face. "That…" he said with a sigh, "is what happens to someone who is too tenderhearted for the horrors of war." He swore softly under his breath. "I should have refused her request."

Lady DuCain joined us. "You would have been hard-pressed to succeed in such a refusal had you tried, John. She was not going to abandon him." She looked at me meaningfully with the last part.

DuCain swore again and growled, "Boy, you had better be worth this."

Lady DuCain huffed then turned to address me. "The horror of seeing you tortured, and discovering that she was unable to help you, was too much for her mind to process. It triggered an emotional shock response. She was able to snap herself out of it the first time, once she realized that there was something she could do to help you after all. But…"

"Wait! She watched that?"

Lady DuCain nodded sadly. "Your screams. They were…hard on her. I suspect that when Remington started screaming, it re-triggered the memories and the corresponding shock."

My screams had triggered this? My heart fell, wishing now that I had been strong enough to hold those screams in, to have somehow been able to protect her from my pain. It was a foolish wish. I could have no sooner held back the screams than I could have held back the sun. But I was still disappointed in my own weakness; it was just one more of my failures that I could add to my long list.

Esther was speaking again. "When she wakes up, she'll probably be disoriented. Give her time to adjust. Don't push her for answers or try to rush her back into normality. If she is ready to talk, fine, otherwise, don't bring it up. Just be there for her when she is ready."

I nodded my head soberly. *Emotional shock!* Now I understood. I had seen it before, on the battlefield in soldiers after an especially traumatic battle; some of them never recovered. I looked down at her again as a new fear seeped into the back of my mind: W*hat if she never recovered?*

"We'll take care of her, ma'am." Thatcher's voice startled me. I hadn't heard him come in. I looked up now to see him watching me closely. He didn't say anything more, but his eyes seemed to be taking everything in and making mental notes. It occurred to me that he was probably judging my battle readiness. Technically, he was team lead, and the truth was that I was far from physically fit for service. Every muscle in my body still ached from the torture, my wrists were bloodied and raw, I was limping with every step, a rib in my side was on fire, and the skin on the side of my head was bruised and split with a trickle of blood coming from where the rifle butt had hit me. Thankfully, he said nothing about it, instead turning from me to address DuCain.

"The corridor and garage are clear, sir. We're ready to move."

"Then it's time. Alistair, if you would continue to carry her, let's get your team out of here."

It was quite likely that DuCain recognized as well that I was not in the best of shape, but he likewise chose to say nothing about it. I was grateful for their silence. There would be time to slow down and care for my own injuries after I was certain that she was safe. And that meant getting her far from Remington and his soldiers as quickly as possible. I shifted her slightly so that I could get to my feet. It was not the easiest of maneuvers between my pain and her in my arms, but I managed.

Thatcher took the point as we moved through the halls of the home I had grown up in. There was an odd feeling of fragility in them as we passed that I had never felt there before. Drumlanrig castle had always seemed such a fortress of safety and security to me. It had stood for centuries against invading armies and ferocious battles. But tonight, as we walked with weapons drawn, the safety and security I had always associated with its walls seemed somehow tarnished by all that had taken place in the last few hours. I wondered if I would ever feel safe here again.

Wren, McLagan, and Knox fell in around us as we left the room. Even DuCain picked up a phase rifle from somewhere and was now expertly working in tandem with the rest of the team to check each intersection and doorway that we approached. It occurred to me once more to wonder about this man that was claiming the title of Alex's father. He had clearly received at least some form of military training.

Thankfully, we reached the garage without incident. Lady DuCain and my mother, who had come with us, held the doors to the jeep open. Thatcher stowed his rifle in the back along with the rest of the supplies and then climbed into the driver's seat. McLagan and Wren took the seats in the back; they kept their weapons with them. DuCain took Alex from my arms while I climbed into the front passenger seat, then he gently lowered her back into my arms. As he did so, he lowered his tone. "I'm entrusting my daughter to you, Buccleuch. You keep your promise to me, boy, or I'll keep mine." He backed away without giving me a chance to respond.

My mother, who must have heard what he said, gave no indication that his words bothered her. Instead, she stepped into the space he had vacated and leaned over to kiss me gently on the cheek. "Take care of her, Alistair, and take care of yourself. Your father and I are so very proud of you."

"What about you?" I asked hesitantly. My family was still in danger and I was torn between wanting to stay and protect them and the intense need to get Alex to safety. They, and the people of Scotland, had just openly rebelled against Remington and the UFC soldiers. This was not going to end well.

She laughed lightly at my concern. "Remington has no idea the trouble he has stirred up. But the people of Scotland will take care of us. Your father will probably take some time adjusting to the betrayal he is feeling; I'll help him through it. You just worry about getting this one to safety. I meant what I said earlier: she is quite a remarkable young woman. Make sure you are worthy of everything she is sacrificing for you."

I laughed with a sudden, bitter sense of loss. "There's no need to continue with the ruse of a wedding now that Remington has..." I stopped as her lips twisted up into a wry smile. She reached out to touch me tenderly on the cheek.

"Oh, my son, you still have so much to learn." Then, not allowing me to ask what she meant by that, she stepped back and closed the door.

Lady DuCain, who was still standing by Thatcher's open door, handed him the silver briefcase that had been at the center of this evening's trouble. "I do believe you'll still need this to maintain your team's cover. I've also placed something in there that Alexandria will need later. You can give it to her when she is ready for it. Now you boys drive safely and take care of her. I'll expect to see all of you at Christmas when we come to visit." She said it with the tone of a mother reminding her kids to behave before she sent them out the door. Then, with a final glance toward Alex, she stepped back and closed that door as well.

Thatcher started the engine, revving it to life as Knox opened the garage's big bay door. With a soft pair of thumps on the side of the jeep, DuCain said, "Get going, boys. Don't stop till you reach the rendezvous point."

With a final nod of his head, Thatcher put the jeep into gear and drove us out into the night.

CHESS. SIXTY-FOUR checkered squares that pre-determine all of the possible moves a player can take. And yet, from those sixty-four squares and the thirty-two playing pieces of this game, there are trillions upon trillions of moves that two opponents can make. Yet, a single move from even the weakest of the playing pieces can set in motion the course of the game toward ultimate success, or disastrous defeat. For that reason, each move must be carefully thought out and thoroughly considered. That is not to say that one must take an inordinate amount of time in choosing their moves; I certainly never do. My mind processes information and calculations faster than the ordinary mind, giving me an edge over most ordinary men. But, while this is certainly helpful, it is not what truly sets me apart.

What one must have in order to be a master of this game, and which it just so happens that I do have, is a perfect understanding of the playing pieces. This, perhaps, more than anything else, is what sets me apart from all the other players of this game of strike and counter strike: I know my pieces in exquisite detail. I know their strengths and weaknesses. I know which pieces should be placed where. I know perfectly which ones can be sacrificed to ensure the better positioning of others. And I know which ones need to hold their positions a little longer so that a better move can be made in the future.

In fact, I am so exceptional at this game that I have successfully kept multiple games in motion for more than thirty years. At any given time, the games I've played have ranged from the simple political maneuvering of seemingly innocuous candidates to the much more intricate military maneuvers that have given me control of nearly a quarter of the world. Grand games and seemingly unimportant games; they are all the same to me. Each one, in truth, is a move in a much bigger game.

At this moment, however, the game that I am most intent upon is the one I have been playing in the background for more than eighteen years. In this particular game, I have chosen my playing pieces carefully. They have been men and women, some strong, some weak, but each one chosen for their specific abilities, deliberately placed where they could be most effective. Their job? Simple: find my missing Alpha and bring it back to me.

For eighteen years, those pawns have sifted through information, observed, waited, and watched. Occasionally, one will send back rumors or scraps of truths that I work to piece together like a puzzle. But always it seems to come too late for me to act upon. It would have been more of an irritant were I not so patient. But I know how to play the long game. After all, it's the only one that really matters.

Last year, one promising piece of information had arrived soon enough to be acted upon. Unfortunately, we knew very little about the particulars of my missing child. Whether it was a boy or a girl I couldn't say. Back then I had been just naïve enough to enjoy the thrill of the surprise when each child was born. What I did know was the approximate date of their birth, that their abilities would be above normal, and the physical and Alpha traits of both parents. In spite of our limited information to go on, my pawn had discovered a boy at Cambridge Base who appeared to fit all of the known specifications and particulars of my Alpha. That child, a tall, thin teenage boy they had told me, could control sound waves and was being studied by the scientists there. But after obtaining the boy, and testing him myself, I had been left with no doubt that he was not mine. It had been an annoying distraction, but not a complete failure.

Following the boy's disappearance from Cambridge Base, the UFC had implemented a new set of safety protocols and procedures that played right into my hands. In their rush to close perceived security gaps, they had left cracks in their other systems that I was able to exploit. I now had pawns in key locations that had previously been unavailable to me. Sobrien had been just one of those pawns. He was a fervent follower, willing to do anything I asked of him, but not very smart in and of himself. Still, with only six weeks to integrate himself into the playing field, he had done well, and had very nearly succeeded in the task I had given him. It was unfortunate that he had gotten himself killed before he had been able to complete his assignment.

My other pawn at that same base had proven much more disappointing. Two years that pawn had been in place. Two years they had woven themselves into the grain of the base's very fabric. At first, it had appeared they might be successful in their task. They had begun sending reports claiming that they had gained access to information about my Alpha and had even fed me a constant stream of promising data that had been delightful. A girl, they had told me. An Alpha with tremulous control over gravity, though it was a control that was increasing regularly. Of course, I shouldn't have been surprised to find this information false. They weren't the first pawn to send me information on a red herring. No. Far more successful than this particular pawn had been the Iranians.

Their special ops force had been another of my pieces in this game; sacrificial pawns whose only job was to gather the information I craved. And to that end, they had performed their job admirably. Finally, it appeared that I had a video of my Alpha, and the boy it showed was exquisite. Of course, I couldn't be truly certain that he was my Alpha until I had him in my possession and could run some tests, but the level of the power he displayed left little doubt in my mind. This child...no, not a child; they had been successful at keeping him from me for so long that he truly had grown into a man. This man would indeed be a weapon to be reckoned with.

Alexander, the woman in the video had called him. A handsome, intelligent young man whose control over gravity waves and leadership of the team around him was already quite impressive, to say the least. It would be interesting to see what more my serum would do for him.

The serum is a creation of mine. An elixir that is, dare I say, uniquely me as its key ingredient is a hormone that only my body produces. And its effect on my Alphas is equally unique; unique and interesting, to say the least. I engineered my Alphas to be strong, but when their natural abilities are enhanced by this hormone, there is a chemical reaction that amplifies the abilities of their sixth lobe. In layman's terms, they see the waves more clearly and have an easier time controlling them. In scientific terms, the elixir bridges a missing connectivity between the Alpha 214 and Alpha 216 axons causing the neuron networks and corresponding synapsis to fire much more effectively. For most of the Alphas we test it on, the added control is only marginal. But for a select few of my children, the control they gain over the waves they see becomes exponentially stronger.

There are, as is always the case when attempting to make changes to neural pathways, a few less desirable side effects that come with the serum. The most common change we see is a lessening of emotional connections to others and an increase in their lust for causing violence and pain. I can live with the lessening of emotional connections: I don't need them to love me, only to serve me. And as for the other, well, it serves to make them all the more fearsome to my enemies, and I have more than enough of those to allow my Alphas to satiate their never-ending desire for violence.

Although I have no true way to guarantee the level of control the serum will add to Alexander's strength, I have reason to suspect that he will react exceptionally well to it. *He is,* I smiled to myself at the thought, *unique in more than one way—a way that none but myself knows about.*

ALPHA RATING LIST

Alphas

α

Genetically modified to have 6th lobe in their brain; can see and control waves otherwise invisible to humans.
*Approximate Population: 200

Betas & Charlies

β **&** Γ

1% of genetically modified who keep enhancements after puberty, but then experience a leap forward in one or more of their enhancements.
*Approximate Population: 300,000

Deltas

Δ

10% of genetically modified who keep enhancements after puberty.
*Approximate Population: 300 million

Echoes

ε

90% of genetically modified who do not keep changes after puberty.
*Approximate Population: 2.7 billion

Digi-Pad 300

BETA/CHARLIE CLASSIFICATIONS

Physical (P)
- Fine Motor (FM)
- Balance (Ba)
- Coordination (Co)
- Body Awareness (BA)
- Strength (St)
- Reaction Time (RT)
- Speed (Sp)
- Endurance (En)

Intellectual (I)
- Cognition (Co)
- Speech (Sp)
- Sensory (Se)

Physiological (Ph)
- Cellular (Ce)
- Chemical (Ch)

Digi-Pad 300

UFC ALPHA RATING REGISTRATION
SECRETARY OF ALPHA REGISTRATION
28839 FEDERATION WAY
LONDON, ENGLAND

REPORT DATE : 23 SEPTEMBER 188

Name	Country of Origin	Alpha Rating	Classification
Alexandria Jaquette	N/A	α/β	Gravity Waves Ph-Ch; I-Co
Callia Ubuqua	Africa	α	Light Waves
Cepheus Jonsson	Norway	α	Gamma Waves
Icarus Argyros	Greece	α/β	Radio Wave Ph-Ch; I-Co
Troy Durnham	England	α	UV Waves
Cody Thatcher	USA	β	P-Co; I-Se
Liam Hadley	Canada	β	P-RT; P-Sp
Reimond Bauer (Rockman)	Germany	β	P-St; P-Co
Aiden Haskell	Scotland	Γ	P-Sp
Bowen Freeman	Australia	Γ	P-St
Dimitri Sobrien	Russia	Γ	P-PS
Huang Zhaohui (Harry)	China	Γ	I-Co
Lakota Wren	USA	Γ	I-Co
Lilith Alcott	USA	Γ	I-Co
Maria Estradé	Mexico	Γ	I-Se
Patrick Paxton	England	Γ	P-Co
Logan McLagan	Scotland	Δ	N/A

PRONUNCIATION GUIDE

Aiden Haskell   Ay-dehn Haa-skohl
Alexandria Jaquette   Owl-eh-xaan-dree-a Juh-keht
Alistair Buccleuch   Ow-lih-stair Boo-kih-loh
Callia Ubuqua   Kuh-lee-uh Oo-boo-kway
Captain Marcellus   Mahr-sehl-uhs
Cepheus Jonsson   See-fuhs Jahn-suhn
Claire DuCain   Klare Doo-Kayn
Dimitri Sobrien   Dih-mee-tree Soh-briy-ehn
Eithine Buccleuch   Eh-tih-nay Boo-kih-loh
Huang Zhaohui   Hwawng Jow-hway
Icarus Argyros   Ih-kuh-ruhs Ahr-ree-yohs
Lilith Alcott   Lihl-ihth Aal-kaht
Maria Estradé   Muh-ree-uh Ehs-staw-deh
Roisin Buccleuch   Roh-sheen Boo-kih-loh
Troy Durnham   Troi Duhrn-haam

Coming 2024

THE
CITY OF
ANGELS

BOOK 2:
THE REGNANT WAR

Chapter 1: Aiden Haskell

NO ONE SAID anything as we drove through the darkness. It had been nearly an hour since we had left my family's property. And, while the first few minutes of adrenaline-heightened awareness had kept us talking and discussing the night's events, the discussions had eventually given way to quiet reflection. With the retreat of the adrenaline had come the reminder that we were each nursing injuries that would need further treatment once we reached base. Thatcher had taken a phaser blast to the arm, McLagan had a gash in his leg, Wren had a deep cut above his eye, and I...well, I hurt everywhere. My muscles were still aching from the torture, my knee was screaming at me, my wrists were on fire, my rib ached enough that it hurt to breathe, and my head was pounding, but none of that mattered to me right now.

Alex was still unconscious in my arms; she was my primary concern. Our escape had been due to her efforts. The number of gravity fields she had been simultaneously controlling there at the end, and the level of control she had maintained over them, was greater than anything I had seen her manage before; it had been truly incredible. She had almost singlehandedly turned the tables on Remington's forces. But it had come at a cost: the effort had left her physically drained. On top of that, the emotional damage she had suffered while watching Remington torture me had become debilitating in the end. She had retaliated at Remington by seeing the shock collar placed around his neck after it had been removed from mine. Or at least that's what I thought had happened. Now I wasn't so sure.

Hearing Remington's screams of pain had sent her back into an emotional tailspin, reminding me just how fragile she was. For all her training and abilities, she did not belong in battle. Estradé had seen that much quicker than I had and had done something about it. But, in spite of Estradé's careful preparations, I had managed to mess everything up by dragging Alex smack dab into the middle of my own problems. I shook my head in self-recrimination; I should have never let her stay.

Thatcher must have seen the movement. "You doing okay there?" he asked softly.

"Yea," I answered. "Just frustrated with meself for letting this all happen."

He looked at me for a long moment before turning his attention back to the road. I could only imagine what he was thinking. He had tried to insist that she be taken to safety the moment he had learned about my situation. It was my fault she had even been given the option to stay, whereby compromising the integrity of our mission. I didn't imagine he was going to be overly forgiving about that. As the silence stretched on, that certainty was confirmed in my mind. I was surprised when he suddenly broke the silence.

"When I was sixteen, my father asked me to check the fence around our prize bull's pasture. It was a job I was more than capable of doing on my own, but about halfway around it, I saw the cute neighbor girl and thought I'd try to impress her by playing bullfighter with the bull. She cheered me on and was rather impressed with my tomfoolery, right up until I misjudged the bull's speed and got caught by the steer's horn right across my thigh. I went flying, landing hard enough to knock me unconscious. My pa, who had been coming to check on my progress, saw what was happening and charged in with his horse to save me from my own stupidity. He ended up having to shoot the enraged bull to keep it from killing me.

"Later, when I woke up, safe in my own bed with only a jagged scar on my leg and a big lump on my head to show for my near-death foolishness, he told me how disappointed he was in my choice and how much the bull's loss was going to cost the family. He also told me that the young lady I had been trying so hard to impress had cared so little for me that she had gone running for home the moment she had realized that I was in real danger. She'd gone there, not to get help, but rather to hide from the trouble that she was afraid she would get into when someone discovered that she had been encouraging me on in my stupidity. I was left to understand exactly how much I had given up that day for so little in return. I felt about as small and worthless as a worn-out horseshoe.

"A few days after that, my mother taught me another lesson that I won't soon forget. What my pa hadn't shared with me was that he was harboring his own wound from the incident. The bull had not gone down with the first blast and my father had been forced to ram his horse into the bull in order to push it off the path that would have taken it over my prone body. In the process, his leg had been crushed between the bull and his horse. He still walks with a limp today because of it. The lesson she made perfectly clear was the difference between the love my pa had for me and the infatuation I had with that girl. One was worth dying for, the other was not.

"He didn't say anything more on the subject after that, but I knew it was my fault and the guilt ate at me until it made me sick. Trying to make up for my guilt, I pushed myself hard to cover the chores he wasn't able to do. I was barely sleeping trying to get it all done, not even taking time to stop for meals. I began to lose weight and constantly had dark bags under my eyes. Finally, one night several weeks later, long after I should have gone to bed, my father found me in the barn frustratedly trying to repair the gate on one of the cattle chutes we were going to need the next day. It should have been a simple fix, but I was too tired to do it correctly.

"He limped over and took the tool out of my hand, forcing me to stop working and face him. Then, without a word, he reached around me to fix the gate with a simple maneuver of the wrench then handed the tool back to me and told me to go put it away. When I came back, he was standing there with his arms folded across his chest, six-foot two of angry cowboy glaring down at me.

"'Son,' he said to me, 'we don't have the luxury of wallowing in our self-recriminations. You did something you shouldn't have, but you've already paid the price of it and learned from your mistake. Now it's time to move on.'

"I tried to argue with him and tell him how it was also my fault that he had been injured and how I needed to make amends for it, but that was when he really got angry with me. He told me that it had been his choice to go into that bull's pasture and that I had no right to try to take the responsibility for that choice away from him."

For several moments Thatcher was silent, then he finally said, "You are not responsible for what happened to her out there tonight."

I shook my head, disagreeing. He was wrong, I was responsible. "Look Thatcher, I appreciate what yae're trying tae say, but I'm the reason yae all stayed. I should have forced Alex tae leave with yae this morning. Then…"

Thatcher's deep growl cut me off. "Haskell, you could have no more forced Alex to leave than I was able to. It was my job to get her to safety; I failed to do that. You do not get to relieve me of my responsibility for my choices or my failures. Alex chose to take the battle to Remington and free her team. You do not get to take the responsibility for her choices away from her either. Remington already made you pay for the choices you were responsible for. Now it's time for you to move on."

"Amen," McLagan added unexpectedly from the back seat. "No bloody noble gets tae claim responsibility for me choices; yae least of all Buccleuch."

I found myself chuckling in resignation. "Okay. I get the point." Then, after a few seconds, I added, "Thank you, for not abandoning us."

"No one left behind, not even yae," McLagan muttered under his breath, making me chuckle again.

The command pad beeped softly, its mapping function telling us it was time to change direction. Thatcher slowed the jeep and began looking for the side trail the pad said was off to the left. It turned out to be harder to find than we expected. We had to backtrack several yards because we missed it the first time.

"Well, at least it will be hard for someone else to see as well," Wren suggested. "Pull in a few meters and let me out.

I'll make sure there are no tire tracks to be seen from the road."

The trail turned out to be little more than a pair of overgrown ruts in the ground that led us into a large copse of trees. In the middle of the trees, Thatcher brought the jeep to a stop as the headlights came to rest on the crumbling remains of an old castle surrounded by a large moat of water. The trail leading up to the castle's old wooden door was a walking bridge too narrow for the jeep to drive onto.

Wren climbed out again, taking his gun with him, and walked up to the door; it was unlocked. He pushed it open and walked inside. A few minutes later, he came back and gave the all-clear. Caerlaverock castle was much older than the one I had grown up in; it was also much smaller. This one had been built in the thirteenth century AD with an unusual triangular shape inside of a man-made mote almost as wide as the castle itself. It housed early Scottish Earls until sometime in the seventeenth century when the drafty, cold place was eventually abandoned. Repair work in the twentieth century kept it sufficiently viable as a tourist site that non-M-Gens were able to take refuge in it during the M-Gen war. Unfortunately, as a result, it took a beating from the M-Gens trying to get at those sheltered inside. The result was that many of the walls had large openings where bombs and other shrapnel had struck, and the interiors of nearly all the rooms were open to the sky above. But it would do as a place of refuge for the night until Captain Marcellus' scheduled transport arrived to pick us up in the morning.

We set up camp between two walls just wide enough to allow for the four-man tent that had been packed. I've always found it interesting that a tent labeled as a four-man tent only truly has room for four sleeping bags with nothing left for the gear. That might have been a problem considering that there were five of us, but it was a given that one of us would be remaining on watch outside the tent while the others slept. Wren offered to take the first shift, stating that he was the least injured in the group. None of the rest of us were up to arguing with him.

Thatcher helped me take the boots off of Alex's feet and then get her settled into the bag at the center of the tent. She only stirred once during the process, her head shifting slightly when I took my arms out from under her. McLagan was asleep in the bag across the entrance to the tent before we even finished zipping up her bag. That left the bags on either side of her. Thatcher took the one on the left; I took the one on the right.

I laid there for some time, staring into the darkness, listening to the rhythm of Alex's breathing, and trying to ignore the aching of my body. I was exhausted, but sleep was slow in coming. Instead, my mind insisted on replaying the events that had brought me so close to losing everyone I loved. At some point, though, I must have drifted off because I woke with a start to the realization that something wasn't right.

"Thatcher," I said in alarm, "where's Alex?"

I heard him reach out to touch the empty sleeping bag between us and then curse loudly. We were both out of our bags and moving in the space of a heartbeat. It was still dark inside the tent, but that wouldn't have stopped us if we hadn't both stepped on McLagan in the process. McLagan yelled in pain and bucked upwards sending us sprawling into a tangled mess of arms and legs.

McLagan began swearing up a storm and yelling at us to watch where we stepped, only to be pulled up short as

Thatcher shoved him roughly back to the ground and out of the way. Outside the tent, the first hints of the pre-dawn morning could be seen in the dark grey cast of the sky above us. There was just enough light in the sky from the crescent moon for us to avoid tripping over anything else as we raced through the corridors shouting for Alex and Wren.

"Up here," Wren's voice called faintly from some distance above. "She's with me." I felt a wave of relief wash through me with those words but didn't slow my pace as I searched for a way to get up to where they were. I found the stairwell in the corner tower and took the steps three at a time, heedless of the rubble that was strewn across them. I only slowed long enough at the top to duck through the fallen, rotting beams of the tower's collapsed ceiling.

As soon as I was beyond the landing and out onto the wall, I was able to see Alex silhouetted against the pale light of the early dawn. She was facing away from me, her attention appearing to be focused on a point far off in the distance. Wren stepped out of the shadows next to me. "I followed her up here about thirty minutes ago." His voice was soft. "She's just been standing there the whole time."

"Why did she come up here?"

"Don't know." He shrugged. "I tried talking to her a few times, but she only looks at me for a moment before turning away again."

Thatcher finally made it, breathing hard as he came through the doorway; he joined us out on the battlement. I could see his jaw twitch as he studied Alex, his mind processing what he was seeing. "Haskell, go talk to her," he finally said. "Find out what's going on." I nodded; it was the same thing I had been thinking.

I could feel the strong chill of the air out on the open battlement as I approached her. It would warm up once the sun had risen, but Scotland was in the grips of the late fall season with early winter fast approaching. On top of the battlement, the cold winds that blew across the moors this time of year were strong enough to lift her hair off her shoulders and stream it out behind her in a continuous dance. She turned to look at me as I approached. Then, without a word, she turned back away to continue watching whatever had her attention out beyond the walls.

Several thoughts passed through my mind in that instant. First, there had been a complete lack of expression on her face. No expression, and no recognition in her eyes. Second, she was shivering but was making no effort to warm herself. It was as though she was not even aware of how cold she was. Finally, standing this close to her, I could feel the faint shifting of the gravity under me. Looking down, I realized that neither of our feet were actually touching the ground, nor were any of the tiny pieces of rubble that were immediately around us. It couldn't have been more than an inch or two, but it also didn't appear that she was consciously making it happen.

What was going on? Hesitantly, I reached out to touch her shoulder. She didn't flinch, nor did she turn to look at me again. "Alex, what are yae doing?" I asked somewhat nervously. She didn't respond. "Alex, can yae hear me?" Again, she didn't respond. She just kept staring out toward the moor beyond the trees. What was she looking at? I followed her line of vision and felt my jaw drop. Barely visible in the shadowy pre-dawn, several vehicle-sized boulders were floating in the air, slowly shifting positions with each other as though they were performing some type of intricate dance.

Any one of them alone had to be heavier than the four hundred pounds she had told me she was currently capable of lifting. All of them together should have been impossible for her. But impossible or not, she was doing it.

"Thatcher?" I called softly. "Yae're goin' tae want tae see this."

Thatcher and Wren followed my gaze out toward the moor. Wren let out a low whistle. Up until this point, it had probably been too dark for him to see what she had been doing. Thatcher looked back at Alex, studying her again for a long moment.

"Inadvertent control," he finally said.

"What?"

"The graph Durnham showed us. Her inadvertent control is much stronger than her purposeful control."

Suddenly, Thatcher walked over and waved his hand in front of her eyes; she didn't so much as blink. He grunted, "She's asleep."

Asleep?! I turned to him in confusion. "Her eyes are open; how can she be asleep?"

"She's sleepwalking. My cousin Jim used to do it. He'd get up in the middle of the night, walk to the kitchen, eat a big piece of the chocolate cake Aunt Mallory had made for Sunday dinner the next day, and then go back to bed. In the morning he'd wake up with cake crumbs all over his bed and chocolate frosting on his face without any clue how it had gotten there."

I thought about the graph General Durnham had shown us. There had been two lines on it, one for the gravity she purposely controlled and the other for the gravity she inadvertently controlled. The second line had suggested that she could unconsciously control much more than she consciously could. I looked back out at the floating boulders. It would certainly explain how she was doing that.

"If she's asleep, then how do we wake her up?" I asked.

Thatcher shrugged. "In my cousin's case, they didn't. They would just turn him around by the shoulders and walk him back to bed."

"Why not wake him up?"

"They tried to the first few times, but they discovered that he would become agitated when they did so, and it was much harder to get him back to bed. So, they quit trying."

Wren, who had joined us and was listening to our discussion, nodded his head in understanding. "Then we walk her back to bed." He reached out and took Alex by the hand. She looked down at his hand as he did so but didn't say anything. Speaking calmly and firmly he said to her, "It is time to go down. Come with me." Still holding her hand, he began to walk toward the tower and the staircase. To my surprise, she followed him. Out on the moor, the boulders settled gently back down. As she walked away from me, the gravity underneath me shifted as well and I felt my feet touching the ground once more. Suddenly standing with bare feet on the cold stone walkway, it occurred to me that this was probably why she had been holding herself off the ground. In my rush to get to her, I hadn't even noticed the freezing cold of the stones, but I sure felt it now.

Wren led her all the way back to the tent with Thatcher and I following close behind. McLagan was waiting there for us. He held the tent flap open with a quizzical expression as Wren led her back to her sleeping bag, but he held his questions until we got her settled. Once she was laying back down, Wren began singing a low, soft song. The words were not in a language I understood, but the purpose was unmistakable; it was a lullaby. Within moments, Alex's eyes grew heavy and then finally closed. Wren let his song fade.

We left the tent as quietly as we could. Outside we kept our voices low as we discussed what had happened.

"Well, if that don't beat all," McLagan muttered under his breath as we finished. I had to agree. "Now what?" he asked.

"Now," Thatcher answered him, "you're taking watch." McLagan grumbled under his breath but didn't argue. In truth, Wren should have woken him up to take over the watch about an hour ago. "As for you two," he indicated Wren and I, "get back to bed and get some more rest before we have to clean up camp and get ready to leave."

"What about yae?" I asked when he failed to follow us toward the tent.

"I'm going to stand watch out here and make sure she doesn't decide to go for another walk. Now get in there; you still look exhausted."

He was right; the adrenaline was gone and my heart rate had finally slowed from the pounding staccato Alex's disappearance had set it to, meaning that there was nothing left now but my exhaustion. As I lay back down beside Alex, I considered what I had seen up there on the battlement; she was far stronger than she knew. But more than that, in spite of the fact that she had clearly been the reason those boulders were in the air, I had not seen any indication that she had experienced any physical or mental difficulty as a result of it. Hadn't she told me that supporting that much weight was both physically and mentally exhausting for her? Wasn't that the reason she had passed out in the clearing and then collapsed again last night? But on the battlement, she hadn't been straining. She hadn't even broken a sweat. I wasn't sure I understood what that meant, but there was a faint tickling in the back of my mind that suggested there was something important in that line of thought; it just wasn't going to make itself clear tonight.

I rolled over in my bag, shifting off the sore rib that had started screaming at me. The only problem with the new position was that it made my knee ache more. I shifted my knee trying to find a more comfortable position, but after several moments I had to sigh in resignation; there wasn't a comfortable position. I gave up and just held still, allowing my body to scream at me while I tried to sleep.

www.ingramcontent.com/pod-product-compliance
Lightning Source LLC
Chambersburg PA
CBHW051307190726
48290CB00001B/41